Because He Lives

Faith, Hope and Love in Action

Catherine Ritch Guess

Photography by Mark L. Barden

CRM BOOKS

Publishing Hope for Today's Society

Inspirational Books~CDs~Children's Books

CRM BOOKS, PO Box 935, Indian Trail, NC 28079

Visit our Web site at www.ciridmus.com

Printed in the United States of America

ISBN (10 digit): 1-933341-33-5

ISBN (13 digit): 9781933341330

LCCN: 2010926159

To

Joseph and Marilyn Chan,
(born Chan, Chhleav and Tor, Sovann)
ជហាន ជហហលពវ ានជ ទឡ្យរ ្រឡ្យវានន

the most selfless servants
of God I know,

in whose honor
proceeds from this book
will go toward the building of a
Senior Adult Center in Cambodia

A SPECIAL THANKS

First and foremost, I wish to thank Esther Gitobu, and her husband Nicholas, for it was because of their interest and encouragement this book sprang from a seed of thought to a harvested work. Thank you for entrusting me with this opportunity, and for having the faith in my ability to make it a worthy literary representation of the love and faith of Joseph and Marilyn Chan in their Christ, and the passion they have for their homeland of Cambodia and its inhabitants. When our paths crossed on June 23rd, 2009, Esther nonchalantly asked if I had ever thought of writing a book of my experiences in Cambodia, to which I answered, "Yes, many times." That question opened the door for what transpired over a Frosty from Wendy's later that evening as Esther approached me about penning a book on the Chan's incredible journey to becoming missionaries. We committed ourselves to prayer over this project.

I was already feeling the power of those prayers and guidance on the way home. That's when I realized how powerfully God had worked in my life that day. I'd attended a luncheon honoring our Southeast Asian ministries and missionaries that day at Bishop Larry Goodpaster's office, I had watched a video of the Cambodian missionaries—all of whom I knew from my past work there—and it was the final day of our Vacation Bible School that focused on Southeast Asia, to which Esther, her husband Nicholas and their three beautiful daughters had come to speak on Cambodia that evening. God's plan had been revealed.

More ironic, my older son Josh—the one I'd held for the first time as a newborn exactly thirty-one years prior to the day—called me the next morning to say how clear it was to see I was following God's call in my life; that he knew I was doing what, and going where, God required of me. With that phone call, I knew that within the next year, I would again travel to Cambodia to live for a time and that within twelve months, ***Because He Lives*** would not only be a Southern Gospel hymn by Bill Gaither and loved by many, it would be a beautiful story of the Chan's faith, hope and love in action in Cambodia. I was reminded of the stories I loved as a child about Corrie Ten Boom and Lottie Moon, and thus hit my computer, instantly writing the prologue and laying out two of the chapters, knowing the rest would come—as did my first newborn grandson, the son of Josh, whom I got to hold six weeks before traveling to Cambodia, and my second newborn grandson, the son of my younger son Jamie, whom I will hopefully hold hours before this book premieres at the UMW Assembly on April 29, 2010.

I literally sensed that scene from the old ***Mission Impossible*** shows, as I could literally hear God's voice saying, "Your mission, should you decide to accept it," to which I abruptly interrupted and responded by saying aloud, "I think I already have!" That was how this book was birthed, to which I can imagine Joseph Chan responding, "Thank God! Thank God! Praise the Lord!"

ACKNOWLEDGEMENTS

To Mark Barden for the wonderful photography to truly make this story jump off the page, and for your constant encouragement and support during this project. Your heart for mission is a gift to the world!

To the Reverend Dr. Romeo del Rosario, country director of the General Board of Global Ministries of the United Methodist Church (GBGM-UMC) in Cambodia, for his most invaluable time, his insight into the ministries of the General Board of Global Ministries through the Methodist Mission in Cambodia (MMC), and his vision for the future of Christianity in Cambodia.

To Chandra Chap for her assistance in taking notes from the Chan's prior to my arrival in Cambodia, for translations and for sharing the traumatic story of her own childhood.

To the families of Joseph and Marilyn Chan for sharing their many stories, with a special thanks to Christina Chan, Joseph's and Marilyn's youngest daughter, also a beautiful and joyous spirit.

To Linat for her sketches to lend visual effects to the story, and for her wonderful translations during my past visit to Cambodia.

To the following persons whom God placed in my path in Cambodia, whose invaluable information and accounts helped set the stage for *Because He Lives* through true-life accounts during the reign of Pol Pot and the Khmer Rouge: Pal Tha - waitress at the FCC (Foreign Correspondents' Club) in Phnom Penh - and her aunt, Mme. Chhouk Tho, who was a former student of Pol Pot; Mr. Seag Sok Heig - Cambodian Department of Tourism; Mr. Sean Rean, former Khmer Rouge soldier and guide at Ta Mok's Khmer Rouge Headquarters; Pastor Sam Om – Pastor of St. John's UMC, a Cambodian congregation in Charlotte, NC, and his sister Mory, both survivors of the Khmer Rouge; and Sang Tola – a GBGM-UMC missionary in Cambodia.

To Vladimir Bessarabov, UN Cartographic Section of the United Nations for use of the map of Cambodia.

To Sam Om, Edna Shum, Rev. Radha Manickam and Richard Tompkins for sharing comments on Marilyn and Joseph Chan.

To Mean Hongly, Chairperson of the Christian Education Committee and Assistant District Superintendent of the Methodist Mission in Cambodia, for writing the names of Mark Barden and myself in Khmer for the book's title page.

To Sandi McGarrah, for whom there are no words to describe. Her passion for Cambodia and its people, for missions, for working with the Cambodian congregation in Charlotte, NC, are all a special calling from God. Not only are you a friend, colleague and former college classmate, you have been a stronghold for this project. Thank you for sharing your article on *The Women of Cambodia*.

To Vera Drye, Etta Rowland and my mother, Corene Ritch, for reading behind me to keep this book on schedule. Your timely assistance was most helpful!

To Lawrence and Carolyn Campbell, who gave of their time and energy to see this book become a reality for the UMW Assembly 2010, and whose support, physically and spiritually, have seen me through many mission projects in both my personal life and the life of St. John's Lutheran Church, Concord, NC.

To friends and family, who so graciously understood the time restraints on this project, and whom I shall look forward to seeing when I come up for air.

To Richard Spencer, my dear cousin. Though our heads have turned to silver, and our bones and joints don't move as quickly and easily as they once did, it is still with the same great fondness that I cherish our visits and our youthful days of sharing the bench and playing on that old upright piano together…*Heart and Soul*. Thank you for setting the scene of Cambodia for me through your own horrific experiences leading into Pol Pot's reign.

And lastly and most importantly, to Joseph and Marilyn Chan for the incomparable hospitality, experiences and ***food***! Your restaurant choices were superb, with memories all their own, especially of the hammock after a delicious lunch of fish in our own little wooden hut! I look forward to my next visit, and many more meals, with you.

Meet Joseph and Marilyn Chan

Along with Pastor Sam Vorn in California, Joseph Chan was a catalyst in bringing Methodism to Cambodia. Without the work of those two, there would have been no missionaries or workers sent there by the General Board of Global Ministries of the UMC. What Joseph and Marilyn have accomplished there is so tremendous. – Pastor Sam Om – St. John's UMC (Cambodian Congregation), Charlotte, NC

(Pastor Sam Om is a former chairman of the Cambodian National Caucus of the UMC, who served as the Vice-Chairman under Joseph Chan at the time of the organization of the Methodist Mission of Cambodia. He is a former Cambodian soldier who also survived the Khmer Rouge, found Christ in the refugee camp in Thailand and came to America. Sam travels back to Cambodia to teach theology and other accreditation courses for the ministers in the Cambodian Methodist Bible School.)

Joseph and Marilyn are an amazing couple. They almost single handedly changed the country with their unending drive to not only raise the money from donations but purchase the land to build the many Methodist missions all over the country. This included staffing, teaching the local people the skills needed to grow food, such as raising pigs and farming, and using tools to help with construction of furniture and building. Their energy is non-stop. They are truly an inspiration. After meeting Joseph and Marilyn Chan 10 years ago, I volunteered as an English teacher at the mission in Siem Reap, where I went back 15 months ago to visit my old friends. I am 80 years old now but I still yearn to return to Cambodia to support them in their work. – Edna Shum, Campbell UMC

Having first met Joseph and Marilyn in 1980 in the Thai refugee camp, we served the Lord there until we left for America, where we again made contact and have served together since 1985. These two dear people were willing to help others first and put their needs last, sacrificing their lifestyle to answer God's call, to leave their two oldest children with their adoptive mother and move back to Cambodia to serve God among their people. They respect other's leadership and others respect them. All they want is to serve God and His people. They have a true servant's heart and don't care about the position or title.

Joseph and Marilyn have become trusted family friends. Everywhere they go people surround them with love and are happy to see them come to visit. Many times I've traveled in Cambodia with Joseph. I've watched him work with people and respect them, even if they are unworthy of respect. He is not one to sit around, but always wants to be helping his Cambodian people. - Rev. Radha Manickam, President – Cambodian Ministries for Christ International, Seattle, WA

Having known Joseph (Chan Chhleav) since 1987, we have attended meetings from NY to California since 1990 to work on homelands ministry. Our friendship was forged over late nights in homes and hotel rooms creating proposals and translating materials into Khmer. The Chans put aside much of the lifestyle of the West as they work. When I travel with them, we follow a simple traditional diet, both healthy and economical. They give of their personal wealth that others may have a chance for salvation. I remember one hotel in Western Cambodia that was $4 for a double and all guns had to be impounded in the lobby.

Chan Chhleav is a personal role model. In 1994, we were in Cambodia together and he arranged a trip to Siem Reap. It was my first trip and road safety made normal travel impossible. After looking at the church site there, a lot of conversation occurred in Khmer and he then told me in English that he thought the road was safe enough to go with two armed guards to Sisophon. I was frankly afraid and irritated, but finally consented to go with him. Of course, within an hour of Siem Reap, we were stopped at a checkpoint by a teenager with a gun. I remember that it had a gas cylinder hanging under it like a bazooka. The guard next to me un-holstered his pistol and ordered the driver to proceed. I closed my eyes and prayed for a quick death. The driver coasted past the teen and no one dared to fire. When I felt the car accelerate I looked up and we were clear.

By the time we got to Sisophon, we met a woman who had just lost her husband in the fighting 7 miles north. We talked with people who were in the middle of civil war zone and I was stunned by their faith. I decided I wanted to be a Christian like that. It was one of the amazing times of my life spiritually and I asked God for forgiveness, as I had not seen clearly from the beginning that this trip had to be done.

I made a commitment to trust Chan Chhleav in the future. Little did I realize that my commitment would be tested in 1996 when we again were going to travel together and civil unrest broke out a week before we left the USA. My foster son's father died of a heart attack after his home was plundered in Phnom Penh. Chan Chhleav prayed with Marilyn and called me that he had decided to go, whether for life or death. I immediately agreed, but my heart was not in it and my prayer was "Lord, let this cup pass from me." In God's goodness the airport was closed two days later and we have never had to test our friendship again.

Joseph and Marilyn are geniuses of liberation. They see salvation as holistic, building an economic engine (fishing pond, land for agriculture, and pig farming) around each congregation that can combat the 70% unemployment rate. The model has not always made sense to professional missionaries, but Paulo Freire (the Pedagogy of the Oppressed) teaches us that liberation has to come more from God in the community than from the outside. The Chans understand this reality and are empowering people through the way that they offer the gospel of Christ.

- Ronald Tompkins, New York City, NY

The Women of Cambodia

The Methodist Church is making a difference in the lives of the Cambodian people, especially the women. After many years of planning, Cambodian women formed their own group, Cambodian Methodist Women (CMW) five years ago in the spring of 2004 in Siem Reap. They elected officers, divided into eight districts and asked the GBGM for help training their women.

The first team of Ubuntu Explorers - 20 women from across the US, sponsored by the GBGM, Women's Division, and led by Sandi McGarrah of the Western NC Conference - arrived in Phnom Penh in September 2006. The Cambodian leadership expected 50 women to attend.Instead 150 arrived. Quite an accomplishment when you consider what they had to do to be a part of this historic meeting. The women had to travel great distances from small villages on dusty roads in crowded open-air vehicles to meet together. They had to leave their oldest daughter in charge of her siblings as well as tend to the cooking, cleaning, and harvesting. Many did not have decent clothes to wear for the big city or shoes on their feet. Since most husbands think of them as property much as women were thought of in Biblical times, it was difficult to leave even for a few days. During the 3-day conference Cambodian and United Methodist Women from the US exchanged ideas, shared life stories, read Scripture, had communion, danced and sang to the glory of God. They made and exchanged handmade banners to be taken back to the districts around Cambodia and the US. They became sisters!

A second Ubuntu team returned in 2007, also led by Sandi McGarrah, to be with their Cambodian sisters. Once again they shared joys, concerns, Bible stories, and a cultural exchange of arts and crafts including cooking, sewing, and jewelry making, and even rice planting. The women divided into districts and made a quilt square, side by side with their American sisters. The group decided to make a sunflower, CMW's logo, on each square. The sunflower has become the symbol of who they are and what they stand for. The women are strong like the stem, standing straight and tall in the daily heat of their homeland. They gain strength in one another much as the sunflower seeds that cluster in a spiral pattern are interconnected to give strength. The face of the sunflower follows the sun just as the women follow the son of Christianity, Jesus Christ. The seeds that feed many animals also nurture the faith of the women with the seeds of God's word for they are the fruit of the plant and give the women the fruit of the spirit. The roots that anchor the plant securely to the ground for nourishment help the women stay rooted in God's word in the midst of many obstacles. The finished quilt hangs behind the altar at their conference meetings as a reminder of their unity with one another and with their American sisters.

It has been said that if you teach women they will teach their children and that can change a culture. The seed that was planted in the hearts of the women in 2004 is a seed of hope that blossomed and is continuing to grow. - Sandi McGarrah

The Fruits of Cooperation

January 8, 2010

Thank Christ for calling us, altogether we cooperate
to do the mission through His plan, He gave wisdom and He reveals.

Thanks to Esther and Nicholas, they are good at communication,
Help MMC to manage, the fruitful result is waiting.

Thank God for sending Romy who works hard to serve Him,
Raises funds to buy land for the construction, supports and cooperates.

Thanks to Catherine and Mark, with the gifts of management,
Searching and managing the true story combining with pictures.

Thank God for He is our guide,
ordaining people according to their abilities,
taking photos and writing on them accordingly
research and put in order as the archive.

Thanks to Chandra for translating from Khmer to English
Although she is busy and lack of sleep, she has worked hard in helping.

Thanks to Linat for struggling with us helping us to achieve.
She took her time to draw pictures to be added to the real story.

Thanks to our brothers, sisters and relatives all,
who try their best to help us
financially and physically support
This is a true story in the grace of God.

Composed by Joseph and Marilyn Chan

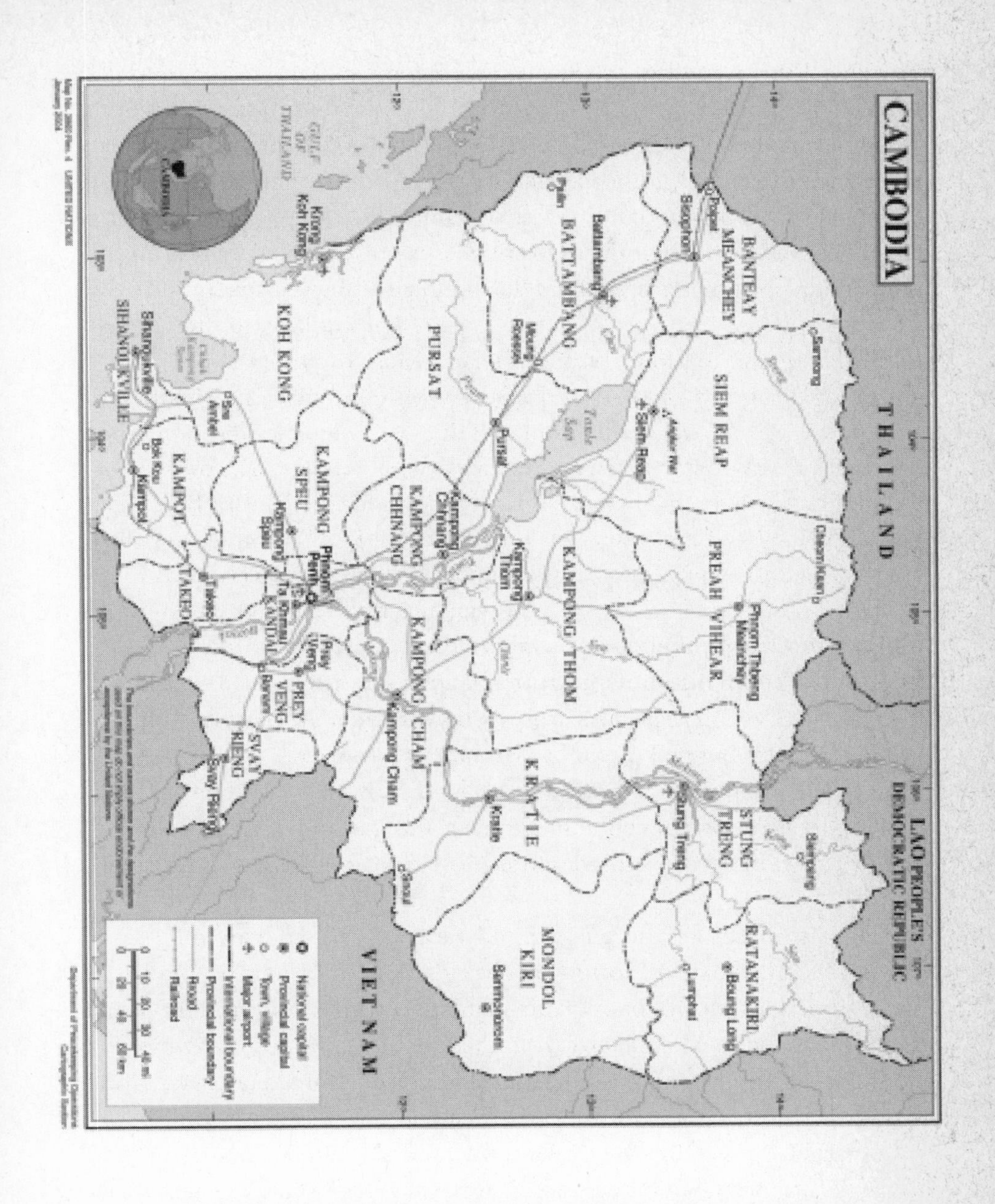

Used by permission of the UN Cartographic Section of the United Nations

Part One

For I know the plans I have for you, declares the Lord,
plans to prosper you and not to harm you,
plans to give you hope and a future.
Jeremiah 29:11 - *NIV*

Do not remember the former things,
or consider the things of old.
I am about to do a new thing;
now it springs forth, do you not perceive it?
I will make a way in the wilderness
and rivers in the desert.
Isaiah 43:18-19

Prologue

Many people have heard of Vietnam and the fall of Saigon that happened on April 30, 1975. Many people have *not* heard of the neighboring country of Cambodia falling into the hands of a communist government under the barbaric leadership of Pol Pot and his Khmer Rouge regime only thirteen days prior to that date on April 17, 1975. In the shadow of the larger picture in the scope of the Vietnam War, that bit of history failed to make the same headlines or create the same stir. Maybe that is because Cambodia, like Thailand, was to remain neutral territory during the Southeast Asian turmoil.

However, Cambodia was so small it found itself caught up in the midst of the war while both American and North Vietnamese soldiers—"secretly" at the time—crossed the Cambodian border to make their assaults on each other, with the Americans also fighting the Viet Cong guerillas of South Vietnam. With no way to protect itself in the process, and strong opposing forces of its political leaders, Cambodia wound up in its own civil war. During the period of time from 1975 - 1979, it is estimated that over 27% of the country's population of seven million were killed, either as a result of ruthless murders or a combination of overwork, starvation and consequential diseases.

With that small vital piece of background information, you are now ready for a beautiful—although sometimes frightening and painful—story of faith, hope and love in action.

There are some people in the world who make you feel better simply by virtue of being near them. Marilyn Chan is one of those people. Playfully cunning as a child—a trait that proved most beneficial for her survival skills during the Khmer Rouge regime—she now possesses the most delightfully pure spirit I've ever encountered, even to the point of being spryly angelic. She is so joyous that even the ring of her cell phone sounds like a child laughing.

One is quick to learn she never appears without bringing something to share, making her also one of the most giving individuals I've ever encountered. Being from North Carolina, I know all about Southern hospitality, but her Southeast Asian hospitality puts mine to shame.

By the same token, if you were pressed to find one scriptural verse to describe Joseph Chan, it would be "for the joy of the Lord is your strength" from Nehemiah 8:10. In fact, the entire first ten verses of that chapter perfectly depict this man, who has literally spent his whole life working, all the while planning in the back of his mind how he could one day "send portions...to those for whom nothing is prepared"—an earlier phrase of that same verse.

To look at Marilyn and Joseph, you would see a missionary couple, grounded totally in the principles of faith, hope and love. You would see a couple whose relentless energy allows them to accomplish more than most couples half their age...who, individually and together, exemplify Christian boldness to its fullest extent...who truly walk humbly with their God...whose accomplishments through their ministry paint the picture of a team who has given their entire joint careers to a life of service. And, you would look into their eyes and see nothing but a life steeped in joy and happiness.

That's when you look at the surface through your eyes.

When you look through God's eyes, you see two individuals who are Khmer Rouge survivors of the communist regime of Pol Pot (named Saloth Sar at birth, meaning "white" because he was so light-skinned), who is reputed to be the most ruthless leader in the history of the world—a truth proven by the world's worst genocide, which took place in Cambodia between April 17th, 1975 and January 7, 1979. You see two individuals who grew up in a Buddhist culture, with their families following rituals and traditions of that religion…whose early years were shaped by growing up in a country that was a French Colonial protectorate…to whom education was important, and both of whom had dreams and goals of one day helping the people of their own country…who dreamed of one day helping end oppression and injustice in their beloved homeland…who lived in a country where *all* religion was banned when Pol Pot took control of Phnom Penh on April 17, 1975…who happened to run into each other in a Thai refugee camp in 1979, after having met one time through relatives twelve years earlier…who gave their lives to Christ while residing in a refugee camp in Thailand…who not only took a leap in faith, but jumped across an entire ocean to reach America and be educated in California's San Jose Bible College, with Joseph continuing his studies at a Methodist seminary…who were bold enough to be involved in UN ceasefire talks for their country, in order to gain the freedom to bring religion back into their country…and who returned to their homeland when it was again safe and have given their all for their Lord, bringing His saving grace and Gospel to the people of their beloved Cambodia.

Plain and simple, you see a couple who both "talks the talk" and "walks the walk."

To fully understand the depth of the story, and the transformation and faith of this missionary couple, you must travel back to the week before Pol Pot and his grisly Khmer Rouge took over Phnom Penh in April of 1975. Through the times, events and history that shaped the lives of these two individuals, I invite you to join me now on a journey down the path of life following the footsteps of Joseph and Marilyn Chan, born Chhleav Chan and Sovann Tor, respectively.

Or as they say in Cambodia: Chan, Chhleav and Tor, Sovann.

Chapter One

April 11, 1975

Twenty-one-year-old Sovann Tor stares in the mirror, admiring her most cherished feature, her beautiful long hair. She's been grooming it to be its loveliest in exactly one week, on her wedding day. This is an arranged marriage, a typical practice among Cambodian families. Knowing little about her fiance's personality, her only thought of him is that he dressed appropriately, and seemed caring and understanding, when he came to ask her mother for permission for the marriage. Sovann has never been out with the handsome lieutenant who will soon become her husband. She's never even talked to him or looked him straight in the eye. None of that matters in her culture. He will be a good provider for her with his promotion to Captain imminent in two days on April 13th, the Cambodian New Year, not to mention the healthy dowry he has paid Sovann's family for her hand.

As is the Cambodian custom the week before the wedding, a sign hangs on the front of her house in Phnom Penh bearing the names of the soon-to-be-wed couple, in case anyone wishes to oppose their marriage. Her mother, faithful in her Buddhist beliefs, continues to make all the necessary arrangements. The monk will perform the ceremony, which would customarily last for days. Her wedding will not be as long, fancy or festive as her older sister's, though, because of the country's civil war between the army of the current political leader, Lon Nol, and the opposing Khmer Rouge forces. Fighting has reached the nearby villages, thus preventing many of her friends and extended family from attending the wedding. Nevertheless, her mother works to make sure it is an event to behold.

Sovann thinks of her older sister who married a military captain nearly eighteen months prior. *What will I be doing in eighteen months? Will I be studying law to help end oppression for the Cambodian people and suppression of women? Will I be studying to be a nurse to help the sick? Or will I be holding my own newborn baby and adjusting to a life of marriage with a man whom I now don't even know?*

Sovann brushes her hair, still staring into the mirror where visions of both the past and the future flash before her in their entirety. They are as clear as the television show in the next room of her family's home. Her mind drifts back to her early childhood when her aunty and grandmother take turns brushing her hair. Born January 26, 1954, she lives with them in her native village of Kralanh after her parents and siblings move to Phnom Penh in 1957, a move necessitated by her father's military position. Her memories speed forward to 1966 when she moves to Phnom Penh to join the rest of her family, when it comes time to attend middle school and high school. Her move to the capital city is influenced by her desire to one day graduate from Phnom Penh's Preah Yukunthor High School, which she does.

The bride-to-be now envisions the person she'd hoped to become back then, peering even more deeply in the mirror at her flashbacks. *I wanted to attend law school*, she melancholically recalls, *to end the suppression of women who have no rights in Cambodia.* Her dream to make life better for Cambodian women, influenced by her extended aunty and role model Muol Chea, still lingers in the back of her mind. (Aunty is the term used to show endearment for a female friend of a family member; in this case, the aunty is her mother's cousin.)

Moul Chea (known as Madame Yao Malang in the community

and government office) is a teacher, and one of the four Assembly Women in the government, who formed a women's group for the purpose of seeking their human rights. Thanks to this aunty, Sovann gets the chance to attend the weekly national women's meeting during her 9th grade, an experience she still remembers fondly. It is during this time—when she hears women speak of how they should help society and saw how they value each person's life—that she discerns her calling to transform society for women, to give dignity to all by treating everyone equally.

Her thought suddenly shatters, as does her dream when her mother refuses her a further education. She walks to the window and thinks of the pawn shop housed in their home. Started by her grandmother, it is now operated by her mother—with the help of her two older sisters and herself. *I cannot complain. It is a business that has done well, and provided us with much, including this home and festive weddings.*

With that, she allows her mind to briefly wander back to the days when her family still lives on the military base and her mother rents the majority of the huge four-floor building in which they now live. It is a time—like now—when the first, second and third floors, each with four rooms, are rented to families. The fourth floor, also with four rooms, is occupied by disadvantaged college students from the provinces whom Sovann's mother allows to live here free of charge. It is not until the college students move out that Sovann's family, and the family pawn shop business, take over the fourth floor.

She slowly meanders back to thoughts of the present as she goes to watch the sunset atop the building's roof, where she has a view of much of the city and its outlaying areas. *All areas I will hopefully one day help by bringing them a world of justice, through the betterment of society for women,* she muses as she tries to tally how many people she's witnessed her mother helping over the years. Faint echoes of distant artillery fire wafting through the air distract her thoughts as they hint at a world she fears will all too soon be near.

Sovann returns to the mirror and the grooming of her incredibly thick and beautiful, long black hair. She has one main goal for this upcoming marriage; she sees it as her chance to actually help transform society. *I can help the military wives. I can teach them to be great women, and teach others to know their rights.*

She is suddenly forced to return from her private world of daydreaming by the reality that, in less than a week, this will no longer be her home. *What will my world be like after next week?* Sovann ponders, entering a whole new realm of daydreams.

A lone man, in his mid twenties, sits on one of the bleacher-type seats of an outdoor amphitheater in Phnom Penh. The "amphitheater" is actually the Mekong River, only about fifty feet away, where it converges with the Tonle Sap River. Running straight back behind him is Sihanouk Boulevard, a divided thoroughfare leading to downtown, with beautifully landscaped trees planted down the middle and on either side of the highway. Traffic is less than minimal—except for the monks dressed in their saffron robes strolling up and down the way—due to the hostile situation of a civil war closing in on the city. Not to be exclusive, the whole of Southeast Asia is currently hostile, but up until this point, the seven-mile radius from the airport to the city has been considered secure. From the looks of things, that situation may soon change.

Sisopath Quay—a wide street lined with tiny businesses, shops and restaurants—runs parallel to the river beside him, leading all the way down to the huge Wat Phnom ("wat" is Khmer for *temple*). Once the city's, if not the country's, most visited area, this scene is the closest thing he's found to a touristy waterfront pavilion in Southeast Asia. He comes here regularly at dusk, when visiting Cambodia, just in time for the nightly show to begin. *People back home would pay dearly for this luxury*, he muses, a half-smile plastered on his face.

His healthy tan, finely-sculpted physique, handsome face with its dimples and pointed chin, dashing blue eyes and black hair—with just a hint of a wave—give him the appearance of a jet-setter seated along some stylish beach on a coastal holiday. Instead of being a jet-setter, though, he is a crew chief for F5 fighter jets based at the U.S. military base in Saigon. Though an American civilian—a plain, simple, ordinary citizen with no formal education—he is employed to work on the base because of his prior experience with the United States Air Force in Thailand and his aviation training afterwards. Although this "amphitheater" and the Mekong don't qualify for a stylish beach, they're as close as he's going to get to a coastal holiday during these tense days in this part of the world.

This "holiday" is actually his leave between government contracts. As usual, he spends it in Phnom Penh, chasing the days *and* the ladies while enjoying the scenery and life, before retiring to a relaxing sunset along the water's edge. Some days he wonders if the reason he's able to find solace here, in the midst of Cambodia's civil war now reaching the outskirts of town, is because his hometown of Montgomery, Alabama, was its own hornet's nest of civil unrest. Besieged by some of the worst encounters of civil rights' issues during the 1960s, this is not "his first rodeo"—as the saying goes. Thus, he comes to this spot to forget the wild world outside the realm of where he sits.

From this vantage point, evidence of Cambodia's Buddhist culture is visible from the huge wat down the street. That culture's superstitious nature is visible on the signs, bearing the words "Happy" and "Lucky" in their titles, of many nearby businesses.

For this evening's entertainment, he tells himself, *it should be no different from last night's.*

All the scenery for the private viewing, which consists solely of a Chinese junk docked along the water's edge, is in place. He has no idea what its inhabitants do during the day, or where it goes; but come nightfall, it's always in this same spot right in front of his ringside seat. People live on it, cook on it and do their laundry on it. Naked little boys dive from its stern into the water.

Right on cue with the setting of the sun, the fireworks show begins with cannons flashing on the far side of the river. It is a prequel to the evening movie, which is watching the war. The sound track is orchestrated by the whistling of artillery shells screeching past overhead, coming over the lone man's right shoulder from somewhere back in the city and dropping a considerable distance inland on the opposite shore. In the semi-moonlight, tracer fire, trailing behind the artillery shells, leaves a silhouette over the water and the landscape. Occasionally flares—phosphorus candles on a parachute—drop on the far side of the water. Those are the special effects. Instead of popcorn, he snacks on shrimp cakes, his favorite Southeast Asian specialty.

But the key point one must understand, he tells himself, *is this is all enhanced by the presence of that Chinese junk out in the water, and kids diving and playing with the backdrop of war going on all around them.*

On this particular evening, there is also something else visible to him. Farther back on the boulevard toward Independence Monument, where foreign war correspondents gather to share information, their unusually brisk pace points to the fact that world-changing news is happening all around them.

Examining the scene around him more closely, he becomes suddenly aware of what has been gnawing at his subconscious the past two evenings. The drone of gibber-gabber about the Khmer Rouge among the townspeople, in hushed tones, causes him to wonder about the current level of security. Although he has no idea what they're saying, he knows something is askew.

A soldier, acting as an immigration police, suddenly appears out of nowhere and asks for his passport. Having no papers or documentation—thanks to the fact the American Embassy pulled the plug on tourist Visas and rescue money for his return to Vietnam just prior to his arrival here—he is taken directly to Prey Sar, a detention center fifteen kilometers from Phnom Penh.

His luck has run out, it appears, as his days of "coastal holiday" look no longer happy. All thoughts of a luxurious waterfront pavilion and amphitheater come crashing to an ironic conclusion. *For this privilege I* am *paying dearly*, he notes, a solemn look plastered on his face.

A five-year-old girl named Chandra plays outdoors with no worries about tomorrow. She knows she is safe because her father is the brave ex-assistant police chief of her family's hometown village in Skuon town, the district capital of Cheung Prey, in the province of Kampong Cham. Due to all the fighting breaking out in the villages and provinces as a result of the civil war in Cambodia, her family now lives in Phnom Penh, the country's capital city. It is considered safe territory.

Her perfectly-shaped round face, accented by her dark brown eyes and her diminutive shape, especially with a hint of resemblance from her father's family, give her the appearance of an oversized china doll. The sun of the hot spring months, drawing to a close as Cambodia nears its monsoon season, kisses her medium-toned brown skin giving it a healthy glow. She is a beautiful child, the apple of her father's eye.

A faint rumble in the distance draws her attention, but only momentarily, as she goes immediately back to her game with all the other neighborhood children.

Chhleav Chan, who is in his late twenties, spends his evening studying—"practicing," as Cambodians call it—lessons for his political science degree. He is not in school in Europe as was his dream. Rather, at the suggestion of his adoptive brother in France, he is in Pyongyang, North Korea, 2255 miles from his home province of Battambang in Cambodia. As distant as that seems, it is less than half the distance it was to Ljubljana, Yugoslavia, where he studied mechanical engineering on a scholarship before coming here in 1974.

His heart and mind share one dream—to carry his learned skills back to his beloved homeland *and* to apply them in order to make his country better and stronger. Following its 1953 independence from French Colonial influence, Cambodia is still seeking to find its own identity. He sees freedom and equal opportunity as the key to that identity.

An extremely astute and intellectual man, Chhleav speaks both Khmer and French, like most Cambodian males who've had the opportunity of a high school education. His two younger sisters are working back in his home village of Poy Char, in Battambang province, to earn money for his education. That is their way of helping, and showing appreciation, for the years he spent his elementary days in school, and then rushed home to immediately go fishing—his means of feeding his family and providing for their needs. It is the only way he knows to support his family when he is forced to take over the role as "head of household" at only ten years old, after his father's death. Due to that unfortunate set of circumstances, Chhleav is not one to "let grass grow under his feet," as the saying goes.

There are days, like today, when he feels an extraordinarily strong bond with his family. Chhleav, the fourth of seven children, thinks of his home, his mother and his siblings, three brothers and three sisters. Separated from them at the age of fourteen, he leaves his village of Poy Char to live in the Buddhist monastery in Battambang so he can attend high school. His mind drifts momentarily from his studies as he thinks back to that time, the first image being of an uncle. (Uncle is the term used to show endearment for a male friend of a family member.)

Thanks to this uncle, who is good friends with the leader monk at Battambang, Chhleav is allowed to live in the monastery, which is next door to the middle school and high school. Though his family is Buddhist, he does not practice the Buddhist beliefs faithfully. The example set by his family, of worshipping at the temple on holidays, and following the rituals and traditions, does, however, prepare him for his work at the monastery, where he becomes a helper for the monk leader.

It is his duty to get up early every morning and cook rice porridge with dry or grilled fish for the monks. Once he's done that, he can care for his own chores before going to school. It isn't until recess that he has a chance to eat his own breakfast. Because there are two groups of students per day at Cambodian schools, he goes early and is finished shortly before 11 am. That's when he follows the monk daily to collect food for their lunch meal before noon.

The Buddhists believe they must offer food to their ancestors, such as Chhleav's family does for his grandparents and their parents before them. This practice pays respect to those who birthed and cared for them, and keeps the souls of the ancestors happy, which in turn is a blessing for the one offering the food.

Chhleav's job allows him to live free at the monastery, for his family cannot afford to send him there. Because he is not studying to be a monk he wears regular clothes rather than the saffron-colored robes of the monk and the monastery students. He is grateful this is unlike the old days when most of the males in a village dedicated their lives, by living in the monastery for one to six months, while studying and obeying the practices of a monk.

Thoughts of his former life at the monastery end as darkness approaches and he is reminded he still has lessons to prepare. *My greatest way of benefiting my people,* he concludes, *is getting an education that allows me to better the society, to give them hope.*

He returns to his "practicing," because education is, as was then, a top priority.

Chapter Two

April 16, 1975

Sovann senses the rapidly increasing danger spreading through the city. The fighting has been so close the past few days that her family can see the bombs. Standing on the top of the house, she sees people looting businesses that have already closed and whose owners have managed to flee the city. People are in the streets running back and forth, some in shock, some crying, some rejoicing, some partying and some packing. Young people are happy as they race through the streets yelling, "Peace, peace!" The sentiment of the older people is, "This is dangerous…there's going to be crisis…stay in the house." The soon-to-be bride is overwhelmed by the chaotic state below her.

"If your fiancé were closer," suggests her mother when Sovann finally returns from the roof, "maybe the two of you could elope and run away together." Her comment is accompanied by an offer of money and jewelry.

Sovann watches her mother remove all the unclaimed pieces of money and jewelry from the pawn shop and hide them safely away, in case they need to leave in a hurry. She spies her mother's nimble fingers even going to the trouble of sewing the valuable items into their clothes. They both freeze in place as a news flash blares from the radio announcing, "The main military office in Phnom Penh has been bombed!" Neither of them speak, for they know that's where the fiancé is working today.

Although most of the military office's inhabitants are injured, Sovann's fiancé is miraculously unharmed and finds his way out of the rubble of the burning building. He immediately rushes to her home to assure her mother he is okay.

"Why did you come here first?" she hears her mother ask. "Why not tell your mother?"

"Tell you first and now go to see her," is the reply Sovann hears.

Still a lieutenant, due to increased military activity the past few days, he has the foresight to escape his office with a stamp pad. He uses it, at the request of the woman who will be his mother-in-law in two days, to take the right thumbprints of both he and his bride-to-be. This practice is used for weddings because thumbprints can't be copied and are considered stronger than signatures. Although the thumbprints are typically taken the day of the wedding, Sovann's mother feels this is a necessary precaution in the event things go even more awry in the next couple of days. She wants to be sure the monk has everything he needs to perform the ceremony.

Sovann thinks how different this is from the dreams she had of her wedding as a little girl. As a rule, the house would be filled with guests—family and close friends—who have come to help with all the food preparations and the decorations for the big event. The outbreak of such close fighting has made it impossible for her grandmother and aunty to come. Her only family guests are her two married sisters, their husbands, and the two young children of her oldest sister—all of whom live in Phnom Penh. A close military friend of her father, along with the friend's family, are also in the house, but only as a safety precaution rather than their interest in helping with the wedding. However, as a sign of appreciation for having a secure roof over their heads, the visiting family works alongside the bride's family to make sure the blessed day goes off without a hitch. From the looks of things, her wedding will not even last the minimal three days, much less longer.

The military friend goes into a room with Sovann's father, also a military man, and the two brothers-in-law, one of whom is a military captain and the other an English teacher. Her father is over the arsenal of guns for Cambodia's army. He has a key to the arsenal and keeps a close check on the guns and their operation; therefore, he is the regulator of all the weapons issued from his military base. Lately he has been doing undercover work, a position which requires that he wear plain dress. Now, as the four men disappear together, Sovann is certain their discussion revolves around the impending welfare of Phnom Penh as the fighting between the Cambodian National Army and the Khmer Rouge—under leadership of a man named Pol Pot—draws closer. Her welfare as a new bride has lost precedence.

She recalls her father's support of her interest in law on the many occasions when her aunty invited friends, in high positions, to share with her about all kinds of law. She remembers distinctly the time Moul Chea brought a lawyer of thirty years to their home. "If you want to change the Cambodian women's social law, you need to get an education in law," the lawyer told her.

A smile of appreciation for her father crosses her lips. *Will my husband listen to me like my father? Will he be interested, as my father is, in my desires to help women's rights?* Sovann glances toward the room the men entered, while recalling her aunty's advice from years before, "If you want to change the society law, it starts within the family by treating each member equally. Every child in the family should have work to do." *Father always listened to what I learned in school and what I learned from the women's meetings. Maybe all military men are like that,* she hopes, thinking of her own husband-to-be.

The four men exit the room as quietly as they entered it. She suspects the shared expression of gloom on their faces matches the gloom they see for the city. It appears all her hopes and dreams, like those of every other Cambodian, will soon become broken and shattered because of Pol Pot and his Khmer Rouge regime.

She sadly watches her oldest sister and brother-in-law, and their two young children, leave to stay with his parents. Retreating to her bedroom mirror to brush her hair, Sovann notices the usual glow of her medium-brown skin is absent. Her dark brown eyes, usually indicative of her playful spirit, have lost their brightness. Even running the brush through her hair fails to cheer her unexplained gloomy disposition.

A lone man sits staring at the walls of a cell that have been his home for five days. He notices a man approaching his cell. It isn't the usual guard, nor is he dressed in military clothing. There is no doubt in his mind this is the last person he will ever see, unless this man is merely the chaperone to the executioner. The mounting fear inside him is not lessened by the sound of artillery he hears getting closer by the hour, nor the bombing he hears down the street.

Without a word, the unidentified visitor unlocks the cell's door, darts his eyes toward the hall as a sign for the prisoner to follow him and says nothing as they stride down the long corridor leading to the back door of Prey Sar, soon to be known as S-24. Terrified, the lone man, who is aware of the many ways of execution he's witnessed during his 6½-year tenure in Southeast Asia, doesn't even know how to prepare for death.

To his surprise, he is led to a car waiting outside the building. The man who unlocked the cell opens the back door of the car for his passenger, and then gets in the front passenger seat. The driver, with the car already in gear, speeds away. From the back seat, the prisoner catches a glimpse of smoke filtering around the outskirts of the city, where the city meets the jungle and the war zone beyond. *The evening movie now features a morning matinee*, he observes, thinking of the mysterious man as the "doorman" of the theater. Still no one says a word until they arrive at Phnom Penh's tiny airport. The mysterious man—the "doorman"—hops out, opens the back door for his passenger and escorts him to a small commercial aircraft.

Within minutes, the lone man is flying above the fighting below. He has no window seat for his own personal air show, or a ticket to tell him where he's going. It isn't long before the sound of the propellers winding down is his only clue he's on his way back to Saigon.

Once there, he heads for the office where he regularly picks up his check, now back pay since he's been out of the country. The "rescue money" he's gone to collect is anything but that. The minute he arrives at the office and asks for his pay, he's immediately picked up by immigration police and taken to the immigration jail in Saigon, on the grounds of an invalid passport since he still has no Visa.

The rumblings, heard in the far distance by a precarious Chandra only days before, are now much louder. In fact, they seem so close that the earth below her feet shakes as she plays with her friends. As she briefly pauses to peer in the direction of the booming sounds, she is fascinated by the bright lights she sees overhead. Some are red and some are white, appearing to her as giant sparklers streaking across the sky.

"Look!" she exclaims to her friends. "They're still shooting off fireworks for the Cambodian New Year!" The comment causes all the children, now mesmerized by the light show in the middle of the day, to take a moment's respite from their game.

She soon goes back to playing, failing to notice the heavy, forlorn look written on her father's face as he watches both the children and the "fireworks."

Chhleav dwells on the North Korean slogan for education he hears in his morning class, reading it aloud until he commits it to memory. "Children are the kings for the nation in the future." Enamored with the fact that the North Korean government supports education and encourages people to do research, he wants to see his country adhere to their system of eight hours for education, eight hours for work and eight hours for sleep and activities with family and friends. Like North Korea, he believes individuals should be rewarded for their efforts.

Even though Yugoslavia is socialist, he admires the fact their government allows people to own houses and small businesses, have vocations, and be involved in government. What impresses Chhleav most about their governmental system is how people get along and work together, and that there is little poverty. He longs to see these same values in Cambodia, so that everyone honors, respects and loves each other.

His ideals are greatly swayed by the communistic thought of the Yugoslavians, a practice he admires, as they "level the playing field"—

to borrow a western expression—of their citizens. It seems a way of thinking that could help his native homeland, where the wealth is spread among so few of the people. The pendulum of that situation is slowly swinging, though, as more of his generation earns an education, lending more professional people to their culture. He sees their efforts as a way to help Cambodia develop and maintain its place in the world now that it is no longer a French Colonial protectorate.

A welcome change after 100 years under their thumb, he thinks to himself. Thailand, once known as Siam, is bordered by the three countries of Laos, Vietnam and Cambodia, which once made up the protectorate considered Indochina. The four countries now make up their own territory, Southeast Asia.

Ah, that I could take the political ideals of Yugoslavia and the educational ideals of North Korea back to my own home country of Cambodia, blending the two ideals for the betterment of a strong nation.

Chhleav comes by his desires to help his country honestly. His father, prior to his death, was a very successful rice farmer. A devout supporter of the Cambodian kingdom and its army, Chhleav's father was known for providing food for the soldiers.

It was nothing, this young student remembers fondly, *to see anywhere from 50 – 200 soldiers show up on our farm at one time.* He recalls how, after a big meal together, the soldiers would take as many bags of rice as they could carry to keep them fed during the weeks ahead. *Twenty to thirty soldiers would carry all the guns while the rest of the soldiers would be loaded down with rice.* It is with great pride that Chhleav thinks back on his father, as he seeks to find his own way to help his country.

Get a good education and remain loyal to my country. That is the best way I can help my beloved Cambodia, he surmises, his deep brown eyes intense on the future.

Chapter Three

April 17, 1975

Sovann awakes to the sound of Khmer Rouge soldiers out in the streets announcing, "Victory! Victory! Peace! Peace!"

She gathers with the rest of her family around the radio to hear the blaring announcement, "Don't worry. We are not going to hurt you. We are looking only for the spies. Do not take your stuff. You will be coming back."

Her mother firmly states, "Don't listen to them." Full of intuition, she immediately takes the mattress sheet and fills it with as many belongings as possible. She makes a point of taking only her husband's plain shirts and not his uniform.

"Why are you gathering up so much?" asks Sovann's father as he watches the Khmer Rouge soldiers outside their house. "The Khmer Rouge soldiers are telling us we'll only be gone for three days while they clear out all the spies and enemies hiding in the city. Then we can come back." He listens with great interest to their continued chants of great news, "For everyone will be equal, no discrimination, no exploitation or oppression, and shared food for the good of each other."

Sovann's mother, whose face is covered with worried anxiety, sends him a disconcerted glare. "Surely you don't believe them."

"I'm going outside to see what is going on." He nears the door leading to the rooftop, with the captain husband of Sovann's older sister instinctively on his heels. Though the family was initially all gathered here "because of the wedding," it seems it's now more conveniently for safety's sake.

Her mother rushes to the door, at the top of the stairs leading out of their fourth-floor abode, locks it and takes the key. "No one is going anywhere until we can all leave together," she insists, suddenly taking over the assumed role of the "commander-in-chief" for their family as she continues to gather all the gold and jewelry she can manage. "We must stay together. Otherwise we may never see each other again!"

Once the sisters have helped their mother finish sewing the rest of the pieces of gold and jewelry into their undergarments or other hiding places, they make their exit. The sisters' plan to load the car is foiled as they realize they'll be unable to buy gas once the tank is empty. They are forced to make their exodus on foot with only a small wooden cart.

Sovann glances at the clock on the wall. *Five o'clock. The hour most workers go home, yet here we are leaving our home.* She takes a last look over her shoulder at all the wedding gifts and all the items for tomorrow's festive occasion. Her mother's staunch command, "Go!" leaves her without a chance to even say good-bye to the world and the future she is leaving behind. She, like the rest of her family, follows the order as they depart with great sadness and uncertainty.

They enter the street—Sovann, her parents, five of her sisters and one brother-in-law—already filled with hundreds of thousands of citizens. The excited joy on the faces of the people, earlier believing "peace is at hand," has turned to fright. The same men, who this morning were announcing victory and peace, are now pointing guns and ordering them to leave and take nothing. Sovann, terrified beyond all her wits, is certain of only one thing at this point. Because their children are all daughters, her parents have always been extremely protective of them, never allowing them to go out alone. When they would go to the movie, all seven of them would sit in a line in the center of the theater, with their mother on the left, and their father on the right. Sovann sneaks a hasty and disdainful peek at the soldiers. She is sure her mother will do everything within her power and means, as "the commander," to make sure her seven daughters stay safe from harm.

When they come to the Chinese Hospital across from Sovann's

old high school on Monivong Boulevard, they see its patients also being forced to evacuate. Throngs of people laboriously attempt to keep up with the crowds as they walk on crutches or roll themselves in wheelchairs. Some, fortunate enough to be pushed on a gurney, wince in pain as they bounce wildly along the gutted, dusty roads. Kind souls with oxcarts try to help, having little room to add anything else to their already excessive loads.

Sovann, whose mind is on anything but tomorrow's wedding, forgets her own minute problems as she notices "the commander" reach out to help some of the patients. Her dream of wanting to bring justice to all the people of Cambodia suddenly becomes the forefront of her thoughts again as she desperately seeks to soak in all she can of a place she knows she will not see again in three days. *If ever.*

The lone man is no longer alone; there are three other Americans being held in the immigration jail, one of whom also works for the military base under contract from the government and was arrested when he went to collect his check. He learns from the other three that a "somewhat secret" evacuation of American civilians and military has been going on in Saigon since the day he left for Cambodia, at the first of April.

From living in Vietnam for the past four-and-a-half years, he knows enough of the language to understand the guards are speaking of sending him and the other military worker, via boat, to Con Son Prison on an island fifty miles off the coast of Vung Tau in Vietnam. *That's the prison reputed to house political prisoners,* he recollects. He's heard some of the stories of the place and the welfare of the prisoners. And he's aware that to the North Vietnamese and the Viet Cong, at this point, he is considered a spy. In a meager sense, he is a mercenary.

He continues to listen intently to the words of the guards, overhearing exactly what he fears. They intend to use him and his co-worker as bargaining chips with the North Vietnamese. Although terror has been the guiding factor of every day he's spent in Southeast Asia, he senses the end of his life is as certain as the end of Saigon.

My collection of Southeast Asian treasures are history, he muses as he pictures himself back in his spacious rented house where it was much safer to live as a native than on the military compound. *Not that any of it matters now.*

He wonders about the whereabouts of the Asians—"agents"—they drop off behind the lines in Cambodia, three or four at a time who are to disperse and infiltrate the countryside, working themselves into the villages. The helicopter would hover a few feet over the ground while he kicks out sacks containing approximately four hundred pounds of rice. He never asks what the "agents" do, where they go, or who gets the rice; the less he knows the better. On those nights, his main concern is scooting back to Saigon in one piece as quickly as possible.

This is not exactly the life he intended for himself. He allows his thoughts to drift back six-and-a-half years when, after four years in the United States Air Force—the last year spent living in tents and doing remote duty as an F105 fighter bomber crew chief in an outback area of Thailand—he returns to the States. Once home, his decision to try marriage, which proves to be worse than war, leaves him with the freedom to attend aviation school for a couple of years. His experience and training land him a great job with Lockheed, but when work cuts back in 1970, so does his position.

Having no ties to hold him down, he decides to go to Vietnam to work under contract for the United States government, imbedded with the military, much like the foreign war correspondents. His work—sometimes on helicopters, sometimes on jets—is whatever is necessary for their present mission. After a certain number of days in Vietnam, he has to leave the country since he's there on a tourist Visa. Between contracts, he enjoys coastal holidays while waiting for the U.S. Embassy to issue him a new tourist Visa to get back into Vietnam.

That's been his lifestyle from January of 1970 until now, until what he suspects is the takeover of Phnom Penh, and the imminent fall he feels reeling toward Saigon, both at the hands of communists.

How many other civilians can lay claim to closing down two countries in two weeks? he mutters to himself sarcastically.

Chandra watches carefully as her father quietly and methodically pulls together as many personal belongings as he is able, making sure not to collect more than each family member can carry. There are no fun and games on this day for the little girl is not allowed to go outside to play. She peers cautiously out a window to see that neither are any of her friends outside. Unsure of what is going on around her, she is certain of one thing. *This is not a game*, she concludes as her eyes follow her father's every move.

When the door finally opens and each person in the family exits the house, carrying as much as is humanly possible, the precocious five-year-old sees the streets full of people. Some of them are loaded down with all their belongings as they walk; some are riding bicycles with their belongings tied on. Still others follow oxcarts or cow carts, loaded so heavily that even the strong animals appear to struggle. She notices men, their eyes looking as hard and cold as the guns they carry, dressed in what appears to be black pajamas.

The street is so crowded they can only take a few steps at a time. It is a human traffic jam, with nothing but wall-to-wall people, as far as her dark little eyes can see.

"Where are we going?" Chandra finally ventures to ask after her little feet feel they won't make another step.

"Back to Kampong Cham," answers her father.

At first she is very excited with his answer, for that is the place she was born and lived before her family's move to Phnom Penh. That excitement evaporates into thin air when Chandra looks up into her father's face, catching a glimpse of something she has never seen there—marked fear. It is a haunting vision she shall never forget.

Chhleav contemplates on how, in order for his dream of equality, peace and freedom to work in Cambodia, every citizen must work hard. Though saddened by his father's untimely death, he is grateful for the opportunity of learning what it takes to support a family. He knows how to farm, fish, make bamboo trays and baskets and harvest rice using a sickle. Though not something he considered so important before, he now realizes he has a deeper appreciation for the fact he possessed all those skills by the time he went to live in the monastery. He sees them, combined with his intuitive and curious nature, as an asset. Therefore, he spends much of his time observing others and learning from them, which he determines to be another useful tool. Even with his graduate education, he is sure these "hands-on" skills and qualities will prove most useful throughout his entire life.

Hard work is primary, he tells himself, looking back on his days at the monastery. He remembers how difficult the adjustment to such a simple way of life is for him at first. *Perhaps that's why I stayed so busy,* he speculates. Now, like then, he is always finding something to occupy his time. He recognizes how, even at that youthful point in his life, his diligence pays off. It is his responsible nature and personality that have made him the class president or a team leader in every school situation. His prominent features, marking him with an air of distinction, have not hurt in distinguishing him for that role.

Allowing his mind and memories to again transport him back to that time, he sees himself busily cleaning up the facilities, washing dishes, cleaning toilets and washing the monk's clothes. The monk is so impressed he entrusts Chhleav with the monk's fund. The monk, who ate well from the good food collected from the rich families of the village, also allows Chhleav to later eat the leftover food, which is better than what the other students have to eat. (It is a Buddhist custom that no one can eat until the monk has first been offered food.)

He envisions the rich students who attend high school, the ones who have a good place to study and are able to go on to the university in Battambang. They are extremely studious and work hard on their major. In sharp contrast, Chhleav remembers how most of the students who live in the monastery are discriminated against, mocked, rejected and laughed at by the rich students. These students share rooms and have to use candles and oil lamps to see to study. They even burn incense sticks to point at their books in order to see to read. In spite of their hardships, most of these students still complete their university studies.

Which then makes them equal to the rich students as they go out to be leaders, Chhleav calculates, still assured that education, hard work and loyalty are the keys to his future of helping his country and its people. *A future of empowering others, considering their knowledge and abilities, and making sure they in turn do the same for others,* he tells himself, vowing to take his responsibility in these areas seriously.

Chapter Four
Five Weeks Later

There is no wedding for Sovann. Khmer Rouge soldiers seize her fiancé the moment they catch sight of his military uniform. It seems his good fortune of surviving the bombing of Phnom Penh's military building has caught up with him.

The "three days" her family has been told they would be away from their home has now turned into weeks. Days pass quietly as people glance to those around them with concern. They try to create silent friendships and a pleasant environment in the midst of their hardships. It is a terribly long and slow struggle just to put one foot in front of the other, much less lag behind the countless scores of persons in front of them. Sovann has lost track of time; she has no idea how long she's been gone, or what date it is. All she knows is her mother was right in her dubious suspicions of the Khmer Rouge's claims.

She notices many families have been split up and assigned to various villages, making sure no one has the luxury of a confidante. *Yet another finely-tuned point of the Khmer Rouge's well-planned and foolproof scheme for managing the people,* she is quick to reason. *In fact, no one has any sort of luxury.*

For her family, they are at least still together as they continue to make their way toward Kralanh, the village where Sovann was born in the Srok Kralanh district of Siem Reap province. Knowing she's returning to familiar territory at least makes it a bit easier every night when they have to find a different spot to bed down along the main road. A few times they've been lucky enough to find an abandoned hut so they don't have to sleep on the ground.

Along the way, Sovann discovers many of the young women have been made to cut their hair by the Khmer Rouge. She's greatly relieved no one has approached her family with that requirement. That's why she's so appalled when, very early one morning, "the commander" awakens the six daughters.

"Quick, cut your hair!" Sovann's mother hastens to order to them. Her voice is soft but emphatic.

Sovann cannot believe her ears. *Not my hair. My beautiful hair that I wanted to be absolutely perfect for my wedding.* She thinks of the evening the week before the scheduled event when she sat in front of the mirror, admiringly taking care of her most treasured physical attribute. Her fingers instantly reach up to the back of her head as she runs them through the long and thick, black hair she'd groomed so long for the never-to-be wedding.

"Cut it now!" storms her mother, handing the scissors toward Sovann's older married sister. "We must look like peasants. Your long hair styles will make them think we are a family of means. Hurry!" she warns. "We must leave soon!"

As the sisters stare at each other in shocked disbelief, Sovann clasps her hands around her cherished locks. *I can't possibly cut my hair,* she vows as she glares at the scissors now in her sister's hand.

Five of the sisters take turns with the scissors as a growing pile of black hair accumulates on the ground. Sovann, with tears in her eyes, watches as their appearances magically change in front of her very eyes. *Only the magic is horrendous rather than wondrous,* she observes sadly. *"Black magic," like the black hair on the ground.*

One look at her sisters proves she was right in her assessment the day before. The Khmer Rouge has robbed them of every luxury. *At least we still have our family together,* she mumbles to herself, *and soon we'll be back in our home village so we'll have familiar surroundings. We will be able to stay with my grandmother and my aunty and have a roof over our heads.*

Her eyes rest on her five sisters, whose eyes and faces are now as bland as their new hairstyles.

"There is no time," insists her mother, looking at the last of her daughters.

Sovann looks pleadingly at her mother for one fleeting moment.

"It's either your hair or your life," states "the commander" with no emotion. She hands the scissors to Sovann.

Finally giving way to the obvious, the remaining sister acquiesces to the command. She remains perfectly still as her worry is no longer losing her hair, but how shabby it will look. A few deliberate whacks and the deed is done. Sovann hands the scissors back to her mother while reaching her free hand to her hair that now barely reaches her ear lobe. She has to fight the tears when she feels the sharp splintery ends. Unable to speak as they begin their day's journey, she is so devastated that even the hunger pains screaming from her stomach go unnoticed.

However, once again, she learns her mother's intuition pays off when, later that day, a family is removed from the line of travelers by Khmer Rouge soldiers. "What you do?" a soldier loudly yells to the father of the family. People walking try to keep their eyes peeled on the road ahead, but the commotion is too loud to be ignored. "You educated!" blares the soldier.

"No," the father pleads repeatedly. "No education. Only a factory worker."

"No factory worker," rebukes the soldier while another one holds a gun at the head of the man's wife. "Her hair and clothes not those of factory worker."

Travelers do not dare look back for a peek at the family who is not seen rejoining the group.

"The actions of the Khmer Rouge are becoming more severe," Sovann's father quietly warns his family that evening.

She hears the intensity in his voice, which lacks the strength it once had as a military undercover worker. She sees the anguish on the faces of her sisters, who now all look like carbon copies of one another. She tastes the pangs of hunger as they eat the last mango her father found in the wee hours of the morning while his daughters were losing their identities. She smells the stench of rotting bodies of persons who have been tagged enemies of a savage regime. Sovann turns to face the steadfast "commander-in-chief" for any grain of encouragement. And she feels the pain of a mother who understands she is no longer in control.

It is with grave difficulty that Sovann fights back the lump in her throat as she reaches up to feel her hair, which is now more like course broom straw than hair. Suddenly she feels like a blind person reaching through the darkness for an object that isn't there as the reality of this nightmarish drama hits her. *My hair is the last of my concerns.*

Travel seems to begin earlier the following morning after yet another sleepless night. As tired as Sovann is from the weeks of walking, she is grateful to be moving. She forces her mind to focus on the task of putting one foot in front of the other while carrying the load of belongings she is assigned. That is, until she happens upon another astute observation, more profound than the one regarding luxuries. *The soldiers were right in their announcement on April 17th that everyone would be equal, would look alike and be treated the same*, she admits dejectedly. *Poorly.*

No one in her family has ventured to mention the gold, jewelry and money with which they've managed to escape. At the moment, Sovann is certain the rest of her family members share her opinion that those items are more of an albatross than an asset. Should they be stopped by Khmer Rouge soldiers, or their treasures discovered, she fears the albatross will become their death warrant. The only positive thought she has is she will soon be able to be with the maternal grandmother and aunty who were unable to attend her wedding, that didn't happen.

She spots both male and female soldiers at the sides of the road ahead of them. Every one of them is dressed in black pajama-style shirts, with the males wearing pants and the females wearing skirts. Except for the black garbs, they look no different from the persons, including her family, walking in the long line.

"What you carry?" one of the male soldiers asks Sovann's father.

"Only a couple of pots, eating utensils and a change of clothes," answers Sovann's mother before the father has time to speak. Her voice is nothing but calm as all signs of earlier alarm are absent from her demeanor.

Two of the other soldiers, a male and a female, rustle through the contents of the mattress sheet. One of them is handling a garment Sovann witnessed being altered with hidden jewels before their evacuation from Phnom Penh.

"Where you go?" asks the soldier rattling off questions.

"To the village of Kralanh," Sovann's father answers.

"No," replies the male soldier whose hand is on the "jeweled" garment. "You go to Phum Prey Thom, in the district of Srok Chi Kraeng in Siem Reap province." He tosses the garment, its secret value undetected, back onto the bundle of clothes.

"But my family is from Kralanh," replies Sovann's mother, trying to explain.

"You go to Phum Prey Thom," repeats the soldier who, up to this point, has been asking the questions. The three soldiers raise their guns to add defiance to their order.

Sovann's family begins moving, taking the road to Phum Prey Thom instead of Kralanh. Even though it is in the same province, it is a destination that will take them several more weeks to reach on foot.

A lone man sits in a coffee shop in his hometown of Montgomery, the capital of Alabama, leafing through the local newspaper's world headlines in his effort to find out what is going on in Phnom Penh and Saigon. There is nothing besides reports of the evacuations. The only information he's found since being home is a small blurb, one that would have gone unnoticed had he not been searching for it, that simply states, "Khmer Rouge takes over Cambodia as their soldiers triumphantly march into Phnom Penh yelling in choruses of 'PEACE! PEACE HAS FINALLY COME!'"

There's more to what I didn't read than what I did read, he tells himself as he folds the paper, puts it on the table and stares out the window. The vision in front of him, as he allows his mind to look past the world outside, is the same one he left at the precise moment he was arrested along Phnom Penh's waterfront. All he sees is the Mekong River rolling slowly past as images of a civil war flash all around him, and naked children dive from a Chinese junk docked along the river's bank into the water of the only world they've ever known...war.

His mind then flashes to the jail cell in Saigon, where an American civilian is being led toward him with fast-paced steps, the determined fortitude in them matched by the mission marked by his eyes. The prisoner has no idea what is going on, but he knows it isn't good. He and his co-worker are pulled from the cell, leaving the other two behind, and marched hastily outside to a military truck where they all jump in the back. Another American, dressed as a commoner in civilian clothes but whose appearance and demeanor say otherwise, hands him an AWOL bag. Suddenly the prisoner understands. The American Embassy has stepped in at the last minute and paid the Vietnamese a dump-truck load of American money to release him and the other man. He doesn't open the AWOL bag, but he's certain it contains everything he needs to get out of the country, including American money.

The next thing he knows, he is at Saigon's Tan Son Nhut Airport seated aboard a Pan Am 707 commercial plane, only the second aircraft he's been on for which he was not the crew chief in the past few years, the first being the one that brought him here only days before. He doesn't look at the other passengers as he moves down the aisle toward his seat. Nor does he speak to the person seated beside him as he fastens his seatbelt. He only stares at the back of the seat in front of him as he reaches up to feel the scruffy stubble that's accumulated on his face during the past several days of being behind bars. His eyes are bloodshot from lack of sleep, his head is reeling from all that's transpired in the last two weeks and his heart is racing faster than the jet's roaring engines. This nightmare is even more bizarre than the ones of the past ten nights' imprisonment or the ones of every flight he oversaw during his 6½ years in Southeast Asia.

Frightened beyond words, he has no clue where this latest nightmare will take him until he lands in San Francisco, California. A lover of music, he peers out the window of the jet and recalls a well-known song, *I Left My Heart in San Francisco.* Divorced, with no children and no job awaiting him, and knowing no life in his own homeland for the better part of the past 8½ years, he feels he left his heart in Southeast Asia.

Confused and not knowing where to turn, he exits the plane with only an AWOL bag containing cash, a couple of personal items and a change of clothes, the latest in Southeast Asian peasant fashion.

The screen of his mental movie shuts off abruptly as he returns to the present. His eyes fall back to the paper, the world's source for the latest news. *Seems America's "secret war" has just become Cambodia's "secret war,"* he concludes wearily while skimming over his country's front page headlines. He struggles to feel any emotion of joy or happiness at being home, breathing in the muggy Alabama air—not so unlike the muggy air of Southeast Asia—as in his mind's eye is still a street lined with storefronts whose signs speak of "Happy."

"There is a happy land, far, far away…" he hears from within, in the Appalachian plain-gospel voice of his grandmother, as the words to an old hymn she sang to him when he was but a toddler dance through his mind. Somewhere, in the deepest crevices of his consciousness, he fears the words "happy" and "lucky" are no longer a part of the vocabulary of the Cambodian people. *At least not those captured by the Khmer Rouge,* he tells himself skeptically as he downs the rest of the coffee, and heads out to find his own place in a world that has not been home to him since he left high school.

It is impossible for Chandra to understand why her family must sleep on the ground, and why they are shooed from place to place. What, at first, was an adventurous game to this little girl is no longer. She keeps hoping for an answer from her father, but she gets none. No one dares to speak for fear of the soldiers in black pajamas pointing guns at them. The closest thing she gets to an answer is the weary, faraway look in her father's tired eyes. Her young mind is incapable of perceiving what thoughts lay behind them.

Her father, longing to look into the beautiful dark eyes of his precious daughter, knows he must not for fear of losing his entire family. Heartbroken that he cannot offer her—or the rest of the family—any comfort, he occupies the countless hours of walking by reflecting on the monumental endeavor of this mass evacuation. Until April 17th, approximately two-million people lived in Phnom Penh; now there are none.

There is no doubt in his mind this is a plan—although ruthless—well thought out and maneuvered, leaving no room for mistakes. The only problem, though, is it *is* one big mistake. *Or at least an inhuman disaster,* he reasons, trying to find any rational reasoning behind the situation occurring in his country. It stands to reason that though the Khmer Rouge has no official headquarters, the wilds of the jungles and remote villages have obviously served its leaders well to allow them to implement such an in-depth operation.

He attempts to make any sense out of Pol Pot being behind all this lunacy and terror. Pol Pot, a man he knows as the principal of his son's high school when they still lived in Skuon town.

We'll be safe once we arrive at our town and people know who we are, the scared little girl assures herself while sneaking a peek in her father's direction. *After all, Pa says we're all from the same place, this Mr. Pol Pot and us. I've even heard some of the people on our walk calling him "Brother Number One." That sounds like a friendly name.*

Their family, along with others also headed toward Cambodia's third largest city, continues to walk toward their destination of Kampong Cham. Bordered by Vietnam on its east and bisected by the Mekong River, it is only seventy-eight miles from Phnom Penh. But it takes many days to get there when they have to carry all their belongings. The little girl hopes they can find another temple in which to spend the night, like they have for the past couple of nights, before being shooed on their way.

Before Chandra knows what is going on, her father is captured by Khmer Rouge soldiers. He is pulled out of line from the rest of his family and the others traveling up the dusty road toward their individual hometowns. From the soldiers' harsh words and the demanding tones of their voices, the little girl decides these bad men recognize her father.

They sound like they mean him harm! she senses, completely terrified. *Because he is from the same town where Pol Pot was a principal, they should know who he is and be aware of his past position in the town.*

They drag him away, leaving a sad and mournful child to never again see her father.

Chhleav thinks of his home daily, missing it terribly, but sure the sacrifice he is making to complete his studies is worth it. He spends all his spare time, which is minimal, making a mental list of the pros and cons of socialist and nationalist republics. Then he memorizes how he hopes to combine them in such a way that he can one day bring freedom to his people.

Little does he know what is happening to the people of his beloved Cambodia. All foreign correspondents—who've managed to stay alive this long—have been evacuated, with a few of them fortunate enough to have been rescued by their embassies. All pipelines of communication are shut off, making sure the world has no idea of the real situation in an already oppressed nation, now under the power of the Khmer Rouge.

Oblivious to the situation, he continues to study and plan how he one day hopes to make a difference in his country. His admiration for a socialistic government grows daily.

Chapter Five
1977

With the arrival of 1977 comes the delivery of a message from the Khmer Rouge stating the workers are going to be released from the suffering, abusive treatment, starvation and killing. Hopes heighten, along with the ecstatically joyful moods of the workers. So does the level of their work, as they prepare themselves to do whatever it takes to again be free.

Ma isn't buying into this, Sovann immediately notices, correctly interpreting the look of skepticism etched on her mother's face.

The message turns out to be no more than a joke, for a reason the workers fail to understand. What they do understand is the fact that men begin disappearing at night, one of whom is Sovann's brother-in-law, married to her older sister, the second daughter of the family. Conflicting thoughts and viewpoints cause a silent turmoil within the work camp, building an insurmountable wall of distrust within the workers as well as the Khmer Rouge soldiers and leaders.

Sovann is sent to another work camp, several miles away from her mother's hut, to a rice field across the road from a Buddhist temple and a wooden pagoda with lattice walls, where the monks once lived before their deaths. The monks' ashes are now interred in decorative tombs that line the road in front of the pagoda, protected by a beautifully detailed and gold-painted wrought-iron fence.

I have no life. No freedom. Nothing. Sovann takes a breath, as deep as is possible with the weakened state of her body in the late afternoon's heat. *Nothing, except the ability to think,* she reminds herself. *They may have brainwashed the children and youth whom they've turned into Khmer Rouge soldiers, but they've yet to brainwash me.* Without lifting her head, while using a hoe to break clods of dirt for the next planting, she darts her eyes upward and sneaks a peek at the hundreds of young workers around her. She wonders how many of their spirits have been broken down, either by loss of loved ones, by hallucinations that accompany the deadly starvation and bouts of diarrhea, or through physical and mental abuse.

A brief, fleeting thought crosses her mind of the dream she once entertained of one day bringing justice to her country, especially for the women. Commanding her hands to hoe by rote, she allows her mind to dwell on the days she longed to go to law school, to be an educated advocate for the women and people of her country. Whenever that dream replays in her mind, it also brings the image of her mother, who wanted her daughters to be teachers at the time. No matter, Sovann dearly loves her mother. She now understands all her mother ever wanted was the best for her daughters. That's why she runs several miles to her mother's hut lots of evenings after she's supposed to be asleep.

They've robbed us of everything. Everything! Sovann wants to scream in outrage. Yet she squelches that desire for only one reason. Expressing herself in any manner, outraged or otherwise, is sure death. It is not an option she minds. In fact, she welcomes that idea, so the possibility of losing her life is not what sways her actions. *They've even robbed us of fear,* she reasons, recognizing she's prepared mentally, physically, emotionally and spiritually to die.

She has considered the idea of taking her own life on more than one occasion, defending her suicidal thoughts with the rationale: *I can't take my own life. They've already taken it. Therefore I cannot be punished for attempting suicide on a life that is not there.* In fact, she has made six attempts on her life, each time deciding she has suffered despair and dehumanization long enough. One time she swallows six pills, sure that will end her vile situation. But she is sent out immediately after taking the pills to dig in a field. It is enormously hard work in the hot sun, causing her to sweat so profusely that the poison is apparently emitted from her system through her pores. Her last attempt—only a week before—also ends in failure at the hands of a friend. It is actually the idea of another female worker, the closest thing she has to a friend in the work camp, to jump off a bridge.

"You really want to do that?" Sovann asks quietly after the friend confides in her.

"Yes," answers the friend.

"I'll go with you. Tonight after everyone else is asleep, I'll go to the toilet. Shortly after you see me leave, you come. I'll be waiting for you just beyond it."

After their long walk to the bridge that evening, the two young women haggle briefly about who will jump first. "You go," says Sovann. "It was your idea."

The other woman, however, becomes so terrified she refuses to jump. Sovann, determined to no longer be a slave to the Khmer Rouge, decides to go first. She climbs to the top of the railing on the bridge, but is pulled back by her friend.

"You cannot," the friend urges.

"Why do you not jump?" Sovann asks, aggravated by her friend's inability to go through with the suicide attempt. She balks for a short while, still wanting to end the unbearable turmoil, before she finally acquiesces to the friend's fear of returning to the work camp alone in the dark. They manage to get back, slipping stealthily through the dark, without being caught. That, too, would mean sudden death, or at the very least, punishment.

A week later, back in the nightmare of her everyday existence, she scolds herself for not allowing herself to get caught. That would have been a fitting, and compromising, solution. She and the friend would have been killed, and therefore not taken their own lives. They would now be in one of the small mounds next to this rice field, where the bodies of all the others, who were killed or died due to the conditions, are buried.

Her thoughts are consumed by the memory of when her family was still all together shortly after they left Phnom Penh. On the route, her family finds some fruit, which they pick and are about to eat when an elderly woman stops them. "You cannot eat that fruit!" the woman yells. "It is poisonous. You will all die. I've seen the people who eat this die in horrible ways." Heeding her warning, they continue on their way, hungry and miserable.

Why did she have to stop us? Sovann wonders. *We could have all died together.* She is filled with anger that every time she tries to end this hell, an inexplicable "thing" or "person" blocks her effort. The fact there is possibly an internal consciousness stopping her, telling her she has a greater mission in life, never fazes her. Unknowingly, she is too blind to see and too deaf to hear.

She focuses on the one reason that keeps her from screaming in outrage. *Checking on my mother*. Her body stiffens. *That is the underlying motive that always stops me when I get the notion to end my life,* she admits. *That's the reason.* At least it has been the reason until today, the day she loses sight of all hope.

Had she been afraid of dying alone, that is no longer a contention. Her older sister, sent to this camp with her young baby—because she was no longer considered married when her husband "disappeared"—has decided she can bear no more pain. During today's lunch, Sovann and her older sister jointly decide there is nothing on earth worth living in this hell for another day. They elect to confront their Khmer Rouge leader this afternoon and tell him the truth about their education, that they are high school graduates.

The rest of the afternoon is filled with no emotion, no anxiety; only long minutes of waiting for just the right moment. From the corner of her eye, she sees her sister drop her hoe. Following her sister's lead, she does the same. They share what they consider to be their final walk, as together they approach the Khmer Rouge leader.

Their plan works. Late that night, when everyone else is asleep, soldiers come and quietly "steal" Sovann and her sister, along with the young baby, away from the rest of the workers. They are escorted to the wooden pagoda, the ultimate stop for those awaiting death. It is not an exclusive honor for them. They are in the company of the wife and baby of a doctor, who also mysteriously "disappeared," and three young children.

Sovann feels no pain or agony over her impending fate. There is ironically a sense of relief. The only anticipation is of the exact moment of the act. There is no loss of sleep, for she rarely sleeps. That is a necessity she has long since learned to forego, like many of the other workers. Sleep brings death. Sleep brings disappearances. *Sleep brings nightmares worse than the ones we live each day*. Oddly enough, she closes her eyes, with the comfort of a wooden floor beneath her and a roof over her head. Although there are holes in the criss-cross pattern of the lattice work, there are at least walls. She is at peace. Sleep comes.

Sovann wakes, but lies quiet and still in the hour before morning's twilight as she listens to the daily procession of footsteps. Because shoes of the workers wore out long before, their steps are barely audible. It is only because of the brush of their clothing as they walk that she knows they are passing by on the small path, only two-hundred feet from the side of the pagoda where she lies, on their way to the huge rice field where they work, across the main road from the temple.

She looks at her sister and wonders whether she too is awake, yet she dares not make a sound. *How long until the baby cries?* she wonders. Sovann remains frozen in place. *What difference does it make? The three of us will be dead soon.* She breathes a silent sigh of relief. Death is no longer feared; it is a welcome exit to the existence now known by the workers. No one has been spared the death of family and friends. No one has been spared starvation. No one has been spared emotional and physical abuse.

For the first time, she realizes her stomach no longer growls in hunger. That is a natural reflex that fell by the wayside months before. It is replaced by an abscess in her stomach that makes it feel even worse when she does eat. Food is not a necessity to her at this point.

Nevertheless, Sovann's other senses are extremely sharp. As hard as she tries, she cannot void them of the smell and sight of death that lies all around her. Meticulously placed in front of the temple, no more than a stone's throw from where she lies in the wooden pagoda, are the tombs sacredly containing the ashes of Buddhist monks from past generations. The remaining ashes and bones of the long-time villagers from this area are buried in one of the several gravesites diagonally across the larger road in front of the temple's tombs. The other gravesites, covered by small mounds of dirt, lie at the edge of the rice field to which all the workers file daily. They contain the mass graves of victims and are used by the Khmer Rouge leaders and soldiers as a means of keeping the workers at bay, taunting them with the presence of ghosts and spirits that remain with their ashes and bones. *The same gravesites the workers, who just left with no breakfast, had to pass as a "warning" on their way to the rice field.*

And then there's the smell of fresh death, among which Sovann comprehends that she, her sister and nephew will soon be a part. That's the worst part of being in the pagoda. Not because of the fear of death, but due to the horrendous nausea she has to fight away, stemming from the rancid smell of the rotting flesh present all around her. Even worse is the sight of bones lying outside in the dirt and bodies partially unearthed, dug up—by the neighboring dogs—when they were left barely covered by the soldiers who committed the heinous act.

The pagoda, whose open door and lattice-style walls would otherwise provide an airiness of beauty and inspiration for the monks who once resided here, is now no more than a house of approaching—better termed as "encroaching" for its current inhabitants—death. Signs of the first morning light peek into the pagoda's diamond-shaped openings from the east, serving as a stark contrast from the circle of gloom that hovers around them, as thick as if it were a protective film enclosing the wooden structure. Still there is no sign of a cup with only a tiny portion of rice, which Sovann and her sister will give to the baby, keeping none for themselves. *What need have we for food at this point?* she questions herself, awaiting a fate that is now imminent.

She lays there, like on the many nights of the past two years when she has been unable to sleep, daring not to mumble a word to any of her family members. A sarcastic laugh nearly escapes her lips. *Why do I worry now?* It no longer matters that a Khmer Rouge soldier is most likely hiding under the hut, or just outside the building, waiting to hear even a word or witness the slightest show of emotion, both of which are signs for certain death from Angkar Leu.

Angkar...the high government who is reputed to be the head of the family...everyone's family, she cynically reminds herself. Instead, it is a feared and mysterious presence acted out in the form of Khmer Rouge soldiers, male and female, whose steel-cold eyes exhibit the absence of emotion caused by brainwashing the children and youth of Cambodia. *Children and youth who, one day, should have had the opportunity to be doctors, professors and national leaders,* she dolefully commiserates.

Sovann heaves a long, but silent, sigh. It is her way of ridding her body of the sorrow for her country, the sorrow for her family, the sorrow for her own state of life and mind from the past two years, but mostly sorrow for the death of this precious child, whose shape she barely makes out in the dawning light. The breaking dawn suddenly also silhouettes the shape of the guard who's been assigned to them as he stands just outside the building.

She stares at the black uniform, wondering whether her mother's hands touched it, dyeing it a deep and dark black, in an effort to earn some superficial appreciation, at least enough to keep her family fed and alive for yet another day. Those worn hands, blackened from the dye, stand out more in her mind's eye than her mother's face as she lies there thinking of how she'll never again be able to run through the blackness of night—hitting the dirt or hiding anytime she spots a flashlight or approaching bicycle—on her way to check on her mother.

Getting herself in this "cage of waiting death," as it has become, is of her own doing. She is thankful that she, like her sister, has an education, making them "too educated" for the level of people Pol Pot's regime wanted for the rice fields and farms. *"Too educated" to live, to know better, is more like it,* she bitterly concludes. She has no regrets of openly volunteering that information. Having no other means of freeing herself from this man-made and ghoulish hell, it is yet another attempt of fleeing from this distressingly depressed state of her country's citizens, who live in a world with no hope, no future. *We'll all die at the hands of the Khmer Rouge one day anyway, so why spend another day in this torturous abyss they've put us in?*

She prays, beseeching the Buddha statue and angels—decorating and painted on the temple in front of her—to protect the mother and father, and sisters, she will leave behind. The prayer is no learned set of words, merely a wish of longing sent wistfully into the air, the only thing she knows to offer her family. *It's all I have to leave them*, she muses with a heavy heart.

A veil of death, from all the monks killed here, still hangs in the air like a shroud closing in around her. The silence is so eerie that it seems earth-shatteringly deafening, making her want to scream for it to stop. One can't help but notice it. She takes a long scrutinizing look at the family members who will soon die with her, grateful they are finally asleep in an oblivious state of being too tired to care.

It has been three days and the eight people are still waiting inside the pagoda. Sovann isn't sure whether she wishes the soldiers would go ahead and perform their dastardly deed or continue to allow her more time to sit and reflect on her life. The past three days hold scores of memories, some pleasant and some remorseful. Nevertheless, the story of her life is continually playing on automatic pilot while she quietly spends her days and evenings in the solitude of these few people.

The days here pass even slower than the long days of work in the hot sun. Even though the first evening inside this "death chamber" brought sleep, the two since then are nothing more than waking moments spent listening to every rustling leaf, fearing the sound to be the tiptoe of the executioner. Sovann learns that senses are heightened when one sits in complete stillness and silence. There is still no fear of the impending death; neither is there the severity of pity for the workers she's held until this point. What little emotions and reasoning power she had left have already died in these four walls, it seems.

She listens as the workers make their daily trek past her in the early morning darkness. Already in a pattern of routine, she knows the next sound will be a soldier arriving with their tiny apportionment of rice in a tin can. Her plate and fork are not luxuries that made it into this cell with her. The stench of human waste reminds her that those are not the only luxuries foregone by being encaged. She closes her eyes and pretends to sleep, if only for herself, knowing it is highly unlikely death will come in the daylight hours.

Perhaps I'm wrong about that, she decides a few hours later, shortly before the workers process in single file to the long, concrete dining hall—across the small path from the side of the pagoda—for their first meal of the day, lunch. The arrival of a soldier on a bicycle, bearing a letter which he hands to the pagoda guard, perks her instincts. *Our death warrant,* she concludes. The eyes of her sister and the doctor's wife tell Sovann they share her thought.

She doesn't move, nor do the others, as they all await the order from the guard who climbs the three short steps leading into the pagoda. Behind him are two other soldiers, who have appeared from nowhere. *His helpers. One for each of the adults,* she decides, reasoning they expect the defenseless children, who are unaware of their fate, to follow voluntarily.

"Go!" exclaims the guard.

The three women rise. Sovann notices her older sister, who was always faster than her as a child, does not win this race. They still await the order telling them where to go.

"Go!" the guard repeats, this time with a flustered attitude present in his voice. "You are free to go."

The three women stand motionless. *It is a joke!* Sovann suspects. *They will shoot us in the back the minute we run. They will use us as an example for the other workers.* Her apprehension is mirrored in the faces of the other two women as they each clutch their babies close to their breasts.

"Go now. We no longer have enough food to feed all the workers and enough people to watch all the camps so we are letting you go."

Still distrusting his words, she takes a step toward the door. The soldiers, their guns down, move back to allow the prisoners to pass and exit the pagoda. Sovann doesn't dare look back; she doesn't want to see the end coming. But she does listen for the movement of the others behind her. She longs to grab hold of her sister and nephew, feeling the need to be physically bonded with them. Yet she does nothing except put one foot in front of the other until she reaches the intersection of the main dirt path running in front of the pagoda.

No one follows them, no one bothers them. The only action by the soldiers is to shoo them on their way, much the same as they'd done when her family stopped to sleep in abandoned huts on the way here from Phnom Penh. Sovann, her sister and nephew walk for most of the rest of the day to reach their mother's hut. Because Sovann is deathly sick, running a high fever with an infection in her left thumb and right shoulder, and her sister is so sorrowful due to the recent death of her husband, they are both disappointed they were not killed.

What they soon learn is they were indeed not told the truth by the Khmer Rouge soldiers. They do not have enough food for the workers, but that is as it has been. The regime compensates for the lack of soldiers by giving more responsibility to the base people. Sovann and her sister are sent back to the rice field to work, but the baby is allowed to stay at their mother's hut in the care of their younger sister, who was injured during the evacuation from Phnom Penh, making her unable to do the harsh work in the fields.

When they return to the rice field, they are each handed a hoe by a Khmer Rouge leader. The look in his eyes is the only order they need to get busy. Little does Sovann realize the hoe she uses in the field each day was made in a metal factory in the southern part of Phnom Penh, under the supervision of a man she met several years earlier—a man to whom she has given no thought since that time.

Chapter Six

Liberation Day - January 7, 1979

Sovann observes people whispering to one another in the rice field, waiting a few minutes between persons as they seem to be passing a quiet message. Knowing the repercussions that can have on all of them, she works harder, trying to make sure the leader knows she is not a part of whatever is going on. Also aware things only get worse in this communist time, she fears what horrible thing can happen to them next.

Then, as the whispers get closer to her, she hears the word "peace." She slows the pace of her work and keeps the hoe from hitting the ground as she makes herself look busy. Her ears are pealed for more about the word that had all but disappeared from her vocabulary. "Peace," she hears again, while trying her best to look disinterested and show no emotion.

The message finally reaches Sovann. "Peace is come…peace is come." She notices the bodies of the workers, who have become so cold-hearted from the punishment of showing any love or concern for another, that they appear to be moving mummies in the rice field. Her immediate reaction is to glance toward the tombs to the side of the field where so many, who died while waiting for this day to come, are buried.

Wary of more disappointment, she forces herself to discount the comment, knowing all too well how people have been tricked in the past as she recalls the last day she heard anything resembling these words—the day her family was forced to evacuate Phnom Penh. *Besides,* she rebukes, *my family is already sad*. Word has trickled through the grapevine, or rice patty as the case is, that they are to be killed before the day is over. She is already on the lookout for any moves from anyone around her, especially the soldiers or Khmer Rouge leaders.

Her mind keeps asking the same questions over and over all morning. *Will they take us all to the same place? Will they take us one at a time? Will they wait until nightfall, like they do with so many others? What horrible way will they find to torture us? Who will they kill first?*

It is not until later in the day when Sovann overhears that a base person, a villager placed in charge of the work camp, heard the news signaling peace on the radio. Although her heart wants to believe the proclamation is true, she is afraid. Even if the gossip is true, she knows the lives of her family can still be in danger. The local people are jealous of her family. Whether rightly or wrongly, they perceive her family to be rich; because of that, they shower them with an assumed air of prestige. There is one particularly mean soldier, along with his mother, who continually threatens her family, making it clear he does not intend for the Tor family—nor their possessions—to leave the Kok Thlok Loeu commune of Prey Thom village, Chi Kraeng district, Siem Reap province.

After lunch, Khmer Rouge leaders come to the field and announce, "Go home! We don't have time to control you anymore. Just go to your family. It is time to be together in families." They then release the workers with no word of what is going on or what has happened.

Sovann finds her sister who works in the same field and, together, they start the long walk to their mother's hut. They are afraid to talk, but quietly plan their escape while keeping a close watch over their shoulders for the mean soldier. The time will come to face his mother when they reach the hut.

She thinks how similar this is to when her family left Phnom Penh in 1975, only this time travelers have nothing with them. People are on foot, sleeping along the streets and trying to find shade along the way under which to rest. *Ah, shade! Something no one has known for nearly four years.* Some people lie asleep against haystacks. As tempting as that appears, Sovann and her sister are more concerned with getting back to the hut as quickly as possible.

It is nightfall when they finally arrive at the village and learn their mother is safe. They wait, as patiently as possible under the circumstances, hoping the rest of their family will soon appear. Three days pass before they are all back together, with the exception of Sovann's oldest sister and her family. "The commander" gives the order they will leave at night, as soon as they find a way to slip away from the mean soldier and his mother. They know the days ahead hold more danger than the days past.

Chhleav leaves the lake near his work camp with the daily catch. This day has been relatively easy, at least from his perspective. He is excited because the distance back to camp is not as far as some days, and he has banana leaves and tamarind leaves to add flavor to the rice for the workers. His heart feels great pity for those who never get to leave the camp, who work there day in and day out. At least his role as the fisherman allows him a tiny freedom, for which he is most grateful, since he has to walk to the lake or other bodies of water each day.

His trait of being nice to everyone, even his enemies, has paid off well for him. Thanks to acupuncture skills he learned from a Chinese doctor he encountered while in university classes in North Korea, he is able to care for some of the ailments of the Khmer Rouge soldiers and leaders, and even one leader's fiancée, earning him a bit of trust and freedom. He knows he is lucky to possess these skills. Otherwise he would be no more than another mound of bones lying in his native country.

Less than a mile from camp, an ominously menacing air sweeps over him. For no reason, at least known to him, his steps become heavy. The usual quietness is so unusually subdued that it screeches at him, demanding to be heard. As he reaches viewing distance of the camp, he sees no workers. No sound of striking metal comes from the blacksmiths' area; no soldiers or leaders are standing guard. He vaguely makes out the silhouette of one lone Khmer Rouge leader as he approaches the metal factory.

"You are free to go," the man says. "Free,"—the word which should send him spiraling in a fit of happiness—gives him a dose of horror for he has met no one on his way here, nor has he seen anyone passing by the lake where he was fishing.

Without any explanation, the leader warns, "Do not head toward the mountains. Go to a city."

Chhleav asks no questions as he lays everything on the ground and immediately leaves for Battambang to find his family. He notices the Khmer Rouge soldier heads in the opposite direction, toward the mountains.

Traveling as speedily as possible, in his anxious state to check on the condition of his family, Chhleav hardly stops for rest or sleep until he reaches the Battambang province. It takes little time to discover his mother has died, and the whereabouts of his siblings are unknown. It takes even less time to learn the North Vietnamese soldiers have pushed the Khmer Rouge regime out of power and declared "Liberation!" for the country of Cambodia.

That means only one thing to Chhleav, whose education—both in the universities and in the work camp—have taught him he wants nothing more to do with communism, under neither the Khmer Rouge leadership nor North Vietnamese leadership. Ignoring the advice of the leader from his work camp, his steps turn toward the mountains—which lead to the Thai border and no communism in its safe haven.

Part Two

Let love be genuine; hate what is evil, hold fast to what is good;
Love one another with mutual affection
outdo one another in showing honor.
Do not lag in zeal, be ardent in spirit, serve the Lord.
Rejoice in hope, be patient in suffering, persevere in prayer.
Contribute to the needs of the saints;
extend hospitality to strangers.
Do not be overcome by evil, but overcome evil with good.
Romans 12: 9-13, 21, *NRSV*

(For the ease of the reader,
Chhleav and Sovann will hereafter
be referred to as Joseph and Marilyn,
as they are known today.)

Chapter Seven

The plane lands, right on schedule, at 10:40 pm on December 31st, 2009, at the Phnom Penh International Airport in Cambodia. I step off the plane, after nearly twenty-six hours of being in the air and losing an entire day. My initial thought is, for the first time in my life, I won't be able to call and wish my family a Happy New Year. Although a menial act, it is a tradition that happens at the stroke of midnight, from wherever I happen to be.

Oh well, I slough it off, *it's only noon on December 31st back home in North Carolina. No matter, I have a greater mission of writing a non-fiction about a Cambodian missionary couple at the moment.* The notion that I can at least exchange wishes for the New Year with the book's photographer, my dear friend and Christian brother Mark Barden who is sharing this experience with me, serves as a satisfactory consolation.

That trivial matter is immediately preempted by the fact that all the pieces of luggage from our flight have rounded the baggage carousel and mine is not among them. My extra suitcase, stuffed to the max with shirts, shoes and bubble gum for orphans, is the first one to come out, but my personal bag is nowhere to be seen. I wait patiently, watching three remaining pieces of luggage circle the carousel several times, until I accept there is no more luggage.

A familiar face, of which I suddenly catch a glimpse behind me, chases away all concern of luggage. Joseph Chan, his face covered in his usual huge smile, clasps his hands and bows his head to greet me. Feeling most welcomed by the vision of him I remember from six years ago in this same spot, I immediately turn loose of my carry-on bag and return the traditional greeting, a sampeah (clasped hands and bowed head) and the words, "Chum Reap Suor." Luggage no longer matters, since my laptop—all I really need to complete my mission here—is thankfully tucked away inside my carry-on. The owner of this familiar face, who speaks some English and has a car waiting outside, is here to take Mark and me to the Golden Gate Hotel, the same Cambodian home we had here on our prior visit.

Joseph accompanies us to the tiny baggage claim area and explains my predicament in Khmer—their native language—while Mark keeps an eye out for my luggage. Just as I finish the last of the paperwork and sign my name, a man appears from nowhere with my new purple suitcase—a Christmas present I received only a couple of days before leaving to come here.

"I believe this is yours," he says calmly in English before disappearing as quietly as he had come.

Joseph, Mark and I glare at each other, assured that I have no worries, for God's angels are already in Cambodia watching over me. *And my work*, I hurriedly pray, knowing I have to walk back through this airport in less than three weeks, to fly home, with everything I need to complete a book—in another eight weeks—about the two most selfless servants of God I know.

One step out of the airport, greeted by the reception of the 80+-degree temperature, is nearly as pleasant and vibrant as the smile on the face of Marilyn Chan, Joseph's wife, who is waiting with their vehicle just outside the main entrance. After the traditional Cambodian greeting is shared by all of us, the first words out of her mouth are "Happy New Year!"

In English! I happily note. I suddenly glance at my watch, terrified I've missed the whole event between getting Visas, going through customs and chasing down lost luggage. "Ten minutes, Mark, we still have ten minutes!" I exclaim.

Mark, the only person I know who thrills over such insignificant things as much as I do, returns my ecstatic smile as he hops in the front passenger seat and I pile in the back of Joseph's late-model Land Cruiser for the seven-mile ride eastward toward Phnom Penh's downtown and our hotel. I share my enthusiasm with Marilyn, seated in the back with me, about how overjoyed we are at all the signs of Christmas on the planes and in the airports. "Signs that are festively decorative, though there is little that speaks of the real 'reason for the season,'" I share, praying that's at least a start of accepting our Christian holiday. Our conversation immediately turns to how wonderful it is to be together again, how much work we have to accomplish in the next several days, how we go about it and exactly what information I need from them.

The conversation from the front seat billows back toward us so that I hear about all the changes here since our last visit. Marilyn, also picking up on that, exclaims, "We now have a KFC!"

"A KFC?" I repeat questioningly.

"Yes, you know, a Kentucky Fried Chicken. They've popped up all over Phnom Penh."

I laugh hysterically. "I've flown all the way to the other side of the world just to be welcomed by KFC?" Mark and I take turns sharing with them that we've both been to the original KFC in Corbin, Kentucky, a fact that thrills them. I get a strange feeling my feet have never left the ground.

Then, as if I'm back in Charlotte—or any other large city holding a New Year's celebration—traffic comes to a dead standstill. Talking stops as Mark and I stare out the front window and spy the cause of the detaining commotion at the same time. Mark, in his role as the ever-ready photographer, whips his camera and equipment from his carry-on for his first assignment of our trip. In front of us, Independence Monument is not only visible as it towers above the street circling it, but it has brightly colored fountains of water shooting up into the air, with the colors changing every few seconds to herald in the International New Year.

A huge lighted sign, spanning the entire boulevard as it hangs proudly in the air in front of the renowned monument, wishes everyone a Happy New 2010—in Khmer, of course, but it matters not. Mark and I decipher exactly what it says. We're so caught up in the moment that a nice, warm shower and the comfort of a real bed are no longer a priority. Like the thousands of Cambodians gathered in the parks stretching down either side of the monument, and others driving their motorbikes, bicycles, beat-up cars or carts—not to mention all the tuk-tuks (Cambodian taxis) carrying paying passengers—who are all attempting to make their way around the circle at the same time, we are enjoying a memorable night in Cambodia's capital city.

What better place to be, especially considering my task at hand, than in front of the monument commemorating an instrumental part behind the reason I'm here? I gleefully ask myself. It isn't until later in the trip I learn of the overwhelming number of people unaware of their actual birth date, only the year, as a result of the country's civil war and the Khmer Rouge's evacuation of Phnom Penh. Those individuals now share January 1st of the year they were born as their official birthday. So not only are Mark and I enjoying the International New Year like the rest of the world, we are also celebrating the world's largest birthday party, a fact unbeknownst to us at the time.

Now fully alert, the enjoyable scenario speedily reacquaints us with Cambodia's driving habit of what appears to be "whoever gets there first hits the gas and goes." When it's finally our turn to circle the monument, there's another huge sign spanning Norodom Boulevard—the intersecting thoroughfare—bearing the words "Happy New Year" in English in case we didn't gather the words of the first sign. The extreme joy I feel at that moment is too great for words, in either English or Khmer. To be in a foreign land, literally sent on a mission from God (or at least His helpers), totally overcome by the vastness of what I must accomplish in the next three weeks, being away from family—including my new firstborn grandchild, friends, and all familiarities of home and my traditional holidays…all of those seem suddenly inconsequential.

And I thought the man showing up with my luggage was a good sign! I laugh in silence, so aware of God's loving arms wrapped around me that I have to fight back tears. *Tears of joy, tears of awe, tears of thankfulness.*

"Do you want me to circle around so you can see it again and get more pictures?" asks Joseph.

"Yes!" Mark and I scream eagerly at the same time, more enthralled than two children in a candy or toy store for their first visit.

This time Joseph turns onto Norodom Boulevard, underneath the English sign to give us a short tour. We pass rows of fancy hotels, Prime Minister Hun Sen's home and several other businesses and establishments—most with colored lights and many with Christmas trees and other familiar Christmas decorations. They are all "signs" visibly bearing proof that Phnom Penh is well past its history as a French Colonial protectorate and its later tumultuous siege under Pol Pot's Khmer Rouge regime.

Pol Pot...Khmer Rouge... I bid my creative writing muse to look past the glamour and festive celebration before us to imagine the events at this same scene on April 17th, 1975, the day every inhabitant of this city was forced to evacuate Phnom Penh for a destination of three years, eight months and twenty days of hell. Instead of street vendors with neon flashing lights, I picture emotionless black-clad soldiers, their guns aimed at anyone who dares stray out of line or look anywhere besides the ground in front of them. Instead of food vendors with sausages on sticks, fruits and rice cakes, I mentally taste the famine of one small can's ration of rice a day per family. Instead of all the brightly colored lights, I visualize a world of total darkness. And instead of all the cars, tuk-tuks and motorbikes crowded around us, I envision an endless line of pedestrians, bicycles and oxcarts loaded down with the only things the two-million residents of that time are able to carry on their backs.

As I hear the repeated clicking of Mark's camera from the front seat, I take in the silhouettes, against the backdrop of all the festivities going on in front of us, of the couple who is the real reason I'm here. I can no longer fight back as tears of humbleness gently leave traces on my cheeks, while I thank God that I've been allowed the opportunity of sharing the Chans' unimaginable story—of both terror and redemption—with the world. It is against this backdrop of celebration, a fittingly joyful expression of life shared by scores of thousands of happy-go-lucky Cambodians, that I completely fathom the magnitude of the story I am here to write, encompassed in the vast harvest of work of these two people who each have their own incredulous and miraculous story of survival. A story which God used to guide them to this point in their lives, to this rich fertile field, where Joseph—once a fisherman for the Khmer Rouge—is now a fisher of men, and his wife Marilyn—once a rice planter for the Khmer Rouge—now plants seeds of faith.

It is long past midnight when we finally arrive at our hotel, where our rooms are on the third floor with no elevator. Our filled-to-the-brim suitcases suddenly feel tons heavier with that tidbit of news. Marilyn quickly steps up to the desk, exchanges a few words with the check-in clerk and returns with two keys for our rooms, side-by-side just past the clerk's desk, on the ground floor.

Thank you, God, for those angels, I utter with the last drop of strength I can muster as I make the few steps to my room, see all my belongings are carried safely inside, close the windows, turn on the ceiling fan and air conditioner, and collapse on top of the bed. *And thank you for Joseph and Marilyn Chan,* I manage as my eyes close.

Chapter Eight

Shortly before the appointed hour of nine o'clock on New Year's Day, Mark and I notice the Land Cruiser in one of the three parking spaces for the hotel but Joseph and Marilyn are nowhere to be found. They soon arrive at our Golden Gate Hotel, along with Chandra Chap, who will be our translator for the morning. I notice they are in the green Mitsubishi truck, purchased ten years ago by Myers Park United Methodist Church in Charlotte, North Carolina for use by the missionaries. Since that is my church, and the church where Mark's wife is one of the ministers and Mark is in the choir, I feel another momentary wave of connection with home for New Year's Day.

Chandra, I soon learn, is the sister of a missionary who now resides in California. "Marilyn and Joseph lived at the home of my brother when they first moved to California. That is how I first met them. I lived with my brother, too, because my father was killed by the Khmer Rouge when I was five years old. We left for America when I was ten.

"After grade school, I earned a degree in sociology and returned to Cambodia for two years to serve as a Christian counselor. Then I went back to the States for a brief period to receive my Master's Degree in social work at San Jose State University. I returned here to be a missionary in my mid-thirties, working as a social worker for one of the country's orphanages and as a Christian counselor at a private counseling clinic." Through our brief conversation, I detect she knows the Chan family well, and is already aware of many parts of their story, making her an ideal interpreter as I begin my first full day of work.

"Where's Joseph?" I ask, equipped with a hefty supply of blank paper and ready for countless hours of note-taking, when I suddenly realize he's gone again.

"Our battery was dead when we left you last night," Marilyn explains. "We had to take a tuk-tuk home."

The angels are at work again, I conclude with a chuckle as I imagine the couple, who recently celebrated their 30th anniversary, enjoying what—a bit humorously in my mind—is probably a much-needed and well-deserved romantic respite. I envision them being whisked away into the night air, a night of celebration, while enjoying the luxury of being chauffeured to their home as they bask in their love for each other and the world around them.

Then, not at all humorously, I suspect I'm right in my analogy that they do need and deserve this brief respite, romantic or otherwise. Staring at my many pages of preliminary notes and questions, there is a gnawing fear that my delving will carry them back to a four-year hell of gruesomely horrific memories and nightmares during "Pol Pot time," and the years following, until their safe arrival in America. It is a haunting fear that sprouted with my first readings about living conditions for survivors under Khmer Rouge control, and a fear that grew with each question I jotted on paper in anticipation of my research and interviews with them. I pray, as fervently as I know how, that the forthcoming pain for them will be one of healing, of recognizing God's grace even more strongly than they already do, and of strengthening their ministry to a country plagued by those same memories and nightmares.

Wasting no time, Marilyn reaches in her computer case, pulls out a stack of printed pages and hands it to me. A quick glance reveals it's the answers to the preliminary questions I've sent them, prior to my arrival, so our time together can reap the most rewards. Chandra, who translated all their answers, sits and helps decipher any remaining questions I still have about the material.

The angels really are at work, I recognize, aware this is time needed to pull together loose ends with Marilyn before getting Joseph's insight from his own story and perspective. Piecemeal images begin to take shape in my mind as I endeavor to visualize all the years of combined living between this couple, shaped by their country's history, and how God has now shaped it into good for His glory. *My work is even more mind-boggling than I'd imagined*, I note, conscious that same God is shaping all this information for my brain in a way I can not only understand and perceive it, but in which my fingers can relay it to the world.

When Joseph finally returns a couple of hours later and announces we're ready to ride, I gather first-hand there is no auto parts store nearby, or gas station on every corner, like at home. Recalling how long it took to find a tire when one went flat—not once, but twice—during one of the days of our last trip here, I'm relieved we're getting on the road by lunch time instead of dinner. As we pile in the Land Cruiser, in which we will spend a great deal of our time during the next two weeks, I pause to reflect that it's still three hours until the drop of the Big Apple's infamous lighted ball. While rejoicing that I'm privy to an extra long celebration of welcoming in another year, a quick prayer beseeching a blessed 2010 for my family and friends precedes the start of an enormous volume of work.

We are barely a few short minutes into our journey when I realize, thanks to the advantage of daylight, what a difference six years has made in the face of Cambodia's capital city. Daylight hours and a ride around the whole of Phnom Penh accentuate one distinguishable fact about this country. The abundant opulence of a wealthy few is indescribable on the one hand, while the dregs of poverty experienced by many are wretchedly pathetic on the other. There is such a broad spectrum between the "have's" and "have not's" in this country that America's rich are poor in comparison, while our poverty class seems rich. A momentary recollection of the first time I witnessed the vast contrast between New York City's Harlem and Fifth Avenue reminds me of the expression, "You ain't seen nothin' yet!"

As for traffic, city buses at home are being replaced by light-rail trains. Here in Phnom Penh, small pick-up trucks of six years ago have been traded for ten-wheel industrial trucks. Tuk-tuks that were once pulled by bicycles, with the driver peddling, are now powered by motorbikes. One of the most interesting sights is still the chickens and pigs being taken on their way to market. Traveling through the downtown of Phnom Penh, pairs of pigs are loaded chest to chest on a rack on the front of a bicycle or motorbike. Chickens are crammed in basket cages on the fronts and sides of the bicycles and motorbikes. One can observe an entire truckload of items—from tiles to pottery and baskets to lengthy metal pipes—being carried in this fashion, often with a sizable load of fruits, vegetables or rice also balanced on the biker's head. Animal activists at home would have a heyday with this method, but when one's annual income is $300—which is the average for Cambodia—one does what is necessary to make ends meet.

"You can't work on an empty stomach," becomes the key phrase of our entire trip. Joseph makes sure we eat before we do anything else as he searches for a suitable restaurant. He and Marilyn are extremely attentive to what our systems can handle in the food and beverage department, giving strict instructions to the waiter in Khmer, and to us in English once the food arrives. Thus begins a recurring habit that happens every day, sometimes twice a day, as they go out of their way to see our every need is met. This is nothing unusual for this couple. It is the same treatment our entire team received from them the last time we were here. It is the same treatment they bestow on everyone, stranger or friend.

Lunch is followed by a quick trip to the market to stock up on bottled water and Coke Light and an afternoon at the headquarters of the General Board of Global Ministries of the United Methodist Church in Cambodia, which houses the office of the Chan's. It is a beautiful facility—one I've admired before—and one that allows me a spacious conference table on which to lay out all my notes. As if the answers to my questions aren't enough of a paper trail, Joseph returns from his office with thirty-plus more pages.

With my stomach filled, my brain is soon filled with segments of two unbelievable lives. Unbelievable for two reasons: first that they are still alive and seated across from me at this table, and second, that they've accomplished more than several committees put together. I listen attentively to each telling of their lives' stories until my head is nodding and my eyes can no longer keep up with my ears. Joseph, the astute man he is, sees it's time for a nap.

My short nap—necessitated by the twelve-hour difference in our time zones, combined with the lack of sleep during flights—turns out to be 5½ hours. Snack crackers, from home, and a partially cool Coke Light, which tastes nothing like the ones at home, become my evening companions as I stare at the stack of papers in front of me. The quiet evening allows me time to read over the thirty-plus pages of typed notes, single-spaced, in an attempt to make any kind of correlation between the episodes detailed on them, the answers to my questions and my background research. Another bout of growing and gnawing fear overtakes me, this time for myself, when I sense I am in way over my head. *I'm supposed to write a book about a couple I barely know, in a foreign country, where everyone speaks a language in which I only know how to count, say "Hello" and "Thank You"?*

I sit stunned for a few moments questioning the best way to dive headfirst into this project. *Didn't My Lord Deliver Daniel?* plays subconsciously in my head while my hand taps the rhythm to that spiritual on the desk in front of me. While sorting through the collage of printed pages sprawled in front of me with my other hand, the question *Didn't my Lord deliver Joseph and Marilyn?* sounds forth, breaking its way into my consciousness as one particular paper grabs my attention. On it is a photo of Joseph, that giant smile wiped across his face, as he stands in front of a sanctuary, a parsonage and a new dorm—his dream for students who need a place to live, as he once did, to further their education.

This project is his brainchild, as were many other of the sanctuaries and parsonages of the Methodist Mission in Cambodia. I recall his words from that afternoon. "At the end of one of my seminary classes at Claremont College in Claremont, California, the professor told us to write out our dream for what we wanted to accomplish in our ministry. I wrote that I wanted to go back to my homeland of Cambodia, purchase land, build churches, complete with parsonages and dorms. When he read my paper, he laughed aloud and said, 'You dream too big!'"

Another of the papers also demands my attention. It is a report written by that same professor, who recently visited Cambodia and witnessed the culmination of Joseph's dream that was "too big." "He had tears in his eyes when he saw this," I remember from Joseph's conclusion of the story earlier in the afternoon.

I read the report again, taking special note of every detailed statement about Joseph and realizing how incomprehensible it seems for such a humble man of such small stature to accomplish so much. I'm reminded of one of my favorite sayings, attributed to John Haggai: "Attempt something so great it is doomed to failure unless God is in it."

He must have known Joseph, I determine with a huge chuckle. My fear turns into a broad "Joseph-sized" smile as I receive the sudden assurance that my Lord—the same one who delivered Daniel and the same one who brought this couple through their lives' struggles and transformed them into the witnesses they are today—will deliver this story. All I have to do is be the hands.

I sort through the pages of answers before leafing through all the remaining reports and articles about Joseph's work and the many accolades for him. There is not a page that doesn't contain something dramatically astounding. As a writer of mostly fiction, I see this story is much more fantastic than anything I can create in my wildest dreams. Another light chuckle escapes as I think aloud, "Who needs my wildest dreams? These pages are all filled with details of Joseph's wildest dreams."

What—only a few minutes earlier—seemed an insurmountable task turns into an attainably reachable—and fun—puzzle as I piece together tidbits of their lives, anxiously awaiting each new and remarkable detail. However, as I begin fitting the pieces of the puzzle together, I become aware of a huge, and most necessary, missing piece. A piece which makes me shudder, for fear of asking Joseph and Marilyn to share it. I have hit on the realization this book is not going to take on its shape, *nor its life,* without this couple taking me to where all the horrors happened.

Do I dare mention it to them? Do I presume to think they'd ever want to revisit those places, not to mention those dastardly nightmares? I tap on the wall of my room—in what has become the signal between Mark and me that one of us has hit a mental stand-off and needs a little help. He meets me in the hallway to hear my dilemma.

"I saw this coming," he says, "as I listened to them share their stories today. I think you need to confront them with this need. It's the only way you're going to get the whole story."

That's when I contact Esther Gitobu, also a GBGM-UMC missionary serving in Cambodia and the one who's handled all of our travel arrangements, who also feels this is a foregone conclusion if I'm to relate their stories accurately. She approaches them with the request, and thankfully, they agree to open their entire life to me, encompassing all the pain and suffering along with all the blessed joys.

When they arrive the next morning to take us to the first two sites of their lives' horror, and share the news of their decision with us, I look into Joseph's eyes and give him his own response to most things, "Thank God! Thank God! Praise the Lord!" We make our plans to leave early the following Tuesday morning, leaving everything we don't need with Esther, checking out of the Golden Gate and my comfort zone, and travel in a huge encompassing circle to all the places of Cambodia connected to the story of this dear and extraordinary couple.

It's decided, I tell myself with a sigh of relief, realizing this will be the most difficult writing assignment of my career. I feel I've suddenly been pushed overboard without a life jacket, fully aware that I will not return to this ship in the same condition I left it. My life will be forever changed once I step out into the water of that sinister past with Joseph and Marilyn.

"Attempt something so great that it's doomed to failure unless God is in it," I recite softly, reassured that God *is* my life jacket as I prepare to enter a world foreign to me...*in every possible way.*

Chapter Nine

"It's Saturday!" I exclaim over breakfast, as giddy as a little girl going on her first visit to an amusement park.

"Yes," replies Mark dryly, as if nothing is out of the ordinary.

"Do you realize this is the first free Saturday I've had in months?"

"Do you realize," responds Mark, who knows me well, "it's the first free *day* you've had, *period*, in months?"

He's right, I tell myself, recalling what a difficult time I had scheduling in a few minutes to visit with his wife and him during the past several months.

My free day—which we know is a joke since it's going to be chocked full of work for both of us—is to be spent at the infamous Tuol Sleng prison, atrociously known as S-21. Its chief leader, Kang Keck Iev (called Duch), has recently completed his trial and been sentenced for war crimes, just days before our arrival. The remainder of the day will be spent at "the killing fields" of Choeung Ek, the place approximately seventeen kilometers southwest of Phnom Penh where those imprisoned at Tuol Sleng were taken to be executed, *if* they managed to live that far.

As Joseph parks beside this massive facility of four concrete buildings—which was heart-wrenching enough on our last visit—I find it ironic that Duch, now a converted Christian of several years, is himself housed behind bars awaiting the final verdict for the length of his sentence, as we prepare to step inside the prison connected with the worst genocide in the history of the world. Feeling the hair rising on the back of my head, I brace myself to enter this world so dreadful that only its survivors—numbering seven by most accounts—can understand the true depth of its hell, and that only survivors of the Khmer Rouge regime can even come close to recognizing what happened within these walls. I know this visit is a test of the faith of Joseph and Marilyn, and I regret they have to bring us here. Yet I also know it is the only way I can tell their remarkable story, along with that of every other Cambodian of that era, fully and accurately.

Facts I'd forgotten, whether consciously or unconsciously, come rushing back to mind as I step out of the Land Cruiser and spy the fourteen short, white concrete tombs, precisely distanced from one to the other on the front lawn of Tuol Sleng Genocide Museum. *Tuol Sleng, a most deceptive name,* I reason, while admiring the beautiful flowering trees adorning the front lawn. Translated from Khmer, Tuol Sleng means "Strychnine Hill;" I ponder at this strange connection to Hitler. Others translate it as "Hill of the Poisonous Trees." Either way, it hints of the grave poison of the minds who controlled this area from April, 1975 to January, 1979, and the poisonously ill-fate of all those who were held here during that period.

The buildings where I stand, a one-square kilometer compound, were once home to Tuol Sleng Primary School and Toul Svay Prey High School. I find it ludicrous that such a fine facility—which, though quite plain, was state-of-the-art for that decade and especially in Cambodia—could be revamped into such a "chamber of horror." My mind, as if presenting its own argument for the case, pulls forth facts I've learned about these heinous leaders. *Pol Pot, a former high school principal who once was a teacher; Duch, a math teacher...* The list of educators and educated persons goes on and on.

What better place for them to assemble, I ask myself, *than a school? A place where they've spent the better part of their careers? A place where they're accustomed to shaping young minds and planting viewpoints?* I begin to look at this entire scenario with a whole new perception. Not understanding, mind you, merely insight as I sense the pieces of this puzzle beginning to connect.

"These are the graves of the last fourteen persons found here," Joseph begins, taking on his assumed role as our private tour guide. "They were discovered on January 7, 1979."

Liberation Day, I note. *The day a second mass of cries spreads through the country yelling, "Peace!" for a nation that would remain oppressed for over another decade.*

"North Vietnamese soldiers, who overthrew the Khmer Rouge on that day, came here immediately and found all this evidence of what had been going on at this place. Our government at that time kept everything here as it was so people of Cambodia, and the rest of the world, could be reminded to never allow such a barbaric regime to ever again take control of a country. When the Kampuchea People's Tribunal began the prosecution of leaders of the 'Democratic Kampuchea'—as the Khmer Rouge regime was called—in August of that year, that's when the museum opened."

Talk about evidence swaying a jury, I determine, amazed they turned this into a museum in such a short period, only seven months later. *But then,* I remind myself, *they did nothing except open the doors that had been closed to the world during that time frame*—a realization that made me shudder all the more at standing in this place of the odious killers' once-trodden footsteps. I stare long and hard at the campus surrounding me. *Halls, which should have been hallowed to all the students who graduated here, are now anything but hallowed in their ghastly memories and convoluted archives. Archives which contain contrived confessions of the prisoners who stayed here. Archives of confessions to anything, whether true or false, that would stop a prisoner's torture.*

"One of the bodies was that of a female." Marilyn's voice trails off in sympathy.

"The bodies were terribly decomposed," Joseph continues. "They'd been left here, one in each of these fourteen interrogation rooms," he explains, waving his arm in the direction of the rooms on the bottom floor of the building to the left, Building "A," it is called, "when the personnel of S-21 fled, knowing they were soon to be captured if they stayed."

He leads us toward the rooms, which I remember resembling old jail cells at home, only worse. "These first rooms were used to interrogate people such as government leaders, professors, anyone Pol Pot considered to be a threat to his power, to his revolution."

I listen to his words while finding it unbelievably sardonic that educators could kill other educators and professors, which I—rightly or wrongly—presume to be based on the pretext that those persons with logical reasoning and educated opinions could see through the ultimate absurdity of fellow educators being behind such a plot. *Not to mention the rumor that part of Pol Pot's grievance with city educators was neither he, nor his teacher wife, could land a position regarded as prestigious as theirs.*

One glance into the closest cell sends me back to the first time I was horrified by this place. *Only this time it's worse. I'm here with someone who lived the hell of this inhuman controller and his band of companions and soldiers. How could so many people be corrupted by his madness?* I wonder, totally bewildered.

My bewilderment broadens as Joseph promptly takes the shackles from the metal bed frame and demonstrates how prisoners were chained. "All they got was a mat, a blanket and cushion." He points to a metal ammunition box on the floor of the 6x4-meters cell. "This was their toilet. Some of the cells had a plastic jug or a metal bucket."

While surveying the floor, I detect the square tan and cream-colored floor tiles, arranged in a checkered pattern. Not sure why, they scream at me with bad vibes of this place from before. *Funny how that one detail is the one that gives me the creeps,* I sense. I then remember it's the blood stains on these otherwise unobtrusive squares that made me uncomfortable before, stains that have obviously been cleaned from the time of my last visit.

"The people in these rooms were blindfolded while being questioned. Sometimes," he adds, holding out his hand, "they would pull out their fingernails while pouring alcohol over them." He uses his other hand to give a visual aid. From what I'd already heard, and now know of this place, that seems tame.

We move to the next interrogation room where Joseph spots a shovel. "This had two uses as a weapon." He swings it in the air. "They'd use it to strike a person's head, or," he pauses, holding the sharp edge of its scoop against the bottom of his nose and pretending to push up, "they'd use it this way to cut your nose where it's very tender."

I wonder how difficult it is for this dear, sweet servant of God to speak to me so openly, so honestly, resisting the temptation to sway my opinion by his own personal feelings. He simply shares the facts. The ammunition box on the floor creates a vision of "Pandora's box" in my mind as I deduce that I've opened "Joseph's box" and "Marilyn's box," both of which have had, and continue to have, their bitter anguish and broken hearts replaced with the love of a gentle Savior. *It is a trait well represented in the lives of these two servants,* I observe admirably, *as it is in the lives of many of the new Christians in this country.*

I give no consideration to the fact that the school's classroom had open windows to allow airflow. That is, until Joseph says, "The Khmer Rouge put in the glass panels to keep the screams of tortured victims from being heard outside." Shivers—a result of imaginary screams bouncing off this row of fourteen windows from the last prisoners in these cells, left purposely to die a slow death before decomposing and who are now buried just a few feet away from me—run up my spine.

"They closed the shutters of all the windows whenever they brought people in or out, when prisoners were interrogated or whenever someone was taken outside to the former playground for torture." His words heighten the dismal picture already in my mind.

While stopping to look in each of the fourteen rooms—where all their inhabitants heard questions such as, "What do you do? Were you a friend of America or Vietnam?"—we encounter three elderly women who've traveled nearly two-hundred kilometers to get here.

"Did you lose family during Khmer Rouge time?" I ask.

"Yes…many," answers the eldest of the three, with great sadness in her face.

Marilyn speaks to them in Khmer to learn they lost many friends and family members in the village where they lived. This is their first visit here, and although grieved, they agree to be photographed with me at this place that unlocks scores of nightmares. As I bow, clasp my hands and tell them good-bye, I pray they can find peace and closure during their day's visit. They smile and seem grateful when Marilyn tells them I'm writing a book, the same reaction I see from everyone she tells. They all seem anxious for the world to know the horror of their situation so that history never repeats itself.

I watch the look of horrified shock on the women's faces as they glare into the next room and mumble quietly in Khmer to each other. Their reactions cause me to hone in on the difference between the expressions on the faces of native Cambodians, and the foreign tourists, who are among the museum's guests on this day. There is a look of understanding in the expressions of the Cambodians, whereas the tourists' expressions are filled with honest, yet blank, sympathetic interest.

Several people notice Joseph doing live demonstrations of the various torture procedures and stop to watch and listen. He becomes the most photographed figure in the museum, his poses and explanations going home with visitors from many countries and several continents. Witnessing this allows me to see firsthand how massive a list the Khmer Rouge would have collected from the contacts of all the people imprisoned here, just by seeing the number of people influenced by Joseph in a matter of minutes.

"Every one of those contacts was tracked down," Joseph continues. "They were all considered enemies of Pol Pot's revolution. The prisoners were forced to give names of all the persons with whom they associated, of their friends and family members."

"How long did they stay here before they were killed?" I ask.

"Political figures, considered valuable informants, usually stayed six or seven months. Other prisoners were generally here only two to four months."

I resist the urge to ask if the time allotment is dependent on food availability, and the need for space to bring in more prisoners. At the same time, I consider the large number of jails in America, many nicer than most people's homes, whose prisoners are continually set free due to lack of space, with new jails sprouting up as fast as schools in some places. I cannot help but think how America's old, dilapidated schools should possibly be turned into jails of learning centers, hopefully creating less of a need for jails and prisons—a thought brought about by an entire generation who lost an education due to the Khmer Rouge.

When we come to the end of Building "A" and its interrogation rooms, Joseph stops in front of what I consider the most heinous method of torture here. What remains is a wooden pole that was once part of a swing on the playground in this spot when Tuol Sleng was still a school. "For Khmer Rouge purposes," he explains, describing the act shown in a graphic picture beside the pole, "they tied the hands of the prisoner behind his back and pulled him up in the air, with him dangling upside down. They'd do this over and over until the prisoner was unconscious."

Joseph pats his hands on one of the two huge concrete urns beside the pole. "Like this, like this," he begins. "They filled this with the toilet water, oh, so bad, and dunked the unconscious prisoner's head in it until he was again conscious. Then they'd continue their interrogation." He literally bends his head over into one of the urns with his hands together behind his back, giving me more of a grueling visual image than I care to see and making my blood run cold.

As we enter Building "B," I fear I will never look at an elementary school playground the same again, nor my grandchildren's future swing sets. That fear is anything but relieved from the rest of the tour of Tuol Sleng, which—thanks to Joseph and Marilyn—becomes a "living" museum.

The ground level of this building is filled with large boards, mounted on bases, which should hold posters and teaching resources for brilliant young minds. Instead they hold rows and columns, butted as closely together as possible, of photographs of the young minds who were wasted as detainees here, later to face their death. I peer briefly into the face of each one. First the young women, all with dark eyes and black hair chopped short, with their dreams of weddings and bearing children cut shorter than their hair; then the young men, such handsome faces, whose goals and dreams are now non-existent. For all of them, they've become blank nameless faces, their only identity the number on the board held in front of their chest. The only distinction is the measure of horror, captured on film, in some of their eyes, and the bruises and scars of torture obviously suffered on their way to "the photo shoot."

I long to hear their stories, long vanished, but I realize there is only one. A story of an existence cut short, like the women's hair, robbed of all education and a chance at life, of having a family, of chasing goals and dreams. Only one story...torture and death. I see the faces of a few elderly women and presume them to be family members of others imprisoned, who landed here merely by virtue of association. *And countless faces of tiny children, their young innocence replaced by the fear of an enemy they didn't even know.* I swallow hard and force the lump in my throat to go back from whence it comes. *That is their story.*

I'm grateful Marilyn appears at that moment.

"You can tell when the various prisoners were killed," she explains, "by the kind of board they hold against their chest in the picture." A quick scan of the group of photos in front of me signifies a difference in some of the boards identifying each prisoner, allowing me to pinpoint which ones arrived at the same time.

We round the corner from one line of photos to the next. Marilyn gives a small gasp. "This is the doctor who was a friend of ours and was killed here. I told you about him when you asked about the people I knew who had been killed at the hands of the Khmer Rouge."

"I can't believe you recognized him," I reply, noting his face is so badly disfigured it's hard to imagine his own mother recognizing him.

"I didn't recognize him," she admits. "I only knew who it was by his name being on the photo." She stares at the picture for a fleeting moment. "His daughter lives in the USA."

A closer look discloses there is a name, written in Khmer, on the photo. *How horrid it must be to run across someone who was once a friend in this manner.* I feel the urge to reach out and take this dear woman's hand as a sign of comfort and support, like one would reach out to a hurting child. At the same time, I glimpse how she's dealing with this in her own way, a necessary therapy. Thus I continue to follow her, wandering from room to room.

Each room adds another dimension to the inhumanity suffered here by S-21's prisoners, all later executed. "Once imprisoned here, the chance of survival was slim," says Marilyn. She tells me of a woman who ran from this place. "They shot and shot at her, but she managed to escape. She's the only one known to have done that."

I am keenly aware that the staggeringly few survivors of S-21 were spared only because they possessed an invaluable skill, useful to Pol Pot's torture. One of those survivors, Vann Nath, is an artist who was kept to paint portraits of Pol Pot, and the horrors committed here. His works hang on the walls, depicting how the various instruments of torture were used on prisoners. They are so lifelike that no detail of what happened here is left to the imagination. As if they're not gory enough, photographs of bodies—tortured to their maximum level and several left with no life remaining in them—also line the walls, adding to my astonishment at what kind of sick person would do such a thing, much less arrogantly display a lasting memento on the wall.

I view each of the paintings, much like I would were they in an art museum. *Which they are, of sorts...the art of terror*. I cringe as I examine each detail and how explicit the artist is in his renditions of what went on here. *Another sadistic satisfaction for a deranged ego.* Two of the paintings leave me in sheer shock; both of them too close for comfort, having just left my first newborn grandson back in the States to come here. One depicts a baby being thrown up in the air to land on a bayonet, with the soldiers involved laughing and cheering. Another painting shows a tree with a plank citing it as the "Juvenile Execution Tree." A soldier is bashing a newborn baby's skull against the tree while the mother watches.

Seeing my horrified expression, Marilyn steps beside me, as if what I see isn't grotesque enough. "They killed people in these ways because guns and ammunition cost too much. This was a way they could save ammunition.

"One of the young girls I knew joined the Khmer Rouge. She had been involved in killing a general's wife and children. I'll never forget her bragging about how much fun it was. 'It's so easy,' she'd say. 'We don't waste our guns. We just throw the baby up and let it fall on the bayonet.' She kept saying, 'I'm so happy! I'm so happy!'

"We were all so scared to be around her. People were afraid of the young soldiers, who were really respectful to 'Angkar' (the mythical voice that didn't actually belong to any one person or really exist, but was referred to as the power behind the entire Pol Pot regime, including Pol Pot himself). People my age were older. We had enough experience to understand what was going on, to see through the evil. But not the young people. They were totally brainwashed. The young soldiers would kill their own families. They were taught, 'You are not my father! You are the enemy!' The one rule that controlled all their thoughts, behavior and actions was, 'Listen to Angkar!'"

She pauses for a moment to allow my mind to digest that challenging fact. "Mothers were made to watch this. If they dared to flinch, they were killed. They were unable to mourn or grieve the loss of their baby. If you saw them kill your husband, you could not move or show emotion. Then they'd kill you."

A bizarre rationale, it seems, for it stands to reason the mother or wife would have been the next in line for execution, mournful or not. But in such a wicked scheme of things, the act of being forced to watch a loved one killed, especially in such a macabre manner, served as yet another way of torturing victims while saving ammunition and guns.

We move to another painting, on the same scale of grisly actions, which portrays a woman lying with her hands and feet chained to a bed. Her nipples have been cut off, replaced by scorpions to bite her, inflicting even more unendurable pain. Suddenly regretting the gift of such a vivid imagination, I find myself—an observer on the sidelines, unable to do anything to help—reliving the scenes of the bayonet, the execution tree and the scorpions, not to mention the other "original" ways these Khmer Rouge leaders created to "save ammunition and guns."

Marilyn understands my unspoken words. "People were killed at random. Women were kidnapped right off the streets and raped. Sometimes, in my dreams, I am still running away from the Khmer Rouge."

We follow the path of paintings, from one former classroom to another, until we catch up with Mark and Joseph, who motion for me to join them. In the room is a wooden contraption, large enough for a person's reclined body, which is sloped at one end. The lower end has chains for securing the prisoner's hands, with shackles braced on the higher end for the prisoner's ankles, assuring the person being tortured is immobile. Joseph slips his wrists next to the chains at the bottom and shows me precisely how the prisoners were tortured, some executed, with this water-torturing device. A large metal watering can sits on the board, where Joseph retrieves it, holds his head back and pretends to pour water down his nose. "Sometimes they put a plastic bag over the prisoner's head, suffocating them in this manner."

The click of Mark's camera, as he shoots a live shot, sends my mind reeling to the click of a gun's trigger, held against a prisoner's head, shooting a live victim. Never have I been so close to such murderous ways; I feel I'm caught up in them at every turn—which I am.

As Joseph continues to demonstrate the various acts of torture committed in this small room, a man stands behind me watching. He is so broken up by what he sees and hears that he cannot speak. Like earlier in our visit, onlookers are astounded in silence as they witness a real, live witness to these abysmal acts.

"This is what it was like under the Khmer Rouge," Marilyn, noticing their reactions, says simply. "You didn't dare look to the left or right, just in front of your feet. If they saw you moving or straying at all from that, you were killed. If you spoke at all, you were killed." She holds an imaginary gun to her body, the click of Mark's camera again driving home that image. "If they said 'Move!' you moved.'"

On the heels of her insight, tourists exit the room in single-file, speechless as her words and action take them back in time, making them afraid to make any sudden moves or sounds. I'm amazed at how this couple, tiny and diminutive, can have such a bold influence on those around them—whether in church, in the United Nations Building or in the most ghoulish chamber of torture on earth.

Following the zombie-like movement of the other tourists, we come to another room, and yet another display filled with pictures. Marilyn faces me. "They took photos of every single person who came through here."

Appalled, I can't believe someone could be so pompous as to take time to photograph all these persons, solely to gratify his own ego at how many have suffered as a result of his actions, when their only demise is eventual execution. I scan the numbers printed on the brochure I received at the front gate, which estimates over 10,000 prisoners came through here in only three years, not counting the children killed, which brought the tally closer to 20,000. *At one town in one district in one city*, I calculate, learning the extermination of lives at this location ended only when they ran out of open grave spaces at Choeung Ek's noted "killing fields."

We come to another photo Marilyn recognizes. "This woman was a minister's wife. She and her baby," who is in her arms in the picture, "were brought here. They supposedly told her they only wanted to ask her some questions."

A brief, but thorough examination of the woman's face proves she knows the real scoop. There's no doubt, from the expression on her face, she realizes life for her and her son is over. As I wonder what phony confessions they forced from her, my mind drifts to scriptural accounts of Jesus' trial and the confessions the interrogators attempted to prompt from him. Her face says she stood firm in her beliefs during her persecution. I cannot bear to look at the tiny child's face, which bears signs of tortured treatment.

A long walk up and down another roomful of boards brings us to what appears to be a publicity shot of a beautiful young woman. Her face is flawless and her black hair is long and turned up, very much the style of the early seventies. The picture stands undisputedly out from the rest.

Marilyn, noting my interest, points to the photo. "She was a popular actress and back-up singer, who was seen a lot with a popular male singer when Pol Pot took over the country." She leans in to me and whispers, "They say the soldiers repeatedly raped her and then placed a bomb in her vagina and blew her up. This supposedly happened to other young women too."

Too stunned for words, having guessed her last words before she spoke them, I stare at the picture, dumbfounded. *Was there no end to their horror?*

"The soldiers were supposedly not allowed to rape the women, and were supposedly punished for that."

I sense that she, like I, seriously doubts the degree of punishment given the soldiers compared to that of the victims. Secretly, I venture as to how many soldiers are still alive to tell their stories, but then I realize their stories are quieted by the fear of now paying, like Duch, for their actions.

A large glass case, resembling an oversized dresser, thankfully draws my attention from the women's photos to one end of the room.

"Their clothes," Marilyn offers subtly. "They were all stripped down to their underwear when they arrived, and then hosed down every four days or so. The Khmer Rouge wanted to be sure they didn't carry any weapons. I've heard that even their shackles and chains were inspected regularly to check for anything the prisoners could use to commit suicide."

I notice no suits, ties or dresses on the shelves of the glass case; nothing besides plain simple work clothes of an ordinary rice farmer or factory worker seem to fill the large display. I find that curious in light of all the persons, considered political figures and educated powers, brought here. Then I recall Marilyn's words. "My mother forced us to cut our hair. We had to look like peasants so they wouldn't suspect we had money."

Obviously the others shared that same idea, I reason, as we come to another board, covered with another batch of photos, one of whom is a man Marilyn identifies as the great singer she mentioned in the story of the woman. He is quite handsome and looks like the Cambodian version of any number of American pop singers from that period.

"He was known all over the country. People loved to hear him sing. He brought a new kind of music to our culture when he was young and was popular for a long time."

My mind plays a flashback of Elvis.

"He was sympathetic to our government, and sang a song which alluded to that," Marilyn continues, causing my mind to further allude to *An American Trilogy* sung by Elvis, relating this man to a celebrated figure in my terms, on my turf. "That action was considered to be a revolt against Pol Pot. If you sang the old National song, they'd kill you. Can you imagine?"

No, I can't! I want to scream. *I can't imagine any of this.* Especially when the next room we enter, now upstairs, is lined with photos and quotes from former members of the Khmer Rouge, from high-ranking leaders of the "Democratic Kampuchea" to group leaders to ordinary soldiers. Their comments are most interesting, and quite intriguing. In fact, taken out of this situation's context, they're astutely logical. What grasps one's attention in this room, though, is a framed plaque containing lyrics for a new National song, the one Pol Pot insisted be sung by the citizens of his country during the Khmer Rouge regime, and which he is considered, by many, to have penned.

Dap Prampi Mesa Chokchey (Glorious Seventeenth of April)

The bright red blood was spilled over the towns
and over the plain of Kampuchea, our motherland,
The blood of our good workers and farmers and of
our revolutionary combatants, both men and women.
Their blood produced a great anger and the courage
to contend with heroism. On the 17th of April,
under the revolutionary banner, their blood freed
us from the state of slavery.
Hurrah for the 17th of April!
That wonderful victory had greater significance
than the Angkor period!
We are uniting to construct a Kampuchea with a
new and better society, democratic,egalitarian
and just. We follow the road to a firmly-based
Independence. We absolutely guarantee to defend
our motherland, our fine territory, our
magnificent revolution!
Hurrah for the new Kampuchea, a splendid,
Democratic land of plenty! We guarantee to raise
aloft and wave the red banner of the revolution.
We shall make our motherland prosperous beyond
all others, magnificent, wonderful!

Marilyn stands beside me and asks, "How could you have a conscience and sing that song?"

I have no answer, except for the subsequent question running through my own mind. *How could you have a conscience and do any of this stuff?* But my heart is so sympathetic for her, and for those who lived—*and died*— this horror, I say nothing.

Joseph, who is carefully taking in every word of these persons and their quotes on the wall, motions for me and says quietly, "When I returned to this country for the first time in 1993, we came here and you could still see blood on the floor. It still had the smell of death. I was so shocked by all that had happened here, I could not stand to see it. Then, as now, I was so thankful to the Lord that saved our lives."

He points to one wall of portraits. I readily recognize that of Pol Pot, having researched him so frequently in prior weeks, and Duch, due to keeping up with the recent trial. Beside them are also photographs of Ieng Sary and Khiev Samphorn, both of whom were prosecuted with Pol Pot as leaders of the "Democratic Kampuchea" after the North Vietnamese liberated the country from Khmer Rouge leadership.

"I met Ieng Sary and Khiev Samphorn," states Joseph matter-of-factly.

My eyes leave their portraits and peer at this survivor. Suddenly this is all becoming too real, too close.

"Once when I was in North Korea, I went to Beijing for a vacation. They were there for a meeting and I heard them speak. When I was forced to return to Cambodia and was at the work camp, we had to attend assembly meetings. They came to one of the meetings to teach people how to improve the country."

My day no longer seems like a history lesson but a "hands-on" experience. I stare at the walls around me and wonder how anyone can think what I see improves anything, much less a population of people.

With each of my ensuing query of questions, in my task's desire to understand every aspect of Tuol Sleng and its victims, Joseph explains with, "like this, like this," or "like that, like that," making sure I have every answer I need. I stand in awe of his knowledge, his love, his deep desire to help the whole of his native homeland. I also stand in awe of his patience in being positively certain I understand every detail. Each time he's convinced I "have it," he exclaims excitedly, "...like that, yes, yes!" His enthusiastic guidance causes me to feel like a spirited tiny child who has grasped the major skill of taking steps or forming words. It is then I recognize what distinguishes him as a great teacher, a great leader, a great missionary in bringing converts into understanding and accepting the love of Christ.

With that in mind, I venture around the entire room, studying each photograph, the bio of each person and a quote (in both English and Khmer) from each one. I notice Joseph is glued to one particular picture. Sensing it to hold major importance, I go to his side.

"Read this," he invites, before reading it aloud to me. It is a testimony to the importance of hard work, not only for the current generation but for future generations. "For our life, we are still working," Joseph states sincerely while obviously deep in thought. "It is good for Marilyn and me to see this now in pictures here. We have to work hard to leave things for those who come after us. We have to respect and care for things, as well as the people…the people of today and the people of tomorrow. God expects us to work hard…to till the soil, to plant the seeds, to reap the harvest." He closes his eyes for a brief moment. When he reopens them, tears faintly glisten in the dim light of what little bit of sun is able to filter in from the outside. "So thankful."

I know exactly what he means, and his words go far beyond what the rice farmer in the photograph is doing. Joseph has farmed his entire life; he will continue to farm his entire life. *Planting, sowing and reaping for the Master*, I muse.

When we reach Building "D" and the last of Nath's paintings, we enter another small room, one I imagine too small for a classroom but which probably served as a storage or resource room. Along its back wall is a glass display case housing the smaller, handheld instruments used to "compellingly" interrogate prisoners in this place.

"They've left out one of the instruments of torture and killing," Marilyn shares.

I stare through the glass case to the ones for which Joseph is explaining their use. "You mean there's more?"

"Yes," she answers, "the palm branch."

My blank gaze is all she needs to perceive I don't understand how a palm branch can be a weapon.

"They used it as a saw," she adds, holding her right hand vertically and moving it back and forth.

Joseph immediately gives me a visual demonstration, holding his neck as far to the side as he can and pretending to saw it, making this method even more inconceivable as I envision the palm trees back home lining Florida's boulevards and shores.

Totally aghast, I shift my attention back to the facility as I notice the ground floors of Buildings "B," "C" and "D" were all converted into tiny brick cells, each one measuring only eight x two meters, where individuals of more prominence were held. Each cell has a chain concreted into it that held the prisoners. Joseph walks up and down the row of cells, each one hardly bigger than my computer cabinet, intently looking for something he can't seem to find.

"When I was here before," he shares, "there was a small plate and fork used by the prisoner in one of the cells. It had been left there because a man, who had his Ph.D in Political Science and Economics, was housed in that cell and had used the fork to pick at the veins in his wrist until he killed himself. There was still blood in that cell."

As with most of the other bloody remains, it has either worn away or been removed. But as with Joseph's other depictions, he is so graphic in his descriptions that it is easy to visualize the scene, even to the point of the doctor sitting chained in his small area, pulling away the skin and picking at the veins until he is able to end his life.

Outside Building "C," Joseph points to one of the rooms of the upper level. "One of the prisoners jumped from there and committed suicide," Joseph explains. "After that, the Khmer Rouge put up this netting of barbed wire to prevent more suicides."

I gaze across the buildings to see the "safety net." I find the Khmer Rouge's logic perplexing, thinking it would have saved them a lot of unnecessary time and trouble to have allowed the prisoners to kill themselves. Then all the soldiers would have had to do was take the already deceased bodies to "the killing fields."

Yet self-inflicted suicide would have allowed the prisoners a freedom of choice, I realize. *This is an important insight into the mind of this madman,* I reason, having concluded from the morning's tour that Pol Pot, and his regime of murderers, literally thrived on the act of killing, clearly influenced by his own insecurity. That, enhanced and fueled by his growing sense of paranoia, is what led to his ruination, when he began to suspect his own cadres as enemies and, consequently, killed many of his own leaders and soldiers, and their families.

A note on the wall in front of me lends credibility to that fact as it tells of Cambodia's Minister of Trade being accused of an association with the CIA, an assumption which triggered an entirely new rash of killing when Pol Pot suspected he had uncovered a whole new realm of spies. *A strange mode of behavior for a man who insists on calling himself "Brother Number One."*

Only one building allows us access to the upper level to view the rooms that once housed what looks to be as many as a hundred prisoners in each room. Exactly like the upper levels of all the buildings, rooms are larger than the downstairs quarters. Long metal rods extend the length of the rooms; each rod is able to secure thirty men or women at a time. Again, Joseph demonstrates the living conditions of the prisoners as he reaches down to the shackles attached to the rods. From the looks of the arrangement of rods on the walls, it appears prisoners were turned in opposite directions, in a head-feet-head-feet pattern all the way up the length of the walls.

My mind is flooded with questions of how they ate and how they used the bathroom, among other issues. As badly as I wish to know the answers, it is easier not to know them.

Building "D" houses what, to many visitors of Tuol Sleng, is the most loathsome, yet unforgettable, sight of all. It is a map of Cambodia, stretched out over the whole of a classroom chalkboard. The Mekong River is painted red, signifying all the blood poured into it and the countryside during Pol Pot's time. Skulls, placed together in the shape of the country, provide a lasting reminder for the visitors of all the torture and killing that happened on these grounds. It is estimated that a total of 17,000 – 20,000 met their demise within the confines of this school-revamped-prison, surrounded by a double-iron fence topped by rows of barbed-wire.

We exit the final building of the compound, with the tan and cream square tiles that encompass the floors of this entire facility forever etched on my mind. I pray I never see these same colors or this pattern of tiles again, for I know too well the array of jolting memories it will conjure.

Now well into the afternoon, Mark and I vote to skip lunch so I can gather all the information possible during the open hours of these two museums of death and killing, and Mark can make use of the best natural sunlight. *Besides,* I decide, *it only adds to the flavor*—definitely no pun intended—*of an existence on starvation-proportioned rations.*

We walk back across the yard of Tuol Sleng, crossing in front of the fourteen tombs, the bodies interred within for whom I now possess a deeper respect and greater appreciation. Joseph solemnly breaks the silence. "My name is on a list here." His comment causes Mark and I to glare first at each other, and then at Joseph. "A friend of mine saw it. His name was on the list too."

"Why was your name on a list here?" I hesitantly ask.

"My friend, who saw it in the archives near the end of Pol Pot's control, said I was reputed to be a friend to the CIA." Joseph's solemn expression changes to one of humored jest. "I told my friend, 'I only speak Khmer and French, I don't even know what the CIA is!' And back then, I didn't." He laughs boisterously before suddenly returning to his solemn expression. "Had Pol Pot's revolution not ended when it did, they would have come after me," is all he says as his voice drops and his face falls to a blank stare toward the compound in front of him.

His final comment warrants proof of the countless accusations—recorded in the Archives of prisoners' confessions still here—that these prisoners were literally tortured so severely they gave their inquisitors whatever it was they wanted to hear, truth or not. They were fed their answers. That meant thousands of individuals were wrongly accused, imprisoned and executed. *As if any of them rightly were*, I cannot help but think while standing in the middle of the location of these nightmarish conditions.

Pausing for a moment in front of the fourteen tombs, I look at them with a slight sensation that they've spoken from the grave, which in essence they have. Their witness to an event of mass hysteria is recorded and written inside. Their voices can be heard in the photos of each person who came through this "security office," who was detained, interrogated, tortured and killed...*after giving a lame confession the Khmer Rouge wanted to hear.* Only then were they spared from further torture by means of execution.

Joseph and Marilyn lead us back to the Land Cruiser to escort us to the grounds of the bulk of these executions.

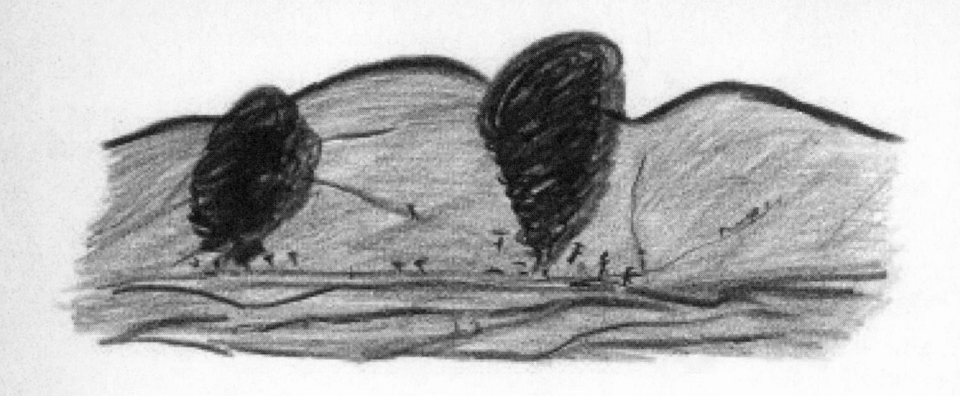

Chapter Ten

Try as I might, I fail to imagine how the seventeen kilometers to Choeung Ek must have seemed on the dusty, deeply-rutted dirt roads for one "going to the slaughter" from S-21. Mental queries of their last thoughts race through my mind, for they were undoubtedly aware, or at least dubious, of their fate and what would happen to their badly-beaten and abused bodies once their "method of death" had been decided. *Maybe not, though,* I ponder, remembering how many stories from Tuol Sleng indicated prisoners were told they were going to work or school, only to be taken away and killed. It strikes me odd they were blindfolded since they "mysteriously" disappeared in the middle of the night, never to be seen again. *Torture to the very end,* I sadly resolve.

During our ride from Tuol Sleng, following the same roads as trucks that carried those facing their deaths, Marilyn shares tidbits of her past, points she feels necessary to our understanding of the prison and "killing fields." "The distrust was the worst part," she begins, speaking of life associated with the Khmer Rogue. "People were forbidden to write…to love. Individuality disappeared. Physically and mentally, I was already dead." She sighs. "Many people felt this way."

She fans herself for a brief moment's respite from the raging heat. "To study meant death. The only people left were the working class from the factories and peasants. The Khmer Rouge sought to kill all the other classes. 'Egalitarian' is the word Pol Pot used.

"The work was hard. We slaved all the way through the daytime and into the nighttime. For many, it was a long slow process of plowing the rice fields with oxen. For me, it was usually a matter of digging up rocks from fields too rocky for plowing before planting rice. Our only food was soup, mostly of water, and rice. Starvation, diarrhea and disease were the deadly consequences of working like that."

The simple act of Marilyn looking out her window to a rice field stirs my heart. She turns back to face me. "There was a 19th century Cambodian prophecy that went something like, 'People shall fight for a grain of rice stuck to the tail of a dog,' ending with 'and a demon king will rule.' That's how we lived. And that lack of food caused people to then turn greedy after Pol Pot's time. We hoarded." Her words take on an apologetic air, as if she felt shamed by that act.

I offer her a smile. "How else would you have been?" I ask, remembering how many Americans hoarded in anticipation of Y2K. "But look at the way things are now. That's over. The Southeast Asian culture of hospitality again predominates, both from what I saw six years ago and what I see now. Everyone is so anxious to reach out and help us." I don't bother to share the rest of my thought with her…that their hospitality predominates even though signs of "Western-ism" are now rampant throughout their country, robbing them again of their unique and priceless culture and individuality. *No thanks to my own country,* I sense woefully.

When the sign for "the killing fields" is in sight, Marilyn becomes even more somber. "They cut people's hearts out and put them in pits." Her comment serves as a warning to prepare ourselves for the upcoming gruesomely visual reminder that approximately two million people perished under Pol Pot's regime.

Joseph turns into the long driveway and a hushed silence blankets the Land Cruiser. Like with the prison, this is not my first visit here; yet this time, it surfaces a whole new realm of emotions and regrets—one of them stemming, I fear, from the birth of my first infant grandson, only six weeks old. Not unlike the baby depicted in the artist's painting at Tuol Sleng, I find it incomprehensible to imagine watching him, slammed into the juvenile execution tree, and being unable to flinch, much less say anything or grieve.

We exit the Land Cruiser in much the same way I exited Dachau on both my visits to that first Nazi concentration camp of Hitler's time...slowly, silently, reflectively. As we approach the 17-tiered stupa, I notice a relatively new sign in front of it. Dated August 17, 2009, its message reads, "May the victims' souls rest in peace." I wager those words, placed here by the Japanese Red Cross, express the sentiment of every visitor who steps foot on this soil.

Following Joseph's example, Mark and I remove our shoes as we reach the top step of the stupa. I know what lies inside. I've seen it before; there is no way to forget it. And even if I could have, all the documentaries and films I've used for research in the past months show countless pictures of this iniquitously ill-famed place. This stupa differs from most Buddhist tombs of its type. Its acrylic glass sides serve as a memorial for the 8,895 bodies discovered here, most of who had once been inmates of the facility from which we have just traveled.

One's eyes would easily skim over the first tier, which holds clothes—all found on the premises after the Khmer Rouge lost power—from bodies brought here. It's the second and third levels, which are at eye level for most visitors, which draws one's attention. The 2nd – 9th levels hold skulls, over five thousand, all found at this exact location known notoriously as "the killing fields." Many of the skulls have been crushed or bashed in, giving evidence of the savage crimes committed against them here. Various other bones are housed on the 10th – 17th levels. Sadly, I conceive what I see is not the whole of bodies killed here; the count ranges from 17,000 – 20,000.

I remember the impact of this place on my first visit, but because of Joseph and Marilyn and the closeness I've developed with their stories, I now feel I know these people whose remains are on exhibit. I cannot find it inside myself to consider this sight morbid, for it is an open cry—literally—to the world to please never allow this kind of macabre genocide to ever happen again. All I can do is stand there and pray.

Joseph, who's been silent this entire time, offers softly, "Thank God that He saved me before this happened...," His words trail off, allowing Mark and me a minute glimpse and private insight into what he experienced during his last few days under Khmer Rouge power.

I stare into the glass case where his eyes rest and note the numbers stamped on the skulls. Careful research has gone into the recovery of these skulls and remaining bones as a means to learn exactly how many people were actually killed here. A small team has stamped and numbered each one as it was unearthed, and placed the skulls in groups according to their ages. Joseph peers at the ones who were the age he would have been back then. I feel everything inside me cringe as I sense the persons who lost their lives here staring at me—literally—through holes where eyes once were in these skulls. That is the moment I begin to grasp the depth of God's miracle that brought this remarkable man and his wife to where they are now. It is a miracle that accompanies His knowledge of His plan for them while they were still in the womb. There is no question of God's power, His redeeming mercy and grace, or His hand in the lives of these two individuals. I am overcome with every emotion conceivably known to man. Like Joseph, I, too am thankful, but for the opportunity to have been chosen to tell their amazing story. There's no questioning it is a divine calling.

I am glad when we finally venture from the stupa toward the "fields." God's power is so evident around us as we view the memorial I fear we will all self-combust if we stand there much longer.

"Long ago," Joseph states, using his right arm to draw my attention over the two hectares of land this place covers, "this was a Chinese tomb. The real Cambodia style of burial is to cremate and place the remains in small boxes. That was not the practice during Khmer Rouge time. Bodies were simply dumped in the big holes you see out in the field behind us." His words, or lack of, explicitly describe the cold, callousness of the Khmer Rouge's respect—or lack of—for the bodies "dumped" here.

Immediately, as I scan the grounds, which are actually measurably small considering the number of bodies found here, there is one thing terribly disturbing to me about this place. It bothered me before, six years ago, but I could not put a handle on it. Now, living on my grandfather's spacious land, I can. There are chickens walking around this place at every turn, most of them a mother hen followed by several baby chicks. At first, I cannot decipher why I am so unsettled by this.

Then, as I begin to count the number of craters, most of which held upwards of a hundred graves each, I realize how earthy and natural, how very common, this place is. A plain, ordinary plot of land, like what I live on at home, desecrated by being made into the scene of such a bloodbath at the hands of insensitive murderers. *This beautiful countryside, made into a mockery of creation.* Verdant green, with trees abounding, it is land that stretches as far as the eye can see. It is a perfect place for a farm, with rich fertile fields.

Fields, that's what is bothering me. It *was* rich fertile fields...*for killing*. That truth further unnerves me. Marilyn stands beside me, saying nothing, but allowing me to come to terms with whatever is going on inside me. She clearly understands how difficult setting the stage for this scenario's inclusion in the book is going to be for me. The task is made easier, though, by her loving smile. We wait together as I finish writing notes.

One of the first things to greet visitors here is the tree trunks, dotted with small, lasting remnants of clothing that once covered the bodies of some of the victims. It is not uncommon to spot a tooth or small bone, lying partially unearthed beside the path leading through the field of mass graves. Signs bearing numbers, coordinated with the numbers on a sheet received at the front gate, allow visitors to go through at their own pace, via a self-guided tour. For some, the tour is short as this, like Tuol Sleng, is not a place for the faint at heart. For others, the tour is a slow, reflective prayer for the years of hell, the unbearable torture and the excruciating deaths of the thousands whose remains are still scattered throughout this plot of land.

For Chandra, who is our translator, it is a time of mourning the death of her father. Only five years old when Phnom Penh was evacuated, and then watching her father arrested only to disappear before her eyes on the way to their home village, she stands silent and still across the way as she peers into one of the craters of a mass grave. Her face reads like a book as she visibly wonders which of the 400+ "killing fields" across Cambodia serves as the grave for her father. She has no idea when or where he was killed, only that—like so many others—one minute he was there, the next he was gone.

I cannot begin to fathom the endless query of questions going through her mind at this point, nor do I venture to try, out of sympathy and respect for her and her family. What I do is offer a prayer for comfort, for forgiveness and for appreciation of a wonderful father for the short time she knew him. My heart aches as I see her, from the corner of my eye, take a tissue and wipe away a tear. She soon joins us, her eyes red and sullen, but her spirit light. I admire her strength and her ability to deal with what must be a continually gnawing question that will never go away. The phrase "without a trace" takes on a whole new meaning for me as I watch her stoically make this visit with us, all for the sake of me having the opportunity to walk in Joseph and Marilyn's footsteps of their tormented memories.

We continue our journey to the remembered tree against which executioners beat children. It remains a spine-tingling sight.

Joseph moves toward it and points to a particular spot on its bark. "When I came here in 1993, you could still see the blood here. The smell was horrible." His comment produces an overwhelming, sickening queasiness as I turn my head slightly to the right. "This is where they threw the babies when they killed them," he continues, motioning toward where my eyes are already focused. A large pit lays open, where it has been unearthed to exhume the bodies of the mass of infants and small children.

The explosiveness of the site is not lessened by the two deep craters immediately to my back and side, one marked as the mass grave of women and children, and the other marked as a mass grave of 166 victims without heads. A sickness of the soul slowly and deliberately seeps throughout my entire body as I weigh, were I in Marilyn and Joseph's shoes, whether I could really truly find it in my heart to wholly forgive the people who did this. Could I fully and unreservedly forgive a bloodthirsty band and their leader of such malicious injustices and murder?

Never before have I faced to this degree, or been so daunted by, the absolute and unconditional magnitude of God's love and forgiveness. I ponder on Duch's Christian conversion and feel exactly like the words of an old hymn, which begins, "I stand amazed in the presence of Jesus the Nazarene, and wonder how he could love me, a sinner, condemned, unclean." Penned by Charles Gabriel, who grew up on an Iowa farm in the mid-1800s, he, too, knew about fields, a point which causes me to remember his words of the next stanza. "For me it was in the garden he prayed, 'Not my will, but Thine.' He had no tears for his own grief, but sweat drops of blood for mine."

I silently query how many prayers were lifted up in this garden, to the only God known to the many victims—whether Buddhist or the scanty number of Christians. Victims who could shed no tears, even while knowing their lives were at the mercy of another's will. I contemplate the fathomless number of drops of sweat and blood that fell on this garden, this field, whose only harvest was the thousands of bodies. Tears instantly flood my soul—not for my own grief, but for the grief of those whose lives came to an end here, or on the way—but I willfully force them to wait for their release until I am alone in my room.

We keep plodding along to where, in front of us on the path, a small rectangular area is chained off. A sign hangs from the chain warning of "Fresh Paint." A careful glance indicates why the area is chained. The traffic of footsteps on the path has unearthed bones and teeth, an important element for tourists to witness.

As at Tuol Sleng, Joseph enlightens us with his perspective as an "insider." Three young adults walk up while he tells of even more horrors about this place and the way the victims were treated. He points to a femur peeking out of the dirt in front of us. "Every time I come, it makes me more thankful the war with the Khmer Rouge ended before I was sent here. Because I was educated, I was a target. It was only my fishing abilities and experience that kept me alive long enough to survive the entire deal.

"My name was on the list at the security office in Tuol Sleng," he shares with the young people, once again making reference to that item still holding my curiosity. I, like them, hang on his every word. "Had the Khmer Rouge regime lasted a few more days, I would be lying under this ground instead of walking on top of it."

His words cast a fearful solemnity to the air around us, leaving us all, including Marilyn, shaken as we comprehend how near this situation really was to all of us. I instantly think of Marilyn's fiancé who was killed, a "military man" of whom I read in her notes the evening before, and consider whether he was among the bodies of bones here. My eyes veer briefly in her direction while wondering if that same question ever crosses her mind.

Joseph abruptly dissipates the silence of our mood when he spots a palm tree with terribly sharp, jagged edges on the branches. "Like this, like this!" he calls to me, motioning with his hand for me to follow him. He reaches out and rubs the edges, encouraging me to do the same. I know indubitably what he is doing. He is offering me a "real" hands-on opportunity to experience just how gory having your head sawed off would be with this instrument of terror, the one missing from the display at Tuol Sleng's Genocide Museum.

The three young people, whom we discover are college students from South America and France, suddenly become a part of our group as they ask Joseph and Marilyn an array of questions, inquiring about all sorts of aspects from "Pol Pot time." When they learn I am writing a book about this fascinating couple, they are immediately enthralled and begin snapping pictures of all our party. Their questions turn to me and we soon ascertain this young man from France has visited a remote North Carolina mountain community, Cedar Mountain, that serves as the setting for one of my novels. He, like the rest of us, is thrilled at the truth of what a small world it really is. Pretty soon, we are all like one big happy family as they are having their photos made with us.

That's until I grasp the total irony of my thought. Never on this spot, whether many long years ago or thirty-five years ago, has there been "one big happy family." *Or any other kind of happy family, for that matter,* I determine, rationalizing that families who came here long ago were mourning the loss of a loved one entombed here. *And neither could there have been happy Khmer Rouge soldiers throwing up babies to land on bayonets, or slamming them into trees. That wasn't happiness; that was madness.* All of my college psychology classes, together, in no way account for this type of action.

Mark, noticing I am totally absorbed in a world thirty-five years before, informs me I need to keep moving if I plan to see the video of this place. As much as I yearn to stay lost in my own private thought bubble—with my heart, my soul and my very pores soaking in all I can from that time gone by in order to adequately relate this missionary couple's story—I know he is right. Yet for me, the stories continue to abound. They float in the air, held aloft by the spirits behind them, they filter through the leaves of the many trees of this former orchard, and they lie on the ground on which we are walking. As "deadly" as this place is, for my writing muse it is bursting with life from its many tales, accounts of the characters who make this place so disparagingly famous, and who come to life before my very eyes. It allows me a key into the private worlds of Joseph and Marilyn that even their detailed stories can not. I am caught up in my own 3-D movie, something writers and artists understand and accept, as I close down my mental screen projector and head for more notes at the newest addition of "the killing fields."

The short video, of which Mark spoke, is a resource added since my last visit. During the past year, a house has been built in which visitors are shown a movie depicting the kinds of activities that happened here. A sign in front of the building sets the stage for what is inside with the words, "Would you please kindly show your respect to many million people who were killed under the genocidal Pol Pot Regime?" This is their polite way of telling visitors to remove their shoes and hats.

Five minutes into the movie, I develop an even greater admiration for this brave, bold couple seated beside me who not only faced everything documented in the film, but have the strength and courage to face the screen and watch it. What's shown on the screen is "a hard pill to swallow," but I resign myself to the fact this is not a matter of one's desire to witness blood and gore, but an attempt to grasp exactly what did happen here. For me, it is to gain a richer and deeper understanding and a greater appreciation of the two main characters of this book. I pray it will hopefully unearth any sliver of light during a most unfortunate slice of history.

According to the details of the film, over three million people lost their lives throughout the whole of the country from 1975 – 1979, during Pol Pot's reign. It states the Khmer Rouge sent 20,000 people to their deaths here, nine of whom were European. Out of the 450 killing fields scattered throughout Cambodia, this one is the largest. My condolences return to Chandra, who has no idea whether her father rests in one of those 450 fields, or was left alone along a path shared by other victims also pulled out of a line of "wandering nomads," unsettled by a conscienceless barbarian.

When we exit the movie, I turn to seize a last fleeting glimpse of the one scene still undermining my thoughts. I feel nauseous as I look back in the direction of the "Juvenile Execution Tree." *In the period of one day,* I decide, *I have been in what must be the two most scandalous places on the face of the earth. "Execution Tree,"* my mind repeats unconsciously. At first I am unaware of any inner thoughts; I am too caught up in trying to fathom how so many people could be so violently swayed by one man's corrupted mind. Then I understand.

No, I correct myself, *today I have been in what must be two of the* three *most scandalous places on the face of the earth. The first is the site of an "execution tree" used for a cross centuries ago, an execution that made it possible for Joseph and Marilyn to bring the Gospel and Christ's salvation back to their native land.*

An earlier interview reminds me of a man's words I'd found hard to believe at the time, but now make total sense. "I didn't think about what we were doing at the time we killed the babies. Everyone around me was shouting, 'Kill him! Kill him!' and so I just did it."

Is that not the same reaction of an angry mob who yelled, "Crucify him! Crucify him!," in the streets of Jerusalem centuries earlier? The same crowd who earlier had thrown off their cloaks and laid them on the street for this man to pass, a man whom they now wanted killed?

For years I've listened to, and even delivered, sermons illuminating the significance of the role played by the aggressive influence of a riotous crowd in the death of Jesus. Now I am staring at a tree where I visibly witness the importance of the role played by the aggressive influence of riotous soldiers in the death of infants. *Riotous soldiers molded by the aggressive influence of a man who had once been a teacher and principal, desirous of having his students to pass.*

That observation causes my body to go limp. My immediate reaction is to embrace Joseph and Marilyn, shielding them from a hurtful and insensitive past with my sisterly Christian love. My gut reaction is to give in to the nausea in the pit of my stomach and the limpness in my body. My heart's reaction is to rejoice in the Lord for He not only protected them with His ultimate shield, but in the process, called them into His fold to be loving and compassionate servants. Servants who loved and trusted Him enough to travel halfway around the globe and obtain the education and training necessary to take Christianity and the Gospel back to a hurting and recovering third-world country—a country left by the communists with no forms of religion. I picture Jesus looking at Joseph and Marilyn and one day saying, "Today you shall be with me in paradise."

"Since this was the last place of rest for so many thousands of people, do their family members ever come here to pay their respects?" I ask Marilyn.

"Yes," she answers with a nod of her head. I have been around her long enough to discern that nod which, angled a bit to one side of her head, serves as an emphatic "Yes!" "Each September, there is a large Buddhist festival called Pchum Ben, when Cambodians go to pay their respect and homage to ancestors who have died. Family members come here to bring flowers, to burn incense and to release the bodies from the hell where their souls are doomed. Monks come too. People cook very good food to give to the monk and ask him to send the food to their ancestors' souls and release them."

Somehow the vastness of God's unconditional love and forgiveness, as I know them, suddenly becomes even more real to me. Fearing the risk of seeming a bit audacious yet needing to know, I stop in my tracks and turned toward her. "When you became Christian, did you continue to follow any of the Buddhist rituals and traditions?"

"No," she answers simply, taking no offense, while confirming my suspected answer. Having grown up in a practicing Christian family since birth, with my ancestors very active in their faith, I have no basis by which to know. Extremely aware of Cambodia's superstitious background, I am keenly interested in whether those practices follow converted believers into their Christian faiths.

I find myself grateful to leave this place, although I am fully aware the memories I take with me, partially due to the book's research, are now forever etched on my mind. *As vividly as the square tan and cream floor tiles I left behind at Tuol Sleng,* I surmise.

As we make our way back to the parking lot, we are accosted by tiny children, barely old enough to speak, who run up to us mumbling unrecognizable words. It takes no time to figure out this is their way of begging Americans for food. Their father has brought them here to take advantage of tourists' sympathetic hearts, caused by what they've just witnessed.

Marilyn is quick to reach in the back of the Land Cruiser and present the children with bananas to share with their family. *Like mother, like daughter*, I muse, recalling the stories of her mother's benevolence.

As the children hastily follow us to the Land Cruiser, reaching anxiously for the small, delicious finger bananas, I find myself elated that the execution scenes of Jesus and the children, from moments earlier, are now replaced by a beautiful scene of Jesus and the children as he said, "Let the little children come unto me." It is truly a picturesque image, one of no comparison with the rest of the day, and one which will remain alongside the horrors of my memories of this place. A warm smile covers my face as I watch these precious children share their reward evenly among themselves. I find it heartwarming that, within only a few yards from the skeletons of so many infants and children, there truly *are* happy children at this place. These children, unlike the ones buried here, will have food in their belly on this day.

As Joseph leaves dust trailing behind us and heads back toward the city, I contemplate on how many people followed the same road we did to get here, yet never left. Their point of no return simultaneously lends freedom more value, making it exceptionally precious. Laying my head back against the seat, I relish in the fact that in one single day, I have been catapulted back decades. In the process, I have been given a minute inkling of how many miracles it took to bring this couple to the place where they are in their lives now, both at home and in their service to God and the world.

An exhausting day—mentally, physically and emotionally—draws to a close as Joseph and Marilyn take Mark and me to the site of our favorite Cambodian restaurant, the Wagon Wheel. Although one would never guess from its name, it serves the best Wiener schnitzel I've ever tasted, even among my several travels to Germany and Austria. To our dismay, the restaurant is no longer there. Tired and hungry, having missed lunch, we reconcile ourselves to the Happy Pizza, also situated on the Sisopath Quay along the waterfront, next door to what was once our favorite old establishment. We sit at a sidewalk table and stare longingly at the houseboats docked along the shore, and the tour boats still cruising passengers, providing a perfectly serene backdrop for the day's end.

Looking back on all that has transpired during this long, full day, I come to a major conclusion. My free day truly *is* a free day, or is at least a day of reckoning with exactly how "free" I really am. It forces me to appreciate exactly how much freedom I really do have and how blessed my life is, and has been. And it makes me want to reach out even more, in whatever way God deems possible, to the survivors of this incomprehensible insanity. Images of the day, even without the aid of Mark's photos, flash through my mind. I mourn for all the victims who were killed, whether physically at the hands of the Khmer Rouge, or by starvation, diarrhea or infectious diseases—all of which became as violent a murderer as the instruments of torture we witnessed being demonstrated by Joseph during the day.

When I finally return to my hotel room, those images, combined with the words of all the notes I've taken during the course of the day, stare back at me with one decisive message. "The way God deems possible," they seem to say, "is to write a beautiful narrative of how God has miraculously taken an account of such outlandish hell and turned it into one of transformation and redemption. A story of Joseph and Marilyn Chan."

A story of faith, hope and love…in action, I hear subconsciously as my fingers peck away at the keyboard, until well into the morning hours, on a story to which only God could bring beauty.

Chapter Eleven

Sunday, the day of rest, is exactly what we all need. Not for the rest and relaxation as much as for the rejuvenation of our spirits, after the emotional drain of the day before. I feel a great necessity of getting my "cup" filled in order to be ready for another grueling week. By the end of the day, Joseph and Marilyn "refill" my Sabbath with so many blessings that "my cup runneth over."

The morning begins with meeting Christina, the youngest of the Chan's three children. A high school senior, she will attend college in California in the fall—a big step for an 18-year-old who has spent the majority of her life in Cambodia even though she was born in the Golden State. It only takes a few minutes to discover she has inherited the child-like spirit of her mother and her father's joy, traits evident in the resemblance of her mother's face, and her father's dancing eyes.

While Mark is busy snapping photographs of our newest acquaintance, a young woman enters the front door of the Golden Gate Hotel. There is something immediately, yet vaguely, familiar about her as she proceeds toward me. Spying a sketch pad under her arm, I know why she is here. The reason for the familiarity is still a blur in my mind, chasing around frantically as it tries to make itself known, but I am anxious to share my ideas of artwork for the book with her.

"Hello. My name is Linat," she says cordially as we exchange greetings.

Marilyn and Joseph join us to make the proper introductions. "Linat is a former student of the Cambodian Methodist Bible School." They offer many accolades about her studies and work as we pull chairs around the coffee table in the hotel's small lobby, making sure we are in the direct line of circulating air from the overhead fan.

Within minutes, she has a list of sketches I'd like for use in the book. She stands to leave, rushing to get home before her husband leaves for work so she can keep her two young children. When she turns to give us one last wave, before taking off on her motorbike, my mind's blur transforms into a sharp image as I recall her as one of the three translators on my first trip to Cambodia. Her hair, now short and styled, along with her professional appearance masquerade my memory of her long, straight hair and traditional Cambodian silk skirts and shirts. I'm thrilled as I inform Linat that she once interpreted our words of teaching into understandable phrases for Khmer Sunday School teachers and children's and youth leaders.

She nods. "Ah, yes! I remember."

Both of our smiles broaden as we realize this prior connection. I extend a final thanks to her, knowing her sketches will now hold even more meaning for me. In my mind, I envision God smiling as He watches this small cluster of His servants, from opposite sides of the world, working together in His name.

"I would do anything for Joseph and Marilyn," she shares quietly. "They have been like parents to me. I could have never gone to school without them. They even allowed me to live with them so I could attend the Bible School."

We exchange business cards. As she rides away, I glance at her card to discover she works for a Christian agency in Cambodia. She is only one of many whose lives have been changed as a result of the Chan's incessant work to further God's kingdom. *And one who is continuing to further that kingdom,* I reason, watching as she disappears in the traffic. Joseph's plan of not only empowering, but making sure the empowered know how to continue that circle, is clearly succeeding. *Joseph, the shepherd, bringing sheep into the fold.*

On the way to church, which in Cambodia doesn't begin until after lunch, Joseph and Marilyn rave about Linat and the strengths she brings to the ministry of her country. I love the association of so many faces bound by the spirit emitted by this couple. There is something powerfully rewarding, simply by virtue of being in their presence, as I share this day of worship and rest with them. Though I have worked in the church more years than they've been Christian, there is a powerful force undeniably controlling them and our path with them, one unlike anything I've experienced in all my years of being in Christ's service.

We drive for what seems forever down a long path, the thick dust and dirt seeping into the crevices of the Land Cruiser to combine with the hot temperature of the scorching sun. The sight of temples and spanning fields are replaced by remote areas of small huts and jungle shrubs.

Marilyn hands me a beautiful purple silk fan and a white paper towel. "You will need these during the service." I take them and nod.

A glance forward reveals the concrete church building to my right nestled between trees and huts. "This is the Emmanuel Methodist Church," Joseph announces energetically. "The land for it was donated by Mrs. Sylvia Savoeun Phon and her husband Moeung Peo, loving members of our church family of Central UMC in Stockton, California."

We are the only vehicle so Joseph pulls into the small driveway and parks in front of the single building which serves as the sanctuary as well as the education center. The sound already pouring toward us from inside the uncovered windows alerts me I'm in for a treat.

We peek inside the back door, but the single room is so crowded with young bodies we are unable to enter. It becomes necessary to walk around the side and enter near the front of the sanctuary, onto the raised area of the pulpit. Having been a children's choir director and music teacher for decades, my soul is truly magnified when I see the number of children packed in the building, singing their little hearts out and making motions along with the words. There is no talking, no picking or hitting on the others, even though they are literally seated hip-to-hip on the floor.

When I earlier inquired about the availability of Christmas trees in Cambodia, Marilyn's response, "They're very expensive," is now insignificant. As I watch the children's eyes, flickering like candles in the night, I look at her and ask, "Who needs Christmas trees and lights when you have these precious children singing? Look into their eyes!"

For years, I've told children their eyes sing and people hear what they see. These animated children prove I'm right. I have no idea what their words say, but I'm totally enthralled by their voices rejoicing with every ounce of energy they have. They are truly giving their all to the Lord's praise and glory. It is an unforgettable experience, which becomes even more unforgettable when the music leader asks if I would like to teach the children a song. I instinctively pull out the old standby from my last trip and lead them in a round of *Halle, Halle, Halle*. They enjoy the motions while they sing wholeheartedly, and we all understand the single-word lyric, "Hallelujah!"

Next, Marilyn teaches them a children's song she has written. Last, their music leader and the children's leader direct them in a short chorus, which they sing in Khmer, Thai, Vietnamese and English. When they reach the stanza in English, their eyes peer at me to see if it meets my approval. My reaction of clapping, nodding and smiling is echoed by them as we together celebrate that we are one in the Lord.

When it is time for them to leave and the adults to enter for worship, some of the children go home, but many flock outside, peeking in the doors and windows to watch us. They are excited to see "foreigners" in their midst. I stare at the beautiful illustration of the Nativity scene on the back wall of the pulpit area, drawn by their youth. At first, it strikes me odd their colors used to depict the Holy Birth are the same ones as in our depictions. My eyes open to the fact this portrayal is not a matter of Eastern or Western influence, but a universal blessing for all. The physical features and clothing styles may differ in the representations, but the gift of the Christ child is the same, also evidenced by the openness and confidence with which both the children and adults sing and rejoice, in their native tongue and musical styles indigenous to their culture.

The minister asks both Mark and I to speak to the adults. We each say only a few words, via translators, to the congregation. I get the sense of what Paul must have felt, as I stand before them, "bringing love and greetings in the name of our Lord Jesus Christ from my family and friends, and brother and sister Christians in America." One of the most striking features of the service is the involvement of lay people as they pray, give announcements and read scriptures. The sacrament of communion is exceedingly meaningful as Joseph helps with the distribution of the elements, even though the cup is filled with red fruit punch, poured from tiny plastic bottles like the ones from which my sons loved to drink as children. The bread is delicious, a carry-over from their days of French influence.

At the end of the service, in which the only words I understand are "Jesus," "Bethlehem," "Hallelujah" and "Amen," I feel inspired beyond measure. The message is the same as the one heard by congregations all over the world on this Sunday still in the Christmas season. Of that, I'm sure, regardless of the many words I missed.

We walk outside to exchange signs and expressions of "Goodbye" to the members of the congregation, who are dressed in as many different styles as there are people present. One older woman, whom we observed working with her rice crop prior to the service, walks only a few feet to her home, which is next door to the church. Reapplying the same krama around her head that she removed to come to the service, she bends as she goes back to work in the rice she is currently harvesting. When she sees Mark approach her, she pauses only long enough to smile for him to take a photo. It is then I notice her natural beauty, enhanced by her smile that transparently reveals her loving spirit. I feel blessed when her smile reaches me.

Other adults stand outside and talk while their children play chase and hide-and-seek among the banana trees and other shrubs. The minister comes out with two boxes for children who were absent the previous Sunday. I stand in shock, recognizing all too well the boxes as he hands them to the children. They are shoeboxes, just like the ones children at my church filled for nearly a month. They are shoeboxes, just like the ones filled by every denomination at home and around the world. And they are shoeboxes which are processed and sent out into the needy areas of the world by "Operation Christmas Child," whose international headquarters is located in my home state, with a large distribution center located only minutes from my house. Having worked in the facility with my youth groups, I know the process through which this box has traveled to get here, as does Mark. Having just had a representative of Operation Christmas Child speak to the children with whom I work, I know these particular boxes were distributed by teams from New Zealand and Australia. I'm not sure who is most excited about the rectangular boxes and their contents—the children or Mark and me. Mark shares the reason for our boisterous excitement with Marilyn and Joseph, who in turn share his comments with the children and adults, who are now clapping with all their might.

It is a more glorious Sabbath than one can imagine, even greater than ones with magnificent pipe organs, shiny bronze handbells or grandiose choirs. *And more riveting than the pro football play-offs,* I muse, thinking of what will take precedence on this day in my own home country.

Even considering the worship services I've attended in Cambodia in the past, I don't think I shall ever encounter another day like this, when I am surrounded by so many kindred spirits of all ages who are so enthusiastically dedicated. I cannot imagine the ecstasy Joseph and Marilyn must feel, having been God's instruments directly responsible not only for this beautiful worship experience, but the freedom to have it in their home country.

As we climb back in the Land Cruiser, I notice there are only a couple of motorbikes and bicycles that arrived between the two services. Everyone else is within walking distance of the church. It is reminiscent of the days when my great-grandparents attended church. Even the musician, carrying his keyboard in a black case as he goes home on foot, lives just a few huts away. Watching him makes me instantly grateful I didn't have to contend with that obstacle every Sunday of my life.

Joseph drives slowly so as not to create a dense cloud of dust as he heads back toward the main highway. Far down the red dirt path in front of us, we spot an image of which I will never tire in Cambodia. A young farmer, his bicycle loaded down with goods—which in this case is green coconuts—pedals his way to the market in order to provide for his wife and family. Knowing Marilyn's inherent way of "reaching out to those less fortunate," I rightly anticipate what comes next. When we pass him, Joseph stops the vehicle and Marilyn climbs over Christina as she exits the back seat in her rush to meet the man. In a moment, she returns with five coconuts, the tops of all of them chopped off and a straw sticking in each of the large, rounded Cambodian delicacies.

"I've never done this on the way home from church before," I share with a hearty laugh, thinking there's very little connected with church—before, during or after— I haven't done in my career. Sipping on the sweet juice, as succulent as it is, is nothing in comparison to the joy I receive in knowing we've helped a young man support his family on this day. *A man whose "oxen is in the ditch," as the scriptures say*; or in my mind, *a man whose children are hungry.*

Little does Marilyn know my love for coconut. A little dark chocolate and a few almonds, both of which I brought from home, and the traumatic hell of yesterday's visit to Tuol Sleng and "the killing fields" turns into a taste of heaven. *Ah, what every writer deserves while enduring such long, tedious hours of research!*

My conscience immediately reprimands me for such a selfish thought. Experiencing how I deserve nothing, in light of so many poor people in this impoverished country, shame runs through me, causing my thoughts to shift back to yesterday's forms of torture. The picture of Duch, and his dastardly character from that period, fills my mind. It is instantaneously replaced by a vision of how I suspect him to appear now that he knows he's a forgiven child of God.

None of us deserve God's love. None of us can earn God's love. But everyone has the privilege to accept God's love, and in turn share it with others, if presented the opportunity. I look at Marilyn, her innocent spirit matching her impish eyes, and Joseph, whose "joy of the Lord" is his strength. *Thank God for their opportunity.* I marvel at their remarkable story of faith, hope and love in action. *Thank God for the one who extended them this opportunity.* I rejoice for the missionaries who've given their lives to the people of Cambodia. *Thank God for their service.* And I wonder at the possibility of someone as cold-hearted and callous as Duch converting to Christianity. *Thank God for stories of figures such as Paul, who prove God's merciful grace and transformation applies to anyone who will accept it.*

My shame of a moment earlier turns to gratitude for such a beloved brother and sister in Christ who have given me one of the fruits of

God's handiwork to enjoy. *No, just like Christ giving his life for me on the cross, I don't deserve it. But here it is for me to accept, and take all I can from it to make me a better, stronger person, ready and willing to reach out and share that Christian example of love with others.*

I smile at Marilyn as I take a big sip of the coconut milk. "Thank God from whom all blessings flow!" I proclaim.

"Thank God! Thank God! Praise the Lord!" replies Joseph, right on cue, with that huge smile that covers his entire face.

What a way to spend the Sabbath! I muse. Sliding back comfortably into the seat, I'm as content as if I were basking in the sun on a deserted island, left alone to my thoughts and this book project…until one giant missing fact slaps me in the face.

"Wait a minute, Joseph!" I exclaim, hastily sitting aright in the seat. "How and when did you get back to Cambodia? You were at college in North Korea when Pol Pot took over, right?" My coconut takes a back seat—literally—as I grab my pen and paper in anticipation of receiving the details necessary to fill in the huge blank.

He smiles warmly and nods. "Yes, yes, like this, like this. I was asked to leave North Korea in December of 1976 and told only that I was returning to Cambodia. Not sure why and not yet finished with my degree, I chose to take what I'd learned to that point back to my province of Battambang, in an effort to help them work in fellowship to build value, respect and dignity for each person. I was so excited to be returning to my homeland, even though I didn't understand the reason. I could hardly wait to get on the ground and surprise my family. I was anxious to see them all and make sure they were alright.

"But it was me who got the surprise. When my plane landed in Phnom Penh, I—along with a woman and two other men who were also Cambodians sent back from North Korea—was immediately stripped of my passport and identification. I was shoved into a governmental car of the Khmer Rouge and taken directly to the southern part of Boeung Trabek district in Phnom Penh."

He shakes his head in sorrow. "On the way to what became my 'home' until Liberation Day, I was shocked at the sight of trash and leaves all over the streets. There was total silence everywhere, so strange…," he pauses and shakes off a cold chill, "and all the schools and markets were closed. Signs of death were all along the road on the way to the metal factory, where they took me to work because of my mechanical engineering degree. It wasn't until I arrived at my destination that I learned of all the murders, and the hideous treatment of my fellow citizens. I discovered that many soldiers and leaders of Lon Nol's military armies were all considered oppressors and corrupters, and therefore killed on contact. Then I heard that some of the first ones imprisoned and slaughtered were the rich, the politicians, the journalists, the professors and the educated men and their families. That's when I really became concerned, especially when I learned the three people who returned with me mysteriously disappeared shortly after their return."

Joseph's pain is audible in his voice. "All I could think about was my family. I wondered if they were alive and where they were. I was heartsick that I was unable to reach out to them and help them." He gives a sigh. "It wasn't until after Liberation Day, when I was finally able to return to Battambang, that I learned my mother had died as a result of starvation and the diarrhea that went with it. My cousin, who was the district leader for my area, was killed by the Khmer Rouge." His voice fades as he concludes, "His two sons 'disappeared' right after their father was killed. They were never seen again."

A sense of pity consumes me, accompanied by a pang of guilt for having ruined his blessed Sabbath. Yet within minutes, his moment of silence is replaced by a replenished joy as he talks enthusiastically about the other churches, and the ministries going on within Cambodia, and I go back to enjoying my fresh coconut. Joseph unknowingly exhibits a dynamic living example of not looking back to the past, but rather, staying focused on the future. It is the past from which he draws to put his Christian faith and his understanding of God's love into perspective.

Mark, who can't pass a White Castle at home without stopping, is also focused on the future. He can hardly wait to get back to Phnom Penh and the Golden Gate so he can walk to the nearest Lucky Burger. Complete with "lucky meals," it is the Cambodian counterpart to McDonald's. I agree to try it, more for the walk than the food.

After our "fast-food fix," Mark retreats to his room to watch the Khmer version of a comical survival show, while I settle down to begin transcribing the many pages of notes given to me by Joseph and Marilyn.

A couple of hours later, there is a knock at my door. I open it to see Marilyn standing there with two fresh coconuts.

"One to drink now," she offers merrily, "and one to eat later."

"Where's Joseph?"

"He's outside waiting. I wanted to be sure you had something good while you were working."

She departs as quietly as she came, leaving me with Christina's cell phone in case I need anything.

Fruits of the Spirit, I muse as she exits through the lobby, *and she is the best fruit of all.* I smile as I recall from her notes that we were born the same year. *It was a good harvest that year,* I joke to myself, *a bumper crop!*

Chapter Twelve

Marilyn and Joseph arrive early on Tuesday morning, their Land Cruiser's baggage area filled to the max with everything we could possibly need to keep us afloat for the next four days. Between the emergency snacks I brought from home, and the bags of fresh fruit Marilyn has packed, not to mention the cases of water and cold sodas in the cooler, I begin to sense we're off for a picnic at the park instead of "jumping ship."

There's even a whole array of fishing baskets and nets, I notice, wondering who in our group is going to have time for fishing. I don't ask questions. I figure the time for that will come later, on their timetable, not mine.

We finally rearrange things to fit all of my writing gear, Mark's photography equipment, and our clothes and basic needs in the back. Once we're all seated and buckled in, Joseph shouts heartily, "Pray!"

Christina lunges into action with words I cannot understand, but which I know relate to our safety and traveling mercies, our success in our mission and the ability to touch the lives of those with whom we come in contact. I suspect that somewhere in her requests is one for strength for her parents as they open all the doors of their lives. That's when I add my own prayer for this imminent task to provide them with a closure that has been absent from their lives for the past thirty-five years. As I stare at Joseph's silhouette, with determination and purpose written on his face as we barrel down the road, I am confident God has already answered all those prayers, and has ordered our steps prior to our arrival for all the destinations included on this trip. Little do I realize *how* well He has ordered everything—even down to the timing and the people we will meet—until we are well into the journey.

Our journey of life, I muse as I pull out my pad and pen, ready to record their steps on paper, thinking how fortuitous it is that Christina's still on school holiday and can experience this slice of history and her parents' lives, as difficult as that may be. *The younger generation needs to know, to appreciate what their families had to live through to survive.* I look at Christina's naïve face and eyes, so young, so tender. *And make sure such a catastrophe never happens again.*

"Do you remember what it was like prior to the Khmer Rouge, in the time following when Prince (Norodom) Sihanouk was ousted from power by General Lon Nol?" I ask, praying my questioning doesn't resemble an inquisition as I urge Marilyn to set the stage for her amazing story. Historically, I know what happened; I've researched the printed facts of the prince's bloodless coup, led by Cambodia's defense minister Lt. General Lon Nol, on March 18th of 1970. But I'm anxious to hear her side of the story as it relates to her past.

"While Prince Sihanouk was visiting in Peking, he was ousted by General Lon Nol. According to friends of my father, who were also military men, Lon Nol was the first president of Cambodia. He was friendly, humble and openly sought to understand the needs and hardships of the people. His governmental platform was more toward restoration, to rebuild the nation. The songs spoke of bravery and being patriotic to the country.

"Even so, there was still crisis, oppression, exploitation, corruption, discrimination, great unemployment, and no respect for employees. Many of the military leaders did not take care of their soldiers, and refused to pay money to help the soldiers' wives. Some of them even had affairs with the soldiers' wives. But many military leaders were also killed by those under them in retaliation.

"Before the Khmer Rouge and the communists finally took over control of the country, many of Lon Nol's men were killed."

We barely make it off the side street, where our hotel is located, onto Monivong Boulevard when Marilyn changes the subject and begins to detail her family's sobering morbid experience on April 17, 1975 as we pass the site where the Chinese Hospital, seen in *The Killing Fields*, still sits. "When we came down this street, there was a woman, dirty with blood on her sarong, sobbing and holding a baby. We learned she had given birth to the baby only the day before and was thrown out of the hospital and into the street earlier on the morning of the 17th."

No farther than we've traveled, I notice the glowing sparkle that is so much a part of Marilyn and her whole appearance is absent as she sits solemnly recounting the facts. "From the items we had brought with us, my mother gave her a sarong in which to hold and feed the baby, and a bag of sugar to make sugar water for the baby. When we went a little farther down the street, we heard of a doctor at the hospital who was about to deliver a baby. Khmer Rouge soldiers ordered him to leave, but the doctor told them he would come with them as soon as he safely delivered the baby. They immediately shot him, right there with the mother giving birth, due to his refusal of obedience to Angkar Leu (the name used during Khmer Rouge time for the top government).

"Angkar Leu wanted the people to believe it was their best friend, that it was looking out for the best interest of the people. It wasn't long before people learned to fear Angkar Leu, for one stray step from the government's orders and you, and your family, would disappear in the middle of the night...if you made it that long."

Her kind face manages a gentle smile, as if to apologize for the scheming actions of an evil force. "Some of this transpired even before April 17th. One of our neighbors had eye surgery, which needed to be followed up with a doctor. All of the doctors were forced to leave the city, which meant our neighbor was left alone with no help and no medicine. Because of this, he went permanently blind."

"What happened to the buildings? Were they simply left like a ghost town?" I ask, regretfully wishing I could recapture that choice of words. As it is, I am sure Phnom Penh—along with many other villages—

had already become a ghost town, and those which hadn't were doomed to do so in the coming months and years. Knowing how much the Cambodians fear ghosts, I want to beg forgiveness for my heartless question, but Marilyn is so engrossed in the much worse horror of that day that she doesn't seem to notice.

"Many buildings were burning as we passed them. This started with the bombing of the military office the day before. Some places exploded as a result of gas combustion. We saw people burning from the fires, unable to receive any help."

I determine her soft smile, barely recognizable but still in place, is her security blanket. It acts as a shield to hide all of her emotions buried inside, yet also as her assurance from God that there is nothing so great He will ever leave her. Her brief pause is a welcome break as my hands struggle to keep up with her stories, which are rapidly segueing from one to the next.

"Because it was so late by the time we left our house, and so many people were trying to evacuate at the same time, travel was extremely slow. We only made it as far as the Law School on Monivong Boulevard by nightfall of that first evening. It was so quiet that our family decided we could sleep on the sidewalk there. However, as we tried to clean off a little spot to make a bed, we saw the body of a soldier of the Khmer Republic, the army in which my father had been. We knew it was a soldier because we recognized the uniform, but there was no head. That's why it was so quiet. We just kept walking until we could find another place to rest overnight."

I shudder, wondering how one could possibly find "a place to rest" after seeing such a sight, especially on the heels of all they've encountered leading up to that vision. My mind drifts back to scenes of New Orleans' Superdome—a place I've been many times before and after Hurricane Katrina—and the horror of that situation, caused by America's worst natural disaster. *That was bad enough,* I remind myself, thinking of all the stories I've heard from survivors of that storm, *but to see all this kind of death, in such a grotesque manner, at the hands of one's own countrymen.* I shudder again, from my own memory of having visited the site of many of the battlefields of my own country's civil war from 140 years earlier. My heart bleeds over such loss of life and destruction, as I think of the many burned towns and homes from that bloodbath in American history. Yet there is still no comparison to what I'm seeing and hearing in Cambodia.

I'm so engrossed in this history lesson that our sudden stop startles me as I brace myself against the front seat. A quick glance out the windshield yields a view of four cows meandering across the highway, their tails swaying as they lean first one way and then the other with their thin bodies and skinny legs. Traffic comes to a dead standstill in both directions, with horns blaring, as the bovines cross the pavement. The idea of blowing horns at cows is beyond me; it is not making these animals go any faster.

"My country, my road," Joseph says.

"What?" I ask.

"The cows," he explains. "They think this is their country and their road. It is the cars who are out of place here."

His comment warrants an audible snicker. *He's right,* I tell myself. *The cows were here first. The cows still travel this road.* It's then I notice something strangely different here. There are no fences to contain the animals. They all wander wherever they want. "Don't the people worry about their livestock wandering onto someone else's property?"

"They'll go home when they get hungry."

I mull on his words, calculating how I don't recall seeing more than two animals, if that many, at any one hut. They are identifiable without tags in their ears. Suddenly I realize there are no leash laws in third-world countries. I note the scenery out the window has changed from wall-to-wall buildings to countryside and trees. Dorothy's famous line from *The Wizard of Oz* plays in my mind as I revamp it to say, "We're not in Phnom Penh any more, Mark!"

Marilyn, seeing nothing out of the ordinary, continues, "Each night was a different stop. We tried to stay on side roads just off the major highway because so many people were disappearing after dark. And it was so hot. We got so thirsty. I remember this one time, not long after we'd left Phnom Penh, when my parents sent my younger sister and me to the Mekong River with a kettle to draw water. When we got to the river, it was full of dead bodies and blood. We kept walking up the river, trying to find a place where the water was not so contaminated.

Before we had gone very far, we ran into Khmer Rouge soldiers who pointed their guns at us and asked, 'Where you go? You want to die?'

"My sister and I were terrified. We knew they were going to shoot us right there and people would find our dead bodies next. My sister told them we were looking for water. They used their guns to point us back in the direction we'd come from, commanding, 'Go!' I was so frightened I nearly dropped the kettle, but I knew my poor father was so tired and dehydrated. I held onto it for dear life and my sister and I ran as hard as we could. The only water we could get was full of blood. It was so horrible but we were so worried about our parents, especially our father.

"When we got back to where our family was, my sister and I said nothing as we boiled the water over a fire. It was so contaminated that it still smelled horrible. We could hardly stand to drink it. My father asked why it smelled so bad, but we told him it was just dirty." Her words cause a wave of guilt to sweep over me at the thought of my bottle of cold water in the cooler at my feet.

"As we kept traveling on that road during the next few days, I continued to see more bodies floating in the river. We knew they'd been in the water for several days because they'd sink at first and then, after two or three days, they'd rise back to the surface."

I reconcile myself to the fact this is not going to be a pretty book, even though it is a beautiful story about a beautiful theme surrounding a beautiful couple. So as not to disturb Joseph's driving, since my place in the back seat allows the advantage of reading the speedometer, I invite Marilyn to continue to share her memories of her family's evacuation of the city. As I had hoped would stem from this adventure, her memory blossoms as she rattles off story after story, each prompted by a particular spot in the road that was a part of their journey. All of them are a part of the demise of her value as a person at the hands of the Khmer Rouge. I look at her…then treated worse than the thorn of a thistle and now a beautiful rose among women.

Within minutes, I have the feeling I'm seated in the theater watching a horror flick, only there's no exit door, thus leaving me trapped inside. The accumulating recollection of her memories, which are a result of this replay of three years, eight months and twenty days, now has

Marilyn spilling her guts—a matter of expression—as she tells of the many people she encountered, living and dead, and the many executions she witnessed. With the passing of each haunting spot in the road, there is another tale of gore and grief. Before we're an hour into the trip, she is literally retracing her steps, with stories "coming out of the woodwork" as they surface from cavernous depths of her consciousness.

"In one village, the Khmer Rouge killed people by digging holes in the ground and burying them up to their chests. The soldiers poured the hot water from the rice over their heads every day. On the day of liberation from the Khmer Rouge, North Vietnamese soldiers found one family still alive and took them to the hospital. This family was found at the commander's house, so the men who did this were taken as war criminals."

From the expression on her face, I can tell Marilyn is as numbed by these stories as I am. "So many people were killed for so many different reasons." She pauses for a few moments. "And so many people were killed for no reason." After another brief pause, she adds, "If an actor had even played the part of a king, he was killed."

With a new string of stories, she begins, "One man piled his wife and children into their car after they had eaten a meal on their good dishes. He then drove into the river. All of them drowned together." Her face shows her own sorrow at the story. "Many families died together rather than having members left alone, or rather than chance living under such wretched oppression.

"This story happened only two days before Liberation Day, at the end of the Khmer Rouge's power. A large crowd of people was taken to be slaughtered late one night. Afterwards, one of them, a teenage girl, woke up in the early morning hours. She got up and began walking only to discover everyone else was dead. Soon she came to her sister, whom she saw moving a bit. She helped her up and the two continued walking through the mass of bodies. They heard movement coming from one particular area. Thinking there must be another person alive, they went to check. They found their father, also alive. The three of them had to be taken to the hospital once Liberation Day arrived, but they survived.

"After Liberation Day, a cave was discovered where Khmer Rouge soldiers had tossed bodies of persons they had taken from the Siem Reap hospital. The soldiers would take the patients, hit them until they killed them and throw them in this cave near the mountain. There was one man who didn't die, but was too afraid to crawl back out of the cave, so he was left there with all the dead bodies. The only thing he had to eat was the human flesh. When he was found, they took him back to the hospital but he smelled so badly, like the stench of a decomposed human, that it made the people there sick. They had to put him off in a room by himself, away from the others."

Marilyn's subdued expression indicates a grueling account is unfolding. "This is the saddest story I know. My aunty told us about it when we went back to our hometown after Liberation Day. They had big open fire pits there and the Khmer Rouge soldiers had thrown a man in one of them, after hitting him until they thought he was dead. He woke up from the heat, crawled out and hid in the trees until the soldiers were gone. Badly burned, he tried to get to his mother's house that night for help and medical attention.

"Because Buddhists believe in reincarnation, she thought he was a spirit and told him, 'You passed away already. Don't come here and haunt us.'

"'Let me in,' he cried from the door, telling her he was alive and had escaped the fire.

"But she refused to believe him, again saying, 'Go away! Don't come and haunt us. If I open the door, it will get us all killed.' She was afraid and didn't dare let him in her house so he crawled back to hide in the forest near the place where all the food was cooked for the workers in that village.

"At night he would sneak there and eat the scorched rice that had been left at the bottom of the pot and thrown away. The Khmer Rouge soon realized someone was getting into it so they followed him and said, 'You cannot live.' They cut him in many pieces and threw him in the open fire pit again."

With each recount of her life and its seemingly countless hellish conditions, each tale more grotesque than the other, I welcome a rest stop and, oddly enough, lunch. My proportion of food is now measured in comparison to what the many poorly-treated families had during those years of dread and starvation.

Our day of unexpected delays reminds us of the One in charge when we finally reach the monastery where Joseph lived and worked during middle school and high school. We arrive at sundown, the perfect setting for Mark to capture Joseph on film with the sun casting an array of gorgeous colors to accent the intricate designs of the pagoda just behind him. As magnificent as the evening's setting of the sun is, it pales in comparison to the radiance of light beaming from the face of this dear servant of God, who, when he was here last, was a servant of the Buddhist monk.

Monks are gathered inside the temple across the street from the pagoda. Their young ages, the oldest appearing to be in his early thirties, reminds me of the execution of all the Buddhist monks, cited to be approximately 60,000, during the Khmer Rouge regime. The fact that all religion was banned from the country at that time makes Joseph's relentless efforts to bring Christianity, particularly Methodism, back into Cambodia all the more incredible.

"No one followed the rituals during that time," Joseph explains, confirming a point I'd already assumed considering the lack of food. "Even if there had been enough rice to offer, people wouldn't have been allowed to observe the traditions and worship. They would have been killed. People were not even able to light incense candles."

Another luxury I'm sure they could not afford, even if they had been permitted to burn them.

The eyes of the Buddhist students watch observantly as Joseph leads two obviously-American tourists throughout the property, re-enacting his every step and stopping along the way to explain every detail of his time there from 1960 - 1968. Other eyes, of students who attend Joseph's former high school, come closer when they spot two foreigners whom they consider wealthy. Like many of the people we've encountered since our short time in the country, they seek financial help.

Once we are back on the sidewalk outside the grounds of the monastery, our experienced tour guide points to the electric lights, whose bases are sculpted to match the décor of the pagoda. "We would come out here to study," he says, stooping to show us how they would use candles and incense sticks to create their light back then.

A young man, dressed in his saffron robe and studying to be a monk, meets us on the sidewalk. "Can I help you?"

Joseph proceeds to also inform the young man how he once lived here and points to various sites around the premises. "Everything is as it was, except for the lights in the monastery. We had to burn incense and hold the sticks toward our books to see to read at night." He looks at the ground. "These sidewalks weren't here and all the streets were dirt."

Like a hummingbird pausing briefly at one stop before flitting off to another, Joseph is on the move again as his arms point to the places where he followed the monk to collect food. "This market was not here then," he states, pointing to the lighted-up storefronts. "There was nothing but houses along the streets then."

Because darkness has set in, we do not retrace the steps he once took through this area. We do, however, pile into the Land Cruiser for a drive-through tour of where he worked to earn his keep. "And the good food the rich people gave the monk," he adds vivaciously.

I smile, having noted how Joseph loves to eat. Smaller than me, he can put away more food than Mark and I put together. *Must be all that flitting around like a hummingbird,* I surmise before concluding that because of his beautifully transformed spirit, his energetic equivalent is definitely a butterfly instead of a hummingbird.

The visit to the monastery proves to be a short stop, but a necessary one to understand the distance he had to travel to be educated and to see a glimpse of his teenage years. When he's content we've seen all there is to see, he continues toward the actual town of Battambang. After all the horn blowing of the day as Joseph sped past the other traffic, it is strange to see signs with the words "No Horn Blowing"—in Khmer, of course—dotting the highway. It is amazing the difference the past five years have made. This road is now completely smooth with a stripe down the middle to indicate lanes. That is a stark contrast from six years prior when it was so rough my head hit the top of the van with each bump.

Once we hit the edge of town, however, modernization ceases as few houses have lights. Most have small fires in front of them. Bikes and carts travel on the road in the darkness with no lights making it extremely difficult for Joseph to drive. This provides an allusion of what it must have been like for Marilyn's family and the other workers during the time of the Khmer Rouge as they had to work in the dark and then travel back to camp, often beginning their early morning walks while it was still dark. There is no moon on this night, creating an eerie darkness unlike anything I've ever known.

It is a good while before we come upon a short, narrow bridge. "During my escape after the Khmer Rouge," Joseph says, breaking the silence of a world of total darkness, "I traveled this way in search of my family. Back then this was a densely-wooded forest, making it harder to find your way. I never did find my family until much later, but when I came to this bridge, I found an unexpected and unwanted surprise. A man held a gun up to my head and demanded to know where I was going. All I knew to tell him was I was looking for food.

"I do not know why he put the gun down, but he did. I ran as fast as I could without looking back. I will never forget this bridge. I remember that story every time I come in this direction."

Visions of headless soldiers and gunmen do not paint a picture of serenity in the still night. To make things more paranormal, a long line of ultra-violet lights appears far off in the distance to our left. They are exceptionally bright in the vast darkness stretching out before us. I watch as the single line multiplies to thousands of lights, covering large areas of land. My assumption of a small airstrip is blown out of the water; there are more lights than at the Charlotte airport. My curiosity mounting, I finally venture to ask what they are.

"Those are lights to catch the crickets," says Joseph matter-of-factly.

"Crickets?" Listening to a lone cricket at home in the darkness is a favorite summertime pleasantry on my back deck. Judging from the number of lights, I'd think the sound of that many attracted crickets would be louder than the Charlotte Symphony. I ignore my temptation to roll the window down to listen for them.

"Yes, crickets."

"What do they do with that many crickets?"

"They eat them."

Our rhythmic banter of back and forth questions and answers is broken as I digest his words, while finding it hard to imagine how anyone could digest the crickets.

"Like the fried spiders I saw the last time I was here?" I finally manage.

"Yes, they fry them and sell them. This place is known for its fried crickets. It's their main business. The fried spiders are in Chandra's hometown of Skuon. They are small tarantulas, called 'a-ping' and they sell for eight-cents each. It's a main source of income for that village."

His answers leave me wondering how many crickets this area catches a night with that many lights, and who could, *or would*, possibly eat that many of the minute creatures. Suddenly, the thought of finding anything to eat to supplement the tiny amount of rice rationed by the Khmer Rouge—which is when the Cambodians began to eat the insects and anything they could find—is as real as the headless soldier, the gunman and the black of night. The scene is set for me to walk hundreds of miles in the shoes of Joseph and Marilyn.

Miles roll by until the silence is again broken, this time by Marilyn. "We lost one of our ministers in this area recently. He was hit by a truck, and left a wife and three children behind."

That incident would be disheartening enough in America, but to happen in a place like this where there are already so few ministers, my heart aches. *Yet another hardship you must understand if you are to walk in the shoes of these disciples and realize their plight of servanthood.*

The darkness is again all we see once we're out of range of the UV lights. I peer over my left shoulder to search for stars. From here, they seem very distant, but oddly, they are in the same exact position in the sky as at my house when I look out at this time of night there. Realizing we are turned in the same direction as my house, as I delight in the beauty of the evening sky, the world seems infinitely smaller.

It is only 8:30 when we finally meet Chandra at our hotel, but due to the darkness, it seems much later. She has spent the day interpreting for dental missionaries at the nearby orphanage. By this time, dinner—*which doesn't matter what it is as long as it isn't fried crickets*—is delicious to all of us, especially Joseph.

Chapter Thirteen

Our breakfast buffet—featuring rice porridge, salty fish and duck eggs—takes a backseat to the privilege of eating with a group of volunteer dental missionaries from America. Chandra introduces us to the group, most of whose members are from the states of Oregon and Washington, and for whom she has served as an interpreter the day before. Joseph converses with the head of the team, a Cambodian man, appearing to be in his mid-40s, who now lives in the Pacific Northwest. It is only a matter of minutes before this dentist realizes he recognizes Joseph from the past. They soon discover they were in the same refugee camp, Kao I Dang, in Thailand following the Khmer Rouge regime.

"I was sponsored by a church in the United States," the dentist shares, "and sent to Chicago, Illinois. Thankfully I was able to attend Boston University to become a dentist. I knew from the beginning I wanted to come back here every year to provide dental attention for the children and the orphans."

His influence to help is a growing ministry of its own, judging from the number of volunteers seated at several tables. It is providential we run into this group, for it allows me to personally see there were a number of "seeds" planted by the missionaries in the refugee camp that actually did take root. The presence of these volunteers provides a mental image of a flower bulb that multiplies each year, springing up with more beautiful flowers each year.

As if that isn't enough of a treat to start the day, we walk outside to a spectacular sunrise behind the silhouette of an elaborately ornate Buddhist temple sitting next door to the hotel. Drones of a male voice echo through the air over a loud speaker, resembling the sound of an old radio station from my early childhood.

"It's a Buddhist celebration," Joseph explains. A few miles down the road, a large tent covered in black and white signals it is a funeral. The décor on the tent is much the same as what I've seen for weddings, minus the bright colors.

"Funerals usually last three to seven days," states Marilyn. "There is usually another celebration on the 100th day."

"How is that different from weddings?" I ask.

"Weddings in the city last a day or two. In the countryside, they also usually last anywhere from three to seven days. Two days prior, the family starts baking the cakes and makes the rice cooked in banana leaves. For the feast, they'll cook three or four pigs. If it's a well-to-do family, they'll have four or five pigs, a cow, chickens and ducks. A high-class family will invite the entire village.

"Cambodian weddings are a very festive occasion. It is a day when the commoners can dress up like royalty. People want to put on a huge show. Families will sell everything they own, even their land, to throw a big celebration. The weddings distinguish how well off you are."

I recall seeing weddings on my prior visit. The wedding party would parade from the groom's house to the bride's house in a grand procession, led by a musician playing a gong along with several players of indigenous stringed instruments and a man, carrying a pig's head on a platter, bringing up the rear. "It is quite an ordeal," I finally reply. "My favorite parts are most definitely the gong and the pig's head. We definitely don't have those at home." I think about the large crowds and the small huts. "Where do all the people stay if they invite that many people?"

"There are no extra beds so they sleep on bamboo mats or on the floor."

"I guess elopement is not an option."

"No," she says with a smile. "Cambodians like any occasion to celebrate."

From the horror stories I've seen and heard in the few days I've been here, I can rationalize why. Yet this is a long-standing tradition that began centuries ago, way before the time of the French Colonial rule or the Khmer Rouge were even thought about. Even in its earliest days, the wealth in this area has been held by only a few, mostly royalty. The idea of "King for a Day," or "Queen for a Day," is apparently nothing new; neither is it privy to a particular country or region.

Thoughts of kings are interrupted when Joseph comes to a stop on a dirt path. His interest lies in the *real* "king," the King of Glory who brought him back to serve the people of his beloved country, I notice as I look at the buildings to my right. A sign at the road announces our arrival at the Tek Thla Methodist Church.

"This was our first church!" Joseph eagerly exclaims. "It began as a mission. Before we built a structure here, people met at the pastor's house." He points to a house on the opposite side of the road, which has a healthy garden to its side. "This was the pastor's house at that time. Now we have built a parsonage beside the church building." He directs our attention to a small house beside a concrete sanctuary, neither of which have coverings over the holes for windows and doors. A young man approaches us. Behind him is a young woman carrying a tiny infant, adorable in his mittens and a cap.

Joseph wastes no time in introducing them to us as Pastor Ieng Pros, his wife, and their first son who is exactly "two months, twenty days old." "He grew up in this church as a youth, attended the Cambodian Methodist Bible School in Phnom Penh, and was appointed to be the pastor here."

As with the group at breakfast, I see how the seeds are not only sprouting, but multiplying, in many areas of ministry in this country. *With lots of help from Joseph and Marilyn,* I learn with his next words.

"When I came back here in 1993, I bought this land. We now own five lots here," he explains showing us the location of the last one purchased by his family in 2002. "This is the first blessing that the Lord provided us. In 1994, Central United Methodist Church in Stockton, California, gave the money for this land and the first church building." Joseph points to a facility that is now open on three sides. In front of the one remaining wall, at the back, there is a large chalkboard with English words written on it. "This building is now used for a classroom for Sunday School. During the week, English classes are taught here at the Christian School. The pastor's wife is a teacher here." He looks toward her as she offers an acknowledging smile in our direction.

"At first, this building had wooden walls, but termites ate them. The wall was removed a few months ago. This is why we are now constructing all the buildings with concrete or handmade bricks.

"The parsonage came second. Built in 1998, it was donated by Mao San Lazarus and his family, members of Central UMC in Stockton. That follows the criteria we are trying to develop for all our Methodist churches. We are first constructing a place to worship, hopefully with a well for the community. The second goal is to build a parsonage, and the third goal is to eventually build a dorm in which students can come to live while they learn, as I did at the monastery in Battambang." Although it is an industrious goal, it is becoming a reality throughout Cambodia, thanks to the dreams, goals and persistence of Joseph and Marilyn.

"Like this, like this," Joseph says, leading me to the new sanctuary. "In 2008, the Korean Methodist helped out so that we could build this new facility." I enter the spacious building which is completely open except for the front chancel area. A beautifully hand-drawn manger scene, done by the youth, is taped to the back wall of the chancel. Plastic chairs are in stacks around the wall, ready to be used for the worship service, and able to be removed for the children's time. Like what we'd witnessed the past Sunday, this is an interesting concept whereby the children come first and worship on Sundays, and then the parents and adults come afterwards while the children romp and play outdoors. It is the perfect scenario for these outlying villages.

My eyes quickly detect an electric keyboard and an electric guitar against the wall beside the chancel. There is a shared amplifier for the two instruments. As I move toward that direction, Pastor Pros says, "I pray for $100 to buy a mixer board for the youth to be able to sing." My mind tells me he may have an answer to his prayer as I marvel that this building has electricity. There are no overhead lights, but there is enough electricity to run the instruments and microphones. Having seen power poles and electrical hook-ups in Cambodia, I know better than to check this aspect.

I immediately turn on the keyboard and begin to play while the pastor scurries to bring me a chair. As I play *Amazing Grace*, we all sing in our native languages, making a harmonious rainbow of sound for the blessing of not only being here, but having the freedom to worship in broad daylight with brothers and sisters of different backgrounds and customs. It is a glorious time. Mark sings *The Lord's Prayer*, while I accompany him, and the others speak it in Khmer. They are thrilled; the pastor has never heard it sung. I ask Pastor Pros for his favorite hymn. He turns to a page in their hymnal and hands it to me. Without the aid of my glasses, Mark laughingly holds the book out far enough for me to make out the first three notes. Having spent my life on piano and organ benches, I instantly recognize the tune as *Pass Me Not, O Gentle Savior*. As I hand the book back and play the hymn, Marilyn and the pastor sing it so beautifully that I can imagine the gates of heaven opening and angels singing along with them. I then rip into a rousing version of *Victory in Jesus*, to which they clap with enthusiastic joy. Wanting to spend the day here worshipping with my friends, but knowing we have much territory to cover, I end with *Because He Lives*, Joseph's favorite hymn. It is a tearful moment for me as we all sing together, our Southeastern accents combining with their Southeast Asian accents to praise God in one voice.

When we exit the building, we have a small congregation consisting of two dogs, several chickens and a pig. "The church's?" I ask.

"The church's," answers Joseph. "But a friend of the congregation built a good wall around the property to keep out cows and water buffalo in order to protect the church and buildings." It isn't until his comment that I notice the tall fence around the premises.

Before we leave, we join hands in a circle—joined around the perimeter by the dogs, chickens and the pig—as we pray together. It is as if they, too, know they are a part of the ministry here, which they are. They are a part of the current plan for a portion of land to be provided for ministers to be able to farm in order to supplement their income. The Methodist Mission in Cambodia has the foresight to realize that in order to continue to grow and thrive, they must make it possible for ministers to make a living and support their families. There is something quite enlightening and heartwarming about the idea of worshipping with all God's creatures together in one place.

"Aren't you worried about them wandering off into someone else's yard?" I ask.

"They come home when they're hungry" is the reply I get.

Like many "half-time" Christians, I muse. *They only come home, to the house of the Lord, when they are hungry and in need.* That, too, brings me to an enlightening thought at the idea of a people who are not so caught up in greed and high incomes that they are too busy to flock to the church on Sunday, as these people do.

As we walk back to the Land Cruiser, we are approached by an older woman, but who is still quick on her feet and extremely spry as she darts from the first house Joseph showed us. "Why didn't you call to let me know you were coming?" she asks in Khmer. She shares a few words with Joseph and Marilyn, whom she obviously recognizes, before tearing off down the dirt path.

"She is the former pastor's wife," explains Marilyn, translating the words of their brief conversation. "When her husband was the pastor here, she planted food for all the people of the church."

No wonder her garden is so healthy, I reason. "Does she still feed the community?"

"Yes," Marilyn answers, listing all the foods grown by the woman and provided for the neighbors.

During the time it takes Mark to snap all the photos he wants of this church and its pastor, along with Joseph and Marilyn, the elderly woman returns with a jackfruit she has gone to pick. I am deeply touched that this woman, who has so little, is so anxious to share with others. *Truly a servant's heart,* I reflect as I offer her a Cambodian "Thank you." After exchanges of hugs with our new friends, we head to our next destination on this beautifully sunny, *and hot,* day of Epiphany.

As I wipe the sweat from my brow, Marilyn hands me an absorbent paper towel. "If it's not hot, it's not Cambodia," says Chandra with a laugh.

Having left the cold and snow to come here, I am quick to reply,

"Hot is good!" And so is the jackfruit Marilyn immediately cuts for us to share.

Details of Marilyn's childhood and early teen years are the prelude to our next destination of Kralanh, the village in the Siem Reap province where she was born and spent the first years of her life. Not sure there is still much from her past left to see, I'm anxious for a glimpse of the covering her mother had built, under which villagers could relax next to the bridge of the Kralanh River.

On the way there, we pass miles and miles of rice fields. "This area is known for its fertile land," states Joseph pointing to all the workers we pass. "If crops are good, Banteay Meanchey and Battambang alone can produce enough rice for all of Cambodia."

"No wonder Pol Pot saw rice as such an important commodity during his time in power," I reply.

"Yes, but he made too great of a compromise with China. He promised them more than what was left over after feeding his own people. That's why we were so limited in our rations of rice daily during the Khmer Rouge regime." His statement leaves me with a great pang for all those who starved during that time, knowing the food was that close, yet so far away. "This year is a small harvest. There was too much water so the rice is almost gone."

We soon come to a road on the left. "That is the road to my hometown of Poy Char," explains Joseph. "It is twenty-one kilometers away. The house is still there. My sister did live there until recently when she moved closer to her son, whom we will visit tomorrow.

"When I was a student living at the monastery, the road here was not good. I once took a canoe down the irrigation canals to and from home for a visit. It was a diagonal route so I was able to go faster than by bus or a bicycle. Back then people used water buffalo and cows to pull the carts loaded with rice. Now a few farmers have machinery." Most of their machinery resembles a simple Merry Tiller with a wagon pulled behind it, on which the farmer sits. "Communities come together to plant and harvest the rice. That's why you see so many workers in most of the fields."

Mark takes countless shots of the fields and the workers until Joseph asks if we'd like to stop for him to get a closer view. That is an invitation too good for Mark to pass up, so we all begin the search for just the right field and workers for the book's photo section. Within a couple of miles, we all spot the "picture perfect" couple not too far away from the road front on our left side. Joseph brings the Land Cruiser to a halt and we all exit in bated anticipation of meeting the man and woman.

He and Marilyn easily jog down the slippery embankment as Mark and I painstakingly and methodically take individual steps to reach the couple. By the time we get to where they are in the rice field, Joseph has already struck up a conversation and asked permission for us to take their photograph. I'm not sure who is more excited, them or us, that we've taken the time to stop in quest of this mission. Well covered from the sun's blaring rays—in long sleeves, pants, a skirt, and wide-brimmed hats—they pause from their work as we exchange greetings in Khmer. Their smiles are both inviting and engaging as they allow us to not only get pictures, but they teach us to cut the rice with the sickle. We all take turns as our Cambodian host and hostess exchange Khmer Rouge stories and Mark and I delight in our new skill. Unsurprisingly, the sun is perfect for the shots Mark needs. Holding up a single grain of rice against the sun, he finds the perfect backdrop for all the posters, fliers and publicity materials about the book so they are truly a portrayal of this country's work, culture and Marilyn's Khmer Rouge experience.

The couple is so gracious. As we tell them good-bye, they speak several sentences to Joseph. He turns to tell us, "They said you've blessed their rice field by stopping here. No foreigners have ever stopped here to speak to them, or show interest. But by working alongside them in this field, you've blessed it."

I have no idea what to say or do except to keep bowing to them as a sign of my thanks for their kindness and hospitality. I reach into my pocket and hand them 12,000 riel, the equivalent of $3.00 US for their time. As I trek back up the slippery embankment, my heart breaks with the realization that is more than a day's wages for the two of them combined. Yet it is the same amount I tipped "Darth Vader" and "Spiderman" each for a fun shot with me in Hollywood on the way here. The only difference is the pair in Hollywood received hundreds of other tips that same evening.

When I mention my concern to Marilyn, once we are back on the road, she tells me I've honored the couple more than any money could pay them. Gratified that I've been able to bring so much pleasure to the man and woman, I am reminded how very little it takes, *only one's self*, to bring happiness to others. It is such a hot day that I can sense a bit of the workers' obstacles caused by the heat, no food, no water and no air moving in a breeze as the sun beats down, leaving one's throat parched and their feet marred in the mud and rice.

Joseph's turn from the main highway signals we are approaching Marilyn's childhood home. She also notes the nearness as she gives me a bit of background before our arrival. "You had to take an exam to pass from elementary school to middle school. The exam lasted three days and covered every subject, and I had to travel a long way to Siem Reap to take it, as did the other elementary students. I passed with extremely high scores, so I could have attended middle school wherever I wanted. I chose to go to Phnom Penh to be with my family who had already moved there because of my father's military duties."

There is no verbose tone of bragging in her voice, although there is a hint of her strong self-confidence that has served her well throughout her life. It is the same self-confidence that stayed with her through the times of despair and depression, keeping her from sinking totally into a hole of no return on the occasions when she, like many others, was tempted to commit suicide during the Khmer Rouge regime.

"I loved elementary school and did well here," she states as we stop in front of the building where she attended school. Still there, it shows many years of use as well as, sadly, four years of abandonment. "It was wooden when I was here," Marilyn says of the brick wall.

"After I left here, I didn't do well in school. Students in the city made fun of the students who came in from the villages. I already didn't like my name because 'Tor' meant 'lion' and 'Sovann' meant 'gold', so people were always teasing me and calling me 'a gold lion.' Even the teachers discriminated against the people who migrated to the city. Because of that I stopped talking to all the students who teased me and looked down on me. Many of the students bribed the teachers to get a good grade but my mother would not do that. She said, 'You will earn your own grade,' so no matter what it was, that's what I did.

"One of the reasons the Khmer Rouge soldiers destroyed so many of the city dwellers is because most of them came from the provinces, which for so many decades, had been discriminated against by the city people who were educated professionals. Some people rationalized that Pol Pot hated the city professionals because neither he nor his wife got the best jobs because they didn't know the right people, and therefore had no influence among the teachers and professors. Even though they were teachers and he was a principal, they never received jobs out of the provinces."

The warmth of Marilyn's smile tells me the repercussions of those days are long gone. "My hobby was reading and writing poetry. I won the prize in 7th grade for writing the best poem. That is still something that interests me today. I have composed a few Christian songs for both children and adults. We use these songs today as a tool to empower and encourage women to be role models for their children. We've also used some of them for training Sunday School teachers and for the women's conferences. They can then be taken home and used by the churches of the women who attend the conferences and training sessions."

Marilyn's smile broadens. "I was a very good student in America. There, I experienced the mocking and ridicule from Cambodian refugees who had also come to the States, but only because I was Christian. Then, however, I knew God loved and cared for me so it didn't bother me. I wanted to be a light for them so they, too, could know God's love." Listening to her remarks about mockery in middle school and high school, and later her concern for the welfare of others during her college years, allows me to see the shaping—pruning—of her life to fulfill her desire to end suppression of women and oppression of village citizens.

The children playing in the school yard visually show me exactly how far she has come from those days. "They still wear the white shirts and dark blue skirts and pants like we did when I attended school here," she says, smiling fondly as she stares at them. I wonder if she is reliving some of her own childhood memories as she watches them on the playground. "Students in Cambodia go to school six days a week, all day long until 5:00, even on Saturdays. There are two sessions, morning and afternoon. The students switch sessions every month."

"Is that why so many children are on bicycles and walking in the streets at lunchtime?"

"Yes, one group is going home for lunch and another is preparing for the second session. School is very different here from the United States. Students are not allowed to ask questions and classes are extremely regimented."

My eyes are drawn to the children on the playground as my mind is drawn back to my own childhood days. Born the same year as Marilyn, I consider the difference in discipline today and then, as well as the dress codes, and think how different America's world of education is from when my generation attended school. Yet theirs is the same. As is my usual conclusion, from having been an educator, I fear we've done ourselves no favors with all the changes in America.

In the time it takes me to jot a handful of notes, Joseph parks the car in front of a long two-story building with four doors across the front. It sits on a corner of two dirt paths, one much smaller than the other. From Marilyn's description of her childhood home, I know exactly where we are. It is a most impressive structure for this country, especially that area and time period. The bottom level is concrete; a wooden upper level has a porch all the way across. There are heavy wooden doors in front of each of the four sections and the windows have wooden shutters.

"This corner is the section we lived in," she states, pointing to the part next to the side road. "The other three sections were rented. At first, we lived in a big house sitting on this spot, but Ma and her sister tore it down and built this. They had a fruit farm behind it down this road," she adds, pointing down the narrow side road. "Next door, on the opposite corner, was my grandmother's house where her sister, my aunty, also lived."

I turn and look down the main road. Bordered on the opposite side from her former house by the Kralanh River, it looks like it goes on forever, but what catches my attention is the swinging bridge several hundred yards from where I'm standing. The "covering" built by Marilyn's mother and aunt is just before it, and across the street from it is the decorative edging of a pagoda, as it stands out against the bright blue sky. Mark takes off for photographs while I follow approximately fifty yards behind him writing notes as I go. To our left are thatch huts, larger than some I've seen on the way here, but nothing like Marilyn's house on the corner. They are spaced evenly apart and several of them have a business in front of them, the business consisting of a single folding table or some items on the ground. Each house has stacks of firewood and charcoal, each stack perfectly arranged and even. There is a sense of orderly neatness in this particular village that I haven't noticed in any of the others on the way here.

Halfway between Marilyn's old house and the bridge, an elderly woman dressed in a green sarong-style skirt and a sleeveless cream-colored blouse steps out from between two houses and follows Mark. It's obvious she has a purpose as I watch her swiftly catch up with him while he is catching picturesque shots. I can tell she is asking him for money. When he shakes his head to indicate he has none on him, she instantaneously balls up her fist and begins to hit him with all her might, which for a short, small-framed elderly female is a lot.

He turns enough that I can tell he is as shocked by her behavior as I am. I look back to see that Joseph and Marilyn are caught up in conversation with one of the old neighbors, while Chandra and Christina are chatting in the back seat of the Land Cruiser. The orderly neatness of the village has somehow lost its friendly appeal. Obviously there are still some villagers who resent "city folk," and obviously Mark and I don't blend in. She finally runs out of steam after several powerful slugs at Mark's right arm, his back and chest, before turning to walk back toward the place from which she appeared.

I move as closely as possible to the yards of the huts to give her a wide berth as I try to catch up with Mark, who by now has nearly reached the covering. Unbeknownst to me, the elderly woman has doubled back around. I am unaware of her presence until I feel a strong fist wham me squarely in the middle of my back. Sensing the same shock as Mark on her first hit, I pivot to see her just in time to have her hit my back again before starting on my left arm and face. The entire episode happens so fast that I never realize I have several skin abrasions from a rock until she has disappeared between the two huts from whence she came.

Catching up with Mark, we share our "battle wounds" with great laughter. It isn't every day you get to praise God in two languages and get beat up by an old lady. This isn't exactly religious persecution, but I decide it's as close as we're going to get to what Joseph, Marilyn and other Cambodian Christians had to endure along the way, as well as the missionaries who are currently serving in Vietnam and Laos. Suddenly I feel a sense of privileged honor at having been "stoned," making the matter even more humorous.

Our laughter is soon halted as students from the pagoda follow us to the shed, also asking for money. I pray we don't get the same reaction when they learn we have none on us. They simply go back across the street and sit on the base of the streetlights in front of the pagoda and watch our every move. Making sure they don't pull the same stunt as the woman, I turn to see that they stay in their place. That's when I notice the number of monks inside the pagoda. This is obviously a school like the one where Joseph lived in Battambang. It is the largest assembly of monks I've seen since my arrival of this trip in Cambodia. Their ceremony is also being spread throughout the community with the aid of a loud speaker. I watch with great interest for a few minutes to witness what I studied in my "Religions of the World" class in graduate school.

Deciding to examine what I've come to see before our "friendly neighborhood greeter" reappears, I turn to the covering, which is equally as imposing as Marilyn's house. What I expect to be some bamboo or wooden shell with a thatch roof is a magnificently constructed concrete shell with an ornate bordered rim running the perimeter of a dark-brown galvanized tin roof. There is a wide concrete walk-through with a long row of steps at the rear, leading down to the river many feet below. Small aqua and dark-blue ceramic tiles cover the ceiling and the floor, on each side of the walk-through, where concrete benches line both sides of the building. Within the entire facility, there is enough seating space for nearly the entire village.

Called a "Sala Samnak," meaning a place to rest, its sturdy columns and superior quality show no wear from its many years of use. *Like Marilyn*, I quickly assess. I find myself more shocked at the beauty of this riverside repose than I am by the "welcoming committee of one." While I am admiring the loveliness of both this contribution and the river, a middle-aged woman comes inside and goes down the steps where she draws two buckets of water.

Mark heads for the bridge while I bask in the peaceful serenity of this place. Except for the sound of crickets and an occasional passing motorbike, it is completely quiet. The sound of the Buddhist ceremony fades into a dull drone in the background as I view the dense forest of trees on the opposite bank of the river. Marilyn joins me, with Joseph only a few steps behind, to make sure we are okay. She apologizes for the actions of the woman, whom she didn't see until it was too late to get to us.

"We're fine," I chuckle. "You're just in time to tell me what is written on the plaque at the top of the building. I can make out the names of your mother and her sister, but what do the rest of the words say?"

"'This place was built for the people of Kralanh to come relax and rest,' is what it translates to in English."

"It's a beautiful gift and quite a tribute to your family." I understand what she meant when she said it was a good thing her family was unable to return to this village when they left Phnom Penh. They would have definitely considered her family rich, meaning they would have probably all been killed.

Marilyn points down to the water. "I had to canoe across the river if I wanted to visit the rest of my family. Some of them live on the other side."

She shares a few more tidbits of her life here before she and Joseph escort us back to where the vehicle is parked. We lose her as she stops at one of the small shops, which looks to be the village general store, on the way back. When we are almost back to the spot of Marilyn's childhood home, the elderly woman again appears. We all rush toward the Land Cruiser and jump in. The woman stands beside my window, while holding a burning cigarette up to her throat and then flicking her fingers at us. She is mumbling something that resembles an incantation.

"What's she saying?" I ask Chandra, with my eyes glued on the woman.

"She's putting a hex on you and saying, 'I have the power! I have the power!'"

"Can you tell her the Power with me is greater than any power she has?" I ask. My question gets a laugh from the rest of the group.

Although I am making light of the bizarre situation, I actually feel pity for the woman. It is obvious she has a problem and to her, I'm sure it appears we are exploiting her territory. Even so, I feel a great wave of relief when Marilyn finally reaches us.

"The woman back there at the store is my cousin," she explains as she gets in and locks her door. "She recognized me and spoke as we walked by. I told her what happened to you." Her words are directed at me. "She said to please apologize and tell you that woman is the village idiot."

"I knew something had to be wrong with her to start pounding on someone the size of Mark," I reply, causing another round of laughter. We then tell Marilyn what the woman did when we got in the Land Cruiser. She and Joseph apologize repeatedly, but Mark and I both assure them that "getting beaten up by a little old lady" is the highlight of our trip thus far. It becomes the joke for the rest of the trip, but I find myself praying for the woman each time the subject arises, even after a staph infection from two of the wounds and a scar from one of them! I consider it a reminder of the many scars shared by Joseph and Marilyn on their way to a jeweled crown, more beautiful than this Sala Samnak built by Marilyn's mother and aunty.

Siem Reap feels like an old acquaintance when I see Angkor Wat sprawled in front of us. The structure, built in the 12th century during the same time period as the Notre Dame Cathedral, is in a class all by itself. Originally a temple and a tomb, and still the largest worship center in the world, it holds the distinction of being on the Cambodian flag. Staring at the scaffolding mounted against the gargantuan eleven-story structure now, which prevents tourists from any longer climbing its massive steps to the top, amidst saffron-clad monks going to pray, I am glad I can say, "Been there, done that!"

As Joseph drives us toward the renowned view of the combination temple and tomb, we are stopped by local authorities. It's a bit nerve-wracking to be pulled over by foreign police when you don't understand their language. *Thank God for Joseph's honest face.* I silently pray when we are soon on our way again in a few minutes.

"It seems we should have been stopped a couple of miles back by security guards since we weren't actually visiting the facility," states Joseph with a bubbly laugh. "I told him we saw no other authorities. We simply drove onto this road from the main highway." He laughs again. "I guess God knew you wanted to see Angkor Wat."

Or knew I needed to get my bearings for the importance of this place to your story, I contemplate silently, chalking up yet another hurdle God has removed in our search of the Chan's past.

Joseph miraculously drives us around the entire perimeter of the temple, pointing out the trails he took to find firewood and cow dung in exchange for food and gold when they were hidden in the forest near here, between the reign of the Khmer Rouge and the time of their escape.

"It was shortly after we were married," interjects Marilyn, with as much excited gusto as if the blessed event had taken place only the day before. She points into the woods toward the direction of the place they made camp in an old abandoned factory.

"So poor…oh, so poor," Joseph says, shaking his head at his own awe of how far they've come since then.

Poor is anything but what we experience during dinner following our visit around Angkor Wat. Joseph and Chandra accompany Mark and me to a noted dinner buffet and show in Siem Reap while Marilyn and Christina visit their family, whom we will get a chance to meet the next day. To many, the place where we spend our "evening out" would be considered a tourist trap. Having experienced it before, it is again worth every penny for it takes the impact of this magnificent beauty and sample of the arts to make me acutely aware of another dynamic of this couple's lives under the Khmer Rouge.

Our overindulgence in fried bananas and shrimp cakes takes a backseat to the elaborate costumes of Cambodia accenting their culture of music and dance. During the array of various dances, all of which portray stories of the country's customs and beliefs, I note the dancers' use of fishing baskets like the ones in the back of Joseph's Land Cruiser. Their fluidity of movement and impeccable body language not only tell a tale, but convey exactly how much skill it took on Joseph's part to feed his family, and then the monks, and later an entire camp of workers and

Khmer Rouge soldiers. It isn't until the talent and intense years of practice demonstrated in the coconut dance that I'm struck with the enormity of the opulent grandeur of Cambodia's culture that fell to the wayside as a result of the Khmer Rouge. Not until then do I realize the caustically drastic impact Pol Pot had on the arts, the education, the culture and the beauty of the entire country during his nearly four years of power. It is an impact that robbed the country and, more importantly, the country's minds of a wealth of knowledge, development and experience.

This was far more than an "evening out," I note as we return to our hotel, with my mind overflowing with nightmares of all we've encountered in only half of our four-day journey of days gone by. My mind ponders on what must be going through the minds of Joseph and Marilyn during this trek down memory lane which, until this week, had been a forever-forgotten past of man-made hell.

Chapter Fourteen

Joyous excitement, more so than usual, is written all over Joseph's face as we near his family's home in the Siem Reap province.

"Can you tell me about the Buddhist shrines and the practices observed in homes?" I ask, searching for an insight into the cultural and faith backgrounds of these two individuals prior to their Christian conversion.

"My parents and also my grandparents had a small Buddha in their houses," Joseph answers. "The Buddha statues were made from bronze, gold or silver. Buddha charms were made from elephant tusks. When my father offered incense or a candle to the Buddha, he would bow and give a benediction. After that, he would carry the incense or candle to the front of the house near the front steps and bow to an angel kept there, using the words, 'Help me, help me.' This is how they worshipped at home. The Buddhist angels at the door were to give protection from harm by keeping evil spirits out.

"Sometimes when my father traveled to other villages, there would be another god in the forest, made of wood or rock. To those, he would offer incense or a candle with the words, 'Help me, help me. I know you have the power to protect me.' Or he would leave a small bit of food and meat, and pray, 'Please protect me.'

"During the times of fighting, most people in the countryside would pick up a handful of soil and put it over their head, and over the heads of their children. My father did this with our family. Then he, like the others who followed this practice, would say, 'God of land, protect me.' There were also prayers offered for the gods of water, wind, and the sun and moon. For the moon, for instance, they would pray, 'Protect me. Make it not to be too dark. Help me to walk.'

"These were practices of most of the Cambodians only in the countryside, not by all Buddhists," he is quick to inform me as we leave the main highway. We then travel down a dirt road, past a number of houses belonging to farming families, until we come to a sign denoting a hog farm. The sign immediately captures my attention for two reasons. First, there are few business signs in the village communities of Cambodia. In fact, this is the first of its kind I've ever seen here. Secondly, it reminds me of my sons' paternal grandfather in North Carolina who once raised thousands of hogs. I instantly sense a genuine and common ground with this family as Joseph turns in the short driveway to a house covered in shiny gray, rippled galvanized tin, both on the roof and on the walls.

It takes no time for one to notice the depth of love and compassion he holds for his siblings and their offspring, a trait accented by the pride he takes in introducing them and sharing a tidbit about each one. The first members we meet are his two younger sisters, who stayed home and worked to enable him to go away to middle school, high school and the university. "My sisters are not in good health," he explains in English, "because they had to work so hard during the Khmer Rouge and afterwards."

I watch more closely, because of his words, as they slowly walk to the outside of the house to join us under a metal overhang, which extends from the front of the house to provide a lovely and spacious front porch setting on the ground under the shade of all the surrounding trees. Mulling over the saying, "Hard work never killed anyone," I decide whoever coined that quote first was not thinking ahead to Pol Pot or his Khmer Rouge regime. From everything I've seen and heard since my arrival, and also during my last trip here, I'm more astounded by anyone who survived the callous and cruel work conditions than by the number of people killed by them. Given how much food and sleep the workers were allowed, the work was bound to kill them, although prosecuted Khmer Rouge leaders now blame starvation, diarrhea and infectious diseases for a large number who died. Right or wrong, my opinion deems there are no acceptable "politically correct" terms for any of the ways the workers died.

Joseph adds credence to my thoughts as he says solemnly, "My mother, and also two of my brothers and their families, died of starvation during Pol Pot's time. Four of my uncles and aunties and some of my cousins also died of malnutrition in the Banteay Meanchey province."

"So basically, the family members we will see here today are all the family you have left?" I ask.

"Yes," he answers firmly, making it clear he focuses on what he has rather than what he does not.

I adore the blissful smiles on their faces. *The joyfulness in his siblings is obviously hereditary,* I conclude, trying to decide whose face is most enchanting. It is fun to watch their expressions as Mark arranges them for a family photograph. Their smiles, already naturally in place, make this a simple task for him. I feel greatly honored when they request I be photographed with them for their family picture.

We truly are one family, I consider with a huge smile now also splattered on my face. *God's family!*

Once Mark is finished, he looks at Joseph's two sisters. "What kind of brother was Joseph?" He waits patiently for an answer as Marilyn translates his question into Khmer.

They giggle like two young school girls and mumble between themselves before answering together in Khmer. "He was the best!" Marilyn translates their excited words to Mark. They continue to laugh, giving us a slight glimpse of the love and happiness they shared before Joseph left to live in the monastery. Again with the help of Marilyn, they add, "When we were only 7 and 4, our father died. Joseph took very good care of us." One of them adds, "Our father was a big supporter of liberation from the French Colonists. People would listen to him because he was a rich rice farmer and very wise. Father worked hard alongside his employees. He took good care of them and fed them well, so they respected him and loved him. Joseph, too, was like that. He learned that lesson from our father."

Joseph, in his humble way, turns the discussion away from himself as he tells us that each of his family members gathered here is Christian. "One nephew-in-law," Joseph states proudly as he points to one of the young men, "is the minister of the nearby Methodist church. My other nephew takes care of farming for the family and helps much of the community."

Their grandfather's influence has passed on to them, I see, I observe.

I am aware the land for this particular church was purchased by Joseph and Marilyn. "Our second blessing," Joseph says humbly. "Thank God, thank God, praise the Lord!" he exclaims softly while bowing his head and clasped hands in an offering to his heavenly Father. "We bought it to honor my family for all their support of me to get a good education. And for my parents who taught me to share what we have with others."

He smiles broadly at me. "So joyful! So joyful! Our goal is to have something for the next generation to consecrate to the Lord." Joseph begins to share with me the one desire he has left for the ministry of his country. "I want to one day see a senior adult center built as a part of the Methodist mission. We already have the land. Now all we need to do is build it."

I am stunned. *This man will definitely leave no stone unturned when he passes on.* The smile on his face radiates joy all the way to where I am seated. *Nor will he leave any task God has given him undone.*

His dream of one day building a center for senior adults, as a ministry of the Methodist Mission in Cambodia, is definitely a need for his country. They have no assisted living facilities, unlike America where they seem to be sprouting up around the country. Neither do they have the population of senior adults we do, for a large part of them were killed during the Khmer Rouge regime. It is a harrowing thought as I look at Joseph's sisters and marvel at how well they are able to care for themselves in their fading health. They are a testimony to the adage, "a product of their environment;" the people in their environment work until their dying days.

It will not be too far in the future when Joseph's dream facility will also be a need of those now approaching senior adulthood. Like the elder generation, there are very few people of that generation still in Cambodia either. Many of the ones who did manage to survive the Khmer Rouge regime are relocated in America, with the largest number of them understandably on the west coast. Though statistics vary somewhat, it's recorded that seventy percent of Cambodia's population is under thirty-five years of age. Therefore, their problems for the aging are quite different from those of other nations—a result of Pol Pot's revolution, like everything else in their country.

Joseph points toward the two newest members of his family, both infants. "We must make sure facilities are in place for them to carry on the Lord's work. In order to do that, we have to put something back now, not wait." His vision, though far reaching, combines what is left in his country's past with its future, thereby compensating for the wide, man-made generational gap.

The two infants are both just as happy and content as can be. They don't have the luxury of pacifiers and cuddly toys, but one look at them makes me wonder whether those items are actually a luxury or a crutch. What these infants do have is love, particularly from their parents and grandparents, and a foundation of faith, hope and love through their upbringing in Christ's family. Those are luxuries not only for infancy, but for life.

Joseph, still raving about his wonderful family, informs me, "I have a nephew and several grandchildren of my sister who aren't here. Some of them are medical students and some of them are studying agriculture."

There is something about his comment that strikes a chord on my heartstrings. Pol Pot and the Khmer Rouge regime left this nation with no professionals, no learned minds and no one to teach the younger generations, at least none to speak of. Their country had to grapple out of the stronghold of illiteracy and violence. Consequently, for many of them, that was only accomplished via their escape to Thailand—or even another continent—where they could receive an adequate education to bring back to their own people, and even then, not until after the North

Vietnamese communists were forced out of the country.

Seeing Joseph open the back of the Land Cruiser, I privately query how many families had relatives, like Joseph, who possessed an education or a skill that could be passed down to others—if they lived to pass it on. Now I learn why it is we've traveled across much of Cambodia with fishing baskets in the back of his vehicle. Joseph pulls all of them out, making a nice little arrangement of them across the dirt beside my feet. He turns to one of his nephews and softly mumbles a few words, none of which I can understand but which I decipher to be a request of some kind. The nephew quickly jumps on his motorbike, heads farther down the dirt path that led us here, and is soon back with a couple of other fishing accessories that become a part of this "show-and-tell."

Joseph gives me a play-by-play description of each basket's use, making sure I understand which ones are for which types of fish, eel and snakes, and in what kind of river, lake or small pond each would be used. "I'd always get my finger caught in this basket," he says with a chuckle while sticking his hand into a long, thin basket. "This nail is what was used to catch the eel, but it also caught my finger on many occasions." He laid the long basket back on the ground and picked up a basket approximate in size to my old wire bicycle basket. "This one I made to hold the fish I'd caught while I kept fishing. It stayed under water."

After placing that one back down, he picked up a small, woven net and cast it out across the ground to demonstrate the proper way to use it. "I knew how to fish on land, in the water and from a canoe. Not only that, I knew how to make all the fishing equipment. That is what made me invaluable to the Khmer Rouge. They did not want anyone to possess any artistic skills. Like the few artists they allowed to live at Tuol Sleng, they only kept the ones who were of use to them, and only one of each type of artist."

It is easy to understand why Christ chose this man for a disciple, I muse, thinking of the other fishermen called by Jesus.

"Because of my background and degree in mechanical engineering, I was placed in charge of the metal factory run by the Khmer Rouge to make the knives, axes, hoes and shovels used every day. This equipment was then sent to the provinces to be used in the work camps. There were blacksmiths who worked with me. Their families and the families of the other metal factory workers were made to work in the fields nearby.

"During this time, one of the high-ranking ambassador's sons was supposed to fish for all of us, but he did not know how to fish or mend the net, much less make the net. I had to do this for him. The chief leader of the work camp was most impressed when he saw me make the net. He then put me in charge of fishing for the entire camp and the Khmer Rouge leaders. I had to catch many fish every day. Thanks to my skill of mechanical engineering, I was able to design and make a tool for fishing better than any they had. I became their fisherman, carpenter and handyman, which made me very useful to them. Because I was so good at what I did, they extended me a little more freedom than the other prisoners, and because I had to walk so far to fish, I was given a little more food. Sometimes I had to walk through the garden on my way to the lake, so I was occasionally able to grab a piece of fruit, or some beans or vegetables," he adds with a broad grin before going on with his fishing tale.

"During communist time, I fish like this." (By communist time, he refers to the time they were held captive, even though without bars or walls, under the Khmer Rouge regime. Their time under North Vietnamese rule, even though still a form of communism, is considered different—even worse—to them.) He took a much larger net, positioned and folded it the way he wanted and then gave it a big toss.

"This is how I was able to catch enough fish for the Khmer Rouge. I'd go out late at night and throw the nets out. I'd get up early the next morning and collect the fish. They didn't know I didn't catch all the fish that morning. That's the only way I could catch enough and stay alive."

His face breaks into a giant grin. "One morning I threw out the net in the lake. When I went to bring it in, I had caught eighteen snakes. They weren't the poisonous kind so I took them back to the cooks. They had asked me to find banana blossoms. I got some for them so they made a very tasty and delicious soup. Everyone was happy because we had a good dinner that day!"

Within minutes, Joseph has clearly demonstrated why his fishing expertise is undoubtedly what saved him from the wrath of the Khmer Rouge. *Even the crudest of leaders knew better than to "cut the hand that feeds you"*—as the expression goes—*much less kill its owner.*

He pauses long enough to fold the nets. "In the end, it was the fishing which saved my life. One day, I had left for my routine fishing duties and while I was gone, Khmer Rouge soldiers came and took the group doing metal work in the camp. They asked if there were any others and the leader, who respected my hard work and the fact I fed them so well, told them, 'Only one and he's gone fishing.' He didn't bother to tell them I was in the middle of the nearest lake, nor I would soon return. The soldiers left with the rest of the workers, all of whom were killed. There were twenty-five families gone when I returned."

Joseph pauses again. His expression shows he has one more thought, which is visibly an emotional one for him. He looks at no one, but only the ground when he again speaks. "At the time, we didn't know they were planning to kill us all. No one in the camp knew. It was only because of that one leader who respected my attitude of hard work, and willing spirit to do the best I could, that he spared my life. Even for bad people, I try to do my best."

What a profound principle! I appreciate his way of thinking and his work ethic, combining to make a meaningful philosophy not only for life, but respecting others. His words apply to students who refuse to do their homework because of their dislike for a teacher. They pertain to employees who give less than their best for an employer whom they judgmentally feel doesn't deserve it. *And regretfully, they are a reminder for church members who don't attend services, don't give or are totally inactive because they don't care for the pastor.*

His words are no more than an alternate way of saying the same old adage, "Always do your best." The words mean the same in any language, no matter how they are phrased. They have the same impact on society, although their effect is not always realized at the time the work is done. And that impact may never be seen by the one who does the work.

Is this not the same lesson taught by Jesus' parable of the seeds?

"There was a Khmer Rouge soldier who got bitten by red ants," Joseph shares, leaving me to chew on his philosophy.

"Ooooh, very bad, the red ants," Marilyn interjects as she gives a hearty shiver. "Their bites were so vicious that a couple, who climbed a mango tree to get the fruit, almost died from all the water blisters caused by the bites all over their bodies. I saw it on the television before we had to evacuate Phnom Penh."

"She's right," agrees Joseph. "The soldiers would climb to the top of the trees to pick the mangos, but the trees were covered in red ants. The soldiers would tie their pants' legs and their sleeves together, and put their krama over their face with only their eyes showing. But the ants would still bite them between their fingers and toes. The water blisters would get so big they made it difficult to hold anything or walk. This one soldier was so badly infected from the blisters between his toes that he got a bad fever. He was so miserable, he thought he would die.

"But I knew how to make a medicine from the tamarind leaves with salt. I boiled the leaves with salt and made him soak his feet and hands two times a day for a week. After about three days, it began to get better. The soldier used the medicine every day and night until the blisters were well. After that, he was so happy that he brought me rice and some sugar palm every night. He was so impressed with what I did that he told other Khmer Rouge soldiers."

Marilyn nods with prideful glee while Joseph continues his story. "One of the soldiers was engaged to be married. His fiancée got a sprained ankle. He brought her to me to see if I could help her. Luckily, a friend who was a doctor from China had taught me acupuncture while I was in Korea. I used it on her and she got better too. That soldier was so good to me. He loved me like a brother. Shortly before they killed all the other families in my camp, he took me aside. He didn't tell me what was going to happen, but he said to me in a very strong and pleading voice, 'Do not go to the mountain side after April 17th. Go to the city.'"

"Is he the one who sent the Khmer Rouge leaders and soldiers away without you when they came to slaughter the others?"

"Yes," Joseph answers. His lone word is delivered quietly and humbly.

While the family members chatter among themselves, I examine Joseph's life and the many instances in which he has visibly been "plucked" from desperately dangerous situations by God's hand. As I count each one, the verse from Zechariah 3:2, "Is not this a brand plucked out of the fire?" resounds. I think of John Wesley, the father of Methodism, who was rescued from the second floor bedroom of his family's burning home at the age of five. He is quoted as having claimed himself "a brand plucked from the fire" throughout his ministry. As I perceive Joseph—among his family, friends and brother and sister Christians of not only Cambodia, but the world—I see "a brand plucked from the fire." Only in his case, the fire is the hell of the Khmer Rouge and everything associated with their wicked regime.

My thoughts linger on his statement regarding his fishing days for the Khmer Rouge, "There were twenty-five families gone when I returned. It was because of that one leader who respected my attitude of hard work and willing spirit to do the best I could, that he spared my life. Even for bad people, I try to do my best." Realizing that to be the most critical turning point in Joseph's life, I ask, "What did you do?"

"When I returned and they were all gone, the one leader was there to tell me to go. It was already Liberation Day, but we did not know. No one told us. The leader again warned me to go back to my home, so I began walking toward Battambang and my native village to try to find my family. With every step, I wondered why they killed all those people. It was like they wanted to keep their thumb over us as long as they could, and if they couldn't, they didn't want anyone else to be able to either."

For an instant I am greatly saddened with the remembrance of Marilyn's words on my first day there, "The Khmer Rouge would rather kill a whole village than to have one enemy left." They are words that have surfaced from nearly every interview here. Then a tiny glimmer of a smile crosses my lips as I perceive the light God showered into the darkness, even during that scandalous time, via a man called "Chhleav." God is allowing me a glimpse of Joseph through His eyes, allowing me to see straight through to this gentle man's heart.

With that, I am struck with another philosophical truth, as surely as if God is speaking the words Himself. *The day those families were taken "to the slaughter" was the day when the ultimate leader, Jesus, told Joseph to put down his nets—literally—and follow him. Jesus, who had given his life, even for bad people, spared Joseph's life. He recognized a notable strength in this humble man through his work and ethics, making him a perfect candidate for a "fisher of men." Like the chief who was impressed with Joseph's ability to not only catch the fish, but make the necessary tools, including implementing one when a needed tool was unavailable, so Jesus called this man to be one of his own.*

Joseph was "plucked" so that he might one day discover the love of Christ, experience his saving grace, and wallow in his mercy. He was placed into a refugee camp where he would reunite with Marilyn, another "brand plucked from the fire." Together this man and woman, Chhleav and Sovann, are the fishing equipment Jesus needs for his ministry to be returned and revitalized in a country that has been forbidden to have any religion. Not only forbidden, but whose leaders were killed if any form of religion was exhibited.

I gaze at Joseph and Marilyn, examining them even more closely with the understanding that they, like every other one of Christ's followers and servants, are not perfect.

Just forgiven, I muse, thinking of the old cliché. *That's all they needed to be*, I tell myself. *God placed them where He wanted them so He could handle the rest*.

The lump in my throat, which has become a frequent visitor on this journey, is again present. Virtues of this man, passed to him by his father and shared by this family, are unmistakably the tools planted in him by God's hands even before he was in the womb. Again, I am staring at a living example of the scriptures, this time from Jeremiah 1:5—"Before I formed you in the womb I knew you."

As if he, too, has a moment's glimpse through God's eyes to my thoughts, Joseph looks at me and says very quietly, "I'm so thankful God called me and my family to be His servants."

He then retrieves all of his fishing gear and repacks the vehicle. There is a moment of awkwardness as I note the forlorn stares on the faces of Joseph's sisters, who sense we have to leave so soon after our arrival. I feel an urge to leave them with something of Mark and me, at least of a spiritual nature.

I suggest to Marilyn that she sing *Amazing Grace*. She begins the first stanza in Khmer, with the other family members joining in. Mark and I sing in English as I think how heady it is to stand on the dirt under the trees, which is what serves as many of their churches in this country, and praise the same Lord together. Like with the reality of pacifiers and plush toys not being a luxury, so too is the building irrelevant when it comes to the act of worship. It can happen anywhere, anytime, as long as two or more are gathered in His name. The exhilaration I feel from our blended harmonies is greater than any notes soaring from the finest, most majestic pipe organ in the world, and I'm sure in God's sight, is just as beautiful.

As the last stanza of the hymn ends, there is an invisible, yet impenetrable, bond between us. We are one. There are no age barriers, no race barriers, no creed barriers...only one Spirit. Mark and I are leaving a gift with them and taking one in return.

We wave good-bye to the family as Joseph backs out the driveway. He speaks to anyone in the car who will listen, "My family is a blessing from the Lord. I could not have done what I have without them." His words mimic exactly what I think of my own family and make me even more aware that though we come in different sizes, shapes and colors, families are our greatest asset and should be treated and respected as such.

I look back on our visit and reflect on his words, "In the end, it was the fishing which saved my life." *In the end, it was Joseph's fishing which saved* many *lives*, I determine, with my eyes focused on his family until they are no longer visible. Being in the presence of his family, and hearing their stories of the past and present, speaks to me louder than anything I've ever witnessed or heard about the rippling effect of God's Light working through others. *Joseph truly* is *a fisher of men, empowering others to be fishers of men, who in turn empower others to be fishers of men. He gets into the boat with them and shows them how, making sure they totally understand before he sends them off into the water by themselves.*

Not only do I experience Joseph's faith, hope and love in action, but also his patience and sense of demonstrating that act. *He is indeed a Master Fisherman*! I look in his rear-view mirror to catch a peek of his reflection. What I see is a vision of peace and contentment shrouded by a sense of responsibility to all humankind, but especially the people of Cambodia.

Chapter Fifteen

Marilyn, like Joseph, exhibits both a sense of enthusiasm and anxiousness as the hour draws near to meet her family. Snippets of details from her childhood slip from her subconscious, laying the groundwork for my visit with them. "My parents were so strict. With seven daughters, they were more protective than some of the other parents. I couldn't ride my bicycle alone to school. We were allowed no social life or fun during our childhoods. We were chaperoned by both parents when we went to the movies. They gave us no freedoms. My mother even bought my clothes." Marilyn offers an understanding smile. "When I was younger, I didn't understand. However, we had no brother to protect us. They only wanted to make sure we were safe." She stifles a masked laugh. "We were never allowed to go to dances either. We weren't even allowed to *watch* other people dance." A hearty laugh escapes. "The joke is that's why none of us sisters know how to dance, not one of us!"

It doesn't take long for me to comprehend that Marilyn was the cunning prankster of the family. Not the troublemaker, just always ready with a practical joke. Yet I soon learn that reputation sometimes backfired on her, like when she got sent to the Central Market with her older sister. "She'd walk so fast I couldn't keep up. One day I finally sat down.

Another time I stopped for water and then hid behind a tree. She'd threaten to go home and leave me, to which I'd reply, 'Go home without me and you'll get in trouble.' She knew I was telling the truth because we were never allowed to go anywhere alone. To get back at me, if we passed a dog, she'd run really fast and then the dog would chase us. I couldn't keep up so it would try to bite me. I hated walking with her because I was so afraid of dogs.

"When we were younger, people thought my older sister and I were twins. One day my sister's friend saw me going to school. Thinking I was my sister, she told me, 'No school today.' I knew she had us confused but rather than offend her, I simply said, 'Thank you!' My sister didn't know and went to school."

"Typical sibling rivalry," I reply with a snicker, recognizing their plight to be universal.

After Marilyn's many stories regarding the difficult challenges of her family during the Khmer Rouge regime, I feel exceedingly honored for the opportunity to meet them, as I hope for even the slightest glimpse into their early days when they still lived on a military base. They graciously agree to meet in Siem Reap, at the home of Marilyn's older sister whose military husband was killed during the genocide.

We are graciously greeted at the front entrance of a concrete house, situated in an area where many of the teachers have built houses on land provided by the school. There are windows and a beautiful sandstone tile floor, adding a hint of coolness to the warm, humid air. I take one glance at the tall, slender woman who moves with quick steps to welcome us inside while she grabs a chair for me, which she places in the middle of the floor to allow me to face all of them.

The sister who ran too fast, I gather from her sprite movements, *and who, with her baby, was imprisoned in the pagoda awaiting death when they narrowly avoided that ghastly fate,* I reason as I look closely at her face and eyes for any hints of survival stories hidden within them.

The sister injured by the wagon who took care of the baby, I decide when another taller, extremely slender woman appears and takes a seat in the line of straight-back chairs placed against a wall purposefully for this visit. Her hair is still long and straight, a very striking feature after all the stories of such short, cropped hair.

An elderly woman, whom I immediately determine to be their mother, comes from another room to join us. Though stooped and bent, and aided by Marilyn's older sister, this woman carries herself in a way that communicates she is still the stronghold of this family. It is easy to see why she was lovingly—and perhaps sometimes not so lovingly—termed "commander-in-chief" of their family during the days of the Khmer Rouge regime. Her hair, clipped close to her head to keep her from being so hot, adds to her air of strength as its gray color points to anything but feeble.

I stand, hands clasped and head bowed, to greet her. My effort is returned by smiling eyes, filled with the tender love and care of a woman who has given her entire being, and undergone much, to protect and raise her daughters. Via Marilyn's translation, I tell her mother—Kim Y Sim, who is now 85—what an honor it is to meet her and what a wonderful family she has. The smile in her eyes extends to spread across her whole face as she gives a politely soft, yet happy, giggle. I fall in love with her immediately.

Having three of the seven daughters together accomplishes exactly what I'd hoped for as stories literally fly out of the woodwork—or concrete, as is this case in Cambodia. *Just like at home,* I think. *When the family gets together for a reunion at the grandparents' house, stories abound.*

Like in America with a family of all girls, one of the first subjects to be broached is weddings. "Families always got together for weddings. Grandparents and all the relatives would come from everywhere and stay because the wedding would last so long. There would be the procession with the gong, the pig's head and a naked chicken."

I recall the wedding processionals I witnessed on my last visit, with huge white tents elaborately decorated with bright yellow and hot-pink ribbons and bows. They are most impressive with the magnificent array of formal dresses and costumes, being a time when commoners are allowed to dress like the royalty, and when families spend all they own, even selling land, to pay for the outlandish festivities lasting from three to ten days. As one who's played for hundreds of weddings, I find myself still greatly intrigued by the man who carried the silver platter with the pig's head atop it during the procession. *I'd like to see the expression on a bride's face at home if one of the groomsmen came traipsing down the aisle with one of those. Or the look on the bride's mother's face if a gong was clanged all the way down the aisle instead of the organ playing a grand processional,* I muse cynically, also wondering about the look on the guests' faces if they learned they were being served "naked chicken" — what they call a chicken with no feathers in Cambodia.

Leaving my mental ramblings of different wedding traditions, I am treated with another "show-and-tell" exhibition, this time from Marilyn's family, when her older sister reaches for a bag and pulls out several huge flat, round rocks that resemble knee caps. The purplish-brown "rocks," I soon discover, are seeds of an inedible fruit, angkunh, that can be used as a medicine. But to these daughters, and other Cambodians, they are a favorite childhood game. Before I know it, Marilyn and her older sister, a teacher, are down on the beautiful tile floor holding up the seeds and demonstrating how to play "Bos Angkunh."

"You can only play the game at Chol Chnam Thmey (Khmer for *Cambodian New Year,* which translates to "Enter the New Year"). The seeds are sold in the market before April 13th, when the three-day holiday begins. You can make the seeds shiny if you want to," Marilyn hastily explains as she counts out a group of seeds. "Each player makes a row using an odd number of angkunh seeds."

Her older sister stands five seeds in a position so they look like rolling wheels. "You take turns rolling an angkunh seed at your opponent's row, trying to make as many seeds as possible fall over. You try to hit the outside seeds first. If you hit the middle seed first, you have to skip a turn and the other player gets to place the seed between their toes and hit you with it." They really get into the game as the older sister puts a seed between her toes and pretends to kick.

"The winner," Marilyn continues, "is the one who knocks all the other player's seeds down first. You're supposed to have two teams, one team of boys and one team of girls, but since we had no boys, it was just us girls."

To see these two grown women on the floor playing this childhood game is beyond fascinating. It is obvious they need no one else to have a good time. The game itself, as far as how it is played, reminds me very much of playing marbles with my cousins when we got together at my grandmother's house as young children. My mind drifts back to my own fond memories until suddenly the older sister is holding up two of the seeds in one hand and clicking them together loudly, while speaking excitedly in Khmer, in words I'm sure she's telling Marilyn to translate. The fun part of this game, at least for me, comes when Marilyn explains, "Whoever wins gets to bop the other one on the knee with two of the seeds." That's when the sister jumps up and bops Marilyn.

The game is tremendous fun for me, but then, I'm not the one getting bopped with the hard seeds that make lots of noise when clunked together. The real reward of the game, though, is watching these sisters return to a joyous time in their lives, a thrill created by some simple product of nature, before the years of hell began.

Simply making do with what one has. Again my mind returns to my own childhood days of playing with cousins at my grandmother's house, using small granite stones, acorns, kernels of corn, anything to make up games and keep us out of trouble. *What happened to those glorious days?* I wonder sadly. A*nd why can't we go back to them?* I ponder, thinking what a small world this is after all, and how great the simple joys of life are, no matter in what corner of the globe they're found. I continue to watch the "home demonstration" while being sorrowfully reminded of the breakdown of modern families. *Technology has done us no favors*. I contemplate on how much I hate seeing the people of America glued to a computer screen or video game, with a phone cord resembling my grandfather's old hearing aid hanging out their ear, and think how much I really do not want to go back to that situation. Like my earlier quandary with Joseph's family, over whether all our toys and gadgets for babies are really luxuries or a crutch, so now I think the same about our modern technology. I long to stay here, to sit and play while sharing family stories, and witness love in action.

Alas, my wandering thoughts are brought back to the present when Marilyn says, "If the seeds make no noise when the winner hits the loser, the loser gets to then hit the winner on the knee two times." She reaches over and pretends to bop her sister's knee. "Oh, and the winner sings and the loser dances."

From the looks on their happy faces, one can't help but wonder whether—consciously or unconsciously—they, too, would like to return to the days when life was simple and plain. *Days before the Khmer Rouge,*

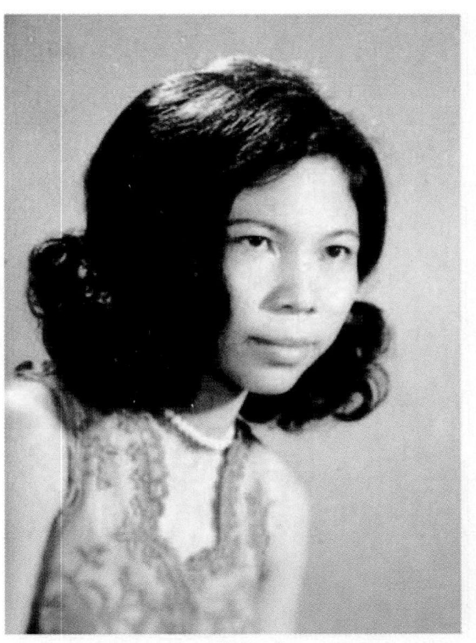

Sovann Tor (Marilyn Chan)

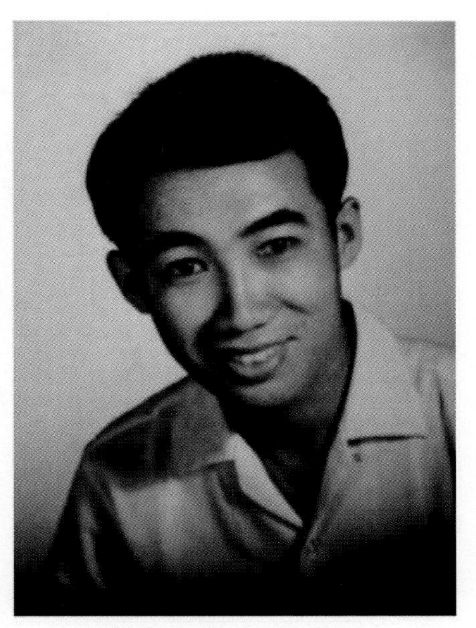

Chhleav (Joseph) Chan

(left to right) Siv Hak, Siv Try (Marilyn's adoptive mother), Nyda Chan, Marilyn Chan, and Joseph Chan

Marilyn and her sisters surround their mother, Kim Y Sim. (above)

Marilyn stands in front of her home in the village of Kralanh. (right)

Marilyn's mother built Sala Samnak (a place to rest). (below right)

Kralanh River (below)

For most of his life, Joseph Chan provided for his family. (pictured above in 2010)

During the communist time, he gathered cow dung for fertilizer and carted it across Siem Reap. (bottom right)

Joseph is an expert fisherman who mends his own nets (bottom left) and makes his own oil "flashlight" for night fishing. (left)

Residents from the village of Prey Thom run to greet visitors that included Marilyn Chan who had not returned since she left 35 years ago. (above)

A former Khmer soldier who spied on Marilyn's family never turned them in because of their kindness during Khmer Rouge times. (left)

Marilyn is reunited with old friends. (below)

Marilyn stands in front of the pagoda where she was kept for three days awaiting execution. (above)

Buddhist temple across the road from the rice field where Marilyn worked. (right)

Memorial shelters at mass graves at the edge of the rice field. (below right)

The rice field today. (below)

Behind the barbed wire fence of the Tuol Sleng Prison, thousands of innocent victims spent their final days before being taken to the Killing Fields. (above left)

Joseph Chan describes how torture was carried out using common tools. (above)

Each prisoner at Tuol Sleng was photopgrahed. (left)

Joseph describes a torture technique to Catherine Ritch Guess. (bottom left)

Hardware used to shackle prisoners' ankles to the floor. (below)

A high school was transformed into the infamous prison also known as S-21. (above)

Joseph Chan demonstrates how shackles were attached to prisoners' ankles. (right)

Prisoners were hung upside down and then lowered head-first into large vats of waste water. (below right)

Joseph shows how prisoners were hit in back of the head. (below)

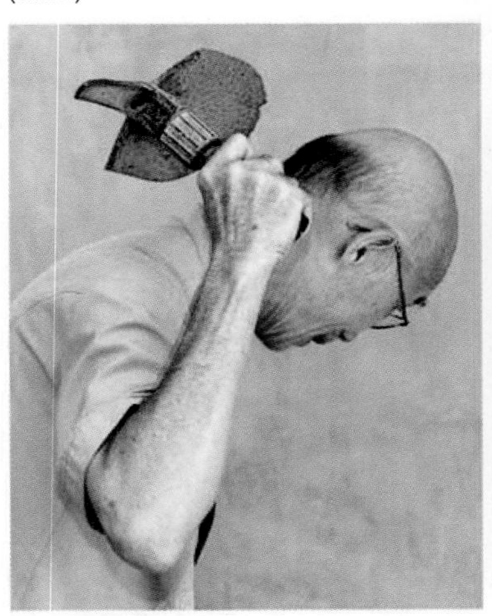

The Khmer Rouge executed and buried in mass graves thousands of Cambodians at Choeung Ek. Joseph points to a picture taken as the graves were being excavated. (above)

Today, he walks among the excavations in the killing fields. (above left)

The sharp serrated edge of a palm frond was used for killing. (above right)

Bones (left) and teeth (below left) are still found on the ground.

Babies were killed by bashing their heads against this tree. (below)

This stupa at Choeung Ek is the final resting place containing shelves of skulls and bones of killing field victims.

Phnom Penh is a place of beauty, character and history.

Independence Monument (above)

Foreign Correspondents Club (FCC) where journalists posted stories during the war (right)

Royal Palace grounds (below right)

Flowers at Central Market (below)

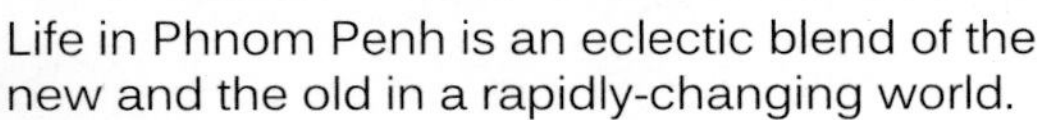

Life in Phnom Penh is an eclectic blend of the new and the old in a rapidly-changing world.

Traditional markets (top of page)... Digital stoplights (above)... High rise condos (below)... Accidents in heavy traffic (bottom right)... Motorbikes carrying anything and everything (bottom left)... Traditional Buddhist monk (left).

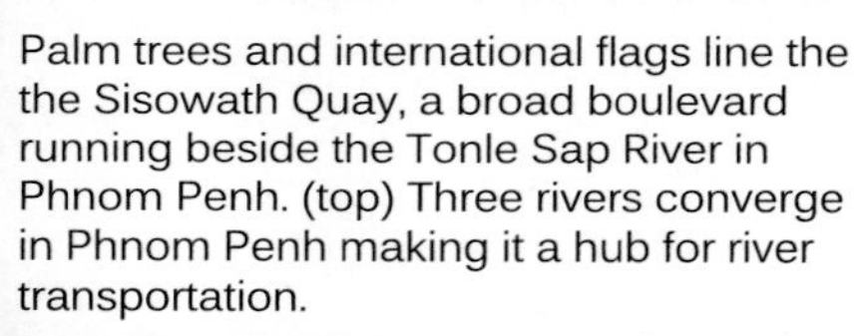

Palm trees and international flags line the the Sisowath Quay, a broad boulevard running beside the Tonle Sap River in Phnom Penh. (top) Three rivers converge in Phnom Penh making it a hub for river transportation.

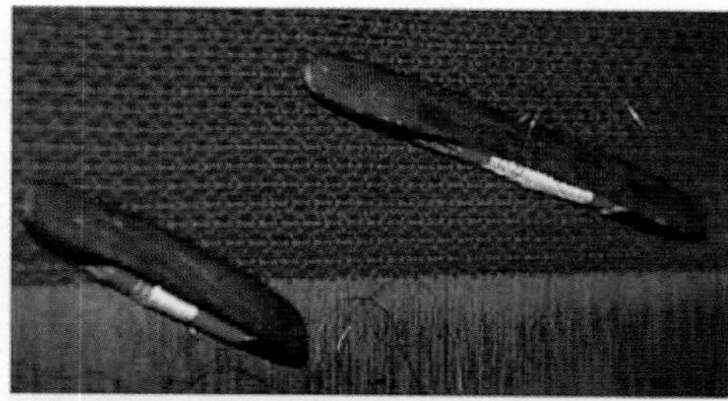

Villages and houseboats dot the banks of the Mekong River east of the center of Phnom Penh. Fishing, farming, and silk weaving are among the trades practiced by the people who live there.

Angkor Wat, the largest temple compound in the world, is the main symbol of Cambodian pride. (top) From its rich heritage to everyday life, Cambodia is a colorful tapestry of culture and tradition mixing the old with the new. Still, at its heart are the Khmer people who have endured countless hardships to thrive in an ever-changing world.

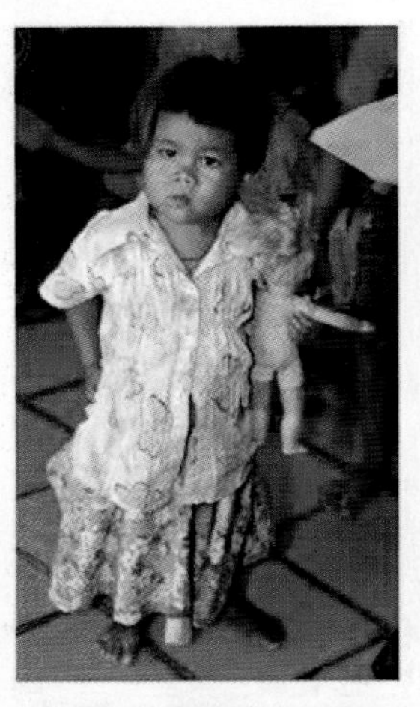

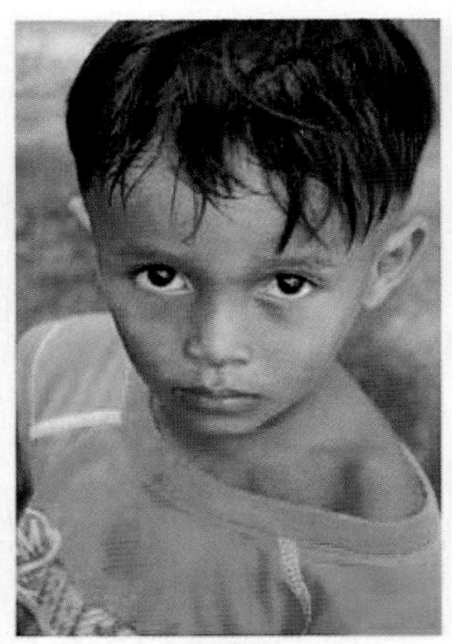

The future of Cambodia lies in the lives of the little children. Joseph and Marilyn Chan have devoted their lives to provide for their health, education and spiritual nurture. Their commitment is making a difference!

I muse. But then, Marilyn's words of how conditions were prior to that time run through my mind. *Days of corruption, days of oppression, days of no song or dance...*

Days not so unlike days in every other country in the world, in one way or another, I must sadly accept. Forcing myself to remain focused on my reason for being here, my attention turns to the reaction of their mother, whose face reminds me of a mother hen watching over her chicks, as she watches the game. She, too, is amused by the antics of her off-spring, even though they are aged fifty-five and fifty-seven.

All actions stop and the seeds are quickly scooped up with the arrival of the youngest surviving sister and her two daughters, ages eighteen and fourteen, who carry 2-liter soda bottles filled with palm juice. *A treat,* I observe from the delighted expressions on the faces of the other family members.

Once the proper introductions are made, I see the women all staring at the feet of the youngest sister. They talk among themselves briefly and then Marilyn relates the story. "One day at the work camp, my youngest sister was digging the dirt to plant potato vines. She dropped the knife she was using and cut all the tendons in her foot."

I am in shock for three reasons as I now also stare at the youngest sister's feet. First, I cannot imagine digging a whole field with only a knife. Secondly, the thought of splicing through all the tendons of one's foot, which is a highly tender area, sounds dreadfully painful. Thirdly, I envision her bare foot on the germ-infested and contaminated soil of that time period and worry about infection.

"She developed tetanus and all the flesh fell off," continues Marilyn. "It took three months to get any flesh back and for it to start to heal." She pauses to catch the Khmer words interjected by her mother. "She was in the Khmer Rouge hospital, which amounted to no more than a clinic. There was no traditional medicine. My mother had to carry my sister on her back to the toilet, and bathe her. There was no one there to help her. She would have just laid there and died had my mother not gone every night, after doing her own work, to care for her."

I glance at Kim Y's face, filled with compassion, and thank God for the strength and stamina she was able to hold onto during those years. From the countless stories I've heard before and during my visit,

I wonder if any of these women seated before me understand the true depth of the blessing they've received. *As individuals and for having this tower of power for their mother.* I look into the beautiful face of this elderly woman. Her smile is so precious it nearly brings me to tears.

"Ma worked hard during the day and with no flashlight, found her way to the hospital every night to care for my sister. She had to wake up very early every morning because if you were late or missed work, you'd be punished." Marilyn's eyes drift from her mother to her sister.

"My sister was only sixteen at the time. After the three months, when her skin began to grow back, the Khmer Rouge forced her to go right back to the work camp. They made her carry dirt. Her foot then became swollen from all the walking and infection. We knew she would lose her foot, or worse, if something wasn't done immediately. Ma was able to use some jewelry as bribery for good medicine. She found an animal skin which she cooked real good. That's what was used for my sister's skin graph."

The youngest sister holds the leg of her trousers up so I can see the scar running all the way up and diagonally across her foot.

Like before, the mother and sisters speak among themselves in Khmer and then glance toward the slenderest sister with the long hair. The youngest sister, sensing her turn is over, takes her seat in the row of chairs with the others as it becomes time to hear the dilemma of this next sister, the fourth daughter born into the family.

"When she was young, she, like my father, couldn't see at night. While we were walking with the other families to the destination where the Khmer Rouge was sending us from Phnom Penh, we'd have to travel until late in the evening. My father and sister would have to walk along the side of the cow cart that carried our supplies, holding onto the edge of it so they knew where to go. One night, the cow cart was so close to the edge of the road that my sister fell into a bush, filled with thorns that stuck in her body. The bush was next to a huge tree, and she got penned between it and the cow cart. Since neither the cow cart nor the tree gave an inch, the vertebrae of her frail body were twisted between them. One of the men traveling with us attempted to straighten her back, but it was still very painful for her. There was no doctor to attend to her so even if she lived, everyone knew she would never be the same again."

This younger sister speaks softly to Marilyn as the older sister, who'd played the game, nods and adds a few words. "She knew that because she would no longer be able to work in the fields, the Khmer Rouge would kill her. She was prepared to die, but they allowed her to stay in the hut with our mother.

"Then in May of 1977, my older sister's husband, who was the military captain, was killed. She returned to the same work camp where we were. Her baby was then eighteen months old and could walk and talk, so they sent her out in the field and made my younger sister stay home and keep the baby. That turned out to be a good thing," Marilyn shares with added enthusiasm, "because until then, the soldiers only gave my younger sister a tiny bit of rice each day since she could not work. They also only gave the baby a wee bit of rice.

"One day when she was home with the baby, Khmer Rouge soldiers came to take all of my mother's belongings. My younger sister saw them, all dressed in black, when one of them jumped down from the tree where they'd been hiding until after they saw my mother leave. He was sent in to scout out the place and find the valuables. But when he saw the baby and how skinny my younger sister was, he had pity on them. The baby was very smart, because my sister worked with him, and he kept saying to the soldier, 'I never get enough to eat, I never get enough to eat.'"

The older sister abruptly jumps up and runs to the kitchen in the middle of the story. She returns with a tin can, the size of a condensed milk can, which is barely half full of rice. As she hands it to me, Marilyn explains, "This is how much they got for the both of them for all day."

I examine the amount of rice and then sympathetically look back to the sisters and mother. It's impossible to fathom myself living on that tiny bit of food every day for only a week, much less four years.

"A family would only get a whole cup. That's why there was so much starvation. Our country was lacking rice because Pol Pot made an agreement to export so much annually to other countries. That meant there was not enough left for our own people."

The older sister makes another comment wasting no time in expressing further thoughts on this matter. From the curtness of her words and the tone of her voice, I fear the situation is worse than what I've already heard.

I wait anxiously as Marilyn turns to me and interprets, "They fed us worse than pigs! Our mother would try to make the food more nutritional for us by adding a banana or papaya root, a tapioca leaf or yam leaves if she could find them and slip them home. We were not encouraged, nor allowed, to use those. In fact, if people were caught with food they did not share, they were killed. When you would see a footprint on the ground, you would know it was a person's. But when you would see a human stool, it was like a pig's stool. No difference!"

My impression of Pol Pot is becoming more demonic with each day and each story.

Marilyn goes back to her story about the baby. "The time the soldier came and saw my sister so skinny and heard the baby's complaint, she feared they would be killed immediately. She tried to make the baby be quiet, but he would not. He just kept saying 'I never get enough to eat' to the soldier. The soldier left after that.

"My sister was sure he had gone to get the other soldiers so they could kill her and the baby, and take everything in the house. But then she heard him tell the others, 'I see nothing.' After that, he gave my sister more rice every day. That's why I say it's a good thing she got to stay home. But still, she was terrified for a long time afterwards. She was afraid they would eventually return and kill everyone and then take everything."

The younger sister and the mother converse with each other and again Marilyn translates. "Even the people who knew us and knew we were good people were jealous of us. They suspected my mother had things. Another reason they were jealous is because we were from the city. People from the city were always made to work harder. They always asked about my younger sister, 'Why she no work?' That's why they reported us to the Khmer Rouge and why they tried to rob us. That was in 1978," she is quick to clarify.

"My mother had an intuition about this too, so she took the remaining gold and jewelry with her to work every day inside her clothes."

I'm still caught up in the food situation. "Did you have eating utensils?"

"Some people had them, and some didn't. We had a plate and

spoon for each of us. When we left Phnom Penh, my mother wrapped what belongings she could in a mattress sheet so she had brought these with us. People who didn't have a plate had to use a coconut shell and their hands. We'd have to take these utensils with us to the work camps so we'd have them when it came time to eat, if you could call what skimpy portions we got meals."

Marilyn speaks in Khmer to her mother and sisters to make sure she is getting all the details. An approving nod from them urges her to go on as the mother reaches over and tugs on the back of the younger sister's shirt. "My younger sister became so skinny from the accident and the lack of food that you could see her tail bone sticking out, even from underneath her shirt."

The mother and sisters watch for my reaction as Marilyn shares this detail. I'm sure I don't disappoint them with my startled look. *Starvation, a crushing blow to her spine, no medicine.* As with the youngest sister, I find it inconceivable this sister, who was only nineteen at the time, could withstand the pain brought on by that combination of adversities.

"But she did find some skill she could do," Marilyn states with great pleasure. "One day she found a palm leaf and made a hat from it. No one showed her, she simply figured it out on her own. She had a real gift for making mats and hats from the palm leaves. People found out and would come to get a hat from her, for she made the best ones in the whole commune. They'd bring her a banana or something special in exchange for the hat, but we could never tell others. We'd have been in trouble because you were only supposed to eat what the Khmer Rouge gave you and allowed you to eat."

I look again at their mother, her face beaming and her eyes still sparkling. *What a beautiful soul,* I think, sensing the natural warmth emitting merely from her presence. "What *did* your mother and father do during the Khmer Rouge time? What was their duty in the work camp?"

"Pa had to cut the hair of Khmer Rouge soldiers and leaders."

"I thought he was in the military, in charge of the arsenal weapons and ammunition," I remark, looking back through my notes.

"He was, but he told the Khmer Rouge leaders he was a barber."

"How did he get away with that?" I ask, stupefied.

"One of the Khmer Rouge leaders in the village where we were assigned was determined to learn the truth about Pa, because they were sure he was no factory worker or farmer. He came to our hut one time with a group of soldiers. 'You are a military man!' he shouted accusingly at my father.

"'No!' my father exclaimed. 'No, I am a barber.'

"The leader ignored him and continued to make accusations and ask questions. But Pa, not to be confused, again declared, 'I am a barber, I tell you!'

"'Then cut my hair,' the leader demanded. My mother and sisters and I were so panicked but none of us dared look each other in the face. We were all sure we would see Pa executed in front of our very eyes, and then they would kill us, so we braced ourselves and kept doing exactly what we were doing without slowing our pace or pausing.

"Fortunately, unbeknownst to any of us daughters, Pa had cut hair at one time before entering the military. That was the only thing he could think to say when he was accused. It was lucky for him and all of us, though. He cut the hair of the leader and did an excellent job, making them all assume he was indeed a barber. If my father had cut the leader or done a bad haircut, the soldiers would have killed him. As it was, Pa gave the man a very good haircut and they made him be the barber in our village and nearby area for the Khmer Rouge.

"But they also made him work in the fields, most of the time with the youth, because he was not able to see at night. He was also older, so he could not work as hard and fast as the youth. It was humiliating for him to be put with the younger youth who didn't do as much as the other adults and older youth. They moved him to that group from the adult group so he could keep up. Because he gave such good haircuts, they let him live."

"So was he separated from the rest of your family?"

"At first he was with us, but then he was made to go to another camp. My sisters and I were split up due to our ages, and my older two sisters had to go to another camp because they were married, but we were not too far apart. Sometimes we got to go back to the old abandoned hut where Ma had to stay to take care of the plantation. It depended on how far away we were working at the time. Sometimes we would be moved to another village to stay for a while until we finished the work there. We did not see Pa as much as we did Ma.

"Ma worked near the village. She was in charge of the plantation farm, which meant she had to raise all the food eaten by the whole village, both the new people and the base people."

"New people?" I repeat questioningly.

"Yes, new people. They were the people, like us, who had been sent to a particular place by the Khmer Rouge. They were people who were not originally from that village. The Khmer Rouge didn't want people to be near their friends and their home towns. Then there were the base people. They were people who owned a hut, house or land in a village and their land was used by the Khmer Rouge for the work fields. Because they were uneducated and unprofessional, the Khmer Rouge did not see them as threats. Therefore, they were given the positions of 'base people' who kept an eye on the workers, like overseers. Base people had a few freedoms, unlike the workers, and got more to eat. Again, because my mother was helpful by dyeing their clothes, and giving them medicine for their children, some people would show her a kindness back. But they wouldn't do that in front of others. It was always done in secret."

Marilyn offers a gaze of benevolence in her mother's direction. "Ma had to work extremely hard. She had to carry the water buckets on her shoulders, and plant the vegetables for all the people by herself. She never got any rest time because when she finished with the plantation farm, she had to dye the people's clothes.

"Dye clothes?" I ask, wondering whether there's anything this woman couldn't do. "How did she get that job?"

"It wasn't actually her job. She simply saw it as a need for some of the people. We were forced to wear black clothes, but of course they didn't issue them to us. People would put their clothes in mud to make their clothes black, but it didn't do a good job.

"Mother was so patient. She was the kind of person who, if she did something, she did it right. And she was the kind of person who, if she saw a need, would take care of it privately. So she'd go out and find some bok (Khmer for *tree bark*), some wine and a green coconut head. She'd cook all that together and then put it in with the mud. It took a long time to cook all that, but it made the dye the best quality to make the clothes really dark black. It was very hard work and it turned her hands black.

"She dyed the clothes for the workers, but when the Khmer Rouge soldiers and camp leaders saw how dark the clothes were, she was then made to do theirs too. But because she did such a good job for them, they'd sometimes slip her a little thing, like a banana or something, or maybe even a potato to feed my younger sister who was at home with the baby. It was those extra things Ma got that kept my sister alive. Ma would never ask for anything, but some people would give. It showed some of the Khmer Rouge regime still had a good heart."

"Or maybe you had God's angels looking out for you," I reply. "It sounds as if your mother would have done anything for you girls."

"She would," admits Marilyn, "and she was able to do lots of things. She could climb all the way up the tree to get a mango for us to share."

One of the sisters says something to Marilyn, which she in turn shares with me. "Ma could also make a good medicine from the coconut shell for rashes and for infections in young children. She helped many people with that too."

I look at the "commander-in-chief" and see daring compassion written on her face. Beneath the angelic face, I know there is a wealth of wisdom. Otherwise, neither she, nor six of her seven daughters would have survived the Khmer Rouge. I examine this staunch woman, along with the stories on my pad, and think about how many talents and resources have been given to this family. *All resources they put to use for their survival skills without even knowing it,* I surmise, looking back on the situation with the benefit of hindsight.

"It seems your mother's background as a pawn shop owner proved to be your family's greatest asset in survival," I note. "More even than your father's history of graduating first in his military class and being involved with undercover work. Tell me about the pawn shop."

"The pawn shop was originally started by Ma's mother, my grandmother. Ma only dealt in clothing and in gold, diamonds and jewelry, things that didn't take up a lot of space. It started because she wanted to help the military people who needed a financial hand from time to time. She didn't advertise because she didn't want people knowing she had those kinds of valuable items in the house. The military people heard about her from other military people on the base and she trusted them more. Her intuition was her method of security."

A method tried and true, it would appear, I conclude from her success in holding onto her assets after so many attempted burglaries during the Khmer Rouge regime.

"People would come to us because we were cheaper. Other pawn shops would charge $5.00 a month for interest on a $100.00 item. Ma only charged $4.00 a month. For clothing, she charged $10.00 a month. She really didn't want to deal with a lot of clothing. We were always busy at the Cambodian New Year. People would come to give us money and get their clothes and jewelry back so they could dress up for the parties and festivities."

"It seems those unclaimed pieces were a Godsend during the Khmer Rouge regime. They helped your family, and many others, on many occasions. Did she actually hold onto some of those pieces until Liberation Day?"

"Yes, when we all met back together after we learned of Liberation Day, we had to quietly escape the hut in the middle of the night in three different groups. She gave each group a piece of gold in case of an emergency. When Joseph and I escaped the final time, after we were married, she also gave me a piece of gold. Because people tried to rob us so often, I carried my piece of gold under my tongue all the time."

"I see her cleverness passed on to you," I reply, impressed at Marilyn's foresight.

She shrugs. "In some ways, the gold, diamonds and jewelry caused our family extra hardships because if people learned about it, they considered us rich and we were persecuted. Ma was able to give clothes to people who didn't have them, and she sometimes secretly gave jewelry to families terribly in need. The only problem was they had no idea how much the jewels were really worth. They wanted gold, having no clue the gems were more valuable.

"My father's sister and her husband, who were primary school teachers in Siem Reap, were evacuated to a very poor and remote countryside. They were sick and starving so my aunty decided to exchange her diamond earrings for some food. But the villager only gave her three bananas since he did not consider the diamonds to be valuable. Thus, the whole family—my grandmother, my aunty and her two children—starved to death. When the husband came back from work far from the village and found that his entire family had died, he was so saddened he lost his mind and lay on top of their grave until he, too, died."

My heart breaks as I see the desperate need for another piece of minutiae often overlooked in helping others. *No wonder Joseph and Marilyn are so firmly convinced that education is primary to helping others if they want the effects to last.*

"Once, when we still lived on the military base and Ma had the pawn shop inside our house, the house behind ours caught on fire. My older sister and I were the only ones at home because our mother had gone to Kralanh to take care of our grandmother, who was sick at the time. We were told to evacuate the house. Neighbors tried to help us, but only because they were hoping to rob some of the valuable items from the pawn shop. I told them I didn't know what to do and that we were only going to take a few things. I quickly scooped up the worst, ugliest clothes we had, along with a few of my youngest sister's baby clothes, and wrapped all the gold and jewelry in them so people wouldn't suspect anything." Marilyn smiles. "Luckily the fire didn't spread to our house."

"I see your cunning pranks paid off."

She says nothing but nods smugly. "We had our own private burglar alarm back then. Ma took an empty tin can and hung it over the top of the door with a small wire. That way we could hear if someone tried to open the door and get in."

"I'm not sure who was the shrewdest, you or your mother. But your cleverness surely paid off on many occasions," I compliment her, before going back to their welfare during Pol Pot's reign. "Were any of your other sisters affected by the circumstances of the Khmer Rouge?" I ask, wondering about the other three siblings.

"Our oldest sister had to stay in the Khmer Rouge hospital for a while," Marilyn explains. "She went delusional from the diarrhea she got as a result of starvation. That happened to many people. The food was not sanitary, there was not enough food and everyone suffered due to lack of sleep. There were no real doctors at the hospitals, so they couldn't take care of the people.

"We could not go see her but we heard from workers at the hospital that she had malnutrition, and bad cramps. Women didn't have periods during that time because of the lack of food. Most young women would just cramp up."

Marilyn hesitates as her focus shifts toward her mother and three sisters who are there. "Our family was extremely blessed. We were so fortunate. We only had one sister to die. She was twelve when Pol Pot took over, and she didn't die until after the Khmer Rouge regime, but her death was a result of something from that communist time."

I see the despondent expression on Marilyn's face and decide to leave that story alone. Yet there is one question left I must ask. "Were you afraid of dying?"

"Always," she answers calmly. The childlike glee is absent from her face. "We were always scared we would all die the next day. We never had any hope we would stay alive. It was so terrifying when they would come and take someone. The Khmer Rouge took the men first. If we had a background with a high school diploma, we were taken. You can't imagine what it was like when they'd come to the camp or village, and someone would disappear. They'd come at night, when less people saw them, and take someone. There were days when you prayed they'd take you, just so you didn't have to be afraid anymore. There was no life among the people. The Khmer Rouge zapped it out of everyone."

I find myself questioning how many miracles have been showered on just the people seated in this room, Mark and myself included. To me, the greatest blessing is we all realize we are blessed and are thankful enough to do something positive with the lives we've been given.

Looking over my list of questions, I recall reading about the lengthy and abusive group meetings that the workers had to attend sometimes after their long hours of work. "How often did you have the community meetings and how long did they last? What was their purpose?"

"If you didn't work hard, they pushed you to work harder!" exclaims Marilyn, so emphatically that I realize this is the voice of experience. "They always told me I didn't work hard, and were always pushing me to work harder. I wasn't very strong then. There were two groups. Group One was made up of the best workers. I was in Group Two. Group

One got a little more food than the people in Group Two.

"We'd have to work until around 9:00 every night and then have a meeting once a week, sometimes once a month, but everyone was made to come to the designated meeting place. Some Khmer Rouge leaders made us meet on the 10th, the 20th and the 30th of the month. Whenever the Khmer Rouge leaders would say, 'Meet!" we'd meet. The meetings usually lasted an hour, but they could last as long as the leaders said. Sometimes they pulled my family aside for a meeting when they'd want to search our hut for the gold and jewelry. And sometimes they'd pull me aside to tell me I didn't work hard enough. When I had diarrhea and cholera, they told me it was because I was lazy before I arrived and therefore didn't work hard, so they gave me no food. Sometimes the Khmer Rouge would give old, worn-out tires to workers to make shoes. I never got those. They were for the people in Group One who they said worked harder."

Marilyn turns to the others to share my question and see if they have any further comments about the group meetings. The older sister immediately rants off a comment, waving her hands as she speaks in such a way that I realize people talk the same with their hands in any language. They skip all the hub-bub of the meetings and go right to the point of the one that sticks out most in their minds. "During one of the meetings," interprets Marilyn, "my older sister told them, 'I'm going to have my baby now!' but they did not trust her because she had a small stomach."

Why wouldn't she have a small stomach, I want to ask. *She's a petite Cambodian, she works over twelve hours a day doing physical labor and she's malnourished. What else would she have but a small stomach?* Instead, I keep writing as Marilyn continues the appalling story.

"'She's lying,' the Khmer Rouge leader yelled at my sister. Because she spoke out in the meeting, they made us stay until midnight. 'Even if you can't work, you have to attend the meeting,' he told her. 'You can just sit.' My sister had to stay in the meeting, writhing in unbearable pain. They kept the meeting going simply because they enjoyed seeing her hurt. It was their way of punishing her for speaking out.

At three in the morning, the labor pains were so sharp my sister screamed, 'The baby will come.' We lived next door to the Khmer Rouge doctor, who was not usually at home, but that day he had come home. He had a good heart, so my mother went next door to tell him. He went right away to get his nurse and asked her to deliver the baby. The nurse didn't have enough medicine to do an epidural, but she did come. My sister had a little boy, who was tiny because she had not been able to eat enough food for herself, much less a baby."

I listen to the intense tone of her voice as the older sister adds another comment, which Marilyn explains. "They made her go back to work in the fields ten days after the baby was born, but she was able to stay closer to home. There was one home where all the babies stayed so the mothers could work, but he cried all the time when she took him there. No one could make him stop. They finally took my sister out of the field and made her stay home with the baby so he didn't cry continually. It wasn't until months later, after her husband was killed, when she was able to rejoin us at our work camp and my younger sister kept the baby at my mother's hut."

My mind questions how all this disparaging information is approached by the schools. I turn to Christina, who attends the private International School in Phnom Penh, and then to her cousins who attend public school in Siem Reap and ask, "Do they tell you all these details in your history classes?"

"Yes," they all answer. Each of the three tells me in her own words how the information is presented, concluding with, "In Khmer history class, they give all the details."

"Do you play sports?" I'm now curious as to whether the students are allowed physical fitness. I've learned during my time in Cambodia that athletics do not hold the precedence they do in our country. The people are more concerned with education, which essentially skipped an entire generation. Residents of Phnom Penh retreat to the lengthy parks along the boulevards in the early mornings and evenings for their exercise. It is a daily and nightly ordeal with "pumped-up" music playing while the people "pump up" their muscles.

"We play a sport and have PE for two hours weekly," shares Marilyn's older niece who attends school in Siem Reap.

I'm enlightened by her answer. Something so trivial seems a big deal to me in light of the situation thirty-five years prior, a time when there was no physical education, only physical abuse.

I ask Marilyn to thank each of her family members for their time and for answering my many questions. Within three hours, I feel I've been through an entire lifetime with them. I can't help but think how those years of suffering under the Khmer Rouge must have seemed like a lifetime to them too.

Closing my notebook, I once again glance down at the foot of the youngest sister, astounded at such a miraculous healing, a healing that can only be God's handiwork. I find myself stunned that this woman is alive, much less able to educate the minds of 11th grade students in Cambodian History. And then I look at the other two sisters who live here with their mother, one of whom teaches arithmetic to junior high school students, and the other who could have taken advantage of the situation to become an invalid, but rather found a skill she could use during the Khmer Rouge regime to help others and keep herself busy. *And even earn secret bits of food for herself and family,* I remind myself.

Once I make sure I have no more questions and have heard all the stories they remember, Mark positions the group for a photo session—the first I suspect they've had in a long while. A shudder of chills runs up my spine, reminding me of the saying people have for when that happens at home: "A cat is stepping on your grave." As I peer into each of their faces, I find myself sympathizing with what they've endured, while feeling inspired by their stamina, their endurance and their stories of survival. It's only then that I'm aware of the reason for the sudden case of chills. It's a subconscious trigger set off, I'm sure, by the sharp contrast between the photos of these women seated together now and the thousands posted on the huge boards inside Tuol Sleng.

These women could just have easily been one of those faces with their chopped-off black hair, giving all the girls and young women the appearance of looking greatly similar. Had their father not been so convincing in his story of being a barber, chances are they would have been victims like the ones on those many boards, their skulls and bones would have been among those in one of Cambodia's 400+ "killing fields" and I would not be standing here at this moment. I pray Mark doesn't capture my thoughts in his photos.

It isn't until this late in our visit when I look down at the beautiful, *and cool,* tile floor—in stark contrast to the one at Tuol Sleng—and see that I am the only one in the room wearing sandals. I am immediately embarrassed that I have shown such disrespect by entering one's home without first removing my shoes.

"It's okay," they all assure me when they interpret my reaction.

I can't understand their words, per se, but I can surely understand their means of trying to console me and tell me not to worry about it after seeing my horrified face. Reaching down to remove my shoes, I suddenly understand the real meaning of "body language."

"Leave them on," says Marilyn. "Really, it's okay."

Smiling graciously, I pack my notes and prepare to leave their family. I'm regretful I'll not have the opportunity to meet the fifth sister, a teacher who lives in Phnom Penh with her husband and children, and is absent from this meeting due to her work. It is she, I learn from the rest of them, who seems to have the best memory of all their lives' experiences, answering Marilyn's frequent calls during my visit with, "Why you don't remember this story?" Neither will I meet their oldest sister who lives in Washington, DC, much closer to my home turf, and has called with stories during my visit.

My eyes drift to Sim, Kim Y one last time as I look past her smiling eyes into the hurt and pain that lie beneath. It is there I see the true woman Marilyn has described to me. A woman whose kind heart is willing and ready to reach out to anyone in need, and who would go to any length to protect her family, making sure her seven daughters stay safe. A woman with no formal education, not even an elementary education, yet a woman with such a keen business sense she is able to care for and educate her daughters, and use her financial gain to benefit her community. And a woman whose keen perception has been a saving grace when others were deceived by shouts of "Peace! Victory!" from the Khmer Rouge, as well as by the North Vietnamese claims of "Liberation!" when they took over and instigated their own form of communism after defeating the Khmer Rouge.

Ending on a light-hearted note, I say good-bye to each of them individually, offering my thanks for their time and telling them I hope to do their story justice. Even though they are not Christian, they are most supportive of the work of Joseph and Marilyn, a fact I find tremendously interesting. Marilyn's mother, in fact, physically helped in overseeing the building process of one of the Cambodian Methodist churches in Khnar Thmey in Siem Reap, including finding resources for it within her own community, and also seeking manpower to help build it and then for its upkeep when Joseph first started it. She has even traveled to Khnar Thmey, Siem Reap Province to see it. I am grateful this elderly woman, in her infinite wisdom, is able to look past the boundaries of religion to see God at work.

As we exit the front door, whose stoop is covered with various sizes and shapes of shoes, I spot a pair of adorable purple sandals, very chic and stylish with two jeweled purple stones on the top of each one. I laugh and tell Marilyn to share with them that I'm swapping shoes with that person, given the fact I'm the only one with shoes on at this point. Knowing I'm joking with them, she laughs and shares my comment. They, too, laugh, still humored by my embarrassment at entering their home with my shoes, while the owner of the shoes cheerfully tells me to take them. I cringe, not about to take the shoes.

"Try them on!" insists Marilyn enthusiastically.

I look at all the faces staring at me, and my feet, and fear I'll offend them if I don't try on the shoes. As I slip my right foot out of my thickly-coated, dust-covered Clark's sandal and into the shiny purple one, I suddenly feel like Cinderella when I realize the shoe is a perfect fit. I'm appalled, for I sense where the rest of this story is going.

"You must have them!" exclaims Marilyn, her family all chiming along in a chorus of Khmer cheers.

When I see nothing will suit except I become the new owner of the purple shoes, I beg to pay for them, or at least buy their rightful owner a new pair. That is totally unacceptable; they are proud they can give me the shoes. I finally grasp the fact it honors them for me to accept their gift, so I graciously take the shoes, wearing them from this sister's house, like a child in a shoe store begging to wear her new shoes home.

In America, I have been known to take the shirt right off someone's back. I guess it's only fair that in Cambodia, I take the shoes right off someone's feet. Wearing my new pair of shoes, I climb in the back seat of Joseph's Land Cruiser, grateful it is dark. That way, no one notices my tears, flowing freely from my cheeks as I now have a real understanding of "walking a mile in someone's shoes."

Chapter Sixteen

It is the thirty-first anniversary of Liberation Day, the day the North Vietnamese took over the reign of Cambodia from Pol Pot and his Khmer Rouge regime. How fitting that, on this celebratory day, we are following the escape routes of Marilyn's family, and of Joseph, when they finally made their way to Thailand and the refugee camp—where they met and which later led to their marriage, Christianity and a new life. Ironically, it is also the day we will visit the final headquarters of the Khmer Rouge, not too far from the resting place of the notorious Pol Pot.

There is much ground to cover, both by miles and experiences, so the day is off to an early start. Joseph stops, while we're still in Siem Reap, to fill the vehicle with gas for our long journey. "Are you giving anything away today for Liberation Day?" he asks the attendant.

"No," the man answers with a smile as the two exchange a few words regarding the importance of this day in their country's heritage.

"Sometimes places give away things to commemorate this day," explains Marilyn. "Like a cola or something."

"Or a drawing," Joseph is quick to add, "where they pick your name out of a box."

"They usually do those kinds of things more in the Phnom Penh area," says Marilyn, "since it is the capital city."

"I am celebrating Liberation Day today," announces Joseph, "but not like everyone else. This is the anniversary of the first consultation for the Methodist Mission to Cambodia, when the Methodist church got its 'official' beginning here. Following a fact-finding team sent here in 1995 by the General Board of Global Ministries of The United Methodist Church, of which Marilyn was one of the seven members, it was decided the need and the situation were conducive to proceed with the establishment of an office for the country in Phnom Penh.

"More than thirty delegates met in Singapore on the evening of January 6, 1997. There were representatives from the General Board of Global Ministries of the United Methodist Church from New York, from the Korean Methodist Church, the World Federation of Chinese Methodist Churches, from the Methodist Church in Singapore and the United Methodist Church in Switzerland, France and Malaysia." He is so moved his voice becomes shaky. "I was honored to be the representative from the Cambodian National Caucus of the United Methodist Church in America.

"We flew to Phnom Penh the next morning, and then attended a banquet that evening to commemorate the organization of the Methodist Mission in Cambodia, with several of the Cambodian pastors joining us for that celebration. I was so joyful…so joyful!" Tears still stream down his face with the telling of this story.

"It wasn't until we went out to dinner that night that I noticed all the flags waving, the banners flying and everyone wearing t-shirts that I even realized it was Liberation Day. I was so caught up in my own celebration that I completely forgot it was Liberation Day. While the rest of Cambodia was celebrating their liberation from the power of Pol Pot, the Khmer Rouge, guns and war, I was celebrating the liberation of my country by a greater Power of peace and love."

Both his voice and his smile are contagious as he shares the details of the meeting that opened the door for the Methodist Mission in Cambodia, telling of the day when all of his prayers toward this end were answered, and his tedious groundwork accomplished its purpose. "By the grace and the great miracle blessing of our Lord Jesus Christ, we were so joyful to be sent to Cambodia where, altogether, we celebrated

His glory and love. We were finally able to bring the peace and blessing from God to all the people in Cambodia. Ours was liberation from the long darkness into His bright light." As Joseph speaks, it is difficult to tell whether the brilliant sunlight and bright blue sky, surrounding the area with beauty, receive a part of their luster from him or whether he is a by-product of their light. My final conclusion is they are all in perfect harmony, inspired by God's reigning Light.

Even so, once we reach the outskirts of Siem Reap, an invisible air of apprehension envelopes us. The closer we get to the mountains, which lead to the Thai border, life approaches a standstill. Traffic and crowded villages give way to open countryside, sparsely dotted with an occasional house or hut. Even the pagodas are few and far between.

There is only one pagoda that possesses their usual impressive air of distinction. It sits far off in the distance, on the top of a mountain, elusive and alone. I wonder if it, like the pagoda in which Marilyn was held a prisoner, sits vacant and was used to kill people. I don't ask.

"Temples and pagodas like that one were very expensive to build," states Marilyn, noticing my intense gaze in its direction. "They had to hire workers to carry huge loads of rocks all the way up the mountain. When you see temples like that one, you know they have been there for a very long time."

I stare at the massive white edifice on the top of the mountain until it is out of sight. With it disappearing in the distance, I feel we are also leaving all traces of civilization behind us. There is little conversation, all of it small talk, as I visualize masses of people—all tired, hungry and dirty—carrying their every belonging on their backs or on a stick wrapped in a krama. *People who are desperately trying to reach a land of civilization, a better world, anywhere but where they are,* I muse. The image reminds me of the Israelites trying to reach a land of milk and honey.

Christina breaks the silence by telling me there is a waterfall hidden deep in the mountain, past a huge forest to our left. I look in the direction in which she is pointing until I spot a mammoth wall of trees. "The mountain is called Phnom Koulen. The Cambodians consider it to be sacred, so a lot of people go there for weekends or festivals. There's a really neat place there where you can go swimming, and there are vine swings." Excitement is present in her young voice of experience. "A lot of tourists go there. You can take a picnic lunch or eat at the restaurant near it, and you have to take lots of water because a visit there takes all day."

"What's it called?" I ask, my curiosity peaked.

"Kbal Spean," answers Marilyn. "It means 'bridgehead.' It got its name because there's a natural bridge there. It's a long walk, two kilometers uphill," Marilyn informs me, "but it's worth it when you finally get there."

Her comment reminds me of how God must lovingly gaze at each one of His children, and how He desires us to look at others. *And how Marilyn looked at Joseph when she saw him in the refugee camp.*

"Whenever we would go there when I was younger," interjects Christina, "I would ask, 'How far, how far?'"

I laugh. The question, "Are we there yet?" is undoubtedly universal among children. Epiphany having been the day before, her question also reminds me of the question asked by the three kings who traveled so far to see the baby Jesus. "How far is it to Bethlehem?"

Perhaps because of our day's destination and the grisly cruelty associated with it, I am also reminded of another question. "How long, O Lord?" This question weighs heavily on me for it must have been the same question asked repeatedly—to whomever their "Lord" was—by the Cambodians who managed to survive under the reign of Pol Pot, Ta Mok and the other three leaders—Ieng Sary, Khiev Samphan and Nuon Chea—so closely associated to the Khmer Rouge killings.

It isn't long before I spot an area that is the scene of a recent fire. *Development has a huge cost, at least to the land and its inhabitants, all over the world,* I surmise. We soon pass another area, approximately three miles farther up the road, where fires for developing have also been set. There is something about the blackened ground, in the midst of the thick forests of hardwood trees, that matches the eeriness creeping into the air around us as we near the mountain range.

That mood is intensified by the sight of a road block ahead. For the second time on this trip, there is something cautiously unsettling about being stopped by foreign police who are speaking an unknown language to the driver of the car. Call it too many mystery novels, or too many American movies and television shows, but nonetheless, it is still a present force. I find myself slightly relieved when Chandra tells me they are only checking for wood. "This area is known for its good wood. So many people were cutting it, and selling it illegally to Vietnam and Thailand for furniture production, they've had to set up roadblocks to monitor it. There are now governmental restrictions on cutting wood in this area."

Thinking of all the drug and illegal immigrant concerns connected with the borders at home, I recognize the problems that arise with every border. That doesn't help me feel safer at the moment. I've crossed both the northern and southern borders of the USA numerous times, but at least then, I was next door to my home country. *And people who spoke my language.* This has a wholly different sensation to it.

Closer to the border of Thailand, a small village of approximately thirty newly-constructed thatch huts appears, literally, from out of nowhere. It is unusual to see a village on the main road. They are typically far off the beaten path, nestled in the trees to provide shade, protection and privacy. Soon we see another complex, this one of apartments closely resembling the government's subsidized housing seen in the U.S.

"The country is trying to 'double-up'," Chandra explains. "They are putting people, who have lost houses and land to developers, along the road fronts of the major highways. The government is subsidizing their housing, and the developers get the whole big chunks of land behind them."

"Progress," is my only reply as I have to face the sickening reality of that word obviously having the same meaning in both larger, developed countries and poverty-stricken third-world countries.

Within three or four kilometers of the Thai border, I get my first look at Cambodian soldiers in their green uniforms. I know, from recent television reports, there is fighting in the border area between the two countries. There is a huge difference between knowing and seeing. Again, I feel a bit unnerved. Yet, considering we are on our way to the final stronghold of the Khmer Rouge, the presence of these soldiers adds to the ominous atmosphere that already surrounds the area.

"Those are the Dângrêk Mountains," states Marilyn as we reach the base of the rising slopes we've watched shooting out of the ground for a good distance.

Unlike our Appalachian Mountains at home, these go straight up. There are no foothills.

"We are entering the Anlong Veng district," she continues, suddenly sounding like the voice of a professional tour guide. Emotion has left her voice as she strictly relays the information. "This is where Pol Pot and the Khmer Rouge regime retreated once they began to feel the heat from the North Vietnamese. People know this area as the Khmer Rouge village. The place we are going was built by Ta Mok. It is called his island. He was the second in command under Pol Pot. Some people say he was the most brutal killer of all the Khmer Rouge leaders."

Considering this is a very dry area with no water, and approximately 125 kilometers from Siem Reap, I find Marilyn's choice of words—"his island"—intriguing. From my research, I remember this area to be the site of one of the first "killing fields" following the fall of the Khmer Rouge's power. It remains as it was then, the final Khmer Rouge headquarters and the meeting place for members of the Khmer Rouge after Liberation Day. It is only six kilometers away, deep in the forests, where Ta Mok is reputed to have killed 3,000 "traitors"—persons of the Khmer Rouge's own movement whom they deemed had become "tainted" or "corrupted"—between the years of 1993 and 1997. Covered in still-live landmines, the area has yet to be excavated in search of the bodies.

I feel a slight sensation as my skin begins to crawl, which I consider most appropriate given the sinister aura created by the topography and the people we've encountered along the way. *And the people hidden along this way thirty-one years ago,* I remind myself. The story Marilyn is sharing with me, and the stories I'm sure I will learn once we reach Ta Mok's house, makes the currently popular vampire series and movies nothing more than child's play.

We reach the northern perimeter of Anlong Veng and I suddenly understand "his island." There is a bridge, built by Ta Mok, that spans both sides of the road. It holds the water in this particular spot, where he meticulously chose to construct a headquarters for the floundering Khmer Rouge regime. Trees, killed by dammed-up water, stand bare and topless with branchless trunks sticking up from the water. Other trees have been cut down and used for the pillars of his secluded "hide-away." A wooden dwelling sits out in the middle of what looks to be a moat, far less imposing than the one at Angkor Wat but still, in its meagerness, a deterrent planned to afford natural protection.

As we turn into the driveway of the place where many wrongly accused "traitors" were "caged"—literally—Marilyn informs me this entire area had been under water after the typhoon of the past September. That adds to the mysticism that shrouds this scenery, which already resembles a bog in a strangely mystical land. The only thing missing is a fog slowly rising up from the patches of water surrounding the weakened tree trunks sticking up from the ground.

No one is there to greet us when we arrive. I simply follow Marilyn inside the first floor of the structure where, directly in front of the entrance, there is a wall-sized painting of the Preah Vihear temple. "This is the 11th century temple over which the Cambodian and Thai soldiers are fighting. It's actually a Hindu temple, but Ta Mok considered the temples an important part of our heritage and was adamant about the fact they should be preserved." Her voice has lost a bit of the edge it had moments earlier, a detail that speaks volumes of what this area says to Cambodians who survived the atrocities of the leaders who met here.

One step inside the large room to which this entrance opens unveils more large murals of prominent temples, painted in long rows down the walls. My recollection that Ta Mok was a monk in his early years makes his empathy for temple preservation conceivable, though it's problematic to find any rationale for his thoughts or deeds.

From nowhere, a gentleman appears collecting money for our visit. I am glad to pay the tourism fee because I'm already "hooked" by what is the last dwelling of an extraordinarily complex man. His offer, in Khmer, of "Do you have any questions?" receives a long list from me, via Marilyn and Chandra. Mark and Joseph, who have been scoping out the outside area, join us just in time to hear the answers.

The guide leads us to a map, the first—and only—painting that isn't of a temple, inside the room. "Ta Mok created this map in 1978 during the time he was appointed Chief-of-Staff by Pol Pot. His desire was for the population to take care of nature and the animals, not destroy them. He told the Khmer Rouge, 'Do *not* destroy the temples! They are the heritage of Cambodia.'" He confirms Marilyn's earlier statement.

"Before 1978, the Khmer Rouge had no solid base, only the jungles and forests. That's why, in that year, they chose this place as their headquarters." As he speaks, another gentleman appears whose dress and the way he carries himself tells me he is not just another guide. Our guide points toward him and utters a few words to Chandra and Marilyn.

"This man works with the Department of Tourism for this area," Chandra translates in English. "It's quite possible he may have more answers to your questions."

"And he speaks some English," adds Marilyn.

I bow to the guide and offer the term "Awkunh," which is the Khmer equivalent of "Thank you." He returns my bow, turns to the new arrival and apparently tells him of my interest in the place and the reason for my many questions. I then turn and bow to the man from the tourism division. He speaks briefly to Chandra before addressing me.

"The Khmer Rouge was very definite in their plans of where guerrillas were needed to control areas, which areas they already controlled and which areas were needed to be gained to have a viable force still in place in Cambodia," he begins in English, pointing to the map still in front of me.

"So the Khmer Rouge did not end with Liberation Day?" I ask, verifying my earlier readings.

"Absolutely not. At least not in this area. This place was established here as a headquarters in 1978. It was only a small place at that time. Ta Mok made it larger in 1981. Even though there was still fighting, the leaders of the opposing parties of the Khmer Rouge and the North Vietnamese began to negotiate with each other. After the ceasefire in 1991, Ta Mok and Pol Pot became enemies, for Ta Mok wanted to continue the communist government. That's why he remodeled the headquarters at that time to make it bigger and better and to include his house. It was then that Ta Mok, who was referred to as 'Brother Number 5,' remodeled the place as you see it now and brought his wife and four children here. He kept a house at the mountains for his personal caregivers."

Our personal guide invites us to see the remainder of the dwelling. "It wasn't until 1996 that the Khmer Rouge finally threw up their hands, saying, "No more power. We lost the world. Up until that time, they continued to fight against the North Vietnamese and stayed in this area to keep the Thai out of Cambodia."

He pauses to give us time to examine the large living quarters upstairs before escorting us back downstairs to where the Khmer Rouge controlled their prisoners. "It was actually Ta Mok who arrested Pol Pot in 1998. Pol Pot was sentenced to house arrest in a very small house, where he was staying near here. Ta Mok was supposedly with him when he reportedly died of a heart attack."

His words strike as loudly as had he struck a gong. Every account I have seen or heard of Pol Pot's death uses those same words, "reportedly died of a heart attack."

"He had heart problems and was, no doubt, under a lot of anxiety at the time because he was being questioned regarding his war crimes. He had recently learned that Ta Mok had just signed an agreement to hand him over to Americans for his trial, but no one is sure of the cause of his death."

My first inclination is this would be an awesome story for one of the many forensic shows ruling the programming on television. *But then,* I correct myself, *it is better to let sleeping dogs lie.* Compared to some of the things I've heard Pol Pot called during my time here, that adage is a polite way of expressing their sentiment.

There's one remaining request of this knowledgeable man who "just happened" to show up at Ta Mok's place while we are here. "I've heard Pol Pot died and was cremated near here. I had hoped to find the place of his burial, but from what I've been told, there is no sign because the local people want to forget about him." In case he is hesitant to share my desired information, I leave my comment with that rather than an open-ended question.

"I know where the site of his cremation is. I put a sign up there myself a couple of weeks ago. It is only thirteen kilometers away."

My heart suddenly pounding, I glance in Mark's direction to see he is as excited as I am. I ask if the guide can give Joseph the directions, which he does. There is a bizarre sensation of seeing the light at end of the tunnel now that I am within distance of reaching my final quest of this Khmer Rouge investigation. In my prior months of tedious research, I feel I have come to know Pol Pot. Not understand, simply know the facts. I am aware of the details of the end of his life, and I have a goal to find where that life ended, if for no other reason than to give closure to this couple. The eeriness of the morning shifts into determination.

The tourism representative further explains that the government of this area plans to make all the local sites connected with Pol Pot, Ta Mok and the other top three leaders—"brothers"— of the Khmer Rouge, including the nearby gravesite of Son Sen, into a historical area. Son Sen was the Minister of Defense and a friend of Pol Pot for forty years. In his paranoia, Pol Pot decided Son Sen was involved with the Cambodian government, and thus ordered him killed. Son Sen's wife and children were also killed. It was that series of murders for which Ta Mok arrested Pol Pot.

In America, there is a saying about "the pot calling the kettle black," meaning an accuser is guilty of the same crime for which he or she is accusing another person. In this case, it is rather "the Mok calling the Pot black." Although a horribly bad pun, it is not intended as a joke, no more than the fact that Pol Pot's cremation happened on a pile of old car tires beside the local latrine. It is merely another pitiable fact of a horrific time in history.

"They are now in the process of developing a new village that will include a museum, hotels and a casino in this area," he adds, calling my attention back to the present instead of the past as he points to a fancy resort visible in the distance.

As Joseph, Marilyn and Chandra continue to converse with him in Khmer, I retreat to the edge of the house and stare out the open windows that overlook the bog. What I see is a most inspirational view, one in which I could sit and write for days. There is a heifer and three calves in front of me, chewing on the vegetation growing in the man-made wetland. Water lilies, the Cambodian sign of hope, sprout up from the water all around the house. It is so peaceful and quiet that it's hard to imagine all the hatred and fighting that once brewed here.

Oddly, Marilyn comes to my side. "This place was once covered in beautiful trees. The trees all died because the water backed up from the dam."

Her simple statement nearly brings me to tears. It is so full of prophetic depth and theology that I immediately turn and envision a meeting of the last of the Khmer Rouge heads in this very room. I hear none of the conversation around me as I imagine the heinous leaders, seated on the floor with no conference table or padded leather chairs, deciding which of their members are "traitors" to be caged outside and then sent to the mountain for execution…or looking at the map to decide which of the villagers to kill next because they have become "corrupted"…or determining which officers are in cahoots with the Cambodian government, deeming them "tainted."

I then look at the people in this room with me, all people whom I love, or for whom I have a deep appreciation or admiration. All beautiful people, like the millions of Cambodians who once lived in this country struggling to hold onto its neutrality in the midst of an unstable war situation, which spilled over into all four sections—warranted or unwarranted, claimed or unclaimed—of Southeast Asia. *Beautiful people who were killed because the evil poison, hysteria and paranoia got out of hand, backing up like water in a dam.*

I return to the hushed inspiration of the view out the side windows, keeping my tears to myself, as I wonder if Marilyn has any idea of the impact of her words. While Mark snaps a myriad of photos and the Cambodian natives share their own Khmer Rouge experiences in their native tongue, my heart commiserates over the events that influenced the individuals who made this place, and what it stands for, so notorious. I pray nothing like this will ever happen again. And I thank God for yet another blessing of an unexpected guest who becomes an invaluable resource.

Before we leave, this man—who has answered all my questions and more—warns us we cannot go to the Thai border today because of the level of fighting there. The temple I viewed in the mural upon my arrival is still the target of a constant struggle. What's more, it is near the small piece of land where people from both Cambodia and Thailand go to market and barter for goods. People have traveled to that spot for years for trade. One reason we have chosen this day to travel this road is because it is Thursday, the day the markets are open. But we discover there will be no market for us today, much to Chandra's dismay.

"Excuse me," I ask as we prepare to leave, "did you lose family members during the time of the Khmer Rouge?"

"Yes," he answers. "Both my parents were representatives of Svay Rieng, my home province near Vietnam. They were working in Phnom Penh prior to 1975. When the Khmer Rouge took over the capital, they were taken immediately. I found out later from my adoptive parents that my older brother and sister also both passed away as a result of the revolution." There is no sign of animosity in his voice, only a desire to make sure what happened to his family happens to no others.

I look back at the man who first began our tour, who is now sweeping the floor. That act, too, chills me. He can sweep away the dust, but not the crimes planned and acted out here. "What about you? Did you lose family?" Joseph translates my questions into Khmer.

The man points down to his left foot, taking away my need for a translator. It isn't until now that I note anything strange about his foot. Trying not to stare, I see it is plastic, a fine material and very well adapted, but still plastic. I watch his face as he speaks to Joseph.

"He lost his foot due to a landmine in 1982," Joseph says as he turns to me. "He was a Khmer Rouge soldier until February of 1982, and was fighting the Vietnamese Liberation when it happened in 1979."

The man offers a few more words while I get over the shock that I'm standing in this place with a former Khmer Rouge soldier, and a man whose entire family was killed by that regime.

"He had been a young Khmer Rouge soldier since 1972," Joseph adds.

I stand there, silent and stunned, at this man, now a guide for tourists to this place of historical prominence, who saw both the take-over of Cambodia by his regime and the loss of it to the North Vietnamese. *Who better to know the facts?* I decide.

"Did you see Ta Mok and Pol Pot?" My question needs no translator as I point to my eyes and say the leaders' names.

"Baht," he answers, giving me the male Khmer term for yes.

The vision I tried to imagine moments before is now a reality as I stand beside a man caught up in all the madness, but who lived to survive the brainwashing of his youth and return to a life of beauty. He holds no hostility toward no one, the man who lost his entire family at the hands of the Khmer Rouge holds no hostility, and both are anxious to make sure I fully understand the way history unfolded itself in not only this place, but the whole of Cambodia. I feel a sudden pity for the people at home in America who are still caught up in the issues between the North and South from a war that ended nearly 150 years before.

Astounded by their openness about all that transpired here, I have no reservation asking my next question to the original guide. "Is it alright if Mark takes my photo with you?" Again I need no translator as I point to Mark's photography equipment and pretend to take a picture. My game of charades is much more rewarding than depending on a go-between.

Again, he answers, "Baht." He even holds his foot up for Mark to get a picture of it. I learn that, during his experience as a soldier, Ta Mok also lost the lower part of a leg due to an injury. It happened around the time Lon Nol's army ousted Sihanouk—a prince at that time—from power in 1970.

An open and honest mutual respect is present in the air. They appreciate the fact that I am so interested in their culture and history, that Marilyn and Joseph are able to revisit a sordid and painful past, and that they are able to be of assistance to my book's progress and research. *Liberation Day, it is,* I muse, as I scan the roomful of persons who lived through Liberation Day and have the stories to tell about all its implications from every side.

Joseph speaks to the two men about Christ and tells them he is a missionary. They both nod and smile.

"On December 12th, all the churches in this area came together here and held a huge Christmas celebration." The simple statement by the tourism representative catches our entire group unaware. I sneak a peek at Joseph and Marilyn, whose faces share the same ecstatic expression as mine. "This was the first year they've done that, but it is going to become an annual event. They even included the nearby orphanage," he adds, much to our delight.

"Talk about liberation," I offer excitedly, praying their annual celebration will soon become the liberation this community remembers and talks about. Our assembly rambles wildly at the hopes now possible for this village and entire area through their Christmas celebration.

What a note on which to end our visit. We say our good-byes while I take a moment to look at the grounds outside. It isn't until then that I pay attention to the fact this abode is not at all imposing. It is actually quite small considering its use. There is no furniture, only a few plastic chairs, which I suspect are for the man who greeted us and his two sons who have joined us for much of the time. The eeriness I experienced before is gone; it is replaced by delight at what this place has become for the community.

Because this place is so far off the beaten path, the guide follows us outside. "Do you need to use the toilet?" he asks, knowing we've spent a good deal of time here and that we're off to the mountainside in search of Pol Pot's cremation site. It's odd how such a simple question can make one realize how, no matter what paths our lives take, whether filled with goodness or evil, we are all created in the same image and have the same basic needs.

Once we are all back in the Land Cruiser, I look at Marilyn, whose face is covered in a soft, reflective smile as she shares my glance. "Beautiful trees are growing here once again," I express quietly. It isn't until then, when another group of tourists arrives, that I realize we've had this place and the guides all to ourselves for the past hour. I also see the tourism representative leave, leaving me to bask in the knowledge that he was placed there at that exact time for our benefit.

The ominous mood from before has dissipated into thin air as we all share euphoric thoughts filled with jubilation over the many connotations this anniversary of Liberation Day holds for us. Once we find Pol Pot's tomb, the rest of our journey will be a downhill ride, literally and figuratively, as we head down the mountain and make our way south, back toward Siem Reap. While the rest of the passengers make small talk about how much we've accomplished in such a short time, and how blessed we are that God has put us in touch with all the right people, I read over my notes and contemplate a few last points of the man who built the abode we just left, the man who put a stop to Pol Pot and, from all implications, took over.

Ta Mok ("Grandfather Mok" in English) is the name he chose for himself. "The Butcher" is the name he earned from Cambodians and the press. The last of the five big leaders to finally be arrested in 1999, just past here at the Thai border, he held onto his declaration of innocence to the end. Even on his deathbed in 2006, before falling into a coma, Ta

Mok gave a statement that he had killed no one, that the executions had been the fault of the others in control. His trial for inhuman charges and war crimes would have begun only a few months later in 2007. A final interesting tidbit is that Ta Mok surrounded himself, prior to his arrest, by a bodyguard of thirty fighters—all hand-picked and all women. It seems he trusted females, as did other barbarous leaders of past centuries, more than men who reputedly often turned in their allegiance.

Putting my notes aside, I breathe a sigh of relief that this dreaded part of my research is over, and that for Marilyn and Joseph, they have closed many doors behind them. There is only one more to close on this journey. I wonder if it is not the heaviest door of all.

We count down the kilometers to the tomb. When we are four kilometers from the site, the mountain goes straight up. The Land Cruiser grinds in its struggle to carry us, as Joseph shifts gears to manage the steep climb. We round a sharp curve and are instantly greeted by signs of bombing and fighting that have happened here, one of them being a deserted, burned car. My prayer, that Joseph's vehicle makes it up the mountain and back, grows to include one for our safety as I suddenly become cognizant that we are surrounded by landmines.

Our eyes search diligently for the tiny road the tourism director mentioned. Joseph stops when he spots a woman ahead of us. He asks her about the gravesite and she points a little farther to our right. We follow her directions to a road so small it is practically impassible. Now our eyes are peeled, looking for the sign the tourism director placed here. I spy what I think is it high on an incline, but there's no way Joseph can drive there. His dilemma is now turning the Land Cruiser around and getting back to where we can walk to it.

We approach a young man carrying a yoke with two water buckets across his shoulders. Joseph stops. "Is this the place of Pol Pot's crematorium?" he asks politely in Khmer.

"Baht," the young man confirms. His answer causes my heart to skip a beat, as do his next words, translated by Chandra. "There was the hut where he stayed, too, but the people tore the hut down."

"The soldiers?" I ask, with Marilyn translating for me.

"Baht." There is no emotion in his affirmative answer. His lack of feeling does not surprise me; the fact he doesn't say something, to reflect how he really feels, does.

Joseph parks the vehicle and remains in it with Christina while the rest of our party climbs out and makes the trek up the hill. The path is extremely narrow and uneven, causing us to have to watch closely for its many deep ruts. To get from the Land Cruiser to the path, we must first cross a small branch, carefully stepping on posts leading to the site. I have the sensation of walking on a tight rope, which I fear may be a bit prophetic, as I slowly balance myself one foot at a time.

As we get closer, I see the sign recently placed here with its exact wording, "Pol Pot's Was Cremated Here. Please Help to Preserve This Historical Site." The small, low to the ground, tomb sits to the left of the sign. A stack of old tires is still visible off to the side, making me wonder if the ones used to cremate him came from this pile. I find an old, rusted nail just off to the right of the path and pick it up, wondering if it came from the torn down hut. It goes in my pocket.

Mark and Chandra busy themselves with their cameras, while Marilyn and I stand there silently staring at the mound of dirt covered by old pieces of rusted tin, held up by old dilapidated pieces of timber. Someone has used a course brush and black paint on an old flat board, creating a makeshift sign that reads precisely, "Pol Pot's creamatorium." There is a Buddhist shrine at the front of the tomb where a few sticks of incense lay. At the base of it, just in front of the rusted tin roof, rest two faded artificial flowers and a weathered beer can, which holds several burnt incense sticks.

The site speaks for itself. *And him,* I ponder as my eyes shift to Marilyn. I know she has come to terms with her thoughts and feelings of not only him, but all the Khmer Rouge soldiers who played a part in her life; it is a forgiveness that came with her discovery of Christ's love and forgiveness of her own sins. Yet this has to be a touching moment for her. *And a test of her faith,* I surmise. *This is where the "talkers" and the "walkers" of the faith are separated like the wheat and the chaff.*

Her face speaks of nothing but kindness and gentleness as we head down the hill to retrace our steps back to Siem Reap. *Their lives have come full circle,* I determine as Joseph carefully maneuvers the Land Cruiser back on the road that brought us here.

Now that I have gotten as close to both Ta Mok and Pol Pot as is possible after all these years, and under the circumstances, my subconscious makes me keenly aware of a perplexingly, but intricately, woven thread that runs between them. Both Pol Pot and Ta Mok were born into prosperous families in their villages. That's a curious parallel, considering city dwellers and rich people were one of the Khmer Rouge's main targets. *But,* I remind myself, *Marilyn told me how harsh the city students were toward the village students, making fun of them and ridiculing them mercilessly. She experienced it herself to the point that she did extremely poorly in middle school and high school after such high scores for entry into middle school. Rich city kids and rich village kids were not considered of the same ilk. Eliminating the rich city dwellers left no one to look down on the rich villagers.*

Prince Norodom Sihanouk, who was indirectly responsible for the Khmer Rouge's increased power as a way of overthrowing Lon Nol's army, once stated, "Pol Pot is mad, you know, like Hitler." Yet in a final interview before his death, Pol Pot defended his actions, stating, "For the love of the nation and the people it was the right thing to do but in the course of our actions we made mistakes." He further stated that he regretted his actions were the same as his inexperience, thus causing mistakes to be made and killing to get out of hand. I refuse to venture how many people's focus became distorted through this period of Cambodia's history. *Or how many people's focus became distorted in historical Biblical accounts in the name of war and love for country.*

As we leave this place that earlier emanated such a baleful feel, I spot a U.S. Army Surplus store on the left side of the road. It is a shop I missed on the way to Pol Pot's "creamation" site, and one I wish I had missed leaving it. There is something bothersome about seeing it right here, especially when I'm forced to recognize that the United States is still one of the few countries that has refused to ban the production of land mines. I cannot imagine who would want to wear any item of U.S. military clothing in this area, in light of the 70's connections. I fight to banish the thoughts of the store and the implications running through my mind of all that was done and left undone by my country, which I dearly love. However, the moment shocks me into a reality that nations, like our individual selves, are not untarnished. With that awareness also dawns the reality of God's unconditional love, a gift made even more unfathomable by thoughts of such heinous acts executed by individuals like Pol Pot and "The Butcher."

There are no tears, no lumps in my throat…nothing. My entire body, and being, is too numb from all I've witnessed and heard during this day to respond. What I feel is such an austere contrast from the beauty of God's creation around me. The initial reaction I finally sense is one of my heart bleeding, aching for not only the victims of this country's genocide but also for the leaders at whose hands those lives were taken. My second reaction I finally notice is the fluttering of butterflies in my stomach, reminding me of the symbolism of new life growing out of Christ's resurrection. One look at Joseph and Marilyn, and their beautiful daughter Christina, assures me that even in the midst of crisis, there is ultimately a butterfly. Not by our own doing, but of God.

The concept is nothing new. It is a fact long known and taught in my ministry. A theological analogy springs forth, as I envision a boxer in a ring, "knocked out" by devastatingly demonic forces. It may lay him out for a few seconds, but before the referee gives the final count, he's on his feet again, this time with a power that can only be given by God. *That's what happened with Joseph and Marilyn.*

As my theological analogy draws to a close, Ta Mok's retreat again comes into view in front of us to the left. The apprehensive air present on the way here is lifted and replaced by a renewed sense of life. We settle back to our cold water, sodas and sandwiches Marilyn brought. Mark and I share our jubilation over crossing a boundary that led us to a dark hell, of which we have come out triumphant with stories and photos to share with people who have never traveled to this tiny country, or are totally unaware of what happened here in the years from 1975 - 1979.

The elusive butterfly has taken flight as we experience God's forgiveness on this entire area and all those involved with the Khmer Rouge's brutal killings. I find myself grateful for the attitude of the new generation to let it go and move on to a new future. And I find myself thankful for the tourism rep whose parents were lost when he was very young, but who cares enough about the welfare of people, particularly in his country, that he dares to make sure this kind of tragedy never reoccurs. Lastly, as my body and emotions return to an even keel, I feel a lump in my throat, caused by the awareness that I have ventured this close to Pol Pot and "The Butcher" and, through others, felt their wrath. A generous gift has been bestowed by God, besides His unconditional love, as He swings wide the door revealing the pasts of Joseph and Marilyn, and their survivals and struggles to get to where they are now.

It is then I'm reminded of several of the earlier comments made by Joseph and Marilyn. "We knew there were land mines in the area, but our need and want for firewood was greater than our fear of landmines." "The Khmer Rouge had planted landmines around all places with water, but people were so thirsty, it didn't matter." "I knew I was in danger, that I could be punished or killed, but the need to check on my mother was greater."

I now understand their words. *"I knew there were landmines in the area but I had to experience Pol Pot's 'creamation' site,"* I utter to myself. *I had to see, to feel…to know*. The miles pass quietly as I think back to the times when I visited Dachau and Hitler's "Eagle's Nest," which—although they took my breath—were nothing compared to what I feel now. I recognize the reason. This is not merely a comprehension of the proverbial bridges Joseph and Marilyn had to cross, but an outpouring of empathy for what every missionary in history has had to face. It is the point when they turn their fears over to God, the moment when they stop being "self" and become "God's instrument." It is the "magical" moment—if you will—when their souls, minds, bodies and hearts become numbed to their own consciousness as they focus on the needs of the world and those around them.

What an anniversary of this Liberation Day, I determine, still amazed this is the day we "happened" to journey toward the mountain and the Thai border. A day we are not allowed passage due to fighting between the Thai and Cambodian soldiers for control of that small area, which for years has been the site of political and military unrest.

I stare at the mountain, over which the Chans finally escaped. The fact of the still-present battling over this border and land control adds to the reality of their plight. Though the Thai border is inaccessible to us, the boundaries of my understanding and insight have been broken. I have crossed from an imaginary vision of what I perceived Joseph and Marilyn's past to be into the real here-and-now of their past, their history and their culture. It is not the pretty motion-picture "Hollywoodized" version like *The Sound of Music*. These are not the Alps. The hills are not alive with music, but still with landmines and gunshots.

In order to allow Marilyn, along with Joseph and Christina, time to eat with her family to celebrate the significance of this day—and their various momentous meanings of the word "liberation"—the other half of our entourage heads to the hotel's restaurant. Since Mark and I have spent a short time in a helium balloon, giving us a fantastic view of Angkor Wat earlier in the afternoon, we're ready for a quiet dinner in order to rejuvenate for the evening's festivities in Siem Reap to end this anniversary of Liberation Day, in the grand style of a native Cambodian.

When our friends return and we climb back into the Land Cruiser, I can't help but chuckle at the thought of an old hymn, *Revive Us Again.* From the laughter and chatter in the vehicle, our two-hour break has certainly revived us for an exciting evening of shopping and celebration. It is a strikingly stark contrast to the repulsively dreadful stories of the morning, giving my emotions and thoughts a field day as they bounce rampantly from one spectrum to the other. *If it's this way for you,* I consider, *think of how it must be for Joseph and Marilyn.* I offer a smile to our translator. *And Chandra.*

"Would you like to know why mother stoops?" Marilyn asks as Joseph exits the hotel's driveway.

Her question immediately unleashes another emotion inside me. "Yes," I answer, choking down tears to speak, although I assume her stooped posture to be from all her hard work in "Khmer Rouge time"—the same reason as for Joseph's sisters.

"She was robbed by Vietnamese soldiers in 1983, while Cambodia was still under communist control. They jumped into her house through the thatch roof and stabbed her eight times." Her words cause my jaw to drop in stunned alarm as her unexpected response creates an entirely new drama and an even more highly-deserved appreciation of this "commander-in-chief." "As with the Khmer Rouge," she continues, "they suspected her to be rich. They figured she still had some of the jewels and gold from her younger years, a rumor created by jealous neighbors. So they took all they could find and left her for dead."

Before I can catch my breath from the shock of this story, Marilyn continues with, "After that, though…"

"You mean there's more?" is what I want to scream in outrage. Instead, I manage to control my emotions and calmly interrupt with, "There's more?" By the time Marilyn finishes the account of her mother, I'm surprised the woman's alive, much less able to join in family functions and carry on with her "head-of-household" ways, as she had done during our visit the day before.

"Several years after Pol Pot's removal from power, in 1985, she learned the whereabouts of the mother of my brother-in-law, who by that time lived in America. She felt compelled to go and check on the woman. When my brother-in-law learned of this, he sent money from the USA for his mother.

"During that time, she had no car like before the Khmer Rouge regime. But that did not matter. In Cambodia, you can go everywhere you want. All you need is to give a car's driver a little bit of money."

"Like when your family came back to Siem Reap following Liberation Day?" I ask, recalling another story she'd shared.

"Yes. Ma asked people for a ride along the way and was able to get there. When she arrived at the province of Kampong Cham, the place where his mother lived, she found out the woman was in need of assistance. My mother, prepared for that, gave her the money from my brother-in-law and also helped her in some other ways.

"However, cars did not run every day, so sometimes people would have to wait a day or two for another car to come by their street. Because of that, travelers expected it to take a long time to get places. After Ma had waited for a couple of days and there was still no passing car, she knew she needed to get back home to care for my father and younger sister. She didn't have time to wait any longer. Eventually, when she saw a tall truck like one of the ones we saw today on the highway, she begged them to let her ride with them. They told her there was no place for her to sit, but she was insistent that she get home.

"She was so persistent, the driver and workers finally allowed her to go along with them, but the only place for her to ride was on the top, holding on as best she could to the load they were carrying."

I cringe, anticipating the dreadfulness of her next statement and wishing I could stop it.

"She fell off. The truck didn't stop to get her when she fell. They kept going because she had already paid them."

"Did they think she possibly died?" I ask.

"I don't know. They didn't even stop to check. But she wouldn't tell my father and injured sister about her fall when she got home. She didn't want them to worry about her." There is a slight reflective pause. "That's how she was. Ma was always concerned with helping others."

Marilyn gives a quiet sigh. "I remember hearing my mother cry so many times when we still lived in Phnom Penh. Every time she heard the bombs in the distance, she cried because of the number of people who had no protection in the outlying areas. They would dig holes and run to them when they heard the bombs. But there was a story of a whole family who died from poisonous snakes in one of the holes. It broke my mother's heart to hear about them. She would often leave us at home, nearly every day, while she'd go to help the refugees left without homes, or who had lost family members due to the bombings. I remember she gave away a lot of rice and money to them during that time. She took food or clothing to the poor people when she heard they were without."

Random acts of kindness before the popular slogan, I ruminate.

"On one of those days when she'd gone to help, a renter of one of our apartments threw his cigarette out. It landed on top of a coconut tree in front of our house and the tree caught on fire. When Ma got back to our street, she couldn't get to the house because of the crowd. She called for the fire chief, who was a corrupt man.

"He asked, 'How much gold will you pay me to come?' Ma then called the military general. He called the fire chief and said, 'I will pay you the bullet if you don't go.' Two or three trucks came right away. By that time, my sisters and I had thrown so many buckets of water on the fire that we nearly had it out."

Marilyn gives a loud chuckle. "The funny thing about that fire was it burned a tree that would never produce much fruit. After the fire, it bore more fruit."

I ponder at the theological significance of that point, but my focus is more attuned to my amazement at the number of people this elderly woman has touched in her life, how many she has benefited, and how many lives have been changed because of her gracious generosity.

I'm reminded of Christians who talk the talk, but don't walk the walk. This woman may not talk the talk, but she surely does walk the walk. And more importantly, her foresight to raise her daughters in such a manner, by providing them with a good role model and instilling strong, solid family values in them, has enabled Marilyn to be able to both talk the talk *and* walk the walk.

Most of all, I thank God for the ability this woman had to trust Marilyn's love for Joseph and to accept that his work and goodness were worth far more for her third daughter's future than a healthy dowry.

The story ends just as Joseph turns into a side street to let us out at Siem Reap's famous night market, which is open every evening from four o'clock until midnight. This evening's crowd is more interested in the celebration than the market. At the precise moment Mark and I step out of the vehicle and onto the sidewalk, fireworks go off, giving us a ringside seat. Mark "oohs," I "ahh," and all the Cambodians wonder what we are doing while I stand there, reminded of "Star of wonder, star of night, star with royal beauty bright. Westward leading, still proceeding, guide us to Thy perfect light."

We're not three kings, I tell myself, *but we are six individuals traveling from Phnom Penh around a large chunk of Cambodia who, like those kings, are in search of the Christ Child as we journey afar to find his Light in this world still affected by four years of darkness.*

My carefree evening takes a traumatic turn when, stepping out from a darkened doorway, a man asks, "You like pretty lady?" I turn to see the male recipient of the question walk swiftly past to join the rest of his group. A subject too common, which receives much attention of late, daringly knocks me from my comfort zone. Yet at the same time, it serves as an example of exactly why the Christ Child came, and why the work of the Chan's—as well as the other missionaries here—is so crucial.

It is strange that, as we leave the heart of the city to go back to our hotel, we pass the king's royal palace (his second home) in Siem Reap. The words to the Epiphany carol remind me that we have indeed found one king on this day. *No,* I hasten to correct myself, *two kings.* The spirit of the real King has also been with us on this entire journey and in all our findings; it is the spirit that surrounds Joseph and Marilyn in their daily living.

Royal thoughts swiftly fade away as Joseph points to a bridge, with lush grassy medians on either side, diagonally across from the king's palace. "Before our final escape to Thailand, right after Marilyn and I were married, I would walk from the old abandoned factory, where we were staying, to Angkor Wat three times a week to collect the cows' dung. It was extremely dangerous walking through the forest, but we were so poor. Everyone said I had the best fertilizer and it made the best gardens, so I was able to use this to market for clothing and gold. The Vietnamese would come every day to buy from us because they said, 'He have the best stools.' They called me 'the Professor of Agriculture.'

"There was firewood I could cut in that same area, both for us to cook with and to sell. I walked many miles every day to try to find food and firewood," says Joseph. "It took nearly all day just to walk to the woods near Angkor Wat to get firewood and then get back home. There was always that bothersome fear of all the landmines in the area, but I just prayed the whole time.

"One evening as I was traveling back home across this bridge, two guards stopped me. They held their guns at me and asked, 'Where you going? What you have in there?' I showed them the firewood and the cow dung. I knew they were going to kill me, but instead they yelled, 'Pass!' Oh, I was so grateful. I got home that night faster than usual."

"Joseph, you have many epiphanies and many reasons to celebrate Liberation Day. These past two days are anniversaries of countless blessings from God," I share with a smile as we pass thousands of people lining the streets to celebrate for the second time in eight days.

"Yes, yes! Thank God, thank God! I have much to celebrate!"

And I realize I have much to celebrate too. The morning's visits of Ta Mok's house and the Khmer Rouge headquarters, Pol Pot's cremation site and the two men—once on opposing sides—all play a role in what I am now experiencing through this couple. *Faith, hope and love in action...in many ways.*

Chapter Seventeen

Having heard many, and witnessing some, of the worst conditions conceivably known to man, it comes time to uncover how Joseph and Marilyn evolved from their backgrounds of all the horrors, and a Buddhist culture, to becoming Christian missionaries back in the country they once had to flee. As we travel from Siem Reap back to our Cambodian "home," I am anxious to break through the invisible hurdle that keeps me one step away from knowing "the rest of the story." How meaningful that on this day—the day after the anniversary of Liberation Day—we will experience traveling the same path that carried them to a new world and a new life, allowing me to have followed in every step of their long journey of survival.

"Tell me about your escape, when you finally managed to get out of Cambodia," I urge, confident their story of struggle is coming to a close.

Marilyn's eyes suddenly show a sense of terror worse than what I've seen to this point. Her expression discloses that their journey was neither "a picnic" nor "a bed of roses," causing me to fear the most traumatic part of her story is yet to come.

"After the Khmer Rouge told us to leave, not telling us why but just to "Go home!" my family finally managed to get back to the hut where my mother was. We arrived in shifts, over a three-day period. It took my father and younger sister longer to get back than my older sister and me. We all waited at the hut until everyone was there. Only my oldest sister and her husband were missing.

"We knew it would be impossible for my injured sister to walk the long distance back to our home village of Kralanh in Siem Reap. Our mother reminded us how dangerous it was for our family because of one really mean soldier who was always badgering our family and whose mother wanted all our belongings, so she went on a mission to find someone with an oxcart or cow cart who could take us. No one would dare help. Even though the Khmer Rouge had lost power in the cities, they were still killing and terrorizing people in the work camps far back in the villages. Specific orders had been sent down the pipeline that 'no one was to help my family escape unless they, too, wanted to be killed.'

"But my mother was persistent and would not give up. She went to every person in the village. There was one woman whose husband had been gone the night before and all day carrying supplies for the Khmer Rouge. He had been absent from the meeting when they warned the people not to help us. My mother went to find him as soon as he returned late that evening, offering him a beautiful ring for payment.

"'I've had no sleep,' he answered wearily. But his wife greatly admired the ring and kept telling him how beautiful it was. She talked him into helping us because she so desperately wanted the ring. He finally agreed and told us to be ready at the morning star. In the wee hours of the next morning, we loaded his cart and set off."

"What happened to him?" I ask.

"I don't know. We never heard. I'm hoping the Khmer Rouge soldiers themselves had to flee and were unable to hurt the man.

"During the Pol Pot regime, my family had felt we were more persecuted than the others in our village, but while we were traveling toward our home along with all the other people leaving the various work camps, we learned we didn't have it as bad as many of them did."

"Sounds like our saying of, 'The grass is always greener on the other side'," I share with her. "The only problem is, there was no proverbial 'green grass' in Cambodia during that time."

"No, there wasn't," confirms Marilyn. "Ma reluctantly agreed to allow my father, two of my sisters and me to go to the Thai border when she finally saw that was our only chance at having any hope for a future. Two of my cousins and two of our friends also went with us. The travel was extremely difficult because we had to walk through the forests. All the roads were patrolled by the Vietnamese searching for people trying to escape. The ones they found were sent back to their villages and homes. So we had to be careful of the wilds of the forest plus the enemy soldiers.

"Along the way, we ran into a man who offered to lead us through the forest to the Thai border. We gave him all the clothes we had with us, except for the ones on our backs, to pay for his services. We were sure we could get new things once we reached the refugee camp. But he deserted us one night and took many of our things, leaving us more lost in the forest. We walked for another month before we finally found our way to Nong Chan, the refugee camp just inside the Thai border. By the time we got there, we had been robbed several times until nearly all our gold was gone. I only had the one gold piece left that my mother gave me, the one I kept hidden under my tongue. It didn't matter because we were unable to get new things there anyway. "

Joseph barely gives me time to digest her words before he begins his own tale of escape. "On the day I returned to the metal factory from fishing and saw everyone else was gone, the Khmer Rouge leader who saved my life was there waiting for me. 'Do not go to the mountains. Go instead to the city.' Because he spared me, I trusted him and did as he said. When I reached Battambang and learned my mother was dead and I couldn't find my family, I went back toward Phnom Penh.

"My plan was to go west to Thailand and escape immediately after the Vietnamese soldiers invaded Cambodia. When I escaped the first time, I offered to help another man reach the border. It turned out to be Mr. Bun Chan Lu, the owner of Phnom Penh's Royal Hotel (now known as Raffles Hotel Le Royal). I had been carrying his luggage for about three months. He liked me because I worked so hard, and he was very nice to me. One morning before daylight, in a light rain, someone yelled out, 'Fighting, fighting!' Everyone scrambled in so many directions that we were separated. After that, we never caught up with each other again.

"I kept heading along the route to Thailand, searching for him. My oxcart broke down soon after that, slowing down my travel. I finally reached the border where thousands of Cambodians were camped out in a refugee camp at Nong Chan village. It was May of 1979 when I finally arrived there."

"But how did you find Marilyn?" I ask, aware that somewhere during this timeframe they reconnected.

"I had been there several weeks when her family arrived at the camp in June. She was only there three days when she spotted me. It was strange because on the day they arrived, a journalist met her and asked if she had a relative who could come and pick her up."

"I couldn't remember anyone besides Joseph who might be a remote possibility," Marilyn quickly interjects, "and I so badly wanted out of Cambodia. I had only seen him once twelve years earlier. We were introduced by my aunty who was married to his uncle. They spoke on his behalf so that my mother would allow him to stay for free in our house in Phnom Penh with the other students. I knew he was studying abroad at the time the Khmer Rouge took over. He was the only person I could think of that I knew outside Cambodia, but I had no idea how they would reach him. I was merely 'drawing straws', as you say.

"It was only about three days later when Joseph and I ran into each other. I was working in the forest near the border where he was looking for the owner of the hotel. There were people everywhere and he asked aloud, 'Why so many people?' He was so close I could feel his breath over my shoulder. I immediately recognized his voice, spun around and exclaimed, 'Uncle!'

"'Who are you? How do you know me?' he asked in a startled voice. My head was wrapped up in the krama so that all he could see was my eyes. I removed my krama and he knew me instantly."

Joseph pipes up with, "I asked her, 'You're still alive?' She asked me if I had come to pick her up. I cried because I felt so powerless. I could do nothing to help her. After that, I stayed close to Marilyn's family to do what I could for them," he volunteers. There is a brief moment of silence as he quietly, but visibly, offers thanks that God allowed him to find the person who eventually became his life's mate.

"I kept trying to locate the rich man who owned the hotel," Joseph continues. "I finally did find his tent. It was big, with five or six people inside. When I didn't see him, I asked, 'Uncle Bun Chan Lu's place?' It turns out that one of the people inside the tent was his nephew, who was the Thai Ambassador's assistant who worked in China. He had come on his vacation and brought lots of supplies to help his uncle and the people. The rich man wasn't there at the time, but when he came back and found out I'd been there, he sent for me to come get food and clothing. I never saw him again after that. I assume he got out of the country safely with his nephew's help."

"There was no housing in the camp except for a few people," Marilyn informs me, "like the rich man's nephew, who had tents. The rest of us slept on the ground under the trees, just like in many of the work camps under the Khmer Rouge. It wasn't long after we were there when some nice new buses arrived at the refugee camp. Thai soldiers, who were patrolling the border, came and asked for volunteers who would like to go work. They said they had jobs for us. Everyone was very anxious to work and move on to a new life. My friends all volunteered to work, as did Joseph. People were ready to do anything to get into Thailand and away from the oppression we had suffered for the past four years, and were still suffering.

"There were several buses a day taking people away, but they took the Chinese and Islams on the first load, telling them they were sending them to Malaysia. Later we learned we were lucky not to be on that bus because most of them died from landmines. It was four or five days later when my family and friends were allowed to board the bus, but not Joseph. He was staying with the single men. They were not allowed to go until another day or two later.

"When it was our turn to leave, we all got on the bus so hopeful and thankful," she continues. "But instead of taking us to the new camp with jobs, the bus dropped us off, far from anywhere in the depths of the thick forests, back in Cambodia. In an area infested with landmines, it was the soldiers' way of leaving us to die on our own. It was a gruesome journey back. The Thai soldiers held guns pointed at us and forced us back into the forest at a place where there was high barbed wire. They cut the barbed wire only wide enough for people to pass through. With their guns held at us, they yelled, 'Go, go, go!' If we didn't move fast enough, they took their helmets and hit us. Everyone was running through, getting cut and scraped from the barbed wire. The soldiers kicked and beat many of the people, and even shot some.

"No one was allowed to take anything with them. If they looked back to try to grab their things, they were shot. We could take no rice, no food, no belongings…nothing. While we were in the camp, if the Thai soldiers wanted to rape or take women, others couldn't help because they would be killed." Marilyn winces. "They raped many women, even with their husbands there and made them watch. They were worse than the Khmer Rouge had been to us." She shakes her head, in an expression of pity for the offenders rather than a display of disbelief of their actions.

"When they dumped us out in the forest, the chances of surviving under the conditions in which they left us were very slim. But what they didn't realize is that, after four years, our bodies, minds and souls were on automatic survival skills. We were too tired and too weak to think, to devise ways to stay alive. We had become hardened, in a mild sense, to "the worst of the worst" living conditions. Because we had to travel so slowly due to my father and my younger sister's condition, Joseph finally caught up with us. It was another of God's many miracles sent to us during that time."

Joseph, with the usual brightness in his voice, immediately takes over the story. "I was so worried, so afraid Marilyn and her family had been killed. The Thai and North Vietnamese soldiers were just as cruel as the Khmer Rouge regime had been. When the first bus left with Marilyn and her family, I was terribly distraught that I was unable to be on the same bus. It was a couple of days before another bus returned to take us away. I feared I would never see her again."

Joseph is an extremely meek person on the one hand; on the other, he has a resilience that refuses to give up, making him the quintessential example of the saying, "If at first you don't succeed, try again." One can sense immediately those things for which he has a passion; this is one of those things. Because of the tenderness in his voice, a question—which really needs no answer since it is already evident in his face and in his speech—comes to mind.

"Did you love Marilyn?" I ask. My own heart flutters with the remembrance of my father telling of the first time he saw my mother, with the words, "When we were both young, my family was visiting your mother's uncle at the same time as her family. I knew then I would marry her someday." Although it was not until years later they reconnected and married, my parents are now going on their 58th anniversary. A solitary glance at Joseph denotes the same expression of compassion I see in my father's face each time he tells that story.

"Yes," Joseph answers affectionately. His smile broadens as he glances in the mirror to see Marilyn's face. "I loved her but I knew I could not ask to marry her. Her mother had a rule that none of the men who lived in her apartments could marry one of her daughters. She didn't want the neighbors to criticize, saying she had a plan to catch available young men to marry her seven daughters. It was her generosity and care for others that led her to provide a need for poor students who had no place to stay to continue their education."

I sit dazzled, realizing Joseph just unearthed another huge puzzle piece, but rather than dig it up now, I prefer to let him finish their escape story. The marriage proposal can come later.

"That's why I was so distressed when they put the families and young women on the first bus, while the single men had to wait for the next bus. I knew she was gone forever. But I kept praying that I would one day find her again."

Care for others is such a dynamic quality of Joseph's that it makes perfect sense that he was not only concerned romantically with Marilyn, but for the safety of her family. He possesses a deep-seeded and genuine regard for those around him, making what he felt and feared grow out of a greater uneasiness for their general welfare. It also strikes me that Joseph, at this point, had no one else since he had been unable to reconnect with his family. They would have had no idea whether he was dead or alive, just as was his knowledge of them. Being the only survivor of his work camp, making him a loner, Marilyn and her family are naturally the only link to his past. *Just as he was the only link that came to mind when she was asked if she knew someone who could possibly sponsor her family,* I remind myself.

"I finally caught one of the buses, thinking it was taking us to a place with jobs. Like with Marilyn's family, it took us to the drop-off point in the forest. I ran as hard and fast as I could through the trees, trying to ignore the reek of human urine and feces. There were bloodied and rotting corpses everywhere. I was so terrified I would see Marilyn among them that I was devastated." The strain and intensity from that situation are still present in his voice.

"My only thought was to find her. It was nearly a week later, when I was walking through the forest and talking with some of the others in my group, that I located her."

The conversation takes on a ping-pong quality as both Marilyn and Joseph begin to paddle sentences of the story back and forth. "The forest was very dense," explains Marilyn. "There could be people practically next to you, on the other side of the bushes, but you could not see them. I was with my family at the spot where we stopped to spend the night. Suddenly I heard Joseph's voice and yelled out to him. It was three o'clock in the morning, but I didn't care."

"I heard her call my name," Joseph adds. "I was so happy. I knew immediately who it was. I took off running toward the sound of her voice as I yelled back, 'Sovann!'"

"He stayed with our family and helped take care of us. We all worked together to stay alive as we tried to get back to a safe place. Every morning we'd get up early and start walking and walk until late at night. It was horrible. The stench from all the dead bodies was revolting, and we could not drink the water because of all the people who died in the water. At night, we'd hear people yelling, 'Help! Help!' when they'd step on landmines as they tried to find water. But we couldn't help them because we would have also stepped on the landmines. This is how we lived for several weeks. I'm not even sure how long it had been, but we finally reached Kompong Thom province."

I know from my map that the Kompong Thom province has the second largest area of all the twenty-four provinces in Cambodia, and it sits halfway between Phnom Penh and Siem Reap. From having traveled to the Dangrek Mountains earlier in the morning, I perceive the distance they traveled on foot, not to mention the hardship of the areas, especially back during that time period. I cannot begin to imagine their encounters, much less their sustenance. Yet, Joseph's story of love and

Marilyn's story of the need to survive prepare me for what I must swallow next, as far as their journey goes.

"We were so hungry while we were lost in the deep forest," shares Marilyn. "We had no food with us so we had to try to find vegetation and fruit along the way. One night while we were asleep, a snake crawled across Joseph's stomach."

"While we had been walking deep in the forest of Preah Vihear province one night, Marilyn's father taught us that if a snake crawled across your body, let it get all the way across and then strike it with the ax." Joseph's comment leaves me with the question of where they'd gotten the ax, but also with the assurance it is a part of another miraculous tale.

"Joseph laid still and quiet until the snake had completely crossed his stomach. My father handed him the ax and he immediately killed it."

"Did you all hear this while it was happening?" I wonder aloud.

"Yes," she answers. "You learn to wake at the least brush of a leaf or the slightest movement. You never know what enemy, whether a soldier or a creature, will assault you. Yes, I heard, but no one moved, except for Pa handing him the ax, until the snake was dead. We cooked the snake and ate it. That was my first time to ever eat snake, but we were *so* hungry. I even ate dog during our second escape attempt. It was my first and only time." Her eyes are full of sorrow and distress, almost to the point of being apologetic. Yet her words stem from a time that no one, unless they have traveled in their paths—barefoot, as they had no shoes—can understand.

"While we were still in the Kompong Thom province," she continues, "we reached Kompong Thom, the capital of the province. It sits on the banks of the Stung Sen River and is a quaint place."

"We'll be there soon," Joseph interjects. "It's where we're stopping for lunch. Like many of the Cambodian provinces, it shares the same name as its capital."

"But at the time of our first escape," Marilyn admits, "it wasn't such a quaint place. It was almost night when we reached the river and we were terribly tired from walking so long that day. We decided to wait until the next morning to cross the river, after a good night's sleep." She shakes her head. "No one slept though. A big storm came and it rained so hard we couldn't sleep. Early the next morning, my father and Joseph made a raft out of bamboo to carry our things, mostly clothes, across. We wanted to keep them dry. When we tried to cross the river, the current was too strong."

"We had to go upstream about three-hundred feet," explains Joseph. "Marilyn's father and I pulled the raft while the others held onto the sides and tried to swim. The water was too high to walk across."

"I can still remember how hard it was," Marilyn adds. "We all nearly drowned because the water was running so fast." She gives a shudder. "I did not think we would make it across. We decided that if one of us drowned, we would all jump in and drown to be together."

Sounds like they had angels watching over them that day, I muse before reprimanding myself for such a mindless statement. *What day* didn't *they have angels watching over them…all day, all night?*

At the moment Marilyn reaches the conclusion of her story about crossing the river, we come to a large concrete bridge. It is closed to vehicular traffic so Joseph instructs us to get out of the car and walk across. The minute I step onto the bridge, I know where I am. It is National Highway 6, a road I traveled previously on a van with sixteen other Americans—including Mark—for a special teaching and mission project. Only then it took over eight hours to cover the same distance we will cover today in a little over two hours. The road is now paved and has been such a smooth ride I didn't even recognize it until seeing this spectacular bridge. Of course, it makes a difference that we haven't had two flat tires like the previous time, due to the rutted and poor condition of the dirt highway once pocked by craters from former bombings.

I well remember this stone bridge. It is an unbelievable masterpiece, built in the twelfth century like Angkor Wat. Its design, eighty meters long and fourteen meters wide is supported by twenty-one pilings, and is an engineering masterpiece. Also like Angkor Wat, it is pictured on one of their denominations of riel, Cambodia's currency. Because it has recently been named as an international tourist site, drivers may no longer cross it. They can, however, do the same as us and walk across it. I wonder how many people have passed over this same stone structure over the past nine centuries, and marvel how it has managed to last this long without major repair or renovation, especially given it was the only thoroughfare for large trucks during that entire time.

When we reach the middle of the bridge, where I have an unobstructed view in both directions, Marilyn points to the east where she and her "escape party" tried to cross it in 1979.

"This is *that* river?" I'm not sure whether I'm more flabbergasted or elated that I'm not only putting the pieces of this puzzle together, but I'm no longer puzzled by the many legs of their journey. I now have a clear picture of the places they went and how they got there. I've traveled not only a mile in their shoes, but hundreds of miles in their tracks. What a life they've lived, how far they've come, and what a difference they've made in so many lives.

I swallow hard as tears form while I contemplate on the task of writing this couple's story. *And hopefully how very many more lives will be affected by their story in print.*

"Come," invites Marilyn as she leads me to a small roadside stand, so close to the road it's practically in the road. Since cars can no longer cross the ancient Spean Kampong Kdei Bridge, though, I don't worry; the vendor is in no danger of being hit. "This place is known for its beautiful wooden carvings," she states as she picks up a lovely, unique wooden purse with a circular shape.

My eyes are drawn to a beautiful clock, which is every bit as intricately detailed as the ones from Germany's Black Forest, minus the cuckoo. The varieties of woods used in each of the creations are spectacular. From the corner of my eye, I spy the most magnificently ornate bedroom suite I've ever seen. The richness of the wood is exquisite, with its uncommon reddish-orange color.

"Is that for sale?" I ask the woman manning this stand, with the help of Marilyn's translation. Her nod serves as my answer. "How much?" I further inquire, rubbing my thumb and fingers together. She recognizes the gesture for "money."

"Twenty-eight hundred dollars."

She also understands American currency, I'm quick to note. The bed, which is king-sized, is massive in its design of lotus flowers and cranes, with so much articulate artwork on the headboard that it tells a story. It is the kind of furniture you see in an estate home in America; it is the only kind of home large enough for it. I hate to think what the cost would be in my country. The craftsmanship is extraordinary. What I witness is uncanny artistic ability, talent and skill beyond measure, a custom work of art fit for a king…and sadly, no way to market it. I now understand why one of Joseph's goals is to educate the people of his country so they have the knowledge to not only know how to market, but become viable competitors in world trade using their unique skills and resources. One last glance at the bed reminds me of Chandra's earlier statement about the beautiful hardwoods, near the Thai border, being cut and sold illegally. Now I see their true worth.

I purchase a small wooden elephant to remind me of this day and its many discoveries before we join Joseph, who is now waiting on the other side of the bridge in the vehicle. He drives only a few feet before he again stops, this time for lunch. Like with the bridge, I recognize this "roadside café."

"Many people stop here for lunch on their way between Siem Reap and Phnom Penh," Marilyn informs me about the simple roofed establishment, with a bar area and many tables on the dirt floor.

There are no walls, except at the back in the kitchen area where supplies are stored. Plastic outdoor tables and chairs, no tablecloths, are the furnishings with a décor of budvases containing small artificial flowers. The food is nothing fancy, but absolutely delicious, as evidenced by the array of industrial workers, travelers and common folk gathered here.

There are outside toilets. Actually, they're three holes in the ground, encased by a structure with three hinged doors. There is a large concrete pool of dirty water with a pot in each stall. That is to pour into the toilet to make it flush. One door is marked for men, one for women and the other is for whom ever gets there first. None of this matters; for such a long road trip, it is a welcome break—even if the road is now paved and the trip is six hours shorter.

Although National Highway 6 is the main—and at one time, the only—thoroughfare between the country's two largest cities, I immediately feel I'm at a roadside stop along Route 66 in Missouri or New Mexico, only fifty years earlier. The afternoon brings fond memories of a time before interstates took over America's most renowned road that stretched across the country. As we enjoy a few moments of relaxation before completing our homeward journey, Marilyn turns to me. "This is the province of the women you met at Tuol Sleng."

"The ones who lost so many family members?"

"Yes. There was much killing here. We were afraid when we were traveling through this area but, fortunately, the people we encountered along the way were most helpful to us. There was a Chinese family who was living in the forest near here after we crossed the river. We were scared of them at first, but they invited us to eat with them. They had very little food, but shared what they had with us. That night, they slept outside and let us sleep in their hut so we could get a good night's sleep. It seems that God put many kind people in our path along the way to protect us."

"Angels?" I ask.

"Yes, angels," she replies with a smile. I'm sure at the time, they were considered Buddhist angels, but now she realizes it was God providing for her and for her family. As if she reads my mind, Marilyn winsomely adds, "Before we believed in angels we believed we were just lucky. Now we know Psalm 91. God sent his angels to protect us." A look of peace and contentment fills her face. Sitting, eating and relaxing in this place, so near where so much of this scenario took place, gives her a chance to not only replay the details in her mind, but share the story of her family's liberation from beginning to the end. We all sit back in our chairs to listen, learn and allow our dear sister an end to the torment caused by the darkest character of her past.

"The workers on the main road learned of the liberation before the ones in the distant villages. It was weeks, the end of February, before some groups learned of their release, even though Liberation Day was January 7th. Some people in our camp had become like my family, but soldiers threatened to kill anyone of them who helped us because the Khmer Rouge wanted to pillage what we had left. This was when my mother paid the beautiful ring to the man with the cow cart. It was still dark when we left. There were lots of people going in every direction. Parents were looking for their children, and the crowd was busy and chaotic. When our family reached the main road, daylight was breaking so I ran along behind the cow cart. I got a glimpse of the bad man. Some of our friends also saw him following us, so they ran after us yelling,

'Let's go!' They told us they'd seen a flashlight in our hut where the man had come to kill us, after he'd slept off his drunken stupor, but we had already gone. When our friends left the village, the flashlight was still on and the man was standing in the hut, angry and disappointed, and swearing to get us.

"He had come to our hut the evening before with some of the other soldiers. They had been drinking heavily. He said, 'We are really sorry for the way we treated you.' I'll never forget his face. He was so drunk his eyes were red. We were all terrified. They finally left and fell asleep just next door to our hut. That's when we took off still in the middle of the night. We knew it was a far walk to this bridge, more than two hours on foot, but we ran behind the cow cart even though we were all in bad health. Near the bridge, we sat down and waited for our father while the man with the cow cart went back. It was a long while before Pa arrived because he was walking with our small wooden cart.

"The next morning we were in a crowd of people in the main road and the bad man found us again. We didn't feel safe. A family who owned a house on the street invited us inside. The owner, who was a Chinese Cambodian, told us, 'I saw that man lurking around your family. Do not go outside. You're not safe.' He felt sorry for us because he saw our father, so sick and so old and skinny, and our handicapped sister. She was so skinny and dehydrated and starving. I, too, was sick and my older sister's skin didn't look good. 'You can't stay long,' he said,' but stay long enough to get your handicapped daughter a little stronger.' He knew he was in danger for taking us in, but he felt so sorry for us."

Marilyn gives an appreciative smile. "When we were finally able to again travel, and the bad man was no longer hanging around outside, the Chinese Cambodian warned us, 'Do not travel together. You must divide into groups.' So my mother rented another cow cart to carry my handicapped sister and told my youngest sister to follow it. Ma, two of my sisters and I were in another group. My father pulled the wooden cart we had from the village. It was filled with our belongings, which had the remainder of our gold hidden inside them. My older sister walked behind and her baby rode on the cart. Ma gave the order, 'The cow cart go first, our group in the middle and father last.' We prepared to leave with her shouting, 'Whoever can go fastest, go!'

"It was early one morning when we left that house and we walked until it was nearly dark. Ma and I had no idea where the other two groups were. With the sun about to set, we saw a house. We glanced at the faces of the people who lived there to see they looked okay. They were kind and allowed us to go up and sleep on their pillowed floor while they slept on the ground underneath with the chickens. We were still afraid the bad man would follow us, so we felt safe and were greatly appreciative. After we carried our belongings up the stairs and lay down, we were so worried about the other two groups that we could not sleep. Yet we didn't know what else to do so we stayed there to let our bodies take a break even though we were terrified for the rest of the family.

"About three or four in the morning, we heard the man ask his wife, 'Do we want to kill the fat one or the skinny one?' They were talking back and forth and we overheard the wife say, 'Whisper! Say it quiet.' The four of us looked at each other in disbelief. We knew our lives were in danger again. Mother stood at the front door to watch for them. Even though I was sick, I was the largest of our group so mother said, 'When they come, you run as fast as you can. I will protect you. Don't worry about me.'

"We stayed completely still and waited for them for a few minutes but they did not come. After that, Ma said, 'I'll tell you when to jump.' She stood holding a bamboo pole ready to protect us. That's when we heard the rooster and realized they were talking about which chicken to kill, not us." Marilyn gives a hearty laugh.

"Ma instructed us to gather our belongings so we could leave immediately. 'Thank you for letting us stay here,' my mother told them. She never mentioned how frightened we were that they were going to kill us.

"'Oh, please don't leave so early. Breakfast is almost already cooked,' the man's wife said. They had cooked the chicken and made rice for us. When we'd eaten all we could, they wrapped the leftovers in banana leaves for us to carry with us."

She laughs again. "That was such a funny story. We still laugh about it every time someone mentions it." I suspect the story and their laughter was a healing dose of medicine, as well as the fattened and cooked chicken, in that time of fear and strife.

"Angels come in strange appearances," she continues, a broad smile still on her face. "Shortly after we left that house, we saw this ugly old female dog. Ma said, 'I believe she's hungry.' She tried to give it some of the rice and chicken we had but the dog wouldn't eat. It became like our protection. If we went, it went. If we stopped, it stopped. It stayed with us the whole time.

"While we were traveling with the dog, we saw a car. It was a Vietnamese cab driver. He was waiting for a group of people but they had not arrived yet. 'You want to go to Siem Reap?' he asked us. My mother was crying because she didn't want to leave the dog. 'Can we take her with us?' she asked the cab driver. 'No,' he answered, 'it's skinny and ugly.' We later decided that was a good thing because the Vietnamese like to eat dog. If it had been a good healthy dog, he'd have kept it, but because it was so skinny and ugly, he didn't. We climbed in the cab and headed toward Siem Reap. Along the way, we saw the cow cart with my handicapped sister and youngest sister. Ma paid the cow cart owner and we took my sisters with us in the cab to the city. "Because there was nowhere to go we had to sleep on the sidewalk. After a few days, Ma began to ask people if they had seen an older man with a small wooden cart and a baby. 'It's broke in the middle of the road,' someone told her. 'It cannot come.'

"My mother took my three sisters to go back and help carry the baby, and the things from the cart, while I stayed with my handicapped sister. They saw the old, ugly dog again on the road. It led them to my father. When they returned to where I was in the city, the dog followed them until we were all together again in Siem Reap. Then the dog just went away. We didn't know where it was going. All of us agreed the dog was an angel sent to protect us because we had done good things for others. My mother gave it food before it left, but again it wouldn't eat."

"One way or the other, God certainly had his angels guarding you," is the only comment I can manage.

"Yes," Marilyn replies softly and reflectively as we gather our belongings to go.

Our bellies full, our legs stretched and our minds and bodies refreshed, we pile in the Land Cruiser to pick up the escape story where we left off, as we travel the last leg of our journey back to Phnom Penh.

We've not gone two full miles when Marilyn points to a pagoda on our right. "When we were walking from Phnom Penh, we spent the night there. My mother found a stainless steel pot with five sections in it. We were able to use the sections for plates once we reached the work camp."

I remember that Marilyn's mother had to cook for the entire village where she stayed and think what a valuable find she had made. *Or, rather, that God placed in her path for the days and long journey ahead.*

As if she could read my mind, Marilyn smiled and nodded. "My family was lucky that my mother found the pot. We also had a fork for each of us."

She looks at me and her kind smile turns to one of trust. "I have a story I want to tell you now. Being here today reminded me of it. When we were dumped in the forest by the Thai soldiers, one of them took pity on my father because he was old and slow. He secretly handed my father his small ax used by the soldiers. It's the ax my father and Joseph used to cut the bamboo to make the raft when we crossed the river," she explains. "The soldier told my father he was really Khmer, so he wanted to help us. He also warned my father that we should all stay together in a group, especially between certain hours because the soldiers would rape the daughters. 'Don't let them get too far away from you,' he advised, 'and keep the ax handy for protection.' We could not believe our good luck."

Joseph speaks a few words in Khmer to her, calling her attention to where we are.

"It was off in that direction," she relays, pointing to our left, "that the snake crawled across Joseph's stomach and he killed it."

"With the ax the Thai soldier gave your father?"

"Yes," she responds, smiling at my ability to figure out the pieces of the story. "My father quietly slipped it to Joseph as he whispered for him not to move and wait until it had completely crossed his stomach." Marilyn and I share a happy moment as we both realize I now fully understand another of their stories.

"It was months before we finally reached the rest of my family in Siem Reap. They were living in an old abandoned factory because someone else was already living in the house that once belonged to my family there. When we did arrive, we learned Ma had received a letter from my oldest sister and her husband. It said, 'We're alive and in Phnom Penh.' She sent Joseph to get them. She also told him the location of the place where she used to hide gold and jewelry in our old four-story house in the city, hoping it might still be there."

"She trusted me," Joseph interjects proudly. "When I got to their old house, I found the hiding place. I knocked on it first to see if it was hollow. The sound I heard prepared me for what I was about to see. Everything was gone. Robbers had left nothing."

My mind goes immediately to the stories of the spoils of war from the Old Testament, and then to the much later stories of pillage during America's own civil war stories, as my heart aches for her family's depressing discovery.

"Everyone considered her rich, even though she never showed it to look at her." Marilyn pauses for a brief reflective moment, as if in her eyes, she was reexamining the scene. "It broke her heart that she had lost everything, but she, like the rest of us, realized the important thing was we were all back together after Joseph returned with my sister and her husband, and their children.

"She did manage to have a few items of value that made it through the work camp. Thus, she took back her role as our protector. She had a strong spirit. She wanted all of us daughters to be teachers. That had always been her dream. She never even made us do many house chores when we were growing up. She did everything all by herself so we could study. She did not want us running the pawn shop. She wanted us to have an education, and be able to educate others."

So that's why she didn't allow Marilyn to go on to school to become a lawyer when she was younger, I reason.

Marilyn gives a small chuckle. "In fact, even though my father never spent time with his daughters, it was him who taught us to cook rice. Not my mother. He was a quiet person, soft-spoken, but he was responsible. We didn't dare to try to be very close with him because he was so very strict and didn't spend time with us. He never played with us, and thought we should not waste time playing." She gave another chuckle, a larger one that hinted that a good childhood story was on the rise.

"When we were children, I'd talk my older sister into playing games with me. I'd make sure I got the seat looking out the window so I could see my father coming down the street on his way home. When I saw him, I'd always have to go get a drink, so I'd leave my sister there at the table playing the game. He'd get really mad and she'd be the one in trouble."

Ever the clever one! I muse, laughing as I think about how much sibling rivalry there must have been in her family with seven girls, with only a couple of years between each. I reminiscence about the same kinds of stunts my own two sons used to pull on each other. But then, if anyone else dared to lay a hand on either of them, he had better watch out.

As I mull over the humorous story, I also reflect over the stress her father must have been under with his undercover position. I recall her earlier words when she'd told me about his work in the military, when he had to ride a bicycle in plain clothes to inspect and write reports on the arsenal. "Had one gun gone missing, he would have been killed." I recognize that his world was occupied by his own personal risk, the risk of his family and the approaching war at the time—all of which I'm sure he kept secretive to his family, or at least his daughters.

"Shortly after we arrived," admits Joseph, "I asked my cousin to speak to Marilyn's mother on my behalf about marriage. It was this cousin who was married to Marilyn's aunty, and had arranged for me to live in one of the apartments."

"My mother, ignoring her rule, asked me if I wanted to marry him. I told her, 'Yes.' People tried to discourage me from marrying him. They said he was too old and poor, that he owned no land. But I didn't care. I did not look at the outside or his lack of possessions. All I saw was the inner beauty of Joseph. It was his character that drew me to him. He was such a good person, always doing things for others, and he was honest. He spoke from his heart so I trusted him. That was important to me in a time when you could trust no one."

"So her mother allowed us to be married," Joseph announces giddily.

"There was no monk because they had all been killed. My mother had to use a priest. There were no fancy festivities, no music and no electricity, only a small wedding. We did have some food…a chicken, I think. And people brought some food."

Her words prove a point I've long believed. The only necessities for a marriage are the bride, the groom, the minister and God's presence and blessing; it is not the elaborate ceremony. My point is further proven by the sight of these two. Never have I seen a more loving couple, who genuinely respect each other, than Joseph and Marilyn.

"We got married on November 9, 1979," Marilyn continues. "It was the anniversary of Cambodia's independence from the French Colonial rule, but no one thought about that at the time." She pauses for a moment as she looks admirably at her husband. "He made hats for us to wear."

I notice a slight blush on Joseph's cheek. "It was only two weeks after our wedding when we planned our second escape," he continues slowly, beginning another adventure of their life's story. "We decided my new brother-in-law and I would go first to make sure it was safe for the others because Vietnamese soldiers were still patrolling the roads."

"They went away and did not come back for several weeks," adds Marilyn. "My sister and I went to the Banteay Meanchey province to find Joseph's other brother-in-law, in hopes that he had heard from them. We walked, letting my sister's four children ride on an oxcart through the jungle. I remember that it was pulled by a pair of black-and-white oxen. I don't know why that fact sticks out in my mind. One day, when it was nearly dark and hard to see very far in front of us, we came to the mountain we had to cross. The mountainside was very quiet and there was no one anywhere around except for our family. We were afraid to stop, so we proceeded until we came to three small paths. Not knowing which to take, I finally chose the middle path. We had barely started walking on it when we spotted two men in the distance. Everything was so hushed around us that we became frightened they were thieves coming to rob us. It turned out to be Joseph and his brother-in-law. After that, we soon left again for our second attempt to reach Thailand, this time determined to reach the United Nations-sponsored refugee camp, which was farther inside the border than where we'd fled the first time."

"We still had a treacherous journey," states Joseph emphatically. "One day while we were walking, four Khmer Rouge soldiers spotted us and came toward us. They held guns, B-40s and AK-47s, in our faces and demanded to know where we were going. 'We are trying to find food for our children,' I told them. Miraculously, they let us go. We were all so thankful we didn't know what to do. Thank God! Thank God!"

"So many people died during that time while they were searching for food and water," Marilyn shares drearily. "There were landmines everywhere, but people were so hungry and thirsty. The Khmer Rouge had planted landmines near many of the rivers and lakes so that when we attempted to get water, we would be killed or hurt. They were determined we would not have anything they didn't give us."

In that sudden instant, her eyes tell the story of many sleepless nights, of long, hot days—and nights—in the rice fields, and the tiring walks to and from them, the starvation from the lack of food and water, and the harrowing counts of their escape attempts. "The escape was so difficult and haunting. Along the route, we witnessed so many dead bodies. Many of the bodies were without heads when we reached the Dangrek Mountain range along the Thai and Cambodian borders. The road there was terribly hard to travel because it is so very steep on the Cambodia side. Once you top the mountain, the Thai side is a kinder slope."

Her words strike me as indicatively prophetic of their escape journey as I reflect on the cumbersome terrain of those mountains, witnessed on our venture to find Pol Pot's cremation site on the heels of visiting Ta Mok's house and the Khmer Rouge headquarters. My musical background prevails as I hear echoes of *There's Within My Heart a Melody* ringing in my mind. *Perhaps those hills are alive with more music than I suspected,* I tell myself as I take the clue for my next question.

"How did you learn about Christ?"

"Marilyn and I accepted Jesus Christ as our Savior in Kao I Dang, the United Nations refugee camp in Thailand, after our second escape," Joseph announces proudly.

"Some people who befriended us in the refugee camp invited us to go to the church meetings with them," Marilyn interjects. "It was so nice to be a part of any kind of group other than a work camp."

It is totally understandable, after the life they'd lived during the years of Pol Pot's reign, that an invitation into a Christian community would have been a breath of fresh air. I think about the refreshing water—pouring down from the waterfall Christina had pointed out earlier—and imagine that moving from where they were, and into a bond with Christian missionaries and Jesus' teachings, would be like standing under that waterfall, letting its cool, cascading water flood one's soul while providing an invigorating and energizing respite from a world of strife. Thinking how any life would be better than what they'd experienced, making it easy to be drawn into a loving community, Joseph proves my theory to be correct with his next statement.

"We were anxious to get away from the communist government. It was not like I had been taught from the Yugoslavian and Korean communist governments. When I was in college I felt that was the best way for our country. Seeing it in action revealed just the opposite. Therefore we strongly sought for peace and freedom with a clear conscience, mind and heart."

"When we finally reached the refugee camp, we felt safe," stated Marilyn. "While walking through the forest to get there, we endured many storms along the way. But they were worth it to get far away from the life we were living in Cambodia. It was a world without hope, meaning, purpose, love, honor, justice and equality. We felt so dehumanized."

"In the refugee camp," continues Joseph, "someone told us, 'If you want to go to another country, you should believe in Jesus Christ.'"

I don't recall that verse in the scriptures, I muse with a silent chuckle. Yet on a serious note, from my many interviews with survivors of the Khmer Rouge, I understand exactly what Joseph means. The words "go" and "another country" are primary to their interest at that time. "Believe" and "Jesus Christ" are merely secondary words, a means to an end. Their only concern is what would forever displace them from the life they had known the past four years.

Those are the same words that have "caught" many of the "Rice Christians" by "fishers of men." "Rice Christians" has become the term for persons who accept Christ solely for the gain of food from missionaries. Although this expression sometimes receives a negative connotation, it has also reaped many rewards, as is evident in the lives of Joseph and Marilyn, as well as many other Cambodian Christians around the world.

"Some of the other refugees told us, 'Whoever believed in God would be able to go to America, Australia, Canada or the United Kingdom.' It was a simple offering and message, with nothing to lose on our part. Think about it, 'Belief in Jesus will be able to take you to America.'

"Then," Joseph plows forward, "on the next Sunday, we went to listen and paid attention to the real message given by the missionaries. We began to attend church week after week, several times each week for a Bible study and were encouraged to read the New Testament for ourselves. At first I had my doubts about this new religion, thinking it couldn't be everything they said. But as we listened to more of the missionaries' messages, I was very much encouraged by the good teaching of the Word. It helped me learn and understand all of this information I had never before heard in my life.

"I became optimistic and hopeful when I read Matthew 6:33, which stated, 'Seek ye first the kingdom of God.' I began to find meaning in my life. When I read I Corinthians 13 about the love of Christ, and later Romans 12:1 – 2, it instructed me to live sacrificially and separated from worldly things. It was hard to just pick up and do everything the scriptures said all at one time. It took a few times of taking a couple of steps backwards and then forwards again. At first, we wanted to receive food and gifts from the charitable organizations. It was only a short while before we became serious about the principles and accepted Jesus Christ. Later, when we truly put our faith in Jesus Christ and fully embraced him as our Savior, we accepted our responsibility to share the message of his love and salvation for others.

"Mr. Nhem Sokun is the pastor who encouraged me to study and teach. At first, I told him I did not know how to teach, that I didn't know the materials, that I was still influenced by my Buddhist culture and ideals of the communist mind, and that I had a negative memory from such a horrible way of life of living in the communist country. But he was a great teacher and he didn't give up on me as he continued to push me in the direction of also being a teacher. 'In Christ,' he taught us, 'there is hope, life, love, value, forgiveness, honesty, faithfulness, respect, peace in heart and contentment.'" His comment receives a nod from Marilyn.

"'Hallelujah!' I finally exclaimed when I fully accepted Christ. I came to see that every wish and desire for all I wanted to have in my life, and for everyone on the earth, was found in Jesus Christ. Through Mr. Sokun's teachings, I continued to open my mind and eyes to further reveal the meaning of life found only in Jesus Christ."

"It was in December of 1979 when we were baptized," adds Marilyn enthusiastically.

"Marilyn, who had also accepted Christ, and I committed ourselves to evangelize the name of Jesus and his salvation for the remainder of our lives. We desired everyone to experience the peace, love and salvation that we had found. At first, we had limited Bible knowledge, so we simply told the others how Jesus had changed our lives and about the hope and salvation we had found through him. At the same time, we continued to learn about Christ by attending church school and Bible studies, by participating in the Christian services and helping out in the community, by spending time reading God's word every day, and by seeking to know Him more and more."

Joseph's enthusiasm grows with each statement. "Under Mr. Sokun's tutelage, I was eventually asked to lead the morning prayers and teach the Bible studies in the afternoons. The missionaries then requested that I lead the devotionals on Thursday mornings for the entire group. Soon after that, I became a lay leader for the camp.

"During the rest of our time at Kao I Dang, after accepting Christ and knowing him better, we lived a simple life and were content with the life God had given us. I served God solely for His glory. I helped out others who were discriminated against, believing if I helped one of these persons meet their needs, someone else would bless me when I needed it. I never expected to be repaid from those whom I helped. I was joyful to help others."

Some things never change, I ruminate as I listen to his final words, which perfectly depict his demeanor and attitude.

"During that time, I continued to see God pouring His blessings out to our family while experiencing increased joy and peace in my heart."

"But just because we became Christians didn't mean there weren't still hardships and struggles," Marilyn is quick to add. "We had been waiting for over two years in the refugee camp for our names to get on the immigration list so we could go to the United States."

"We later learned our names had been removed from the list because of my studies in the socialist countries of Yugoslavia and North Korea," explains Joseph. "We prayed fervently every day and night for God to help us find a way to immigrate."

"While we were still living in the refugee camp," Marilyn continues, "and our faith was growing stronger and stronger, we had a visitor come to our house one night. He secretly asked us to join the Khmer Rouge. A very persuasive man in his twenties, he told Joseph he would become a Khmer Rouge Ambassador for the communist party if he would join. After his visit, we prayed every day, asking for God's mercy, grace and wisdom. We were terribly frightened and feared for our lives. Even more so, we were extremely concerned about the safety of our first child, our son Nyda, who was only three months old at the time and had been born in the refugee camp.

"This visitor came several times after that and threatened that we would never be able to go to America. No one knew about him. We told no one, not even our mother, relatives or friends. We did not even ask the church members to pray for us about this. Just the two of us knelt on the ground of our small hut in the refugee camp every night. We prayed that God would open a door to get us out of there and prevent us from being harmed by this Khmer Rouge visitor. During the day time, we were extra careful because we knew we were being watched closely. Our lives were in danger again. We kept asking ourselves where we could go to escape the Khmer Rouge leaders."

"We are so grateful for Marilyn's adoptive mother," shares Joseph. "God sent this woman to us in the refugee camp."

"There was an older woman, Siv Try, in the camp," Marilyn explains, "who had lost her husband and four children due to the civil war. The only one she had left was a six-year-old son, Siv Hak, with whom she had been pregnant when separated from her family. She was on the immigration list but the only way she could get to America was if she had family to go and help her because she could not speak, read or write English. The only thing she knew how to read was the Khmer Bible, which she learned by attending church in the refugee camp.

"A Christian friend in the refugee camp, Sa Vorn, introduced her to us. Siv Try had a great love and respect for Sa Vorn because he was such a good person. He encouraged her to accept me as her daughter and told her she should love Joseph as much as she did him because Joseph was also a very good man. She accepted Sa Vorn's word and notified the immigration officer that she had found her daughter."

"Is this the same man, now called Sam Vorn, who served in Lon Nol's army prior to Pol Pot and who is now a United Methodist minister in Modesto, California?" I ask.

"Yes," answers Marilyn with a huge smile and that affirmative side nod of her head. Then, continuing with her fascinating account, she adds, "We knew there would be a struggle to prove my relationship to Siv Try because of the extremely difficult screening process. When the day arrived that the immigration officer invited us for the interview, we were worried about what questions she would ask us."

"We asked the congregation to pray for us," interjects Joseph, taking over the story. "Marilyn had to memorize every detail regarding her adoptive mother so when questions arose, there would be no hesitation or doubt of them being related. When we entered the room for the interview session, Marilyn was so panicked she was out of breath. The next thing we knew, the officer stood up, walked toward us, lifted Marilyn's hair and touched her earlobe. She then went over to Siv Try and did the same thing."

"'Their earlobes are similar. You are really mother and daughter. You are accepted!' the officer suddenly exclaimed in a loud outburst," states Marilyn with animated vigor. "We could hardly believe our ears. We knew then God had blessed us and been in charge of that screening."

"Thank God! Thank God!" exclaims Joseph. "We were so joyful, but yet so scared something could still happen. It was too good to be true. We arrived in the Bronx in New York City on January 6, 1982. We immediately began English classes because it was so hard. At first, we didn't have electricity and could not communicate with anyone. It really was a strange new world because *everything* was different."

"That sounds much like your time in the work camps when you weren't allowed to speak to anyone." But then I know from experience how much tougher the same situations are in a foreign country. I try to imagine myself in Cambodia with no friends and no translator. That's when his exact words hit me. "You arrived in the Bronx on January 6th?"

"Yes," Joseph and Marilyn answer at the same time. "With our adoptive mother and her son, and our son."

"That was your own epiphany!" I exclaim. "How prophetic was that? You were not supposed to arrive in New York until then. Like Jesus at the wedding in Cana, your time had not yet come. You arrived at your new home on Epiphany!"

"I never thought of that," says Marilyn with a laugh as she joins in my excitement.

"Do you realize everything of significance and every bridge you've crossed has happened on a date that shares an anniversary with another monumental anniversary, whether good or bad, in the life of your country and the Christian faith?" I begin to list all the shared dates and events.

Marilyn picks up on what becomes a game of lists as I continue to place pieces in this ever-increasing puzzle of their life.

"That's when you changed your name the first time, to Siv Sovann instead of Tor Sovann?" I reason aloud.

"Yes. I had to change my name for the Visa," answers Marilyn.

"What about when you married Joseph? Did your name not change then?"

"No. In the Cambodian custom a woman does not take the husband's name. That's why it was no problem for my maiden name to be changed to Siv Sovann before coming to America. Since we were married in Siem Reap, we didn't have paperwork, only thumbprints."

"So Joseph was able to travel with his own birth name?"

"Yes," he answers with a nod.

"It was nearly six months before we actually felt released from our fear," states Marilyn, a hint of trepidation still in her voice as she continues her story. "It was not until our plane took off the ground in Bangkok, Thailand, that we knew for certain God had truly made a way for us to finally escape the Khmer Rouge and communism. We prayed the entire time until the plane took off from the ground. Once we were in the air, we praised God for His protection, wisdom and faithfulness. Tears were streaming down our faces. We were overjoyed!"

"Thank God! Thank God! Praise the Lord!" exclaims Joseph with the glimmer of a tear of joy.

Their tempter was a real test of faith, I contemplate, *with Marilyn's adoptive mother serving as their 'open door.'*

"We were finally safe from this Khmer Rouge leader who wanted us to be ambassadors in Senegal, South Africa. Marilyn and I refused to go back to Cambodia during that time. But we did promise God that we would one day go back to spread the gospel. We did not return until 1993, after the ceasefire agreements and we felt it was safe to go there," Joseph concludes, leaving me speechless.

There is no way to respond to such a remarkable story, when they've said all there is to say. I look behind me in the direction of the mountains, now far away in the distance, that eventually carried them to freedom.

On second thought, those hills really were *alive with music,* I determine as words to an old hymn, *He Keeps Me Singing,* floods my soul. I'm sure this particular hymn and tune—written by Luther B. Bridgers, a fellow North Carolinian who was an ordained Methodist minister and who traveled abroad to do mission work in Belgium, Czechoslovakia and Russia—no more "happened" to come to mind any more than the other events of this day just "happened." Although Bridgers' well-known hymn was penned precisely a century before in 1910, when his wife and three sons were killed in a tragic house fire, its words still ring as true for the lives and experiences of Joseph and Marilyn as they do in my heart, along with the melody that brought the parallel to my attention. In the silence of the moments that follow, I sing the hymn—written by a man, who also lived a life of faith, hope and love—silently as I read over my "divinely inspired" notes.

There's within my heart a melody
Jesus whispers sweet and low,
Fear not, I am with thee, peace, be still,
In all of life's ebb and flow.

Refrain: Jesus, Jesus, Jesus,
Sweetest Name I know,
Fills my every longing,
Keeps me singing as I go.

All my life was wrecked by sin and strife,
Discord filled my heart with pain,
Jesus swept across the broken strings,
Stirred the slumbering chords again.
REFRAIN

Feasting on the riches of His grace,
Resting 'neath His sheltering wing,
Always looking on His smiling face,
That is why I shout and sing.
REFRAIN

Though sometimes He leads through waters deep,
Trials fall across the way,
Though sometimes the path seems rough and steep,
See His footprints all the way.
REFRAIN

Soon He's coming back to welcome me,
Far beyond the starry sky;
I shall wing my flight to worlds unknown,
I shall reign with Him on high.
REFRAIN

Yes, I decide confidently, *Joseph and Marilyn may not have that melody ringing in their hearts, but they know those words. They've lived them.*

"Wait a minute!" I exclaim, suddenly leaving my pleasant daydream behind. "When did you change your names to Marilyn and Joseph?" I look at Marilyn. "And when did you take Joseph's last name?"

Marilyn smiles such a beautiful smile that it gives me chills. It is a smile that, without a doubt, says she surely "knows the sweetest name that fills her every longing."

"We needed American names when we arrived in the United States. I thought Marilyn was a beautiful name and we really liked the name Joseph."

That's appropriate, I figure. *Mary and Joseph would be names they know well and Marilyn sounds a lot like Mary. And they certainly fit the model of two strangers coming into a foreign land. Rather,* I decide, *they fit the role of two refugees hitting town, which is the image I have of Mary and Joseph arriving at Bethlehem instead of the picture-perfect couple on all the Christmas cards. The fact that both couples have a baby makes my image of Joseph and Marilyn even more picture-perfect.*

"It wasn't until a few years later," Marilyn continues, "that I took Joseph's last name. I got tired of people asking if we weren't married."

I laugh, understanding that would be the typical reaction of nosy American women, especially in a fundamentalist church, at that point in time. The fact that Marilyn knows *two* sweetest names that fill her every longing, Jesus and Joseph, is a touching reality.

"Is your adoptive mother still alive?" I ask.

"Yes, very much so," answers Marilyn. "She takes care of our house in Stockton. Christina will live with her when she goes to college in California in the fall. Our other two children were older when we returned to Cambodia as missionaries so they wanted to stay in the States. They have a close kinship with her so she watched over them, enabling them to finish their education in America, when we came back here. We feel blessed that they both still live and work in California and will be there when Christina goes."

The bright smile on Christina's face serves as a sign of confidence at having friends and family nearby when she arrives to a new world. Although Joseph and Marilyn will accompany her to the States, and Marilyn will stay for a short while to make sure she's settled, this is a brave new venture for their youngest child.

"God blessed us so richly by sending Marilyn's adoptive mother to us," Joseph adds proudly.

"As you blessed her by being her ticket to her own family and freedom," I remind him with a heart warmed by their story of faith, hope and love in action.

Chapter Eighteen

It is a restlessly somber day, and one which allows me to fully comprehend—as much as is possible for a foreigner coming in thirty-plus years after the fact—the reality of what Marilyn encountered each day of her life for the more-than-three-years she existed in a work camp. (Notice I did not say "live," for it was an existence, nothing more.) The drive to her former village and work camp sites also provides me an indication of exactly how long and tedious their evacuation from Phnom Penh to this place was, for we are still several hours away from the capital city by car on a good paved road. *Not to mention all the time it will take to work our way out of all these dirt paths leading deep into the forest and jungles of these hidden villages,* I remind myself.

Joseph makes a left turn onto a small path that is hardly wider than our vehicle. There are no shoulders, or even edges, on the road. It simply blends into the trees and growth on each side.

"This is it. This is my village," states Marilyn softly, though without apprehension.

I feel a humbling rush brush over me as it seems we are literally leaving the real world and floating away, transformed into a world we can see, but which is not really there. I am reminded of the set for the play *Our Town,* as I try to imagine what this must feel like for Marilyn. It is her first time to visit this place since she lived here all those years ago. For me, it's like I'm sitting in the audience of a theater, watching the action of a drama behind a black scrim, and then suddenly being whisked away into the setting behind the curtain.

The poverty level of this area is as poor as I've witnessed in this country. Many of the huts have no roof; some have roofs and no walls. In front of me, a woman is walking onto the path from the yard of one of the nicer huts. Balanced on her right shoulder is a long wooden pole with a basket, heavily laden with bunches of ripening finger bananas, on each end.

Marilyn lunges forward, pokes Joseph in the back and hastily mutters something in Khmer. He immediately stops the Land Cruiser in the middle of the dirt path. She opens the back door, crawls over Christina and gets out excitedly. We all watch as the two women say a couple of words to each other. The village woman carefully drops her load to the ground as she and Marilyn embrace. Marilyn then turns back to us and energetically blurts out something in Khmer.

"That was the person assigned to spy on Ma's family when they lived here," Christina translates.

My jaw drops. We drive into a faraway place, seemingly forbidden judging from the time it took to get here, where this survivor of the Khmer Rouge has not set foot in thirty-one years—since Liberation Day—and the first person she spots is the very one who kept a constant watch on her family. *Her enemy of enemies,* I reason. What are the chances? For one who leaves little to chance, I recognize God's hand immediately and sense the rest of our day "behind the imaginary scrim on this stage" will be just as miraculous. Emotions churn inside me like a continual round of fireworks going off. I cannot imagine what Marilyn must feel.

I am certain God is looking down on this act of forgiveness and reconciliation between two of his children, one who recognizes Him and one who doesn't, with great joy. Mark and I are both too overjoyed for words. It is apparent God has ordered our steps for this entire trip, but especially this day.

We all jump from the vehicle with Mark snapping photos with every step. It is difficult to tell who in our entourage is most excited. Marilyn begins making introductions as we each show our respect with a sampeah and the words, "Chum Reap Suor." The woman beams and returns the greeting. She is just as thrilled at this "chance" meeting as we are as she continues talking to Marilyn.

"She's asking about Marilyn's mother," Chandra shares, keeping us abreast of their conversation in Khmer.

The two women chat for a few short minutes while other family members, several of whom are young children, appear from the hut. I reach in the back of the Land Cruiser for cookies I've brought from home for "emergency" binges. At the moment, my only "binge" is to offer these children a treat. By the time I return to the yard, only ten or twelve steps, the number of children has grown. I break the large cookies into halves and give one to each child. The smiles on their faces are much more filling than any cookies I could have eaten.

They are as fascinated with Mark's camera as they are with the cookies. Only one boy is camera shy, but by the time he's finished his cookie, he warms up to being a part of our large group shot. I have Marilyn ask the woman if I can pick up the wooden yoke and place it on my shoulder for a photograph. A nod is the only invitation I need to lift the load, which I soon learn is much heavier than one would imagine. Laden with enough bananas to make a week's living, the weight is extremely cumbersome just to hold, much less walk to the nearest market miles away.

As I place the pole and baskets back on the ground, Marilyn states, "Cambodian women have very strong necks. Men, too." Her comment reminds me of the scripture about the sparrows and the lilies of the field. God clothes us with what we need. That is what enables the Cambodians to also carry rice in huge bundles on their heads on top of a krama, or the women to carry a heavy clay pot filled with water. From the first time I ever set foot on Cambodian soil, I have marveled while watching people carry all their loads balanced on their heads, whether walking, peddling a bicycle or riding a motorbike. It isn't until now I understand the complexity of that task.

Marilyn reaches into the Land Cruiser and then discreetly hands her former "spy" a bit of money. That's when I also notice the village woman reach into one of her baskets and pull out a large bunch of the bananas. It is a captivatingly unforgettable moment.

As our group heads back to the vehicle, another woman sprints diagonally across the path. She recognizes Marilyn and comes to ask how her mother is. I consider how remarkable it is the village women remember a person after such a long while, given the type of setting in which they existed. But then, given the workers are probably the only people who ever stepped foot in their village besides themselves, perhaps it isn't so abnormal they recognize her; this is not a transient community. I'm filled with rejoicing when I learn this woman was the leader of the work camp, and consider how ironic it is that the two persons who were her worst enemies are the very ones to run to welcome her. *All those extra things Marilyn's mother did for the community did not go unnoticed,* I see. That notion causes me to wonder if these two women remember any of the other workers who lived here or whether the rest were merely nameless faces.

There were typically only twenty families in a village or work camp, which normally ranged from 100 – 200 workers; that's how communist "communes" work. *And it's how the base people were able to keep an eye on the "prisoners without walls."* It dawns on me that all the new communities we've seen rising up along the way to Thailand consists of only fifteen to twenty huts, just like the old communities and villages. People here still know their neighbors. *And their neighbors of thirty-five years ago.*

My mind briefly mulls over that perception. *People here still* do *know their neighbors,* I repeat silently, while watching the crowd around Marilyn multiply as villagers leave their huts, or their spots under the trees, to come and see this wondrous thing which has happened. It makes the story of the shepherds, coming to the manger to see the child, so realistic I have chills. *Oh, if only they will come running to see the real Christ child,* I pray.

Then I stare, no longer blindly through a black scrim, but at the beautiful scene unfolding in front of me. The scene, which only moments earlier reminded me of a drama behind the scrim, fully comes to life. Just as the curtain opens in a Broadway production for a huge musical number in order to give the audience a glimpse of the lives and times of the show's characters, so this curtain has now opened as the villagers begin to fill the stage of our theater—the dirt path— and give us a glimpse into the life of their setting. We don't have to worry about the middle of the road being our stage. Unlike the roads at home, we are the only travelers here except for when the villagers carry their "wares" to the market. The only one carrying "wares" to the market this morning is the "spy" and at the moment, she is the main character.

My prayer from a second earlier of hoping they would one day run to see the Christ child becomes the main theme of this production, for the villagers truly *are* running to where Marilyn is offering them the real Christ child. Another trip to the back of the Land Cruiser shows she has come prepared with a bag of props for this production, in the form of medical supplies.

I quickly decide the back of the Land Cruiser is loaded down with more "fishing equipment" than just Joseph's. She begins to distribute small, sealed plastic bags containing antacids, pain relievers, band-aids and antibiotic creams. This "fisherwoman" explains in Khmer the uses for each item to their listening ears. The people are intent on her every word; their faces are overflowing with appreciation.

As what must be the remainder of this village's residents approach her, there appears to be a lot of hub-bub centering on the presence of one of the few men. He is dressed in farming clothes, like the rest of the village, including a hat to protect his head and his eyes from the sun. People are speaking to him and there is considerable conversation bouncing back and forth between him and Marilyn.

"He's the village chief," explains Chandra, picking up on their dialogue.

The equivalent of our mayor at home, he is swift to make us feel welcome. I am interested in the deep conversation going on between Marilyn and him, as are the villagers who are watching with eager eyes.

"She's explaining to him that she's Christian," Chandra tells me.

I eagerly watch for their reactions to Marilyn's words, which to me will speak louder than their words I cannot understand. Marilyn has an instant "in" with these people for they all know and trust her. She speaks their language. They have a shared background, albeit from two different sides. They trust her because her mother was good to all of them. Her mother dyed their clothes, she raised their food, she washed their dishes and cared for their children.

She was their servant, I muse, *just as Marilyn is God's servant to them now.*

Marilyn makes yet another trip to the back of the Land Cruiser, this time for "nets" to catch the young fish. She returns with a box, containing approximately thirty children's books, all of them Bible stories or stories about God's love written in Khmer, which she hands to the chief. The box also contains writing tablets and pens (it is too hot for crayons).

She is offering them Living Water from a well that will never run dry, bread for their soul, I note.

The village chief bows gratefully and gives Marilyn a huge smile, which is mirrored in the faces of the other people. Then he points to his eyes. Ever ready, Marilyn makes one last trip to the Land Cruiser. This time she comes back with a smaller box filled with reading glasses she's bought at the market, or that volunteer missionaries have brought from home. He tries on every pair until he finds a pair that works for him. The box is passed around as others search for "eyes" that will allow them to see clearly.

See clearly in more ways than one, I speculate while offering them my own glasses.

Mark, who knows my desperate need for my reading glasses, hastily asks, "What are you going to do now?"

"You're going to be my eyes," I am quick to tell him. "All I need to read here are the menus and I can't tell what they say anyway!" I laugh heartily, thrilled beyond measure that I can help the cause. "Besides, I can get more when I get home. The sun is bright enough here that I can see during the day. At night I'll simply have to write bigger notes."

The chief nods excitedly to Marilyn, still thanking her for the books and the other gifts.

"He promises to read the books to them," Chandra translates.

His comment causes me to realize, even with their new "eyes," most of these people are illiterate, just as they were when Pol Pot and the Khmer Rouge saw that as an asset to making them no threat to their revolution. Their new glasses only help them see the world around them. The depth of theological ramifications revolving around that conclusion astounds me as I understand the village chief will soon become their leader in another way. *A way more important than he can ever imagine,* I conclude, praying for him, this village and its people, and the books.

With Marilyn, the other main character, leading the crowd from Act 1 to Act 2, we all follow her to the next set on the stage. "All the people in this village were the base people," she explains in English as we walk a hundred yards or so to where her family's main camp hut once stood. The path is so dusty the red dust attaches itself to us and our clothing with each step. It's easy to see why the palm trees and other greenery are completely covered in a reddish-orange layer, hiding their true colors. My guess is it will stay this way, or gradually worsen, until monsoon season hits. Theologically thinking again, I visualize the "dirt" of our lives being washed away, Christ's redemptive love being our "monsoon." Figuratively thinking, I imagine this same dirt hiding the true colors of all the inhabitants, workers and Khmer Rouge, during the time Marilyn lived here. Through the scenery and the drama occurring here, God is allowing me to see and comprehend far beyond what meets the eye.

It feels we are now transformed into a scene from *The Pied Piper* as the children and all the adults follow us for what is probably the most excitement this village has experienced since the announcement of Liberation Day, January 7, 1979, or whatever day afterwards when the breaking news finally filtered to this area. Marilyn points to an opening beside one of the huts, where a large banana tree stands towering above the other small trees. The villagers listen intently as she tells of the time she shared with many of them; but it is a new story—at least from her side of it—for all the younger generations which, from the looks of it, is a goodly number of them.

"This is where the hut stood where her family stayed during much of the Khmer Rouge regime," Chandra shares. "The hut is gone, but the banana tree was in the back of it."

The banana tree is still strong and bearing fruit. *The person who lived in the house is still strong and bearing fruit,* I determine, looking admirably at Marilyn as she holds up both arms as if to say, "This is where it happened. This was where my family was imprisoned."

Like the Khmer Rouge, the characters of that time are gone, the "set" is disassembled and the stage is bare. Yet there is now another production, another stage, and the current players are being offered food and drink, where before they were dared to have any at the risk of their life.

That poses the question of what happened to all the fruit from the banana tree since the workers survived only on such small portions of rice. It is a question I know must remain solely with me until we are again in the vehicle and away from the villagers.

The cast, with Mark and me included, make our bows at the final curtain call. Only our bows are made to each of the other players rather than an audience. Although originally intended as a private showing solely for Mark and me, the real benefactors of this presentation are the villagers, the "catch" of Marilyn's nets. Though they will still swim freely in their pond—theoretically the village around them—they will hopefully one day find their way into the proverbial basket, like the one Joseph made to hold the fish that have been caught, and too become "fishers of men."

Mark resumes his role of the photographer as he snaps shots of the various cast members, all now elated to be a lasting image of this production. Like most plays and musicals, it has a beautifully happy ending, totally different from what I had feared for the day's episode. The author of this play is God, and it is a holy script, one greater than any of us captured in the photographs could imagine.

When Mark completes his task, we again bow and leave the characters with the words, "Chum Reap Lear," meaning good-bye, rather than "Bravo!" We make our stage exit and head back to the Land Cruiser to again enter the real world. An awe-inspiring moment, everyone is all smiles and waves as we leave a trail of dust, and love, behind us.

Out of sight and earshot from the village, my earlier question leaps to the forefront of my thoughts. "What happened to the fruit from all the trees, like the banana tree behind your house?"

"The base people were occasionally allowed to eat some of it, or it was given to the pigs, or it rotted. The Khmer Rouge would rather see the pigs eat it than us." There is no hate, no cynicism in her voice. She merely states the fact with no expression, a response I cite as a mark of closure for her.

"Base people were allowed to eat whether they worked or not. But not the workers. One couple was killed because they secretly ate leeches. People were so hungry they would eat anything they could find, but because they didn't share with the group, they were slaughtered."

A smile of satisfaction lights up her face as she moves past that horror to an enlightening story, one that makes an impact on what I've just witnessed. "When we lived here, the baby of the spy crawled into the cook fire one day. After that, my mother cared for the baby. The spy treated us nicely after that. Through that, I learned that an enemy can be changed into a friend."

Her satisfaction turns into a blank stare. "In 1978 we were moved to another hut in the village. The soldiers took us aside at the noon meal and had a private meeting with us. They told us to move immediately, giving us only a couple of hours to be moved and back at the work camp. We decided it was so they could dig around and look for our things, which they suspected were buried somewhere in the ground like most other people did with their valuable items.

"We were moved so many times while we were here. The Khmer Rouge would come and tell us to go to another hut, or another place, and give us hardly any time to be gone. Everyone suspected it was because the soldiers hoped to rob us. They thought if we had no time to pull our belongings together, they could steal our valuables." A wisp of a smile returns to Marilyn's face. "But they never found them. We got to the point we could move at an hour's notice. Ma kept all the gold and jewelry safely stashed inside an old black cloth. She took an old palm frond, which had curled up as it dried out, and tucked it amongst the holes in the thatch walls. That way, it was a natural camouflage and no one ever suspected it being a vault for our valuables.

"When the really mean soldier and his mother kept trying to rob us, Ma knew she had to find a place they would never think to look. She actually figured a way to hide the gold and jewelry where they wouldn't dare look in the small toilet we had for my injured sister."

The mother who should have coined the popular phrase about "random acts of kindness" was crude in all the right ways. Marilyn's story adds to the countless list of ways her family found to survive, thanks to "the commander."

As the curtain closes on this "stage" of Marilyn's life, and we leave this remote village to follow the path Marilyn walked to the work camp and fields, I contemplate on how the people in this village are the very same families who have always lived here, minus the families of workers who resided here temporarily—against their will—during the Khmer Rouge regime. I find it interesting that many places in America have become transient communities; here, the only "transients" to ever darken the villages, and live to tell about it, are now back in their own home towns and districts.

My earlier prediction about this being a miraculous day is correct. Nothing that has transpired thus far can be explained as circumstance. It is entirely evident God gave his beautiful servant not only a necessary closure, but a new beginning. He has opened the door for her to plant more seeds in this place where she was once overworked and underfed. I pray the Christians are again overworked as they push that door open further, thus allowing many others to discover Christ. But one thing is for certain. Their souls will no longer be underfed as they become spiritually fed.

I reflect on the scene we have just left. This small village of "one-time base people" has made a memorable impression on me. And I dare say we have also left them with a lifelong memory. "You are the first person to return to this village," is the welcome the people of the village gave Marilyn, in regards to her days as a communist laborer there. I venture to think she shall be the last.

Joseph retreats to the larger dirt path, the main highway for this area, where he takes a left turn from the village and weaves us deeper into the wilds of a jungle-covered never-land, the likes of which I have never seen. The narrow road is covered with such thick, dry dust that it hurts one's lungs to breathe it. Even with the windows closed, it blankets around us, seeping into every tiny crack and opening of the vehicle like an ambiguous haze designed to keep out invaders. A thicket of tall unkempt shrubs and bushes line the path on both sides. Trees shoot up, some seeming from nowhere, with layers of branches spreading far around them, making an umbrella over the already-full ground covering. Other trees shoot straight up, in the middle of a clearing, with giant balls of thick green foliage on the top. One can quickly assess the ease with which enemies and guerillas could hide, stage ambushes or carry out assaults on entire villages from these naturally camouflaged hideouts. Although the landscape is strikingly beautiful, it also holds an ominous and obscure aura of secrecy.

With no forewarning, Marilyn offers a quiet afterthought. "Most of the people who lived in that village and worked in our work camp were from Phnom Penh or Siem Reap."

Her words, few and delivered with no emotion, cause me to stumble upon a reality I'd yet discovered. "So how did the people from Siem Reap get here? Was every town evacuated the same way as Phnom Penh?" I shudder in expectation of her next words.

"Yes, every town," she said, giving me the sideways nod I recognized as an expletive to further affirm her answer. "Khmer Rouge soldiers went into every place the same as they did in Phnom Penh. When they finally took over the capital, they were in complete power."

Not until now do I realize the massiveness of the Khmer Rouge's revolution, suddenly cognizant that the evacuation of Phnom Penh, although definitely the largest maneuver, was but one of a myriad of pieces of their devastatingly cruel plan. Even though I'm aware of the 400+ "killing fields" throughout the country, they now become alive as the horror of what I've witnessed at Tuol Sleng and Choeung Ek becomes a far-reaching massacre, leaving no mile of the country unscathed.

"We are going to a place where twelve young women drowned," Marilyn informs me, leaving my thoughts of annihilation behind.

"Did the Khmer Rouge kill them?"

"No, they were on a boat with other people going to work. There were eighty-six people on the boat when it went down in the big river. The twelve young women were unable to swim to shore. It is a well-known and very mournful story for all of us who were workers. We understood their daily life. We all remember the story. It was like we were in the boat and went down with them."

She pauses while I make the connection that this trip is not about me seeing the spot where the young women drowned or are laid to rest. It is about Marilyn paying her respects to them, thus adding another dimension to her closure of this situation. I sit back and say a prayer that, though this may be painful for her, it is releasing the many staggering memories that have lain trapped in "Marilyn's box"—her equivalent of Pandora's box—for all these years. I envision a wooden box, like the ones from the market, with its lid half open as the dreadful reminiscences of her past hang in the balance, half-in and half-out. Only her box, instead of the ornately-designed patterns of mother-of-pearl and eggshell, is covered in splatters of red with background images of the landmine skull warning, black pajamas and guns with bayonets. With each encounter of this day, one of the memories slips from the box, making its heavy load lighter as another of the faded memoirs rustles between its openings, seeking their chance to also be set free.

It is a vision not so unlike the ones of many people, not only in Cambodia but in every country, as they try to hold onto the things in life they cannot control, letting the haunts of their past spread like venom through their beings until they are completely poisoned. With Marilyn, and also Joseph, this is a beautiful vision. They are allowing God to handle the excess baggage from the past, turning each recollection into a treasure, no longer buried, but free to touch the life of another. My own heart feels lighter, simply by virtue of being a part of this experience with them.

Now, as Christian missionaries, this is a harvesting of the "fruits of the Spirit" which they can offer to others, who are in desperate need of the reaping of their own spiritual fruits and gifts. I think of myself, born into Christianity and serving in a church from a very early age through my music. It matters not whether our life of service is one year, five years, twenty years, fifty years or more. We are all children in God's eyes. We all are in need of tilling the soil of our own "fruits of the Spirit," no matter how good or bad our lives have been. We are God's garden, and like farmers who need to change what crops go in what fields from time to time, so the same is necessary in our Christian journeys. The day, which began as a sobering experience, is now a time of rejoicing as the horrors of "Marilyn's box" vanish into "refurbished" treasures, making room for her box to be "refilled" with God's blessings.

Marilyn interrupts my thoughts to inform me that we are on the way to the rice field where she worked most of the time under the Khmer Rouge regime. "I used to run from the field back to my mother's hut at night," she shared quietly, as if she were still concerned someone might hear her words. "I could not sleep at night so I'd wait until everyone was asleep. Then I'd sneak out. If one of the leaders saw me, I'd tell them I had to go to the bathroom. Once I got out of sight from the camp, I'd run as hard and fast as I could. If there was a moon, I could not go. It had to be completely dark. And while I was running, if I saw a flashlight or someone riding a bicycle at midnight, I'd have to hide on the ground until I was sure it was safe to move again. If they saw me, I would be punished or killed."

"You went alone?"

"Alone. I didn't trust anyone to go with me. Besides, many of the others were afraid of the dark and of ghosts and the many snakes. The Khmer Rouge leaders used to tell us there was a really big tree where there were ghosts. Cambodian people are terribly frightened by ghosts and spirits so they would never stray far from the camp. But I was not afraid of either ghosts or snakes. I was more concerned about my mother than I was about ghosts. Besides, I always wondered if the Khmer Rouge only made that up to keep the workers from running away."

Her suspicion is well warranted, as well as the snakes serving as a natural barbed-wire fence running along the ground. The Khmer Rouge used the superstitions and fears of the uneducated people to their advantage.

"Sometimes at night while I would be running, I would hear something. I would stiffen up and get goose bumps, and hold my breath. Some nights when that happened, I would be terrified, but I would pretend to be okay and strong because I so badly wanted to check on my mother." Marilyn's words became a bit faster with a hint of trepidation in her voice. "My worst fear was leeches. There was water everywhere and I had to be so quiet walking through it. We had no shoes and the leeches would get on the bottoms of my feet. I'd try to shake them off, but they would stick to me. I was so afraid of them." Her words stop for a moment to give her enough of a break to shake off the goose bumps that accompany her memories.

"There were many tombs near the camp," she finally continues. "There was even a small burial ground at the edge of the rice field. Many people were so terrified of it they wouldn't even pass it to go to the bathroom, especially at night. Many times at night, and sometimes even during the day while we were working, I'd take people far away from the tombs so they wouldn't be so scared."

Rising up from out of nowhere, an imposing temple comes into sight ahead of us on the left. In front of it are many ornate tombs. "This is the place with all the tombs?"

"Yes," Marilyn answers solemnly.

The simplicity of her answer, combined with the tone of her voice, adds a fixated eeriness to the already tense moment. It is a gorgeously bright sunny day. The rays of the sun hit the gilded edges of the naga-shaped corners in such a way that had Marilyn not just described the effect these massive structures had on the underprivileged and overworked workers, they would be a most magnificent sight. (Naga is *neak* in Khmer, meaning a deity, which in Buddhism typically takes the form of a large snake or serpent.) I examine the building in its entirety as Joseph makes a left turn onto the small side road beside the temple and the ornately elaborate tombs, each one unique in its design. Although the road is not much wider than the path that led to Marilyn's hut, this one is lined with several long buildings on the right and a wooden pagoda on the left behind the foreboding temple.

Only then, when my eyes have a clear vision of this scene, do I understand the reason for the inexorable terror of the workers at this sight. It dawns on me that all the monks were killed. The temple would have been completely vacant at that time, with the remains of all the monks of this area cremated—or worse, left to rot—at this spot. In effect, it would have appeared to be a "ghost town," even as it does on this day in the broad daylight.

As Joseph parks the vehicle to the side of the road next to the now empty white buildings, and we get out, the aura of death still surrounds this forsaken village. The air is permeated by a stillness that truly is haunting. Marilyn walks in silence toward the wooden pagoda. I follow her as the others quietly move to other sites to take photos.

She stops approximately ten feet in front of the opening for the door and stares at the entrance she had intended to be her exit from this earthly life. Instead, her exit from this pagoda transcended the way for her entrance into a heavenly existence, albeit several years later during her time on earth. The intensity of the moment is as magnanimous as if it were an earthquake; it literally feels I can sense the ground shaking beneath my feet.

I listen intently as Marilyn shares the bone-chilling story of the pagoda and the man on the bicycle who delivered the "freedom" letter. My body shudders and my throat swallows hard. I've heard of the "Hell's Angels" bikers at home, but this man is my rendition of a "Hell's Angel" biker in Cambodia during "Pol Pot time." To add to the incredibly ominous flavor of the story's ending, I wonder whether Marilyn has ever considered that Christ was in the tomb three days before his resurrection. I refrain from mentioning that, deciding it more productive to discuss the matter with her after she sees her life in the light of black-and-white pages of the finished book.

When I finally get past the theological implications of this entire episode, time seems to stop in place as I try to make any sensibility out of what happened here. *How strange, and utterly conscienceless, it seems to take people to the pagoda—a part of the temple grounds—to kill them.* My psychological reasoning cannot help but wonder if these brainwashed individuals, in their sick minds, weren't trying to play God. From their actions, it seems their wieldy power had so taken over their hearts and desires that it is totally inconceivable to them that there is any Power greater than themselves.

There is a great sense of melancholy as Marilyn sighs and adds a coda to the story. "For my mother and the rest of the family, the worst part was the mother of the mean soldier. When they took my sister and I to the pagoda to kill us, his mother said to my mother, 'They will kill you next. Why don't you go ahead and give me your things…all the gold and jewelry?' Because of that one soldier and his mother, my whole family feared each day would be our last."

A power play, I reason. *They are so jealous of what they suspected Marilyn's mother to have, yet they probably feared the revenge of the other base leaders to whom she had done so many favors and helped in so many ways. From dyeing their clothes, to planting and cooking their food, washing their dishes and making medicines for their sick children, she had made herself indispensible to the rest of the base people.* I look at Marilyn's expression. *Indispensible or not, some of those soldiers were so brainwashed they killed their own families,* I swiftly remind myself, knowing it would have been impossible for Marilyn and her family to trust him or his mother.

She walks away, toward the long white building that was the dining hall when she worked here. For what seems hours, I stand frozen in front of the pagoda, unable to tear myself away from the well which springs endless stories from however many people ended their life in this spot. *Vibes from the past,* I sense, as I stare at the ground around me where Marilyn described the scenes of "fresh" bodies and unearthed bones; I imagine the vile smell of death. It is the moment of truth when I finally discover what it is I have returned to Cambodia to find, the moment I truly experience the depth of what Marilyn endured at the point of her worst nightmare. The effort to put one foot in front of the other, treading over hundreds of interrupted lives, is excruciatingly painful as I pull myself away to join the others who are now walking toward the rice field across the main road from the tombs.

Three workers, two women and one man, are in the field. Like the rest of this day, it's as if they are planted here for our benefit. I manage to reach the others just in time to see several gravesites, whose small mounds of dirt are covered with low hipped roofs made from thin sheets of tin. They lie at the edge of the rice field where all the workers would have had to file past daily.

"There were no coverings here then. These are the gravesites that terrified the workers, especially if they had to go past them to use the bathroom."

"So this is where you walked people past the graves you told me about?"

"Yes." Marilyn's answer is nearly inaudible.

We continue walking until we come to the workers. Marilyn explains she worked here during "Pol Pot time." The man hands her his hoe and allows her to recreate the scene she once enacted on this same ground. Soon the women hand Mark and I their hoes so that we too may journey back to the past alongside our dear friend. As enriching as this moment is, it is also a chilling piece of history that takes my breath away.

"What does it feel like, Marilyn," asks Mark, "to be working in the same field where you once were?"

"Like I've never left," she says blandly, yet with a slightly pleasant smile. "I feel like I'm here working again. Thank God I have a life to see this place again." She looks past me at the pagoda. "The Khmer Rouge people here were innocent. I feel only pity for them. They only did what they were told." Her eyes meet mine. "People asked me how I could come back here. They cannot understand. This place no longer holds me a victim."

Jesus rolled the stone away, I relate to the tomb of three days. Her beautiful loving and forgiving spirit speaks to me. "Marilyn!" I exclaim, so loudly and suddenly the workers, even though they have no clue what I'm saying, stare in wonder. "Can you believe this? Once upon a time you sowed seeds right here, in this very spot. Now you're back in Cambodia, still sowing seeds. Only this time you're sowing seeds of faith."

A huge smile breaks across her face; it matches the huge tear streaming down my face. Mark trades his hoe for his camera as he takes photos of Marilyn, of Joseph and of the workers. It is, oddly, a blessed moment for everyone in the field as we take turns working the soil by hand. In the scorching heat, in a field that covers hectares as far as the eye can see, I begin to comprehend how long and how hard the work is to plant and harvest this field. *All day, starting at dark and going past dark, every day*, I remind myself.

Marilyn gives the hoe back to the young man and asks him the whereabouts of the grave of the twelve young women. Her face has a strange glow as she turns back to us. "One of the women was his sister."

My huge tear turns into a spirited gushing inside my entire body. Mark and I stare at each other in silence. Not disbelief, simply awed silence. Our journey now becomes a quest as we rush for the Land Cruiser and head in the direction he tells her. It winds up being a long search, filled with many twists and turns through jungles and cornfields. Way past the area of cell phone reception, in a land where we know no one, and in a place that no one knows where we are, I get the creepy sense we could disappear into nothingness just like so many others here did. It is a creepy thought, yet one that must be turned over to the One who brought us through all the other places we've visited during the past four days. *Not to mention all the illustrious characters,* I comfort myself.

An hour passes before we ever find where the twelve women are buried. There is no marker, not even a mound of dirt...simply a few people pointing to a spot between two huts in the middle of a jungle. Another hour passes before we find enough people along the way to direct us out of the jungle. We are overjoyed when we come to the end of a path and see the tombs, the temple and the pagoda where Marilyn was held—all back across the dirt road from the rice field where we began.

The workers are still there, having made too little progress to speak of since we'd left them. "Is this what you did the entire time of the Khmer Rouge?" I ask.

"I was fortunate," answers Marilyn. "I got to spend most of my time digging in the field and using the kandeav (*sickle* in English) to chrot (*cut* in English) the rice. There were so many rocks in the fields that the only way we could plant the rice was to dig holes. Sometimes we had to pick up the rocks and other workers had to carry them to the sites of the dams and dikes. One of my sisters had that chore."

"What did you do in the time after the rice was harvested?" I ask, knowing the rice crops are greatly dependent upon the monsoon season.

"When the rice was harvested, we had to do other work. The Khmer Rouge built dams to irrigate the land so we'd have to help dig dirt to build up the dam. Others would have to carry the dirt to the site of the dam. Sometimes we would dig the potatoes that grow naturally in the ground and sometimes we would plant corn. We never harvested the corn because the Khmer Rouge did not trust us with the corn."

"So you never got corn the entire time you were under their communist control?"

"No, never. The only time we had a potato is when someone would secretly slip one to my mother for my injured sister." Marilyn pauses for a slight second as a smile wipes across her face. "There was one time a year when we'd get to eat. It was like a festival in those days. When the rice was harvested, we actually got to eat three meals a day with plenty of rice. We even got to have a dessert of sticky rice on the 10th day, the 20th day and the 30th day after the harvest. Everyone looked so forward to that. It was the only thing we had to look forward to. I can still remember how good the sticky rice tasted back then." She pauses as the enthusiasm in her voice drops. "But then after that, we would go back to getting only two meals a day. There was no breakfast. The lunch meal was rice, but at dinner, the meal was so watered down you could hardly taste the rice. The Khmer Rouge told us the only thing we were going to do at night was sleep. We didn't need much nourishment for that. 'You only get rice in the middle of the day when you still have work to do,' they told us."

Marilyn gives a long sigh. "No one would have minded working every day," she shares, "if we'd been given dessert, or even enough food, and some rest. There were no complaints from anyone on the days we ate the sticky rice."

Her words bear a strange truth as they remind me of the famous saying by Benjamin Franklin, "A spoonful of honey will catch more flies than a gallon of vinegar." Only in this case, it was "You catch more workers with sticky rice than a meager bowl of watered-down rice soup." Which probably explains why Marilyn was so successful at her job in the refugee camp at Kao I Dang as the clerk for the care feeding center for sick people and for children under five years of age.

Chapter Nineteen

"Did I tell you about the time the Khmer Rouge tried to force me to marry one of their soldiers?" Marilyn asks blandly as we near Phnom Penh.

Spellbound, I stare at her. "No!" I finally manage in utter shock as I wonder why this slice of tantalizing information is just now surfacing. But then, given the volumes of stories she's had to dreg up from her immense library of memory banks recently, I should be more surprised she remembers it at all.

"It happened in 1977. One night four or five Khmer Rouge soldiers called me to a meeting by myself with them. They informed me I was going to marry a man whose father was the Khmer Rouge leader who was the informant against my father and family. They gave me no choice but to marry the son of that bad man. The only reason they wanted me to marry him was so I would have a child to grow up and work in the fields."

That's a brilliant plan! I think scornfully. *Kill a few, bear a few more. What a way to breed a new generation*. I find myself more dumbfounded with each new detail of this story.

"It was not uncommon for them to make the 'new people' get married with the expectation they were to have a child within twelve months. Only this man was not one of the new people." She stops, leaving me hanging with bated breath for her next sentence.

"What happened?" I anxiously ask.

"I tried to explain to them that I didn't want to get married. 'Why?' they asked me. I luckily remembered the very first group meeting when they said, 'A refugee woman cannot get married unless the man knows how to do all the farmer's work. The woman has to know how to do *all* the work.'" Her words halt, again leaving me hanging.

"What did you do?"

"I talked them out of it."

Now I am stunned. Here is an assembly of Khmer Rouge soldiers ready and willing to kill or punish the workers for the least reason, and this single weak female gets out of one of their "arranged marriages" with no consequences. Her spunk leaves me rightly astounded. "How?" I ask, so eager for each next detail that I feel the need to bribe her to get more rapidly from one point to another.

"I told them I cannot marry this man."

"And?" My head leans forward as I mentally try to pull out the next tidbit of the story.

"They ask why."

I have the routine by this point so I continue with my questions. "And you told them what?"

"I told them they did not want me to marry this man."

"Why wouldn't they want you to marry this man?"

"I told them they were always fussing at me for not working hard enough. I said, 'I know when I have a baby, I not work hard for Angkar and I want to work hard for Angkar. So let the others who are good workers get married first.'

"They said, 'The only reason you don't want to get married is because you don't have beautiful clothes like a queen.'"

She can't dress like royalty on her special day, I recall from her comments about weddings.

"But I told them, 'No, it's because I want to be a good citizen and work hard for Angkar. If you want a hard working child, you need to find a mother from Group One." Her reasoning leaves me stunned. Seeing no forthcoming question for a change, she continues. "I told them they complained about my amount of work at every meeting, so they could not possibly think I work hard enough to marry this man who is the son of a Khmer Rouge leader."

"And you convinced them?"

"Enough that they brought the young man in and asked him if he loved me."

"And his answer?"

"He told them, 'No.'"

"And that was it?"

"They asked him if he wanted to marry me."

"And he again said, 'No?'"

"Yes."

I feel completely entangled in the Cambodian version of "Who's on first?" with Abbott and Costello. "Let me get this straight." I go through each segment of the outlandish anecdote to make sure I understand the nearly comical quality of it, which would have been anything *but* comical had she actually been forced to marry the man.

She nods her head as an added affirmation of her answer. "He said he hated me and wanted another girl who was an active worker. That's what I later heard from one of the work leaders who was a good woman. She said to me, 'You are lucky. He worked hard for Angkar, killing and punishing many people.'"

Once again, Marilyn's brilliant cunningness has played to her advantage, I surmise, as I add yet another example to my notes of how her sisters' resources, given to each of them while they were still in the womb, rescued them from an intolerable—*or worse*, I shudder—situation. I am so flabbergasted I cannot even respond to Marilyn's words.

I sit back and think of the never-ending horror stories that are a product of the Khmer Rouge period in history and endeavor to imagine what kind of sick minds would sit around and dream up this kind of nonsensical way of life. Marilyn hands me a slice of pomelo, my favorite Cambodian fruit which resembles a grapefruit but is sweeter and has a more delicate texture. One taste of it quickly brings me back to the natural goodness and beauty of God's creation that was still present in this country, albeit overshadowed, during that infamous time. And a goodness and beauty that is still present all around me here now.

I spend the next few miles in silence, contemplating how many Bible stories and historical events are memorable due to the beauty and wonder God brought out of the most unimaginable and reprehensible of scenarios. This exercise proves to be a much-needed mental balance. It enables me to continue the difficult task of hearing and writing the hardships, suffered by the entire percentage of population who managed to survive the insanity going on around them, during the Khmer Rouge's power.

Before long, I deduce it was God, and not Marilyn, who nixed that marriage. It appears Joseph was to be the groom of this couple's "arranged marriage" made in heaven.

Speaking of "made in heaven," I decide to offer my thanks for a trip filled with people and places that could have only happened at the hand of the Almighty, thanks to lots of prayers on Joseph's part. "Joseph, not only did you plan the perfect itinerary, you are also a good chauffeur," I acknowledge with a grin. "God's hand put us in good hands."

He gives a jovial laugh. "I was once the driver for the king."

"Really?" I return his laugh, thinking he is joking with me.

"Yes, for about two months in New York City in 1984."

My laughter stops cold.

"The United Nations had a conference, which the king normally attended each year. My adoptive brother was close with the king, so the king called him to see if he knew of a good driver who would also be a good confidante. My brother immediately answered, 'Chan, Chhleav.' He called me and asked if I would be interested. Of course my response was, 'Yes!'" Excitement is building in his voice.

"I went to New York from Richmond, Virginia, where I was serving as a pastor at the First Nazarene Church at the time. Marilyn and I had already met King Sihanouk the year before when he invited Cambodian representatives from each state to visit when him while he was in America for the same conference."

"While Joseph was in North Korea studying," interjects Marilyn, "after Lon Nol led the coup to oust King Sihanouk, the king had a 64-room house in North Korea. He invited the Cambodian students to dine with him on Sundays, so Joseph ate with him every Sunday." Joseph nods his head, as if it's an ordinary occurrence to share a meal with the king, while Marilyn continues to talk. "He was a great musician and composer. He'd sing and play the piano for the students."

"Really?" Now I am intrigued.

"Yes. He could actually play several instruments, including the saxophone and accordion. When he was 80-years-old, he was still playing the piano and singing. He even starred in a movie. His son, our present King Sihamoni, is a ballet instructor. He studied in Czechoslovakia. They were both extremely talented and naturally supportive of the arts."

Not only does Joseph wine and dine with the king, he is serenaded by him, I muse comically, amazed this gentle man was so close to royalty. "I'm in good company, Joseph. I've dined with you and serenaded you, too! And you've chauffeured me all over Cambodia. You've made me feel like a queen!" He and I share a congenial laugh.

"In 1991, when he was in New York," admits Joseph, "King Sihanouk told me, 'You must continue to be a Christian leader to help the Cambodian people. The Christians give to the people, not take from the people.' There was a big banquet at that time, which I attended, for the ceasefire agreement. I was privileged to present a letter from the Cambodian Ministry for Christ and the Cambodian Christian Services, signed by the presidents of those two organizations, to King Sihanouk in New York City. The letter, also to be shared with the four political party leaders in Cambodia, read, 'We strongly support the ceasefire and we request that you please let the Cambodian people have freedom of faith.' I later got to attend the ceasefire talks in Paris for the same purpose."

There is no boastfulness in his speech as Joseph shares this great honor, for he is a man who truly walks humbly with his God. *And talks humbly for Him,* I note, considering his reason for appearing at the ceasefire meetings.

"I have pictures," he adds as a footnote. "When we get back to Phnom Penh, I will show you."

"You really *are* a good chauffeur," I repeat, this time with a hearty laugh. *Just as God's hands placed us in good hands, so He placed His mission in Cambodia in good hands.*

It took going to the wilds of Cambodia and back--driven by the king's personal chauffeur--to fully appreciate the lives of not only this missionary couple, but several generations of people who beat the odds and survived a madman and his cadres.

On the outskirts of Phnom Penh, Joseph stops to refuel the gas tank. I pass my soda can to Chandra as she exits the vehicle to stretch. "Would you throw this away for me, please?" I ask. Going back to my notes, I hear a loud "CLANK" on the ground. My head turns quickly toward the direction of the sound to see my can now lying on the ground beside the Land Cruiser.

Chandra, seeing the startled look in my eyes, says, "There is no trash can."

That's when I see men with brooms, resembling large wire whisks, sweeping the huge dirt parking lot of what is the Cambodian version of a truck stop. I find it difficult to believe this is how they deal with trash, but at the same time, I see it as a means of giving another person a job. I see it also means we are again nearing civilization. That means one thing: restaurants.

The one thing Southeast Asian cities have more of on every corner than America is restaurants. There are more in Phnom Penh than in New Orleans, which has restaurants every few steps. The passing of frequent restaurants is the cue that my stomach is crying for food. I say nothing for I am sure Joseph and Marilyn have a wonderful game plan for dinner. I am not disappointed when they take us to a huge restaurant just before we cross the bridge into Phnom Penh.

The meal of fried rice with crab is unbelievably good and quickly becomes my favorite dish of the entire trip. Both Mark and I are seafood freaks, so Joseph and Marilyn make sure we taste "the best of the best" this restaurant has to offer. Like most restaurants in the country, this one has an open-air section. There is a row of booths at the very back whose outer wall is screened, making it the most magnificent screened-in porch Phnom Penh has to offer. Our large booth sits over the Mekong River, allowing us a view that is every bit as good as the food.

As the six of us sit there devouring our delicious food, looking like we've never eaten before in our lives, my writing muse is quick to alert me that two members of our entourage traveled this same road, with no food and no beautifully inspiring view. Another one fished near here to feed a camp of twenty-five families, plus the Khmer Rouge leaders who oversaw them.

I take a purposeful look at all the servers and the customers. *There's not a person in this entire place whose lives were not affected by what happened during the Khmer Rouge regime.* I think about why I am here, experiencing "the worst of the worst" while eating "the best of the best" that the entire country has to offer. My eyes scan the crowd again. *Including Mark and me,* I quickly remind myself, adding our names to the lists of affected persons.

Joseph ends our dinner and our trip with the perfect statement. "Whatever I always did, I just wanted to help out with honesty. The result came with many good blessings." His comment receives a hearty "Amen!" from both Mark and me.

We've come full circle, I muse, *for my guided tour, but also for Joseph and Marilyn's life.* Our journey of the past four days has proven much more than a time for seeing and learning. It has been a time of nurturing, reconciliation, remembrances, closures and personal growth. *And a bond between six lives that can never be broken.* Tears well up behind my eyes.

A lingering question, which has gone unnoticed between all the other fast-paced conversations and four years' worth of details, raises its weary head as I look out across the river. "I know that when you escaped to America, your plane landed in San Francisco and you flew on to the Bronx from there, but what took you back to California?"

"Yes, yes, like this, like this," Joseph begins with his endearing phrase that is merely a way of emphasizing what he is telling me, making sure I understand. "We only stayed in the Bronx for nine months. After that, we were able to locate Marilyn's sister and her husband. They had been sent to Arlington, Virginia from the refugee camp. We moved there, taking our adoptive mother with us. While we were there, I was able to complete an auto mechanics course at a technical college. After that we moved to Richmond."

"Our first daughter, Sodani, was born in 1984 while we were living in Richmond," states Marilyn with excited eyes and her usual beaming smile.

"We kept involved in church in every place where we lived," continues Joseph, sharing his wife's proud smile, "continuing to pray, learn and study the Bible every day. In Richmond, a Nazarene church asked me to be a full-time pastor for a 200-member congregation of Cambodians they had. I felt I needed more training so I sought a place where I could get a formal education. God opened a door for us to go to San Jose, California, to study at San Jose Christian College.

"It was a miracle. I could not apply for a grant for education until I had been a resident for one year. But the director of the City Team, an organization to help the poor, saw how desperately I wanted an education in Bible studies and how hard I worked. He said to me, 'Go! I will pay for your first year.' I could not believe my ears."

"So we hopped into our old car with Nyda and Sodani, our adoptive mother, her son, and two other 'adoptive' grandmothers we 'inherited' while in Virginia," Marilyn adds with a laugh. "The families of these two women were not happy about them going to California with us, but the women had become so close with our adoptive mother from Cambodia, and so badly wanted to go, that they moved with us."

"We drove cross-country, all the way from Virginia to California," says Joseph. His laugh indicates there are many stories and experiences that happened along the way, but my watch indicates there is no time for those. "After that first year I got a loan, which I paid back for many years, but I graduated with a Bachelor's degree in theology in 1987."

"I wanted to go to college there too," shares Marilyn, but I became pregnant and then suffered a miscarriage. "After Joseph graduated, I was able to attend classes and earn my Bachelor of Science degree in Basic and Advanced Early Childhood Education in 1991. I graduated one week and Christina was born the next!"

"That's quite an accomplishment," I reply. "You got two things to show for all your work." We share another laugh.

"That's when I felt the call into full-time ministry. I had been involved with the church and ministry the entire time, but at that time it had been a passion. When I realized there was more to it than that and accepted God's call," states Joseph, "I began my ministerial courses of study, for which I completed the Five Year Course of Study at the School of Theology at Claremont College, in California, under the direction of the Division of Ordained Ministry. That was in July of 1996, after I had been a part of the organization of the Methodist Mission in Cambodia in January of that year."

"On your own private Liberation Day," I add, causing Joseph to laugh.

"Yes, yes!" His eyes twinkle as they dance with excitement. "During our time in California, we ran into our Cambodian friend Sam Vorn, who was by then a United Methodist minister. We became actively involved in his congregation at Central United Methodist Church in Stockton, California, where he was the pastor. We soon joined that church and that is how we came be Methodists."

"Wait a minute! Sam is the one who had been in Lon Nol's army before the Khmer Rouge take-over, and he is also the one who introduced you to Marilyn's adoptive mother in the refugee camp." I'm thrilled to have made the connection.

"Yes, yes!" Joseph again exclaims, this time with even more glee at my understanding of his stories.

"Sam is still a pastor for a Cambodian congregation at Centenary United Methodist Church in Modesto, California," Marilyn informs me with a smile. "We've now been friends for 31 years."

"There are many Cambodian immigrants on the west coast," says Joseph. "I was asked to serve as a part-time pastor there."

"Both Joseph and I worked as bilingual teachers for the immigrant children. In addition, Joseph taught an adult English class in Stockton," explains Marilyn. Her face becomes expressionless. "I wanted to go back to Cambodia. I longed to see my family, so I went back for the first time in December of 1992. Joseph returned in December of 1993 for the first time, after the ceasefire and the country's ability to vote. Although we were anxious to take Christianity back to our country as soon as possible, we discovered it was not yet stable enough for us to begin God's work there at that time. Therefore, Joseph only planted seeds by purchasing two plots of land in the Tek Thla village of his native Banteay Meanchey province. The following April, in 1994, Sam Vorn's Central United Methodist Church in Stockton donated money to build a small wooden church on the land. They also donated money to provide water year-round for the community. That well is still being used by the entire community today."

"That is the church and well we saw where we sang with the minister, and the former pastor's wife gave us the jackfruit," I say, making another connection.

"That's right," Marilyn confirms. "That is where the Methodist church got its roots in Cambodia."

"You literally *did* plant seeds with the purchase of that land, Joseph. Its roots grow deeper and its branches become more widespread with each Sunday's service."

With that, we leave the restaurant as I give thanks for their "mustard-seed-sized faith" and their determination to see their proverbial "trees" bear fruit. Although I had a great appreciation for this couple when I arrived in Cambodia this time, based on my work with them on my prior visit, following in their footsteps and their ministry the past four days has given me an even greater appreciation for the work being done, and the gospel being spread here. I feel I have what I need to share a story of two individuals who, together, are a testimony to what can happen when the virtues of faith, hope and love are put into action.

When we finally pull into one of the three parking spots at the Golden Gate, it seems we've been gone a lifetime. *It has been a lifetime,* I conclude, *at least a huge chunk of the lifetimes of Marilyn and Joseph.* I am relieved to learn that my same room is waiting for me as I head in that direction with my suitcase, computer and armload of notes.

My mind, reeling from all the notes, non-stop excitement and experiences, screams for a break. Mark is faced with the same problem as we meet in the hallway, both asking at the same time, "Want to take a tuk-tuk ride around the city?" The frantic pace and workload has left us both in need of a "chill pill," which is a hard thing to find when it's still close to 100 degrees outside at night.

We head for the front door of the Golden Gate, laughing about which tuk-tuk we'll take since we've been accosted by at least a dozen drivers every time we near the door. The laugh is on us, however, as we hit the parking area—which only holds three cars—and see not a single tuk-tuk.

"I cannot believe all the tuk-tuks that have been here this whole time and the one time we need one, there is none." Immediately, upon my speaking the word "tuk-tuk," one barrels around the corner at the end of the street and comes to pick us up. Our bout of laughter serves as our "chill pill," removing us from our piles of notes and hundreds of photos. Knowing they will still be on our respective desks when we return, we tell the driver to take us to Sisopath Quay where we can relax and watch the nightlife of the weekend.

The calmness of their nightlife is incomparable. Houseboats, some with lights hung around the edges, are docked along the waterfront. A few fishing canoes, with a small tent covering, are also dotted down the river's edge. There are a couple of tourist boats cruising the river in the hot, but very pleasant evening air. The scene vaguely reminds me of a story once told to me by a dear cousin who sat in this same spot to find relaxation from the helter-skelter of the worldcLet me.

Although there are thousands of people, most of them are comfortably seated at a sidewalk café, or lounging in the restaurant bars. Many are lying on the grass or playing with their families on the landscaped parks running down the middle of the boulevards. It is such a pleasant change of pace from the life at home. Everyone here is taking a "chill pill" and life is good.

Although my eyes are taking in the serenity of the moment, my mind spontaneously and unexpectedly replays the evacuation scene of Phnom Penh. I see these same people in front of me, but with bicycles and oxcarts rather than tuk-tuks, motorbikes and cars. Instead of all the laughter and playing of families with young children in the parks, I envision eyes filled with terror and children's precious little faces covered in expressions of anxious fear. Instead of all the vendors lining the way with flashing neon-colored toys and balloons, I witness lines of Khmer Rouge soldiers, their bayonets flashing in the bright sunlight. As badly as I'd like this mental picture to disappear from my mind, I know it is necessary to make me understand the reality of what happened here nearly thirty-five years before. I stare in silence and allow it to play out in its entirety as we take the tuk-tuk back to the hotel to get Mark's camera. My "chill pill" turns out to be the chills that run up my spine from the mental scenes in front of me as I imagine hundreds of cross faces, their owners dressed in black pajama-style uniforms.

Once we've arrived back at the Golden Gate and Mark has his camera in hand, we decide to walk the streets to allow him to capture both still and action shots of the city's nightlife. Even that makes me think of all the shots that rang throughout the city during the Khmer Rouge's evacuation of all two-million residents of Phnom Penh in 1975. *All of whom, at the time, were actively involved in a city that stood still for almost four years, except for the persecution and killing of the country's citizens who had the abilities and capabilities to be the most beneficial to Cambodia's welfare.* I find myself amazed the country has come this far in its ability to leave that reign of terror behind, prompted largely by the spirit of the younger generation whose attitude is to move forward and work together to make a positive-minded country, one that can benefit all its citizens instead of an extremely-wealthy few.

Once Mark has his photos, we spend our time checking out the shops still open, looking for nothing but admiring every item. Rarely getting time to go "window shopping" at home, I find it ironic that in order to do that, I have to go all the way to the other side of the globe. All too soon, that "cat crawling on your grave" sensation runs up my spine. Trying to shake the eerie feeling, I pick up a hand-crafted Cambodian boy doll in one of the stores and approach the sales clerk. "How much?" I ask, hoping she understands me.

Her impeccable English shocks me, as does the cost of the doll, but I realize this is a fair trade shop and the money is all used in some form of mission work in this country. She asks me what I'm doing in Cambodia. When I explain about the book on the lives of Joseph and Marilyn, we get into a conversation about Christianity.

"My best friend is Christian," states the clerk. "My husband and I have been talking a lot about attending a church lately because of a nice lady who came in here last year. It was right after my daughter was born. The baby was very sick and I didn't have money to buy medicine or food for her. We feared she would die. I was so frightened. This nice Christian lady came in and overheard me talking to someone about my daughter. She asked if it were alright to pray with me. The next day she brought food for the baby and for me, as well as some other items, and money for my daughter's medicine. Today the baby is perfectly healthy thanks to that lady."

Knowing full well the reason for the earlier eerie sensation, I ask, "Do you remember what the woman looked like?"

"Yes," she replies, giving me a full description of Marilyn.

I leave the store with the doll and my second "chill pill" of the evening, this time with goose bumps from randomly experiencing Marilyn's work of faith, hope and love in action.

Chapter Twenty

There is one view of Cambodia I've not encountered, either before or during this trip. It is one I feel would be most beneficial to my understanding of Cambodia, much as it was to Mark Twain's understanding of America. Yet is a view I dare not mention for I'm afraid it will be too much trouble for this couple who has already gone overboard in making sure I have everything I need for the book. Therefore, I leave it in my subconscious as I spend my final Sunday worshipping with Esther Gitobu and her daughters at the International Church with hundreds of missionaries and volunteers from around the globe.

As we head for her vehicle and lunch after the service, Esther asks, "Would you like to take a boat ride?"

I nearly fall down the flight of stairs in my shock. That is the one view I need, the one from the Mekong River. *I guess God thought I needed that view, too*, I laugh silently as Mark and I at the same time yell, "Yes!" As badly as I've wanted the view, he's wanted the photos, so we're both soaring at this opportunity.

"We'll go at four o'clock so you see the sunset on our way back to the city." Esther, who with her husband was the instigator of this book, is also the one who has handled all the many underlying details of this trip's success, such as the four-day excursion with Joseph and Marilyn. She strikes again, as aware of this need as I am. She immediately contacts the Chans to make sure they can join us.

To add to the excitement, our noontime meal is a delightful treat at Hagar, a restaurant owned and managed by an Australian—whom I'm privileged to meet while dining and whom I also saw involved in the worship service. He began the upscale operation to get teenage girls off the streets and into a reputable and viable learning experience and business. It is the restaurant where Joseph and Marilyn brought Mark and I on New Year's Day, but where we were unable to eat due to the holiday.

The food and atmosphere are divine—making this place totally out of my price range in America—but the real treat is when Esther introduces me to the owner and I learn he is only months from opening the same kind of operation for teen males. As I carefully scan all the various buffets to view the beautiful presentation of food, I notice many congregants from the church are also here. This man's intuition serves many purposes. It fills the bellies of the hungry, it gives Christians a meeting place for fun, planning and camaraderie, and it gives young people a new life grounded in Christian principles.

Mark and I stand at the water's edge looking like two kids going to the circus for the first time. Our group is surveying the few boats whose families open their "homes" to make money by cruising tourists up and down the river. None of the boats look entirely safe, but we find one coming in with a group and decide it sways to the side less than the others. Esther quickly bargains with the "homeowner" to get the boat for an extra hour for us to have our own private party on the Mekong River. An admirer of Mark Twain's works and his river settings—all of which I've visited—I jokingly feel like the reincarnated Asian version of him, since their culture believes in reincarnation.

Climbing aboard the houseboat from the river's edge is an excursion all its own. We finally manage to get to the upper level of the boat without anyone falling in the water, and set out for a glorious evening of no cares. Our upper deck is furnished with several plastic chairs and a long table, on which Marilyn lays out an assortment of fruit, including my favorite, the pomelo. There is a sofa and two vinyl upholstered chairs at the bow of the ship, along with a Cambodian flag proudly waving in the wind.

As we pull away from the shore of the Tonle Sap River and make the turn where it converges with the Mekong, I notice a huge building on the waterfront towering above Phnom Penh. At the top of it, a name blares overtop the city in huge red lights: NAGAWORLD.

"What's that?" I ask, having missed it during our many jaunts up and down Sisopath Quay and the nearby boulevards.

"That's the new casino," Esther replies.

Something about her reply "rips me at the seams," as the expression goes. Casinos have wormed their ways into many outlying areas of America, as well as the "hot spot" cities. That is troublesome enough, but to see one here, in the midst of such a poverty-laden area where people are more naturally influenced by the "get rich quick" scam, it tugs at my heart, not to mention my morals. But then, like in the rest of the world, the casino owners are capitalizing on tourists and those who will "spend it all" in hopes of "making it big."

Leaving a proverbial sour taste in my mouth, this is not the scene I had hoped for from the advantage of my river view. But that is soon erased by the peaceful quiet that exudes from the numerous tiny, sleepy villages alongside the river. *This,* I recognize, *is a far cry from what was going on here thirty-five years ago with artillery lighting up the sky and bombs going off everywhere.* Houseboats, and fishing boats on which people live, are docked all up and down the river. Men pull in their day's catch as we pass boats along our way. Teens and children dive into the water and play water volleyball, one group even with the luxury of a net. Mothers tote babies on their hips while young siblings run naked beside them. I sense I'm aboard a time machine that has just entered a zone pictured in my geography books from when I was a young child, decades ago. I immediately fall in love with this place and momentarily wish it were a point of no return.

The setting sun puts on a spectacular show as it drops behind the city of Phnom Penh leaving only barely visible glimpses of neon signs in the distance. A fisherman coming home from his day's work waves to us in the glare of the sun's last rays. Ahead of us, on the right shore, flickering lights grasp our attention.

"That is a weaving village," explains Marilyn. "Would you like to stop?"

Our reply, and a little bit of extra money paid to the boat's owner, has us soon climbing the steep steps dug into the river's bank that takes us high above the Mekong to a tiny village of eight houses, all of which have women sitting at looms weaving beautiful silks. We wander amidst the looms, admiring the craft and workmanship of these workers. No one minds the chickens roosting atop the looms; the chickens do not mind our visit.

"Do they sell their work here or only at the market?" I ask.

Marilyn translates and soon one of the women displays an entire array of scarves, purses and fabrics. By the time we trek back down the steep steps and again wangle our way onto the houseboat, Mark and I have bags of gifts for friends and family, and the women of the weaving village have money to provide for their families for several weeks. There is something surreal about the entire experience, including the perfect timing of the sun's close of the day.

As we return to Phnom Penh, I smile at the sight of the sleepy little villages that have now closed their eyes until the morning's dawn. It is a spectacular visual of God singing them a lullaby and putting them to bed, exactly as I had my newborn grandson before I left. My urge to be stuck here, past the point of no return, shifts as I realize I have a beautiful family waiting at home of which I long to be a part.

I was correct in my verdict that a boat ride was necessary to see the whole of Cambodia. Esther got me on the boat; God took care of the rest. I have a firm opinion that an author must know what he or she writes. They must live it to make the story come alive. I get off the boat assured that I know the story. I know Cambodia...*and I dearly love it and its people.* Now I fully understand the drive that brought Joseph and Marilyn back to their home soil and water.

When we return to the hotel, Joseph takes Christina home while Marilyn stays with me to clarify some points that are still unclear. She hands me a plastic sleeve filled with photos, which I dump on my bed and begin to leaf through with intent eyes.

"Marilyn!" I exclaim. "*Where* did you get these pictures?" I'm in shock as it dawns on me that the photos of her were made before the Khmer Rouge took over Cambodia.

She literally beams from ear to ear. "I escaped with them when we left Phnom Penh. They were flat and didn't take up extra room so I took them."

Staring at the photos for what seems an eternity, totally amazed and marveling at the fact she still has any part of her past from the time prior to Pol Pot, my smile grows to match hers.

"One time when the Khmer Rouge came into our hut trying to rob us, they threw all my family pictures away. I told them they could not take my pictures.

"'Angkar is your only family now. You have no other family,' they told me as they scattered the photos on the ground outside our hut. I was so angry I ran out of the hut and grabbed up all of the pictures, even the negatives. One of the soldiers came up to me and held a gun to my head, but I didn't care. Those pictures were the only thing I had and they were the only thing that mattered to me. I wanted to remember my family, not Angkar, even if it meant they killed me."

I'm so stunned my words blurt out before I can stop them. "I can't believe they didn't kill you."

"Looking back on it now, I cannot either. But they had robbed me of everything that was mine." She looks down at one of the pictures of her when she was a teenager. "My pictures are still important to me. Once when my family moved, I filled my suitcase with only pictures. My sisters asked me why I took my pictures off the wall instead of taking my clothes. I told them, 'Clothes can be replaced, pictures cannot.'"

My astonishment matures to an appreciation of her vision and her foresight. *And her most treasured possession,* I tell myself, *her family.* What strikes me most about the photograph is her long, black hair fashioned in an early 70's hairstyle. Her dress in no way resembles Khmer village or factory "vogue." I can easily understand why her mother so adamantly forced her daughters to cut their hair.

By this time, Joseph returns with more pictures, and a palm leaf to demonstrate how Marilyn's mother hid the gold and jewelry inside the thatched walls of their hut. All of his pictures—although taken after their escape to America—are quite impressive, but the one that thrills him most is of the first consultation when all the representatives from various Methodist churches and organizations gathered on January 7—Liberation Day—of 1997 for the establishment of the Methodist Mission in Cambodia. In fact, all of the photos depicting something to do with the growth and mission of the church—coming out of a communist period in an under-developed country—are more impressive than the one of him with King Sihanouk.

"It's amazing everything you've been involved with, Joseph," I express as I admire the many photographs.

"When we began to count our blessings," says Marilyn, "we saw that God was with us all the time, even back when we were in the forest and during our survival."

"He blessed me with many different skills that allowed me to be useful to the Khmer Rouge," Joseph states.

"He protected my family from all the robbers and people who wanted to do us harm during the time of the Khmer Rouge," notes Marilyn, "and he brought Joseph and me back together in the refugee camp and blessed our marriage and family."

"He introduced us to a wonderful adoptive mother who took Marilyn as her daughter in the refugee camp and allowed us passage to the United States. Once we arrived in America, He made it possible for us to earn our degrees. When we moved to California, He provided us with a wonderful shelter in which to worship and a home in Stockton. Then in 1997, I was allowed to attend the global conference in Singapore to represent Cambodian Christians. It was only a few days later when the General Board of Global Ministries of The United Methodist Church met in Kansas City, Missouri and the Secretary acknowledged us and appointed us to return to our home country as missionaries." Joseph becomes teary-eyed.

"Once we arrived back in Cambodia, we were able to buy lands for the various Methodist offices and also land for Cambodian Methodist churches with our own salary. God blessed us greatly in this way, so we were able to offer the land we purchased in Sisophon in the Banteay Meanchey province back to God for our first church building. We refer to this as 'our first blessing' following our return to Cambodia.

"In 1994, when I made a second trip to Cambodia, one of my 'adoptive grandmothers' who moved with us from Richmond, Grandma Thap Duch, presented me with $1000 to buy the land in the Siem Reap province where our church, parsonage, Sunday school room and now dormitory are located. Her son gave me another $400. Then through the generosity of the Central United Methodist Church in Stockton, we were able to build the wooden worship building and Sunday School room there. We call that 'our second blessing.'

"Siem Reap is our model for what we pray will one day be in all of our districts of the Methodist Mission in Cambodia. We have a completely integrated farming model there, as well as a regional community training center. The church is training many young leaders in all areas of church work. It is what you call 'a work in progress.'"

Joseph is correct in his assessment. I have never seen a more progressing work in any church, much less one in a third-world country. It is amazing to watch the ministry of the Methodist Church unfold, having witnessed it six years ago, seeing it now and perceiving what its future holds. He looks at me and in a voice filled with compassion for his country's people, says softly, "There is still one thing I would like to see built in our Siem Reap model."

"What's that, Joseph?" I ask.

"A center for senior adults. We have the land. All we need is the money for the building. Esther Gitobu's husband, Nick, has helped me with many ideas for it. There is not another facility of that kind in the entire country. Now that we have all these other ministries in place for our children and young people, it is our greatest need."

As I sit at the desk of my hotel room and the two of them sit in chairs at the edge of my bed, I feel more elation and prominence than were I seated at a long mahogany table in a fancy conference room. I am watching history in the making, for I deeply believe Joseph and Marilyn will also realize the completion of this goal in their lifetimes.

I close my book of pages filled with notes as I swallow the lump in my throat. Seated with me are two of God's "movers and shakers."

His presence is so divinely wrapped around them that I sense the glow of their radiant light shining all about me. I have several missionary friends, all of whom I greatly admire. But none share the devastating story of survival that it took to bring them to this point. None of them have had to escape to another country, to gain what they needed to allow them to see a dream eventually happen back in their own country. And none of them have suffered the level of persecution, or the ostracizing, from their own people as have these two individuals.

A thought from earlier during this visit, regarding Duch of S-21 and the text of the hymn *I Stand Amazed in the Presence*, trickles through my brain. I stand to wish them a good rest of what's left of the evening as I stand amazed in their presence. A glance at my watch shows it's well after midnight. *The morning of my last day here,* I recognize regretfully. We've covered so much ground and material in the past nearly three weeks that it's unbelievable. I do a final check over my long list of questions prepared before the trip here, and all the additional questions accumulated during my visit. There is only one we haven't covered and it's most fitting that it's the last one. I sit back at the desk.

"Joseph, you've gone from being a fisherman and a farmer to being a missionary appointed by the General Board of Global Ministries. You are now the District Superintendent for the largest district in your country, with the most provinces of any of the districts. Within that district in the northeast of Cambodia, you have five provinces, including Kampong Cham, Kratie, Mondol Kiri, Ratanak Kiri and Stung Treng, which places you in charge of many minority groups.

"Many of the items on your original plan for the mission of your country have been accomplished and a good number of the others are on their way to being a reality. Simply by virtue of surviving the Khmer Rouge regime and all the hardships you encountered, you are both walking miracles. You've dreamed big, worked hard and reaped rewards of your labor. What are your remaining goals for Cambodia and what do you still hope to accomplish?"

As much as Joseph and Marilyn have enjoyed sharing their faith and their blessings thus far, their animated expressions tell me I've hit the jackpot. *An appropriate ending,* I surmise while thinking of the adage, "The best is yet to come."

"When Marilyn and I came home in January of 1998 to serve as missionaries appointed by the General Board of Global Ministries," Joseph begins, his face as seriously intense as his ideals, "we titled our vision 'Build Trust with Hope and Love' with the Cambodian people. It was our desire for them to know and love Jesus Christ who promised peace, salvation, love, contentment and wisdom to survive each day in a troubled world. We wanted to make it possible for students to study to become great leaders with integrity, to be godly men and women for their families and for society. That would enable them to use their talents and skills to provide for their families and thereby reduce poverty. It would also allow them to help their children so they, too, could earn an education for many generations to come, so that poverty would continue to be less of a problem.

"We had been gone for eighteen years, so we knew it was not going to be an easy task," he concludes.

"Do you realize you've just outlined the very same goals you had for your country when you were studying in North Korea?" I ask. "These are the attributes you originally thought would be attained through a Socialist government."

"Yes," Joseph answers simply.

"But now, having survived a communist government that turned out to be your worst nightmare instead of your ultimate dream, you are watching your goals be met one by one."

"Yes," he answers again, this time with tears glistening in his eyes.

Joseph then hands me a report written by one of his former professors at Claremont, a Methodist college and seminary in California. I read over it to see the various ministries that are now in place in Cambodia via the support of the Methodist Church and thanks to the endless efforts and hours of Joseph and Marilyn. He then hands me two pages stapled together. "For my last day of class at Claremont College, all the students were to come in with a vision of what they hoped to accomplish in their ministry. The professor told us, 'Dream big!' When I stood to give mine, the professor laughed. He said, 'You dream really big.' Then he warned me that what I had outlined would never be possible, so I wouldn't be disappointed in my ministry and accomplishments.

"That professor visited Marilyn and I in 2000 and wrote the report you are now reading about what we had accomplished here through the MMC. He came here to take the information back to the States to use for various publications and articles. During that visit, he witnessed that many parts of my vision, my 'dream too big', had come to fruition. He stood here and cried when he saw the programs that had developed in Siem Reap.

A glance at the papers outlining his "big dream" lists the description of his vision on the front page. The back page is a well-drawn and scaled diagram of his vision. A quick tally proves over half the items listed are already in place with several others in planning stages for future use. There are already churches in most of the twenty-four provinces. An increasing number of them now have worship buildings and community wells. Toilets are being added to many of them. Some have parsonages. Land is being purchased for additional churches throughout the country, making sure there is enough property for the pastors to farm as a supplement to their income to insure they can support a family on their meager salaries. The Cambodian Bible School offers classes for the local pastors allowing them accreditation, and it is working on a number of theological studies, with the aid of teachers coming from the States and other countries to offer courses. The first dormitory, donated by St. Luke's UMC in Highland Ranch, Colorado, is underway at the Regional Community Training Center in Siem Reap. Although it is not yet completed, it is currently being used for church services, computer classes and as a parsonage for the pastor. Through the combined efforts of all the Methodist organizations involved in the Methodist Mission in Cambodian, vocational schools and a grade school (preschool through 12th grade) are not only in place, but are growing and having continued success. There is a mechanics' school, a sewing school and a cosmetology school to name a few of the courses of study in the vocational school, all of which include ways to market a business or a trade.

Marilyn chairs the Women's Program, which began in January 1998. Later that year, in September, the first Women's Bible Training was held in the Singapore Methodist Church in Phnom Penh, in which 110 women from the different districts participated. Thanks to funding by the Women's Division of GBGM-UMC and the United Methodist

Women's (UMW) Mission Giving, the Bible training is still run by missionaries from Singapore. Various other Methodist agencies work together to empower the Cambodian women through training sessions in community building, education, literacy and health care, as well as faith and Bible teachings. Similar programs in India, which had found much success, serve as the model for many of the women's classes. This training is also supported by the Women's Division of the GBGM-UMC.

The women's program has developed to the point that, in 2004, it began to provide small grants for women to start projects that would generate income for them and their families. Leaders help recipients of the grants to fully understand their skills and also develop strong business principles. "Our goal is to improve the quality of life for Cambodian women," states Marilyn. "We strive to help them become self-sufficient, as well as provide an education and health care for their children."

During our visit, we have been privy to watching women raise vegetables, and weave baskets, hammocks and silks as a part of these projects. I fondly remember my previous visit, when I was fortunate enough to have taught leadership, teaching skills and music—along with a team, including Mark, from the Western North Carolina Conference—to women from the various provinces. Our trip to the outlying areas has allowed me to see the seeds we sowed then sprouting into budding and blossoming projects within the congregations of the Methodist Mission in Cambodia. The participants, who were provided scholarships enabling them to attend those sessions held at the Cambodian Bible School—their equivalent to a church-supported university and seminary—are now teaching those same lessons to the women in their own areas. All of these joint efforts, from people around the globe, demonstrate the action of "paying forward" is turning into a huge success. It is truly a vision of empowerment.

Other successful projects—also a result of UMW Mission Giving—are the animal banks of cows and pigs, which allow recipients to raise them for profit as another source of income. Jobs are being created in the church's effort to reduce poverty. As an outsider looking in, it is easy to see the reason for much of the success with projects in Cambodia. Marilyn is an insider; she has "been there, done that" and still has emotional scars. The people trust her as she shows them such caring compassion and lives the example of moving forward.

This is a blessed progression, having evolved from a time of animosity from their brother and sister Cambodians because Joseph and she had an education and had been able to escape. As people witness their genuine love and compassionate empathy, doors open and things begin to happen. It is a beautiful scene to behold as this couple not only shares the values of their experiences and education, but they actually work hand-in-hand by getting down in the dirt with their people to plant new seeds of faith, and ways of income.

There's a strange saying, "The proof is in the pudding." As if what I see is not proof enough, Marilyn's next answer about retirement is "the pudding." "Will you stay here when you retire in another year?" I ask.

"It is our dream to stay here and work with the people. Joseph hopes to open a garage, using the auto mechanics' degree he earned in Arlington, Virginia, and I hope to start a flower and plant nursery."

I laugh, with a nod of my head, thinking how grimy and dirty both of these jobs are. These two are not afraid of getting a little dirty. They well know the lesson that all good things grow from the bottom up. In their lifetimes, they've been to the utmost bottom and they've been resilient enough to rise to the top. As they retire and move forward, there's no doubt their faith, hope and love will continue to be in action, whether in Cambodia or America, or some point in between.

"Can you see a difference between the time you returned as missionaries and now?" I ask, wanting to perceive it from their viewpoint.

"Yes," Marilyn answers confidently, giving me that nod that acts as an exclamation point. "Women are more knowledgeable, making them more confident. As they learn more, they are also developing courage to try new ideas in their families, their communities and their churches. They are hungry to learn more about the Bible's teachings and are open in their faith."

The progress is evident no matter whose eyes are looking in, witnessing the leadership, skills and work of this couple. Developments brought about by their diligence and efforts didn't start the moment they returned to Cambodia though, or even upon their call to ministry while still in America. As during his days of study in North Korea, Joseph still seeks answers to bring peace and justice to his country. He speaks briefly about his views of religion then as opposed to now. Though Buddhist traditions are no longer a part of his life, he makes an interesting parallel to Christianity, connecting his past and his religious background to the present.

"Timothy 5:4 says, 'But if a widow has children or grandchildren, these should learn first of all to put their religion into practice by caring for their own family and so repaying their parents and grandparents, for this is pleasing to God.' To me, that idea is similar to the Cambodian parents' beliefs and practice."

One only needs spend a few hours with Joseph to see that this verse truly is engrained in his spirit and in his ministry. No matter where we are, Joseph is reaching out to someone in need. He, along with Marilyn, is the most caring, selfless servant I've ever had the privilege of meeting, which is saying a lot given the places I've traveled and the wonderful individuals I've met. They are such an example to everyone they meet, and if there was ever a couple who walked in the path of Christ, it is Joseph and Marilyn Chan.

Their Christian influence is not only felt by the people in Cambodia though. At their house in Stockton, California, Bible studies are held by the Cambodians of his church there, and his adoptive mother cooks for the participants. Their choir practices for each week's Sunday service are held at the local park, but if it is too rainy they practice at Joseph's house. What is most interesting about these musical rehearsals is they all have a barbecue together, with members bringing meats, rice, pickles and salad. *And I thought the Methodist churches in America liked to eat!*

"At our house in Stockton," Marilyn shares, "I plant the flowers and Joseph plants the fruit." From their very nature, I am sure those are not the only seeds they plant; they are both gardeners, planting seeds wherever they go.

"How does it feel to see Christianity growing in your country when it is dropping in numbers of active members drastically in other countries?"

"I am very excited and believe God continues to bless Cambodia," Joseph responds. "Back in 1991, the Cambodian Ministry for Christ conducted a meeting for global Christian leaders. It was amazing to learn that so many people were praying for freedom of religion in Cambodia. We still pray that we will become 'the light and salt' for our neighboring countries and will shine to different nations. As people prayed for the gospel to get into Cambodia, our Christian brothers and sisters are now praying that we will carry the gospel out and be witnesses to the world.

"We hope to soon see Christian members involved in the government. For many centuries, there have been few Christian believers in our country. There have been many countries, such as South America, North America, Korea, Malaysia, Japan, China, Chile, Argentina and Australia who have been helping us to build buildings and big businesses. Canada, the United Kingdom, Sweden, Finland, Norway, Russia, Switzerland, Germany, Singapore, Thailand and Vietnam, and many more countries pour resources into my Cambodia to help restore and rebuild our land. All these countries have given financial aid and human power to help with nearly everything necessary to human basic needs. We are most grateful for the love for humanity shown by these countries. Now we see it as our turn for Cambodian men, women and children to reach out to others."

The smile that is so much a part of who Joseph is begins to appear. "Our government now recognizes that Christian organizations built churches and are training children and youth. They understand we are helping people to grow, so we are now able to worship freely in our country. Laos, Vietnam and Thailand are also growing in Christianity. But because our government is more open to our work, our spreading of the gospel and our growth, United Methodist missionaries met here in 2008 to discuss the goals and needs of these other countries, as well as Cambodia. No more do we have to practice religion underground here, but a couple of our missionaries are moving to Laos, where safety and persecution are still considerations."

"How can Christians around the world best help to make sure the growth of Christianity continues in Cambodia?"

These needs are so engrained in Joseph's consciousness that he takes no time to answer. "In my opinion, the educational system needs to continue everywhere. In the Bible School, we should have agriculture school, mechanical training, business school and a retreat place. We need to develop our great educational system for all koon Khmer (Cambodian children) to have free education for the next twenty years. This way, we can train koon Khmer to become great leaders for their family and nation, and to be Christian models for the next generations and others in the world. Train them to know God and obey his commandments all their lives so they will then train their children to follow Christ. This would put the ball in place for the next generations.

"I see the need for elementary and vocational training as important as our need for churches and clinics," he continues. "Our ultimate goal is to see all koon Khmer grow spiritually and to know they are created in God's image for His glory and pleasure. They must learn to know and seek God first in life and in all they do in order to receive and know the fullness of His blessings."

His remarks prove the needs of Cambodia are the same as most third-world countries. Whether struck by natural disasters or devastated by war, the needs are great. The greatest needs are always training skills, inspiring and motivating creativity and also creative ways to market, which thus create jobs and reduce poverty. Clinics and wells, as well as schools and churches are high in priorities, as well as agricultural development in both land and animals.

Their spiritual needs are much the same as developed countries where Christianity has long been the national religion. Society and culture have brought these countries to the point that, in many ways, our countries are on the same playing field in regards to building stronger Christian communities. Joseph and Marilyn outline goals and needs that apply to many of us, and give us a guide of how to go about God's work in our own areas. They set the precedence for placing faith, hope and love in action in our own homes, churches and places of business.

The Methodist Mission in Cambodia (MMC) sponsors many various ministries and missions, not so unlike the many offerings available in America. One can visit them and readily experience the body of Christ through the many arms and legs, the parts of the overall body—all of which work together like a finely-oiled machine, thanks to the cooperation of five branches of Methodism. This is a unique situation, of which

Joseph and Marilyn are an integral part, after having been instrumental in its development. Two decades have seen an expanse from three Methodist churches to over 150 today. Twenty missionaries, Methodist and United Methodist, serve beside ten ordained deacons and a hundred lay leaders. One has but to attend any function at one of these churches to see that the flame, which goes with the cross on the United Methodist logo, burns brightly in Cambodia.

There is the Singapore School, a private school located next to the Cambodian Bible School, located in Phnom Penh. In the past six years, the Singapore School has grown tremendously. The school now has an enrollment of 840 students, with a proposed goal of 1000 within the next five years. That is their ultimate limit. Class sizes are large, with forty students each. However, there are no discipline problems as we wander through the halls and visit the classrooms. The level of respect between the students and teachers is a welcome scene to what we are generally accustomed to in the States.

The headmaster, Steven Yeo, is from Singapore. One needs only spend a couple of minutes around him to discover he is a powerhouse and incredibly articulate. He is personable and caring, setting the tone for the school and making it easy for students and faculty alike to relate to him. Being a past educator, I adhere to the principle that you can always tell the kind of leadership at the top by the students' behavior. If that holds true, Steven Yeo is top notch.

The school now has a canteen that runs three shifts of students through daily, with offerings of fruit, instant rice and instant noodles. This facilitates a more hygienic lunch situation for the children and teens than their previous situation. Students buy coupons in advance, which are given out each morning. That way, everyone—whether on free scholarship or not—receives a coupon each morning so no one knows who is free and who isn't. This prevents ridicule.

A focus on moral principles has been implemented for the first time during this school year. Two of the posters, which have cute animals to attract the attention of young students, strike me as particularly important for children of Cambodian culture. "I will look at people when they speak to me" is foreign to their customary behavior. Typically, Cambodians look at the ground when they speak to people. A particular goal of this principle is to build trust between the students, which will reach into their adult lives. Another poster's words, "I will ask questions if I do not understand" is also a new way of thinking for a nation whose people are wont to keep silent rather than let it be known they do not understand.

Another new addition to the school is the formation of the Boys' Brigade and the Girls' Brigade. Both of these groups are Christian-based and are very much like the Scouts in America. They offer leadership training and life skills training. As with the scouting programs, the participants earn badges and get to pin them on so this is an exciting extra-curricular activity for the students.

Their dress code, as has been Cambodia's custom for decades, is still white shirts and blue skirts or trousers. Everyone is clean and neat, and clothes are pressed. Thirty percent of the students are from poor and needy families, but even they pay a little for tuition to give them ownership. These students are non-distinguishable from the others.

A major change in the school in the past six years, and my favorite point, is the court for physical education on the roof. Because the school is limited in its space, it can only grow up. This means middle school and high school gym classes have a great view of the city, with a tall, heavy-duty metal fence all the way around the play area. Remarkably, the surrounding areas provide a gorgeous cycloramic scene, showing the more developed areas of Phnom Penh. The young children still have a small play area in the front courtyard, allotting them space and privacy congruent to their size.

Another of the arms of mission, and one that pulls at the heartstrings of the entire world, is the orphanage run by the Methodist Mission in Cambodia. The reverberations of the needs of this facility are far reaching, as are its benefactors, run through the General Board of Global Ministries. For our visit, I have been requested to present a check to the orphanage, on behalf of the Red Bird Missionary Conference in Beverly, Kentucky. Itself located in what some refer to as "the black hole of America" because of its own poverty level and the fact that it is nestled in a huge coalmining area, this check for over $400 has been lovingly raised by only four young girls who heard about the Cambodian orphanage and wanted to do something. They are the members of a children's Sunday School class taught by Joan Campbell at Warren's Chapel United Methodist Church in the Redbird Conference. It is a humbling experience to know the area from where this money came, which is one of the poorest in my home country, and see the children, who are among the poorest in Cambodia, whose lives it will touch. *Children helping other children, all of whom are blessed by this act of kindness and love.*

The orphanage is a sad reminder of the infamous dumpsite in Phnom Penh where many mission groups flock to see the ultimate poverty level of this third-world country. The stench of the garbage, much of which is shipped in on barges from many other places—including the U.S.—is sickening. Notably worse than the stench are the thousands of Cambodians who live at the dump, many of whom are infested with AIDS. Children rummage through the trash for any morsel of food they can find, any stitch of clothing to wear or plastic to recycle—if they're not fortunate enough to make themselves a pair of sandals from a plastic cola bottle first.

At its current site, LADS (Light At the Dump Site) is a MMC program whereby a small number of children from the dumpsite are educated during the day. To compensate a child's family for allowing the child to attend school, they are paid a small amount each month, which is considered to be a fair equivalent of what the child would pick up in recyclable materials in the period of a month. For starving families, a child's work—finding items worth cash—is more valuable than an education. Therefore the families must be trained before the children can be trained.

A shocking fact, the dumpsite—which has been the feature of many media articles and television news broadcasts—will soon be moving. Volunteer mission groups, who for years have thronged to the site for a first-hand realization of the state of the country's poverty, are currently being dissuaded from visiting the area. Phnom Penh, like other major cities of the world, is branching out so rapidly in its building projects that the dumpsite is now needed for more buildings. Bordered by the river, the city is limited in which directions it can expand, which means one of the available spaces is the dump.

This is a grave predicament if my prediction of the Cambodian method of eminent domain is correct. "Have any provisions been made concerning where the people who currently live at the dumpsite will go? Will they be moved to the new dump site?"

"No," is the answer I regretfully receive from Esther.

"How can you move to something less adequate than a dumpsite? Where will they go?"

Sadly, neither of us have an answer to that question. I have a nightmarish vision of the evacuation of Phnom Penh, only to a smaller extent, as I imagine throngs of families relocating to another place. I silently question whether the government has made any provisions for their situation, but my fear of the answer is greater than my desire to know.

There is one thing I know for certain regarding the move of the dumpsite and the relocation of its thousands of inhabitants. The job of Cambodia's missionaries will become more demanding as the needs, of those who are already among the world's worst poverty cases, become much greater. Given how the various Methodist churches work together under the auspices of the Methodist Mission in Cambodia, there is no doubt they will be able to put Christ's mission first as they set out to meet those needs.

As I mull over the various ministries and church-related agencies in Cambodia, I get a sense of looking at the scope of the entire country from above. The phenomenal view of Phnom Penh, as seen from the fenced playground atop the building of the Singapore School comes to mind. It is an imagery I appreciate. Bars and fences closed the world to a one-time school known as Tuol Sleng. The fence at the top of Singapore School, a successful and growing Methodist ministry, opens the world to its students.

It's an odd thing, those bars. There's a saying that "everyone finds religion behind bars." There's some thought that many find religion in a refugee camp when they're hungry following a war-savaged time. There's a sure fact that two individuals, who survived perils worse than pen can tell, saw the Light in a place called Kao I Dang in Thailand and followed that same Light around the other side of the world, and back, so those in their native land could also find that same Light. Their story of carrying that Light to others is called…faith, hope and love…in action.

Chapter Twenty-one
Present day

A lone man sits in his home in Montgomery, Alabama. Each day passes slowly, as the mirror shows a life that has been lived hard. "Rode hard and put up wet" is the American expression for it. He looks back, remembering the years when he was hardly wet behind the ears, to a time when he'd completed his necessary training to be a crew chief for fighter jets, and he boarded a plane to Southeast Asia. *Saigon…even its name is no longer the same,* he melancholically muses, thinking of how it's now called Ho Chi Minh City.

Although the most hellacious period in his life, it still holds the fondest memories of a youthful heart. He wonders how the people in that part of the world are doing, as a part of his heart reaches out to them as it always does, and he wishes he could go back for one last glimpse of being happy in a land influenced largely by their belief in luck and good fortune. Thirty-five years have passed since the day he was escorted from Cambodia and sent to Saigon, where he was one of the last Americans to narrowly escape that city before its fall.

A glance down at his now gnarled fingers, which no longer allow them to glide over the piano keys to play *Heart and Soul,* remind him of the toll his days of "wine, women and song" have taken on not only his appearance, but his entire being. *And then there's the matter of Agent Orange,* he recalls, looking at the oxygen machine on which he constantly relies. He thinks of the times when C-123 antiquated-type cargo planes flew along the perimeter of the military base and the airfield, like crop dusters, leaving behind a trail of pesticides the consistency of a thick fog, meant to kill off all the foliage in the area so the enemy had no place to hide. *Apparently they didn't take into consideration exactly howcc many other people had no place to hide while they were doing it,* he determines, taking another deep cough.

"How do you feel?" asks his mother as she enters the room.

"Not a day over 80, but I wouldn't change a thing," he answers as briskly as his 63-year-old body will allow.

He doesn't bemoan his days and years spent there; rather, he sees them as a pivotal turning point in his existence. An existence leaving him forever changed. An existence far from easy, and not always full of happiness and good fortune; yet an existence which he understands can't be lived out filled with regrets. There's no doubt in his mind he is blessed, a realization that crosses his mind daily. He's unable to even comprehend the number of occasions on which he could have died, as he recollects thoughts from Southeast Asia he's kept inside until now. They are thoughts renewed by the article he sits reading about two Khmer Rouge survivors, Joseph and Marilyn Chan, who are now missionaries back in their home country of Cambodia.

"You know," he finally says, "I can't begin to imagine what they experienced, their agony, their terror…none of it." His eyes reveal his thoughts are light years away as he focuses on a bleacher seat approximately fifty yards off the Mekong River. "Most people could never understand it, but as hellish as it was, it was also a beautiful time. You saw life from a different perspective. I've learned about the Lord in a lot of ways since that time." He smiles reflectively as he pauses to catch his breath. "There is no reason or explanation for me being here now other than divine intervention. I feel I was fully protected by God. That's the only way I can explain how I got out."

Although his life may not have always mirrored it, he holds a deep belief in God, one that deepens with each passing day. With those same passing days, there is not one void of thoughts from a lifetime long ago and far away, a place where a piece of his heart and soul remain—Phnom Penh, Cambodia.

A young woman sits eating dinner at Happy Pizza along Phnom Penh's busy Sisowath Quay. She stares across the Tonle Sap River to the island that lies between it and the Mekong River on the other side. There, towering above the shoreline is a tall, white building under construction, its foreboding dominance demanding the attention of onlookers. *My home,* she muses, anxious to one day live in her newly purchased condo on its fifth floor.

It, like the many other high-rises appearing all around the city, bears witness to the fact that Phnom Penh is rapidly growing and expanding. She reflects on how different things look from the day her family was forced to evacuate thirty-five years prior. Even the city dump, which has been the object of many television specials and media stories, is being moved to make room for developers, lending way to many more high-rises and markers of the western world's influence.

Whether it be foods—such as burgers, pizzas, or the traditional Cambodian fare—or businesses—such as tailors, spas or nail salons—the country's superstitious nature is still very much evident in the many signs whose business names don either the word "happy" or "lucky." Chandra, though, dressed in a t-shirt bearing the words "Have faith in God" in her native Khmer language, relies on her Christian faith rather than mere luck or good fortune as the source for her happiness.

As she takes her last bite of pizza, she also takes one last look across the water's edge to the white high-rise. By this time next year she will be moved in, once again a Cambodian citizen. She looks forward to her continued involvement with one of the country's orphanages as a social worker, while continuing her work as a private counselor at a counseling clinic. Her main goal is to help the residents of her beloved country move past the hurt, sorrow and depression of an era of mass genocide and communism, leaving many of its residents with Posttraumatic Stress Disorder (PTSD). No longer must she fear thinking openly and having goals and dreams, or helping others find and reach theirs—as did her family under the Khmer Rouge regime.

Cambodia, like every other nation in the world, will be plagued by its natural disasters and economic ups and down, and by changes in rulers and governments. It, and its inhabitants, will face the same stumbling blocks as every other country caught up in the midst of "development," which benefits the wealthy rather than the common man. Although Liberation Day is over thirty years past for this land, there will forever be visible signs of a tragic history of a civil war and genocide unlike the world has ever known.

The natural allure of the countryside, the ancient rich culture, and the beauty in the faces and in the hearts of the people, making this such a unique land, are disappearing all too swiftly with modernization, which makes this nation also a part of the globalization process. With that change, the younger generations have moved past the events contained in this book, and share the desire to leave the past in the past and move forward. They have returned to drawing from their traditionally rare and vast history, combined with all Cambodia's remaining secluded beauty, to claim the bragging rights of a country for which they can hold up their heads and cherish a great pride.

The people who are fortunate enough to have survived the hell of the communist years—which finally led to the re-establishment of the constitution of the Kingdom of Cambodia in 1993—attempt to walk their paths as if nothing ever happened. Among this group is one couple who walks softly, touching the lives of everyone with whom they come in contact as they introduce them to the Christ who has turned all their nightmares into days filled with God's richest blessings. This couple, like everyone else in their beloved Cambodia, will face more changes and hardships during the courses of their lives here on earth. But at the end of each day, Joseph and Marilyn Chan will continue to turn their faces toward the brightness of the Son, the Light of their world, who guides them daily from a mortal world of darkness to the eternal light. They can walk each step boldly, and face their every tomorrow with confidence, because He lives.

Because He Lives

God sent His son — they called Him Jesus,
He came to love, heal and forgive;
He lived and died to buy my pardon,
An empty grave is there to prove my Savior lives.

CHORUS:
Because He lives I can face tomorrow,
Because He lives all fear is gone;
Because I know He holds the future
And life is worth the living just because He lives.

How sweet to hold a newborn baby
And feel the pride and joy he gives;
But greater still the calm assurance:
This child can face uncertain days because He lives.
CHORUS

And then one day I'll cross the river,
I'll fight life's final war with pain;
And then as death gives way to victory,
I'll see the lights of glory and I'll know He reigns.
CHORUS

Words by William J. and Gloria Gaither. Music by William J. Gaither.

About the Photographer

Photographer Mark Barden is no stranger to capturing images on the foreign mission field. Since 2000, when he became the Director of Mission/Outreach for the Western North Carolina Conference of The United Methodist Church, he has used his telecommunications background to tell the stories of people all over the world. After becoming the WNCC Director of Communications in 2006, Mark continued to feed his passion for missions by volunteering on various mission trips, always bringing home a plethora of stories and photographs. From the jungles of the Democratic Republic of Congo and Sudan to the rice paddies of Cambodia to the snow-capped mountains of Armenia, he has continued to interweave the two of his greatest loves, missions and photography, into a tapestry that tells the story of God's love for humanity.

Born into a Methodist parsonage family, and a grandson of Methodist missionaries, Mark grew up with the church touching multiple aspects of his family's life. With a committed faith, along with degrees in communications, he followed God's calling into broadcast journalism and eventually college teaching at the University of Mississippi and Murray State University. Eventually his desire for parish ministry led him back to North Carolina to complete ministerial studies at Duke University. Before joining the conference staff, Mark spent 15 years as a pastor in local churches in the Western NC Conference.

Mark is married to Barbara Jean Barden, Minister of Education at Myers Park United Methodist Church in Charlotte, N.C.. They have one son, Chris, a student at High Point University in High Point, N.C.

About the Author

Catherine Ritch Guess is the author of twenty-two books, all of the inspirational genre, including fiction, non-fiction and children's titles. In addition, she is a composer and a frequent speaker/musician for a wide range of conferences and events. After serving as an Organist/Minister of music in local churches of the WNCC for over 35 years, she is now appointed the Circuit Riding Musician through the Western North Carolina Conference of the United Methodist Church, a position which allows her to serve globally through her writing, speaking and music.

One of the FACES of *Interpreter* magazine in 2004, and the Profile of the UMC for September 2009, Catherine spends much of her time reaching out to others around the world. Through her children's series, ***RUDY THE RED PIG***, and the non-profit Rudy & Friends Reading Pen, Inc, she promotes children's literacy to natural disaster areas. Her latest venture is a comedy series featuring Miz Eudora Rumph, whom she portrays using the simple mountain wit and wisdom of her Appalachian grandmother.

Catherine is currently working on four other titles, scheduled to release soon, as well as researching her next missionary book. Her most treasured activity is spending time at home in North Carolina with her family—including her two grandsons, both currently under five-months-old—on her grandfather's land.

www.ciridmus.com
www.catherineritchguess.com
www.mizeudora.com